Planet of the Orange-red Sun

Series Volume 6

The Renegade Tower

Planet of the Orange-red Sun Series

Volume 6
The Renegade Tower

by Vic Broquard

Second Edition; ISBN: 978-1-941415-23-8

This is a work of fiction. All characters, organizations, and events portrayed in this novel are products of the author's imagination and are used fictiously.

http://www.Broquard-ebooks.com
Broquard eBooks
103 Timberlane
East Peoria, IL 61611
author@Broquard-eBooks.com

Artwork by Crooked Willow Studios.

For Morgan and L. Ron Hubbard

Table of Contents

Part I Formation

Chapter 1 Adjustments

June 1245, the survivors of the coup in Valen Castle, Westerlings, finally reached their new safe house, Hacienda Valen, on a hilltop overlooking the white sandy beach of Villa del Rey, where the mouth of the Alcantara River met the great ocean of Tierra. Five families, including the widow of the assassinated Lord Paco Valen, fled the castle during that night, fleeting for their very lives! These were the closest associates and advisors of the late Lord Paco, who lay dead on the floor of his private study, slain by his cousin, Pedro Valen, the head blind leader of the coup and who now sat on the throne of all the Westerlings lands.

All twenty-six had the gifts, that is, the *mentales* gifts, of which telepathy was perhaps the least. All were tower trained and highly skilled with their various psi powers. Lord Paco's Grand Plan had almost succeeded! They had been so close! So close to conquering all the lands of Tierra, after which they would then open Tierra to the vast wonders and technologies of the aliens from Rigel-3. So close and yet so far. With the exception of five of these, they had all made huge sacrifices towards this goal, horrible sacrifices which now made them nearly physically helpless. One might say foolish sacrifices, but to the adults, the lofty goal to which they almost reached was worth the effort. Now they had to pick up the pieces of their shattered lives, if that was even possible.

Fons Valen, forty-five, was their unchallenged leader, for it was he who had somehow saved them all, bringing them cleverly to safety and to his elegant hacienda. That he was also the eldest of the twenty-six also played a significant role in everyone's tacit acceptance of his leadership in all things. Second in command was Roberto Valen, a younger brother of the assassinated Paco; he was thirty-three. The two trusted advisors of Paco now became the advisors to Fons: Amado de la Parte, forty, and Donato de Portales, forty-three. Fons had also been the Lord of Arabella, the largest city on their southern seacoast, once the capital of the old kingdom of

Almendia, and some eight hundred miles further east along the southern coast. Fleeing Valen Castle, he essentially abdicated his throne there, either that or be assassinated himself, if he ever returned to Arabella as its ruler.

When they left Valen castle, Donato's advice had been heartfelt and wise. "We need a place where we can all live as an extended family. We must stick together. Think of how we look. Together we stand a chance of surviving this mess." Under Fons' guidance, they were doing just that. Twenty-one of the twenty-six simply could not survive on their own. They had undergone extensive physical modifications to their bodies to help Lord Paco convince hundreds of other Midlands and Easterlings *mentales* gifted to get similar modifications or die from a hideous virus, which was a hoax Paco had dreamed up. Now these twenty-one had to live with the results of those modifications.

Each had five-inch in diameter, ornamental, golden lip plates. Their lips had been slit and the plates with four retaining dowels inserted. The women's plates also had colorful gemstones embedded in them. The plates limited their speech, making it difficult for others to understand them. However when removed, their lip loops were highly sensitive and when licked, caused almost uncontrollable sexual arousals. This was the least of their modifications. All had their feet reformed so that their ankles pointed downward, only their toes could lay flat on the ground. They wore the toe shoes or toe boots, in which only their toes were on the ground, and a tall metal spiked heel touched the ground just behind their toes. Walking in these was limited to two or three inch steps at most and made for highly treacherous walking and at a snail's pace. Even just standing was most difficult.

The women insisted on continuing to wear their pipe corsets, giving them the twelve to fourteen inch waistlines they found so desirable. The men had already discarded their pipe corsets for the freedom of breathing and movement they regained. None of the women could bend except at their hips. The heavy steel boning prevented such and they wore them at all times, except while bathing. The men looked sleek and trim now, though their waists were slowly expanding. The women also had enormous gold and gem encrusted earrings that hung from one-inch gold disks inserted into their ear lobes. These dangles reached down to lie on their upper chests, impressively.

The worst part of all the modifications had been the removal of their hands. The medical machines had amputated them and modified their stumps at their wrists, turning them into one-inch cones, rather aesthetic in appearance and also highly sensitive to touch, which again was highly arousing in bed. All wore cheap alien prosthetic hands that translated nerve energies into physical actions of the hand. However they could feel nothing with them, and they worked very poorly. Worse, they slid off the arm stump, if more than a pound of force was used. The men constantly were pulling their hands off while trying to lift heavier items. None of the men, for example, could draw their swords, not even remotely, let alone wield it. Great concentration and patience was needed on their part just to manage to handle forks and spoons while eating. As one of their daughters said, "Our lives are pathetic. We are nearly helpless."

Part of their helplessness was solved upon reaching the hacienda. Fons arranged for each one to have their own personal assistant, paid to help them with their many physical needs, from dressing, to bathing, to going to the bathroom, to eating. Whatever was needed, these assistants provided. That eased their awful situation somewhat.

The twenty-six survivors included the widow Adora Valen, now thirty-seven, and her children: Paco Junior, seventeen, Imelda, sixteen, Lucinda, fifteen, and Rafael, thirteen but he had not undergone body modifications because of his age. Lord Roberto and his wife Natalia were both thirty-three. Their children were Chico, fifteen, Ana, fourteen, and Fidela, thirteen, who was also not modified. Lord Fons, forty-five, and his wife Delfina, forty-three brought their children: Hermina, twenty, Andres, eighteen, and Gracia, sixteen. Both Andres and Gracia were also not body modified because Fons wanted heirs who were not helpless as he was. Advisor Amado, forty, and his wife, Consuela, also forty, brought their children: Benita, eighteen, Estavan, sixteen, and Donica, fourteen.

Advisor Donato, forty-three, and his wife, Adelita, forty, brought their children: Raul, twenty, Renato, eighteen, and Anita, fourteen, but she was also unmodified having only recently come of age.

Further, most of the children were already engaged – a lot of planned marriages between these five families. Soon after arrival at the hacienda, Fons allowed the six couples to marry, an action that raised the twelve's morale a great deal. Pino married Benita. Estevan married Imelda. Chico married Lucinda. Renato married Donica. Raul married Hermina. Ruperto married Ana. Already the thirteen year olds were "in love," namely Rafael and Fidela. Only Anita, Gracia, and Andres were still single and available. These five had not undergone the modifications.

The eleven families each took over one of the large private suites of the hacienda as their new home. The hacienda was quite large and sat on a hill that overlooked the ocean below to the south and part of the town to the west. Along the northern outer wall of the rectangular complex sat a row of domestic suites, each with two small bedrooms, a living room, bath, a dining room, and a kitchen with attached pantry. The north wall had ten of these suites, with another two along the east and west walls. The other half of the east and west walls had six much smaller servants quarters and a laundry room. The long southern wall housed gaming rooms, studies, and two huge living rooms that could also serve as dance halls and Great Halls for important, large scale meetings. Behind the north wall lay a long stable and hay and grain loft.

The roofs were all the typical Westerlings, red overlaying tiles. More important, the entire central area was a beautiful formal garden with a pond at either end. Awnings covered the first eight feet out from the suits, providing protection from the rains and allowing one to walk all around the complex without getting wet. There were numerous entrances with ornate iron gates which could be locked and barricaded if need be.

The stewards of the hacienda were Eugenio and Esmerelda del Mira, who oversaw nearly fifty staff. These included gardeners, maids, cooks, stable hands, and the many personal assistants.

Even with the staff, the new arrivals complained. "But dad, we look like freaks. Even if we try to go into the town, everyone will think that we are ghastly freaks," Hermina complained bitterly.

"Ah, so I suggest we begin to make our lip plates, your delightful earrings, and our toe shoes and boots the latest fashion statement. That's why we've brought along the machines and supplies. In time, I am sure we can get some of the locals here to want to look like we do. Give it time and you'll be the height of fashion again, dear Hermina. However, there is nothing that we can do about these pathetic alien hands of ours. Chins up; we'll make do somehow and get by. That goes for all of you; we must plan for the future. We rebuild, gain new allies and support. One day, we will return to Castle Valen in triumph! You, all of you, are Valen's true heroes. Never forget that."

"Once we get settled in, we are going to take our next step in rebuilding. We have twenty-six highly gifted *mentales* here. We are going to form our own *Círculo de la Torres*! It will be called the Renegade Tower! We will act in secrecy, spying and learning all that we can."

The day they arrived at the hacienda held far more for them than a mere safe haven from which to rebuild. No, something vastly more significant happened, wholly unexpected. As Esmeralda introduced them to their staff, she eventually got down to the maids. "My god! Esmeralda?" Fons protested what he saw standing there, the three hired maids! The older woman definitely had no arms at all, not a trace; her blouse had no sleeves. The two teen-aged daughters also had no arms and were standing on a single leg!

All of the men and women of the Westerlings had black hair and black eyes. The men wore theirs cut short, while the women seldom, if ever, cut theirs. Westerlings hair was always thick and lush and with the women, quite long. These three were no exception; their hair fell to the backs of their calves, thick, lush, and perfectly straight.

Esmeralda had then introduced them to Dorita dela Handro and her daughters, Alicia, eighteen, and Juana, seventeen. The mother was rather pudgy and short. She was thirty-eight with an oval face and thick lips with bushy eyebrows, echoed in her daughters. Alicia was thin and stood almost six feet. Her face had high cheekbones and an oval shaped nose. Fons thought if she were whole, she would be quite a beauty. Juana stood on her one leg, two inches shorter than her sister. Her face was round more like her father's. Both teens had the thick lips of their mother, which were shaped into a perpetual smile, even if they were not intending to smile. All three's eyes were bright and alert. Then came the startling discovery of their yellow eyes with brown speckles. *Mentales* gifted! After that, it had been a whirlwind of startling discoveries.

None of the three had ever had any tower training, as was require of all the *mentales* gifted. Valen Tower, about fifteen hundred miles to the northeast, was far beyond their reach. In essence, they were self-taught. None had the germanium amplification crystals the twenty-six wore at all times. Yet, these three were quite able to perform their duties as maids, according to Esmeralda. They soon found out why. Dorita had quite powerful *mentales* gifts, which included telekinesis, knowing what another wanted to know, the ability to dominate others, and the rarest of all gifts, that of a katalyein, a catalyst telepath! While Dorita's raw, unamplified psi powers were huge, those of her daughters dwarfed hers!

The two teens could only move around by hopping on their one foot. Yet, they possessed enormous telekinetic powers, which they used to move the things and to perform the actions they needed, including eating and bed making, for example. While they also knew what others wanted to know, they also had powerful teleportation skills, which they called jumping, to differentiate it from the hopping that they did. They were physically unable to walk from their home down near the beach up the hill to the hacienda where they worked as maids for the last two years. So they simply teleported there, taking one hop out of their front door and landing before the doors of the hacienda. If this were not enough, their katalyein skills surpassed those of their mother!

Alicia proved this in a rather startling way during their

first meeting with Fons, when she was desperately pleading with him to keep their jobs here. She used her katalyein skills to erase the trauma he'd suffered when he received all his body modifications. He'd previously thought all had been utterly painless. Via Alicia, he found out the opposite, and after she finished, he felt a huge burden had been lifted from him. He was more alive and happier than he'd been in years.

The story told by Dorita of how they got this way provided a huge clue that Fons and the other men were about to pursue. Esmeralda knew Dorita since childhood, having played together. She had her arms back then. She married Geraldo dela Handro, a fisherman, a deep sea fisherman. A year after they were married, he had returned home with a most unusual fish, the diablo rojo he called it. They both ate it and found it both delicious and mouth-watering. After that, Dorita felt funny. Her arms ached, but his did not. Before long, her arms began to wither and soon she couldn't use them at all. They visited all the doctors but no cures were found. One day Dorita rose and found her arms lying on her bed. They'd fallen off, much like a snake sheds its skin!

After that, her eyes changed from black to yellow and her telekinesis powers manifested themselves, giving her a way to survive. Then she got pregnant with Alicia, but when Alicia was born, she had no arms and only one leg! Yet she had the yellow eyes. As she grew up, her telekinesis skills blossomed allowing her to do whatever was needed. A year later, Juana was born similarly. Fons was impressed to learn that one time Alicia even moved Geraldo's fishing boat onto the shore so he could clean its hull — an enormous weight that would have required many men and blocks and tackles!

Fons learned that Geraldo continued to bring back more of the diablo rojo fish and the four continued to eating it. This suggested to him that by doing so, the three were somehow getting stronger psi energies. Even more impressive, the girls loved to swim and they hopped to the beach as often as they could.

Further, all three were incredibly naive and knew virtually nothing about the *mentales* gifts and the towers. It was like they were raised in a vacuum, Fons thought. Only

Brom Tower possessed any women with the katalyein gift, for it was extremely rare. Likewise, the teleportation gift was almost as rare. Yet here he had three with the catalyst gifts and two who teleported easily, to say nothing of the raw telekinetic powers these three possessed!

It was imperative that these three be properly trained and given their amplifying crystals. He was forming a new tower and these three had to be a part of that! To that end, he had them move into one of the three unused master suits, giving it to them as their new home, to say nothing of offering them a five-fold increase in their salaries as an inducement to stay here. That same day, he talked to Andres afterwards, "Andres, we need to see what Alicia's and Juana's children might possess. Unless you are totally opposed, I want you to start courting Alicia. It could well be your children with her may become the most powerful *mentales* gifted on the planet!"

"Dad, she's only got one leg," he protested a little. "Well, at least she's otherwise attractive. I'll see," he finally consented.

"Thank you, son. A Renegade Tower with our own katalyein and teleport specialists – this is way too good to be true," Fons replied.

"Maybe our exile isn't an exile at all," Roberto added with a wry smile. None knew far out in the ocean south of Villa del Rey, the God called Calder had awakened.

It was now June and a number of positive steps had been taken. First, Alicia, Juana, and Dorita had used their special, untrained skills to remove the traumatic black masses on all the twenty-one who'd undergone body modifications. That alone brought them all a renewed vitality and willingness to live, in spite of their physical limitations.

After that, the four men worked on the missing critical training of the three. An untrained telepath is both a danger to others as well as himself. Considering how incredibly valuable these three were, they chose to train them on all five forms of psi attacks and all five forms of defense. This took them much of late May and early June to accomplish. That finished, they were then given their own germanium crystals and taught how to use them. Given their physical limitations, their crystals were not covered in silk pouches, but allowed constantly to touch the skin of their chests, attached to a gold chain.

During this time, Fons had their wives closely inspect Alicia and Juana's bodies. Why? Their leg was centrally located in line with their spine. Fons worried this unusual orientation might mean these teens could not reproduce. That fear was soon dispelled. Although the men were in another room from the women who were performing the close examinations, because they were in close rapport with them, the men saw what their wives saw.

Alicia did in fact have two legs, sort of. Her legs began where all legs did on either side of her pelvis. The two legs looked perfectly normal for about a foot when they began to curve towards each other, joining into one at the knee. A single lower leg began at the knee. Never had anyone seen such a strange sight as this. More importantly to the men was the obvious fact these teens were capable of having children. Now they could begin planning for the future in earnest.

They'd met Geraldo dela Handro twice now. To say that he was happy and pleased with the sudden great fortune for his family would be an understatement. He was constantly thanking them. He was due back any day and would be bringing them some more of the diablo rojo fishes, as requested by Fons. The four men met to discuss their next move.

Fons said, "Okay, we know Dorita ate the fish and received her gifts after that. My thinking is we should try this on one of our children and see if they too end up like Dorita, a powerful katalyein and telekinetic. If so, more of us could make this change. Think of the power we hold here."

"True, true, but what about breeding Andres to Alicia and seeing what their children become?" asked Roberto.

"That project is coming along. Let's focus on what we are going to do with the fish Geraldo is bringing us soon. Some of us must eat it and see what happens," Fons replied.

Donato spoke up, "Look, we know Dorita was perfectly normal when she ate it and became transformed. Should we try that on a normal woman first and not one of our modified women? Geraldo was not modified and showed no signs the fish had any effect upon him. Still, we ought to test it on one of our men. It might have something to do with Geraldo, not with men in general. We need some controlled studies. What about getting Gracia to volunteer and perhaps Rafael? You would still have your heir in Andres, Fons." This was a sticky subject. Fons had always argued against Gracia and Andres ever having any body modifications. But would he be willing to risk Gracia in this experiment?

"Damn, Donato. Okay, I admit I see your point. We need a controlled experiment. We should also have a pair of our modified children also eat the fish. What about using Anita? She's not been modified."

"She is the only one in my family who hasn't been. Each family should have one member who is able to help all the others, though with our personal assistants, that need is lessened. Fons, you have two that aren't modified. The rest of us only have one," Donato countered.

Fons sighed, conceding the point. "Okay, Gracia and Rafael. We don't have other unmodified boys, so it has to be him. What about a modified pair? Who do we choose?"

Amado spoke up, "We should spread the tests among all four families to be fair and honest about it. It would have to be either Renato and Donica or Ruperto and Ana, if we are all going to stick our necks out on this experiment. I suggest Ruperto and Ana because Ruperto is younger than Renato. If the changes do happen, youth may be able to adapt better."

After more discussion, they opted for these four. "How are we going to convince them to do this experiment?" Roberto asked.

Fons replied, "I think we can make a strong case, if they are transformed similarly to Dorita, then their lives will be vastly easier to endure, what with such an enormous telekinetic power. Right now, all of us are having a bitch of a time with these hands. They are pretty darn well useless, if we are going to be honest with each other. Hell, I've given up trying to feed myself. It's so much easier letting my assistant feed me. Plus, they've all seen the immense power Dorita wields. I think that might convince them, but lord knows about Gracia! She's a proud fighter and is unlikely to want to chance losing that."

"I see your point. Where are they at now?" asked Donato.

"I think Alicia and Juana took Andres and Gracia to the beach. Something about teaching them to swim," Fons replied. "Andres is following through on my request to attempt to get Alicia to fall in love with him. He's agreed to marry her if she does. He knows as well as we just how powerful their children may wind up being. He's fully behind our cause. We can talk to them at supper. We can talk with Rafael, Ruperto, and Ann now, if you like."

"Have we given any consideration to mating someone with Juana?" asked Amado.

"Who have we left for her?" Fons asked.

Meanwhile, the four teens were getting ready to go to the beach. "We've never been to the beach or swimming, Alicia. What are to bring? What do we wear?" Andres asked.

"Well, all you really need is a towel. Most people go swimming nude. The water is always warm in the summers, though some wear their underpants. Juana and I have to go nude because we don't have underpants like mom does. We're freaks," Alicia answered sincerely.

"Hey, I don't think you are freaks. Your bodies are, well, different. Nude? Isn't that rather embarrassing?" Andres countered and asked.

"We are freaks, Andres. Everyone always stares at us and thinks so. We know what they are thinking. You'll see. Doesn't matter if it is embarrassing for us or not, cause we can't do anything about it. At least now, most who know us respect the fact we can swim. Still, we are used to it, Andres. We've been stared at all our lives. We just have learned to ignore what we can't change. Come on; let's get going."

"But how do you carry your towels? I can put them in my bag for you," Andres asked.

"In our mouths, silly. Where else? Nobody has ever carried our towels for us. Why would you want to do that?" Alicia asked. Again, Andres realized they were naive about social interactions. He suspected that was probably because so few people ever truly interacted with them.

"Where we come from, it is only polite for men to assist women, in this case by carrying your towel for you," he replied.

"Even if we don't really need you to carry them?" she asked somewhat confused.

"You bet. Like with your chair when we first met. Men are expected to assist a woman with her chair; men are expected to open the doors for the woman they are with."

"Even when they can move their own chairs and open the doors themselves?" she asked.

"Exactly, that's being polite to the fairer sex," Andres added.

"But we are not fairer sex; we're freaks really."

"You are both beautiful young women who have some obvious physical differences from the normal woman, that's all," Andres attempted to again be polite.

"Well then okay, there's our towels. Come on. We want to go swimming," she consented.

He stuffed them into his bag along with Gracia's towel too. "I'll bring the carriage around."

"Why?" asked Alicia. She was the more forward of the two sisters.

"So we can ride down to the beach," Andres replied, thinking that was obvious.

"Why waste time? Besides then you have to mess with the horse. Come on; just put your arm on my shoulders and hang on. Gracia, you grab Juana. Hurry up. Time is wasting," Alicia requested. Andres did as she asked, slipping his hand under her long hair, correctly figuring he might accidently pull it when she began hopping. Gracia did the same with Juana. Alicia then did a little hop, but as she came down to the ground, she landed herself and Andres on the sandy beach. Momentarily, Juana and Gracia appeared beside them.

"Wow! That was incredible, Alicia. Thanks!" he complimented her, very much impressed with her effortless teleport.

She smiled. "Follow us. We're going to our favorite spot over that way," she nodded with her head. She and her sister began taking smooth, small hops in the sand heading closer to the waters. At least fifty men, women, and children were on the beach or out swimming, but mostly children. Nearly all were nude. Andres noticed she was going at the right speed for him to walk at her side. "See," she whispered, "we can move alongside of you two feet'ers. That's what we call your kind," she giggled.

As they moved down closer, several other teens called out to her. The most typical response was either "Hey, here comes the mermaids" or "Hey, the freaks are back again." Alicia whispered, "Just ignore them, Andres. We do." He found that hard to do. She picked up his and Gracia's thoughts. "You mean you really want to go over there and beat them up for insulting us? Why?"

"Because those are not polite things to say to anyone, especially you two, who can't change the way you look. They need to be taught manners and not go around insulting people." Alicia raised her eyebrows.

They stopped a few feet from the water's edge. Crystal blue waters lapped upon the white sands. The day was sunny still. Alicia and Juana began to get undressed, using their telekinetic skills, which must have seemed like magic to others who were staring at them. Andres and Gracia followed suit, a bit embarrassed to be undressing fully in public. "Spread your towel out like so. When you get tired, you can come up and lie down on it and soak up some sun until it clouds over," she explained.

"I suppose you both should just walk out into the water a ways. It is nice and sloping. We can't do that, because it's much too hard to hop, so we just jump out into the deeper water where we can then swim. Come join us; we won't go into water over your heads," Alicia promised. She and Juana did another of their jumps and appeared some fifty feet out into the water where they fell into the waters. Taking deep breaths, Gracia and Andres began walking out to them. When they got close, they saw the two teens were indeed swimming, rather swiftly at that. Their whole bodies seemed to undulate up and down as their leg propelled them along, much like a fish, the two thought.

After a time, Alicia swam very close to Andres, missing him by inches, allowing her long black hair, flowing in little waves down to her ankle, to drift across his chest as she changed direction slightly. He was roused. "Oops, that's never happened before. I'm sorry," an embarrassed Alicia exclaimed and came to a stop, struggling to get her foot on the sand beneath the waters so she could stand not far from him.

"I'm sorry, Alicia. Like I said, you are one attractive woman," he replied. "I guess it shows."

"But how can that be? I am a freak; no one else reacts that way," she said growing a little confused and wiggling some to remain standing. Andres moved to her and put his arms around her stabilizing her.

"That's all in your mind, Alicia. You just think what all the others think. You are beautiful," he whispered, running his hands down her sides. He felt emotions stir in her she'd never felt before. At just the right moment, thanks to his light rapport with her, he gave her a gentle kiss on her thick lips and felt even more emotions and knew he'd awakened her passions, long suppressed.

She started to say, "But, I am. . ." He cut her off with and even more passionate kiss, and she began to respond gradually and then with a fierce passion long suppressed, now suddenly released. He felt her touching his mind. "You really don't see me as a freak, do you?" she whispered.

"Of course not, a little strange, but a beautiful young woman." He kissed her again and suggested they perhaps lay on their towels a while. Instantly, she jumped them both to their towels. Carefully, she sat down on hers, tossing her wet hair to one side. Then she laid down on her back. Andres followed suit, rolling over on his side to gaze at her.

"You really don't think I am an ugly, misshapen freak, do you?"

"Nope." Again, he ran his fingers gently over her belly.

"I like you touching me. No one has ever done that to me before. Juana and I figured ages ago no one would really like us — you know, like this. We never had a boyfriend or really any friends at all, just mom and dad. Can you kiss me again? I really liked that, if you aren't embarrassed to have others seeing you do it to me," she whispered. Andres complied, ignoring some distant snickering and snide comments from some other teenage boys.

She changed the subject. "You know these crystals make a huge difference for Juana and me. Before by the end of the day, she and I would be so utterly exhausted it was all we could do before falling asleep each night just to get into bed. We had to eat though; we always felt like we were starving to death."

"Right, that's typical, Alicia. You see, you and Juana use a whole lot of your psi energies just living and doing what you have to do. Each of us has only so much psi energies available each day. When you use it all up, you feel utterly drained, exhausted, and are so tired you have to sleep. Of course, after a good night's sleep, your energy is fully recharged. Also using your gifts burns up calories and you have to eat a lot. That's why you both are so thin; you use so much each day."

"We have so much to learn, don't we, Andres?"

"You are learning very rapidly and very well, Alicia."

"But I can't be your girlfriend, Andres. I can't do like all the other girls do. Look there, she, she has her arms around her boyfriend. They are walking along together. I can never do that. You best forget about me," she stated, but he sensed the underlying grief.

"You can hold me with your powers, but I think I know a way that you can walk beside me and not have to hop along. Come on. I'll show you. Gracia, see if you and Juana can do what we're doing." They stood up, she with a sort of jumping motion to get to her foot. "Okay, we lean tightly together side by side. I put my arm securely around you. Now I will be your missing leg. I step and now you lean on me and take your step, right like that." She did so, feeling him taking the weight of her body against his. After a few awkward steps, she got the hang of it.

Beaming, she grinned, "I am walking beside you, Andres, like the other girls do! Juana look, we can be like other girls, like this!" Juana was just as pleased as Alicia was.

"Oh," she exclaimed. "You'd feel better if we were doing this with our clothes on."

"Well, as a matter of fact yes I would. Do you mind?"

She didn't. A few minutes later, dried off and clothed again, he tossed his bag over his left shoulder and took her securely with his right hand, and they again began just walking along the beach, enjoying the view. Andres found it difficult to ignore all the catcalls sent her way, but she didn't hear them; she was totally engrossed in "being normal" for the first time in her life. Juana felt similarly walking beside Gracia.

After a time, she whispered, "Andres, do you really like me?" He stopped and gave her another passionate kiss. Juana giggled a little and Gracia smiled at her brother.

"We can walk like this around the hacienda too, not just the beach," he whispered.

"I would really love to – with you, Andres. I didn't think a boy would ever want to kiss me and hold me, not ever, not really."

"I know. You and Juana have had a most difficult life so far, but now that's all changing for the better," he replied.

"Hey, look! There comes papa's boat now. Can we walk that far? I'd like him to see us walking like normal people do," Alicia exclaimed. They continued down the beach. Going up the rise to the docks was a bit more difficult, but Andres was insistent they do it normally. Then they walked down the long wooden docks where Geraldo was just tying his boat up. He stopped and stared at his two daughters. When they finally got close, they saw tears streaming down his face.

Alarmed, Alicia cried out, "Papa, what's the matter? Are you hurt?"

"No, dear child, I am crying because I am so happy to see you and Juana. You are walking, not hopping!" She and Juana beamed and then hopped quickly up to him. He threw his arms around the two teens holding them tightly for a time.

Andres and Gracia moved up and allowed the girls to retake their positions at their sides, which also supported them so they didn't have to use some telekinetic energy to remain standing without wobbling a little. Geraldo said, "Well, I have got four of those special diablo rojo fishes your father wanted. Let me finish unloading the other fish and I'll bring those four to the hacienda straightaway."

"Thanks.Dad is really excited about them. Your girls

took us swimming for the first time today. Gracia and I have never been in the water before, but your girls sure can swim well," Andres said.

"Aye, that they can. I swear that they swim as good as the fishes in the ocean. That's my girls," he said, proud of them.

"Well, I suppose we ought to be heading back now. Care to walk a little ways before you jump us back, Alicia, Juana?" Andres asked.

"You bet!" The four began a slow stroll back down the docks and into the city streets. The two teens held their heads up proudly; for the first time in their lives, they felt like a real person. Later as they tired, they jumped back inside the hacienda. They then hopped into their suite to brush the sand out of their hair and change for dinner.

As Andres and Gracia headed to their suite to do the same thing, Gracia said, "Well done, brother. You are giving them back their lives. It is such a good feeling helping others, isn't it? I hope we can help lots of other people. I feel so alive just now, don't you? She really did turn you on back there, didn't she? You weren't pretending."

He flushed, "You're right. I am fascinated by her. She's something else." Gracia smiled.

Fons interrupted them, "Gracia, may I have a word with you in private as you are brushing out the sand from your hair?" Andres stepped into a side room to change.

"As you know, Geraldo is bringing us some of those special fish of his, the kind that has apparently allowed these three to gain their immense powers. We want to run a series of controlled tests with the fish. We want to have two sets of a boy and girl eat the fish, one set being those who have been body modified and the other set being unmodified. Ruperto and Ana have agreed to be the body modified test subjects. Rafael will be one of the unmodified pair. Gracia, I would like you to be the other one."

"But dad! I don't want to become, well you know," Gracia began to protest.

"I know, dear, but we've taken one child from each of the families, excepting the de la Parte's. Probably nothing will happen. Yet on the chance it does happen to you, think of the immense power that you will be gaining? Power you can use to truly help other people and make a huge difference in their lives." He played his daughter well, knowing how much she truly wanted to help others. He always thought it was a shame her *mentales* gifts didn't include the many healing gifts.

"Well, I suppose I really ought to do it then. Put that way, how can I refuse, dad? Do you think just eating these fish will do anything to us? We're *mentales* to begin with. Dorita wasn't."

"That's what we want to find out. Does it affect us? Does it affect only women or can men be affected too? We have so many unanswered questions about this find of the century. This potentially *dwarfs* all Paco Valen ever did. Thank you, Gracia." She smiled and finished her hair.

Later after dinner, Geraldo prepared one of the diablo rojo fishes while Dorita, Alicia, and Juana watched him. The other three large fish were being kept in ice, teleported down from the far north where the ice and snow never melted. Ice was terribly expensive, but needed in this case. Fons hovered over Geraldo, taking notes as best he could with his ill-working hands. For his part, Geraldo felt important, outlining in detail just how he'd prepared them for Dorita so long ago. He always cooked fish the same way so there was not a memory problem. He dished out four portions, which he claimed were the size Dorita and he had eaten that fateful evening. "We ate another meal about this size from the fish the next day for lunch."

When the plates were ready, Fons sent for the four test subjects. Their fathers were with them, and all four adults took more notes, struggling mightily with their hands to do so.

"Geraldo, you are right, this fish is about the best tasting fish that I've ever had," Gracia exclaimed, licking her lips. "Juicy and tender, almost like chicken."

Alicia grinned, "Of course, it is the best fish." Another bite of the flaked morsel rose up to her opened mouth. Andres sat beside her watching and admiring her.

"It is good," Ana added, struggling with her fork in her prosthetic hands, dropping about one out of every two bites as they hit her lip plates instead of her mouth. She bravely didn't say anything, but continued to work at it. Ruperto was having similar difficulties, and they wished that they had their personal assistants helping them. Fons didn't want anyone other than themselves to see what was going on. This was too vital a discovery to have others possibly knowing about, not yet anyway.

Chapter 2 Visitation

No sooner had they finished eating the diablos rojo fish when the room became filled with a bluish-green light, startling everyone. "What's happening?" Andres called out, drawing his sword and moving between Alicia and this light, intent upon protecting her. Gracia followed suit, moving before Juana. Amid the pale light, a form slowly took shape, appearing as an eight-foot tall man with a fish tail where his legs ought to have been. His hair was quite long and tangled, and sheer power radiated from him. Calder had finally decided now was the time to appear.

"I am Calder, God of the Seas and Waters. Too long have I slept in my warm waters. My world has forgotten me. Now that will change." He looked at Alicia and Juana and said, "Welcome my lovely Daughters of the Sea. Long have I watched you while you were swimming, waiting for this day, when others of your kind would see you for what you are, powerful Daughters of the Sea. Andres, you have my permission to court Alicia, if she wishes it and if Geraldo and Dorita agree."

He turned to the four speechless men. "You men of great power, you seek to have more Daughters of the Sea but for the wrong purpose. Challenge not the land dwellers of your kin, for they are half-blind. Most of the world is sea and fresh waters, from which all life comes, upon which all life depends. The power of water truly controls the world of men, though they no longer see this. Long have I waited for men of great power to come to my Daughters of the Sea and to recognize in them a taste of what Calder can do for his followers."

"Build thy tower here as you have planned, but seek not to overthrow the land dwellers by force of arms. In every city, town, and village that sits aside waters, build a Temple of Calder. Place with in these temples one or more of my Daughters of the Sea that she may bless those who trade and travel upon the waters, and that she may heal and cure those who believe. Build large fleets of sailing ships. Through trade along the entire coast of Tierra, in time, thou shalt control all thy world."

"My High Priestess shall choose other maidens to become your needed Daughters of the Sea. Trust in the wisdom of her choices. She alone shall have the powers to control all the waters of Tierra, brining water to the deserts, calm stormy seas, or even raise tempests against those who oppose us. Through her shall come the healing of men, peace, and prosperity for all."

"Fons Valen, Roberto Valen, Amado de la Parte, Donato de Portales, wilst thou accept my will and change the path you are following to that of mine?"

A few key phrases resonated in their minds. *Challenge not the land dwellers of your kin.* This was hard to swallow, they all wanted revenge upon Lord Pedro; they wanted to recapture Castle Valen for themselves. Food for thought: *The power of water truly controls the world of men.* Each man considered himself as fitting Calder's conclusion about themselves: he was powerful. *Long have I waited for men of great power.* That he was suggesting they were to *build thy tower here as you have planned* was most comforting. They were on the right path with their proposed Renegade Tower. However, they could not see how they could gain anything by *seek not to overthrown by force of arms.* How else could then win? Building lots of temples and having one of his Daughters of the Sea running them didn't appeal to them. In their minds, *healing and curing* was of little importance in the larger scheme of things. However, what did get their full attention was *in time, thou shalt control all thy world.* Adding to that was the pledge this High Priestess would have the power to *raise tempests against those who oppose us.* To these men, that suggested immense power, a force they could use to control the world.

"I accept, Lord Calder," Fons replied both firmly and with conviction. Hastily, the other three men agreed as well.

"So be it. Our time has come at long last. Gracia, I accept thee as my High Priestess; through you shall my powers flow. Train well my Daughters of the Sea to come, that they may serve mankind well. You alone may choose these new maidens to become Daughters of the Sea. When you have chosen one, feed them servings of my special fish, diablo rojo. Unto you, Gracia, I give the greatest of powers."

He turned his gaze upon Andres, who was still standing protecting Alicia. "Andres, thou shalt become the Supreme Guardian of the High Priestess and all the many Daughter of the Sea to come. Protect them well. Choose other men to become Guardians and husbands for the Daughter of the Sea. Choose them wisely, as you would for Alicia."

"Gracia, Andres, let no man or woman influence thy choices. Be thy own council in these matters."

His powerful gaze then fell upon the four men and Andes and Gracia. "Be not introverted. Look out upon the city. There are others here who are ready and will assist you, just as there are those in other coastal cities and towns and even river towns. Choose them wisely. Healing and trade shall by thy weapons of conquest. Build thy fleets, spread Temples of Calder far and wide, and thus shall yea be rewarded."

His half-man, half-fish image dissolved before their eyes, leaving the bluish-green glow behind. Then it too dimmed and disappeared, leaving a very speechless group staring at the room's wall where Calder had been standing.

Juana broke the silence, "Mom, no wonder Alicia and I love to swim so much! We're Daughters of the Sea!"

"So you are. I always thought that you two were my little mermaids. The God has indeed blessed us all," Dorita replied, very proud of her girls.

"Well, this changes things a little," Fons said trying to remain calm. He'd just had a conversation with a god and he found it more than a little unnerving.

"Ha, a little?" Donato exclaimed. "My god, man, that was a god!"

"I, I never thought gods and goddesses were real," Amado choked, as he swallowed hard.

"Does this mean I won't get to be one of them?" the shy voice of little Rafael asked.

"Yes, what about us, Ana and me," Ruperto asked. "He didn't say anything to us. Are we off the hook, dad?"

Ana kept quiet. She didn't want to become a freak like

Alicia and Juana, but she also could not go against her father's wishes. That was why she ate the diablo rojo, hoping and praying that somehow it wouldn't affect her. Her life was miserable enough with her toe shoes, alien hands, and lip plates. Besides, all she wanted to do now was to make love with Ruperto in their bed with satin sheets. She could hardly think of anything else.

Fons took charge. "Well, to my way of thinking, we have three areas to work on if we are to follow Calder's charge. We four should continue our efforts to get our Renegade Tower up and running. Probably we should take charge of getting this proposed fleet of new boats built and trading established. Andes and Gracia, you are obviously in charge of these temples, building them or whatever, finding the guardians, and daughters of the sea things. We will relinquish control of these things to you, along with the diablo rojo fish. If you two want help or advice, ask us."

"Dad, he did say we are supposed to do these things ourselves," Andres replied. "I am beginning to see why but I can't quite put it into words. Oh, Geraldo, Dorita, may I court your beautiful daughter Alicia?" he asked politely, recalling Calder's words. Right now, he was fascinated with her and wanted to spend all the time he could with the young woman.

Geraldo slapped him on his back heartily. "Son, I have waited eighteen years for a man to come along who appreciates my daughter for what she is. Yes, you have our permission, son. I can't tell you how much it has hurt me to always hear her being called a freak behind my back."

"Thank you, sir, ma'am," he replied jubilantly. "Alicia, come on. Let's go for a walk in the gardens, shall we, my charming Daughter of the Sea?" She giggled and rose from her chair. He put his arm around her shoulders slipping it beneath her long, thick black hair. She took small little hops alongside of him, keeping pace, as he led her out of the kitchen and off towards the gardens. Night had fallen, but still the fragrances from the many flowers were heady. Overhead the two moons of Tierra shone dimly.

"If you walk slowly, Andres, I can hop beside you, almost like I was walking with you," she whispered.

"Here, let's really walk together, Alicia. Lean on me liked we did. Right. Now you are walking with me," he whispered back, planting a kiss on her temple.

A little later, Juana and Gracia joined them. She was also helping Juana walk at her side as they had done earlier in the day. "I'm scared, Juana. What is going to happen to my body? Will I become like you?"

"I don't know, Gracia. We were born like we are. Mom told us her arms withered and fell off. Maybe that will be what's going to happen. She told us for days she was terrified and so helpless. Well I can imagine how she must have felt, you know, though we've never been that way. We've always been able to make things move for us. If you end up as I am, don't get scared. Alicia and I can help you learn to hop and jump. I remember when I was just trying to stand up and move it was hard to learn at first. A little scary, but mom was always there for us, holding us with her powers so we didn't fall down."

"I think all parents do that as they help their babies learn to walk, Juana. Still I can't imagine how terrible it will be not to have arms and only one leg. It scares the crap out of me," she admitted.

"It is normal for us, so I suppose in time it will be normal for you too, Gracia. I can see why Calder chose you though. You are kind and considerate and really do want to help people. Alicia and I want to help others, but they all think we are freaks and won't let us. So we just bless papa's boat when he goes out to sea. Maybe you can fix it so we can help others, Gracia," Juana suggested.

"I'll try, only I am so scared of this. What if I can't even walk? What if I lose my arms and can't lift or move anything like you and your mother can? What if everyone then thinks I am a freak? I am a trained fighter, Juana, sworn to protect others with my sword and skills. God, Juana, I am so scared right now!"

"I can feel it in you too, Gracia. Come on. Smell the flowers. They are so beautiful here. Carlos does such a wonderful job with all the flowers." Gracia took a deep breath, sensing the many fragrances fighting each other for recognition in her senses. Still, beneath this simple pleasure, her fear was quiet real. It took all her will power to keep it from turning into terror.

"Oh here you are, Gracia. Fons told me what happened! Are you all right, dear?" Delfina made her painstakingly slow way through the gardens towards her daughter and Juana. "Let me see you," she demanded in a motherly way. She put her alien hands on her shoulders a bit too hard. Gracia flinched slightly from the rather hard bump, but knew that her mother couldn't feel anything with them and didn't realize how hard she'd touched her.

"So far mom, I'm okay, just really scared," Gracia admitted. "I've been always looking out for you and Hermina since you got so modified, but what am I to do if I change? I'm frightened."

"Well, Fons did say the god promised you immense powers dear. That must mean you will be quite all right. I think it is good this Calder fellow is giving us women more power. I've always had to be in the shadow of your father, doing what he asked of me. Like I am now, I rather wish I had stood up to him and said no, but women are supposed to support our husbands," she sighed and admitted what she'd not really said openly before, only hinted at with her two daughters.

"I know mom. All you can do now is try to make the best of it," Gracia attempted to console Delfina a little. She felt how awful her mother felt, but was powerless to do anything about it. While they were all cooped up on the barge coming down the Alcantara River to Villa del Rey, she feared her mother might take her own life. She was so terribly depressed about her awful physical helplessness. Now after Alicia worked her magic on her, that fear was gone, but she still knew how awful life was for her mother and the other twenty. She wished there was something she could do for them, but as always, she knew she couldn't, probably not even with the supposedly great powers she might soon get.

They talked a little more and her mother left them, moving off slowly and carefully in her toe shoes. "She cares for you," Juana whispered.

"I know she does. Juana, I am getting really sacred now. Can you please stay with me in case something happens? I trust you more than anyone else, except Alicia and Andres."

"Sure, let's get you to your bed. You look a bit tired or something."

"I know. I don't feel quite right, and the more I stand here, the more frightened I'm getting." Slowly the two made their way to Gracia's suite she shared with her brother, Andres. As they walked along, both spotted the two passionately kissing beside one of the ponds and didn't disturb the young lovers. Juana grinned, very happy for her sister. It also meant perhaps one day she too would find love, which until now she had known she'd never have.

The two women climbed into bed together at Gracia's insistence. She fell into a deep sleep, but her body began to sweat and to twist and turn. Juana sensed something was happening to her, but just knew it was best not to wake her. She rolled onto her side and kept watch over her, sending Gracia soothing thoughts.

In the morning, Gracia was too weak and scared to get out of bed. Juana volunteered to bring her something to eat, but it had to be more of the diablo rojo fish – that Juana instinctively knew. She hopped out of the room and to the kitchen, where she found her dad was already cooking a bit of the fish. "Morning Flower Blossom," he called out, using his pet name for his youngest daughter. "I figured you'd need some more of the fish, so it's about ready. How is your friend Gracia doing?"

"She's had a rough night. Something is happening to her. I just know we need to get more of the fish in her," Juana replied.

"I knew that too, Flower Blossom. So I got up a little early to fix some. Here, you can take it to her." He held out a plate with a fork alongside the steaming fish. He felt Juana's telekinetic grasp on it and let go carefully. He watched amused as always, as the plate seemed to move across the room on its own, his lovely daughter hopping along behind it taking her usual ambling small hops. He felt nothing but pride.

Later Juana sat on the edge of Gracia's bed and lifted

her up a little, placing a pillow behind her, and then fed her the fish. As soon as Gracia finished, she wanted to lay back down and soon fell back asleep. Juana took the empty plate and fork back to the kitchen and joined Alicia and Andres for breakfast. Both wanted to know how his sister was doing and Juana told them.

"Well I suppose I ought to tour the city, Alicia. Calder did say we'd find others out there who might be willing to help us," Andres suggested. "But maybe we'd best wait until Gracia gets better. She might need our help."

"We know the city. Juana and I can take you, but I think you are right. We should stay by her side right now. I can feel her fear even in here in the dining room," Alicia replied. That did it; the three headed back to sit beside Gracia, though she was still sleeping and sweating, her hair mounded above her head out of the way. Andres wiped her face off with a cold washrag. They watched and waited.

Close to noon, she woke a little, complaining that she was starving. Andres rushed off to bring her more of the fish, while Alicia and Juana talked soothingly to her, trying to calm her panic and fear. Gracia knew something was happening to her, but she couldn't tell what yet. She kept looking at her arms, but so far, they looked as they always had, strong and well-muscled. After feeding her the fish lunch, Gracia again fell into a deep, restless sleep. The three continued to watch over her. Twice, Delfina made her slow way into her daughter's room to check on her.

Mid-afternoon, her fever broke and Gracia woke. She sat up in her bed and noticed the three watching over her. "Thanks," she whispered. "I feel really funny, but better. Look, I still have my arms; they don't seem any different. Andres, turn your head; I'm not wearing any panties." He did and she pulled down the satin sheet and screamed. Of course, Andres turned to look as well.

From her waist down, she looked exactly as Alicia and Juana. Her upper legs were now somewhat bowed and merged together just above her knees. She had only one lower leg and foot now, just like the two teens! "Oh my god!" she exclaimed after screaming wildly. Her lower leg and foot were almost twice the thickness of her original legs and feet, just like the two mermaids.

"Wow, you are just like us now," Alicia stated the rather obvious.

"How am I ever going to walk again?"

"We will teach you to hop like us," Alicia promised sincerely.

"I have to use the commode really, really badly. Andres, help me, please," she wailed.

"I'm right here, sis. Let's get you to the edge of the bed. See if you can stand on it. Put your arms around me." She swung her leg around and scooted to the edge, putting her foot on the floor.

"My god, Andres! This is so weird! Hold me; don't let me fall!"

"I got you, sis. See, you are able to stand mostly." She was wiggling wildly, her arms going in many directions finally latching onto him. "Got you. See. Now see if you can hop a little to the commode. If you can't, I'll carry you."

She tried a little, but was too scared, and he lifted her up and sat her on the commode. A bit later he carried her back and laid her gently on the bed, she again pulled her disheveled hair up above her head. She let out a long sigh. "Thanks, Andres. I am *really* scared, but hungry, really hungry. More fish please. I seem to be craving it right now." Alicia hopped off to get some more. This time Andres fed her and then she fell into a deep sleep again.

Alicia whispered, "Maybe it's not all done yet." The three continued to watch over her, but Delfina and Fons came by to look at her new leg and then left. Delfina, though, left crying softly to herself.

The four men had not been idle. They met all that morning working on the details of their proposed Renegade Tower. "Look, do we or don't we use a woman as the venerada?" Fons asked. "I for one would like a man in that position, as it was before Amy Blackwell's Ultimatum forced us men out of power." The others agreed with him. If they were breaking all traditions and forming up an illegal tower, they might as well make it the way they wanted it. As the eldest,

Fons appointed himself the Venerado of the Renegade Tower. Roberto would become the Capo of the *Círculo de mentes*, their tower circle. He would wield the combined psi powers flowed to him by the other circle members.

A circle usually had nine other technicians and another who was their Regulator, whose job it was to keep the ten's bodies calm, relaxed, all tensions removed with blood pressure, heartbeats, and breathing all normal. The four men chose Natalia, Roberto's wife for this position, because she had training as a Regulator, though no one knew if she could still perform those duties without her hands. That unspoken problem faced them all. Could they even become an operational circle without any of them having hands?

Next, they needed to pick nine others who had technician training and who had strong psi powers. Each of their children had the training from Valen Tower, so that couldn't be used to eliminate some. For hours, they debated which of their children had the most potential. Each father argued for his, though several put in supporting words for Adora's children as well.

Finally, Amado said, "You know, since we are breaking all known rules, why are we limiting the circle members to just nine? We've got twelve good candidates in our married children. Why not have Capo Roberto wield the combined power of twelve not nine? He should have more power available than any other circle."

"But could Natalie monitor thirteen at once? Ten is pushing it, as I understand it," Donato countered. "Maybe we ought to have two Regulators. Anita is only fourteen, perhaps a bit too young for this, but we could have either Consuela do it or my wife, Adelita, as the second Regulator, perhaps giving them only a few to monitor."

After some discussion, that idea was accepted. "Say, all this is dependent on Ruperto and Ana not turning into something strange, like Alicia," Amado pointed out. "How are they doing? We did feed them that fish last night."

"Ruperto and Ana are showing no signs of anything; neither is Rafael. Something is happening with Gracia, but we knew that would be happening," Donato answered. "Still, we ought to keep an eye on them for a few days to make sure. Gentlemen, we really are getting ahead of ourselves a bit. What about the physical tower itself? We have to have a safe, secure tower in which to work, to setup security networks, a comm network, and such."

"True, true. It doesn't have to be one of those five story affairs. Crap, we can't go up and down the stairs, if we did build a tall one, not hobbled like we are. It needs to be level with our hacienda, only made from thick stone," Fons answered. "A place free from all outside distractions, that's the key. It doesn't need to be all that large either, just enough for all the circle members to sit comfortably. We best use chairs and not pillows as in the other towers. Our women with their pipe corsets can't deal with that, and it is just too damn hard for us men even to sit down on the floor anymore, not in these boots. We shall sit in chairs. The tower needs to be, say, twenty feet across on the inside and doesn't need to be taller than the hacienda, not really, unless we want an observation deck or we want our tower to be plainly visible to all the city."

"Hey, there's something to be said both for and against our tower being visible to the city," Amado countered. "If we keep it low, most might think it is merely a grain silo. If we make it plainly visible, we might be asking for trouble and then again, we might be gaining stature among the local lords and ladies."

"Once we are online, the other towers will know our location. We can't keep that a secret. They could put pressure on the Lord of Villa del Rey to shut us down," Donato advised. "So we need to get the lord backing us, somehow. That means we must provide some service he needs badly enough to defy Valen Tower's requests to shut us down."

This, the men discussed for some time before they realized Calder had given them the answer: provide protection for the coming fleets and local healing. "Of course the sick and injured will have to come to us, we can hardly go to them," Fons declared. "Now we need to get a construction crew hired, an architect, and stone cutters. I'll send for Eugenio and see if he can put us in touch with some who can facilitate this project. Of course we're going to have to find a lot of germanium crystals to use in the networks." This led to more discussions. Slowly but surely, the project began to take shape in their minds. Soon they hoped it would begin to appear in the physical world.

It was after supper that Gracia again awoke. Once more, she was feverish and begging for more fish. However, her arms were getting somewhat weak, causing her even more panic. Andres thought it remarkable that as stressed as his sister was she could still eat. But then, he thought, the fish was responsible for the many changes her body was undergoing. All three took turns sitting up with the sleeping Gracia, mopping her forehead during the night.

As dawn came, Andres was with her, but in the morning light, he could tell that she would likely be losing her arms too. Both looked more like dried husks around ears of corn than human arms. His own stomach tensed as if in echo of his sister's. She awoke and he again fed her. "My arms, my arms, oh god, Andres, not my arms too," she whispered between bites. Once full, she again drifted into sleep. He refused to leave her side, and Alicia brought him breakfast and sat with him. She sensed how much he cared for his sister and really admired him for it. Never had she met such a caring man before.

At noon, her fever again broke and she awoke. She tried to sit up, rousing both Andres and Alicia who were half dozing. As she sat up, the dried, withered husks that had been her arms fell off, leaving perfectly healed but empty shoulder sockets. She again screamed in terror and shock. Andres wisely said nothing, but gently mopped her forehead. She calmed down a little. "I got to use the commode! Oh god! I can't do anything. Andres, help!" He lifted her up, carried her to the commode, and helped her. Then he carried her back to her bed, sitting her on its edge.

"I'll go get her one of my dresses," Alicia volunteered. All realized that now none of Gracia's clothing would fit her. "You are one of us, Gracia." She hopped out of the room.

Gracia began crying, "Now I am a freak too, Andres."

"Sis, you are not a freak; you are still you and I still love you too. Give it time. I'm sure Calder would not allow this to happen without giving you powers to survive. Give it time. Alicia was born this way, so she had lots of time to learn."

"Andres, you can't imagine how helpless I feel right now. I can't even walk," she cried.

Andres replied, "Neither can Alicia or Juana and they get by very well. Give it time, sis, give it time." He had no idea what else he could say to her and just sat beside her and held on to her, sensing she needed that more than anything else at the moment. He was right. Before long, Alicia reappeared holding one of her slipover dresses in her teeth as she hopped into the room.

"Just slip it on over her head. We don't wear panties so we can more easily use the commode. Besides, none fit us. There, Gracia, you look good in it," Alicia complimented her.

"Alicia, I'm terrified!"

"I know, I know. Give yourself time. You'll catch on," Alicia suggested. Just then, Fons and Delfina came slowly into the room, followed by many others. All wanted to see what had happened to Gracia. In her fragile emotional state, Gracia broke down totally, embarrassing all the looker-on'ers, who quietly left as quickly as they could. Andres continued to hold her. The three said nothing and allowed her to sob.

At last, she stopped crying. "Can you see if you can stand a little?" Alicia suggested.

"I suppose I best try something, but it is so terrifying!" Gracia whispered. Andres let go of her and stood, ready to steady her or catch her. She scooted to the edge of the bed a little and pushed off, getting to her foot, at which point, she wiggled and wobbled a little, but her face showed visibly the utter panic that she felt. At last, she whispered, "This is so weird! I feel so strange, so helpless. I have to hop, don't I?"

"To the commode," she said bravely. Taking uncertain little hops and wiggling her torso about, she made it, but Andres had to lift up her dress for her and get her long tresses out of the way. "Andres, I'm really scared I can't do this," she whispered, hoping Alicia and Juana wouldn't overhear her. "I'm not like them. I'm scared to death!"

"Don't worry. I'll always be here for you. Look, I am now your guardian. I look after you, not mom, dad, and the others. They have to handle their own affairs now. I'm dedicated to Alicia, Juana, and you. I can't imagine how scary this is for you, but I can see something positive about it."

"What can possibly be positive, Andres?" she whispered back.

"We're supposed to find more women to become Daughters of the Sea, and they are going to have to go through this too. So you are getting firsthand knowledge of it and will be in a better position to know what they will be feeling and thinking. That way you will be able to help them through it. Alicia and Juana were born this way, so they can't really know what you are going through exactly."

"You're right. I can see that, but it doesn't make it any less frightening to me. I'm so utterly helpless right now and so scared."

"You'll be all right. Come on. Let's get you hopping more. I won't let you fall, I promise, sis." She lunged forward enough to get back on her foot, wiggling a little to get her balance once more. Slowly and carefully, she hopped back to her bed.

"God, I'm tired of sitting in the bed. Let's see if I can get out into the garden for a bit," she suggested. She watched Alicia and Juana hopping easily towards the bedroom door and sighed. They made this seem utterly trivial, so easy. It wasn't! It was frightening! With Andres at her side, she bravely attempted to hop after them. Once she got going, it wasn't too bad. Turning was more challenging and sitting down on a garden chair really spooked her.

Finally sitting and watching the cloudy afternoon sky, she sighed and said, "You know, my upper legs are so funny now, they are sort of springy. Guess that'll help." Meantime, Alicia chatted about the flowers, trying to get Gracia's attention more outward than inward, hoping that would help some.

Eventually, Gracia suggested she try to hop around the whole garden. Again, she sort of lunged up out of her chair, wiggling frantically to keep her balance. Andres wisely allowed her to see if she could keep from falling. She recovered. Taking a deep breath, she began hopping around the garden area, a rectangular area some two hundred feet by seventy feet. As she hopped along, her hair bobbed up and down as well as her well-endowed breasts. She saw Andres noticing them and stopped. "You *would* be looking at them," she teased him.

He chuckled, glad to see her smile a little. "Come on, no stopping; you're about a third of the way. We need to get you strong enough to go on a tour of the city with Alicia and Juana."

"That'll be the day," she said rather antagonistically. Then, she had another thought, "Glad there are no stairs! How do they handle stairs?"

"We can't. We jump them," Juana replied, meaning she teleported up or down them. "We hop as much as we can, Gracia. We get too fatigued and tired if we have to use our psi energies too much. So it is really important you get hopping down well."

By the time Gracia returned to her original chair having hopped some five hundred plus feet, she expected to be utterly pooped. She wasn't, but sat down anyway. "Well, I made that one."

"Super, sis. You did it and I didn't have to catch you."

"I very nearly fell three times. Turning is a bitch, but I did make it, didn't I? It's a start."

"You did really well, Gracia," Alicia praised her. "There are several different ways we can hop. Let me show you." She demonstrated a small one, her feet barely left the stone floor, but her motion was fairly smooth. "The one thing to watch out for is not to take a big hop. Even we lose our balance and have to use psi energies to keep from falling. If you don't jump up so high each time, then you don't bounce so much."

Juana added, "And don't try to go too fast. If you do, it is very easy to lose your balance and have to catch yourself with your psi energies. Well, once you get them," she added, realizing Gracia didn't have them yet.

Just them Esmeralda came up to them. "Ah here you all are. My, Gracia, you do look like the two sisters, don't you. Well, I came to say the seamstress will be here soon. Your father is ordering all three of you some new dresses, but you three can tell her how you want them made. He wants all three of you to dress similarly and as fancy as possible. Ah, here she comes now."

A middle-aged woman carrying a bag of sample materials came walking up to them. After introducing her, Esmeralda left them, returning to her duties. With some discussion, they settled on a light blue satin material. "The dresses have to be easily slipped on over our heads and no lower than our knees. It's too hard to use the commode," Alicia explained to the seamstress. Unlike the form fitting gowns worn by the other women here at the hacienda, the dresses worn by Alicia and Juana were more like sacks. The seamstress suggested a more form fitting style that had buttons across the front, making it easier for the women to see to button them with their telekinetic skills. At last, Alicia and Juana agreed to try one and see. Later, if it worked out, they'd order more of them. Compromised reached, the seamstress left, promising to return in two days with their first ones.

"I'm hungry again and thirsty," Gracia said after the seamstress left.

"Okay sis, then let's hop to the kitchen and rustle you up something."

"That's a long ways," she countered. Andres insisted, and again she lunged a bit to get up out of her chair, but she didn't wobble as much as before. Once sure of her foot, she followed after the other two, who hopped on ahead of her, telling her to try to mimic their hops. "This is still awfully scary, Andres," she whispered, focusing on her hops.

"Of course it is, but you are doing it. That's what counts. Keep up the good work."

Andres fed her more of the fish, a glass of juice, and then some tea. After that, they headed back to the garden once more. For the next two days, Andres kept her at it, hopping all around the hacienda. Steadily, she continued to improve. The dressmaker returned with the sample dresses. Excitedly, Juana and Alicia headed off to see if they could put them on by themselves, while Andres put Gracia's on her and brushed out her hair some. "There you go, sexy. Take a peak in the mirror," he suggested. Again, she lunged up a bit, getting to her foot. Once secure, she hopped over to the mirror. Andres purposely didn't follow at her side. "See, you just soloed," he pointed out. She smiled and looked at herself in the mirror. The dress accentuated her prominent bust. In comparison to her bust and hips, her waist looked small and shapely, though hardly the pipe corseted sized of the other women here in the hacienda. Still, the dress was attractive, and she loved the color and texture of the satin, even if she couldn't really touch it.

"See if you can solo your way back into the garden, sis."

"It's still frightening, Andres. Don't let me fall, please." She began hopping again. He stayed back this time, but was ready to dash forward and catch her if she stumbled. She didn't and was pleased she made it all the way. As she got there, Alicia and Juana came hopping up very animated.

"We just love these dresses! We can put them on ourselves. Now we three look alike!" Alicia stated the obvious. The dressmaker was pleased and took their order for another six of the same color. The Daughters of the Sea would always dress in sky blue satin gowns, because Gracia decided it mimicked the sea and sky.

Andres kept Gracia at it for the next few days and she steadily got better at her hopping, though she still continued to eat more of the diablo rojo fish, though in lesser and lesser amounts. Finally, Andres decided it was time for Gracia actually to walk out into the city, if only for a little ways. Besides, he was anxious to explore some of the large city that had grown over the years to close to twenty-five thousand, though there was a noticeable lack of men in their early twenties, victims of the ill-fated army. Every city had this same lack, however. It was a sore point many local lords had with Valen Castle and Lord Valen, well, the late Lord Valen.

"Okay, sis, today you are going for a walk in the city with us," Andres announced.

"Oh god no! I'm not ready! That's way too scary!" she looked up pleadingly at her brother.

"I'll be at your side all the way. No more loafing around for you, High Priestess," he teased her. Begrudgingly she lunged forward a little to get onto her foot. She still wobbled a little as she got her balance, but it was vastly better than her first attempts days ago.

"We'll be with you too. If you do get too tired, we can jump you home," Alicia promised, knowing that Gracia needed that bit of security right now. She still had not received any gifts that would help her handle herself if she began to fall. With Andres on her left and Alicia on her right and Juana beside her sister, the four left the hacienda for Gracia's first hops into the city as a Daughter of the Seas. They took it slowly. Three women hopping alongside Andres made quite a sight. Everywhere they went, others stopped to stare at them, much to Gracia's embarrassment, but she had little time to think about that. She had to concentrate on her hopping, determined not to take a fall and have to make Andres catch her.

Most of the homes and shops in this section of the city close to their hacienda were made from the same grey stone with red tiled roofs. Many had signs hung over the front doors, advertising various crafts and shops. Of course behind each building was a garden. Everyone had a garden in Villa del Rey. Further everything in the city shut down between one and three each afternoon for a garden break. This was a custom from before the massive climate change, when the afternoons were extremely hot. Now their climate was balmy all year round, but the custom was still followed by everyone.

"My leg must really be stronger, Andres. Before I could never have hopped this much without a long break," Gracia admitted after she'd hopped three blocks.

"You are doing really good, sis," he praised her. She smiled and continued her hopping, trying to mimic that of the two women next to her. After another two blocks, Andres began to relax a little; Gracia was doing fine.

Just then, three teens hailed them, two men and a younger woman. "Juana! Here you are at last! I've been looking all over for you," one called out. The group stopped as the three came jogging up to them. "Where have you been? We've been looking everywhere for you."

"Hi Emelio, Renata," Juana said shyly.

"We now live in that new hacienda," Alicia added. "Oh, this is High Priestess Gracia Valen and her Guardian and brother Andres. This is a friend of ours, Emilio Cuelo and his sister, Renata. Sorry, don't know you," she said to the older teen, who looked to be eighteen.

"Guess what, Emilio? Alicia and I are now officially Daughters of the Sea priestesses. Now we really can officially bless ships," Juana announced proudly.

"Wow! Juana, that's the best news ever! You, a real priestess. I knew you had it in you," Emilio replied, genuinely enthusiastic over her good fortune. "Oh, this is Diego Rique. He's why we've been looking for you. His father is about to go to sea, and I promised him to get your blessing before his dad sailed. It's really important his dad has a good trip and catches a lot of fish. I can explain more, but we have to hurry. He's supposed to sail anytime now; it's high tide. Can you jump us there, please, Juana? Please?" Emilio was almost begging, Andres noted.

"Sure we can. Alicia, you bring Gracia and Andres. Emilio, you and Diego and Renata hold onto me," Juana said. "Which dock?"

"Six."

"Er, how is this thing done?" Diego asked confused.

"Put your arm over her shoulders, yes, like that. Renata hold onto me and I put my arm over her other shoulder, see. Okay, Juana, we're ready," Emilio said hastily. Juana bent her leg a little and started to do a short hop. All four vanished and appeared on Dock Six.

Andres moved over between Gracia and Alicia, putting his hands on both women's shoulders. "Don't worry about landing, sis. I'll catch you."

"You better! This is really scary and freaky," she whispered. "Do I have to hop too, Alicia?" she asked panicking a little.

"It will be easier for you if you take a little hop with me; you'll land better. One, two, three." Alicia called out. They hopped together and Gracia landed behind the other group. She wobbled a little, but Andres quickly stabilized her. "Come on. Let's follow them. It must be that large sailing ship." With Andres still between them, they hopped along after Juana and the other three.

As they approached the ship, Diego called out, "Hey dad. Juana has come to bless your trip." His father was a weathered seaman and rather busy barking orders to his four crew. Already the mooring lines had been dropped. He nodded to Diego, but said nothing.

"May Calder grant you a safe voyage and allow you to catch many fish," Juana pronounced. Using their old *mentales* gifts, both Andres and Gracia noticed she'd placed this blessing into the actual ship as opposed to saying it to a person. "There, it's done, Señor Diego. Your father should catch many fish now."

"Thank you, Juana. I certainly hope so. My future rests on it. Come on. I'll buy you all a round of ale at the pub," Diego offered. "That's the least I can do for you, Juana, and your friends here. Emilio didn't say there were three of you."

"Well, I don't know," Juana replied, looking at Alicia and Andres, then Gracia. *Should we?*

Alicia sent, *It's customary for those who receive a blessing to thank those who gave it.*

"Sure, thanks, Diego. We're new to the city. Where's the pub?" Andres replied for the group.

I don't know if I can make it! Gracia sent him in a panic.

Sure you can. I'm right here with you, he sent back, calming her a little.

"It's a few blocks from here. I'll lead the way," Diego replied. Both Andres and Gracia did sense he was very relieved and pleased they accepted. Emilio, on the other hand, was extremely pleased. Andres suddenly sensed why! He had a crush on Juana!

Diego and Emilio led the way, but Renata fell back to walk long side of Juana. "Is it true that you are now really a priestess of the sea?"

"Oh yes. Gracia is now our High Priestess, but she's only just become like Alicia and me. She's just learning to hop now. It's her first time out of the hacienda since she got her leg. These are our new priestess dresses. Do you like them?" Juana asked.

"Yes, very much so. You look really good in light blue. I

bet the dresses were very expensive. I wish I could become a priestess too, just like you, Juana. I've been working at it. I healed a dog last week and helped a boy who broke his arm three days ago. Priestesses are supposed to heal people, aren't they?"

"I think so, but I'm not sure," Juana answered her.

Gracia felt obliged to speak up for her Daughter of the Seas. "We are still learning what all we can do to help others, Renata. You really want to become a priestess like us? We don't have any arms anymore and only one leg and have to hop everywhere."

"I suppose that must be awful, but if you can really help people, cure them, heal them, make it so the fishermen can catch lots of fish and have safe trips, then that's what I want to do. If I don't do it soon, I think our foster parents are going to marry me off to some man I don't even know. Maybe Emilio and I will have to run away or something."

"How awful!" Juana replied. They hopped on in silence, Gracia focusing on not falling down. Six blocks later, they arrived at Billy's Pub, and Diego held the door open for the group as they hopped or walked inside. Andres carefully stayed at his sister's side all the way. At this hour, the place was nearly empty, and they took one of the larger tables. He pulled a chair out for Gracia, making sure she was able to sit down without looking too awkward as she did. Then he sat beside her, ready to help her sip her ale. Alicia sat beside him on the other side, Juana beside her. Diego, Emilio, and Renata sat opposite them. Now each got a good look at the other.

Of course, being Westerlings, they all had black hair. However, they all had yellow eyes with brown speckles; they were *mentales* gifted. Both Andres and Gracia noticed immediately none had their germanium crystals and therefore were probably not tower trained. Renata was fifteen, and like all Westerlings women, her long hair was her pride and joy, falling to her knees, straight as an arrow. She had an oval face and was rather cute, but there was a gap between her two front teeth appearing when she smiled. Her brother looked a lot like her, except his hair was short and a bit bushy. It didn't even reach his shoulders. Both he and Diego carried a short sword.

Diego wore his hair quite short, and he already had a small, black moustache, rather frequently found in this city. He also had a small goatee as well. Yet he was handsome, cutting a dashing figure, well-dressed, the opposite of Emilio and Renata, whose clothing looked rather worn, but not threadbare. Diego was eighteen, while Emilio was a year younger.

After pouring everyone's mug from the pitcher he bought, Diego said, "Here's thanks to our priestess!" He raised his mug and took a sip. Emilio and Renata followed suit. Alicia and Juana used their psi skills to lift their mugs to their mouths, while Andres held Gracia's to her lips for her, before taking a sip from his own. He felt obligated to explain, "She's only become a High Priestess and Daughter of the Sea a few days ago. She's not yet received all her powers from Calder."

Diego looked at Gracia and said, "Well, this Calder could not have picked a more beautiful High Priestess! Say, aren't you some of those new folks who've moved into that empty hacienda on the bluff?"

"That's us." Andres replied.

"Well, I can't thank you enough for coming to bless dad's ship. I am sort of in a pickle barrel right now. You see I'm dad's youngest son, and I absolutely hate going to sea with him and fishing! I got trained as a fighter, but dad's had a run of bad luck, and if he doesn't bring back a good catch this time, he's going to make me have to go with him and help out. He's got to fire one of his crew, replacing him with me. Those guys have been with him since I was a lad. I don't want any of them to lose their job. Of course, if he does have a good catch, then I'm off that hook and onto another hook, possibly an even worse hook."

"What do you mean, Diego?" Gracia asked. Sitting down at a table made her far more comfortable, though slightly embarrassed her brother had to help her sip her ale.

"Like I said, I got trained as a fighter. Now I've been asked either to join the new army the new Lord Valen is building up at Valen Castle or to join the Villa del Rey Guards. I don't want to join the army, that's suicide! I don't want to join the city guards either; the pay's rotten. Say, by any chance do you need any security men to help guard your hacienda?" Diego asked.

"Well, Diego, quite possibly. Dad might and I might too," Andres replied, thinking about what Calder had said about forming up guardians to help protect the Daughters of the Seas.

"Hey, that sounds ideal," Emilio put in. "Can I apply too? Renata and I are fosterlings. We've no idea who our parents actually were. Our foster parents are about to kick us out of their house. They claim we are old enough to make our own way. Renata's right, mom's about had it and has asked dad to find her a husband. I told her if it came to that, we'd run away, but I don't want to leave you, Juana, not really." He started to say more, but stopped slightly flushed, embarrassed to say more in front of everyone else.

"Say, have any of you had your tower training yet?" Andres asked, suspecting he already knew the answer.

Emilio hung his head, Renata, likewise. Diego replied, "Señor Andres, around Villa del Rey, only the very wealthy and the lord and his family have enough money to travel all the way to Valen Tower for that. Hardly any of us with the yellow eyes have. Sorry, but I hope you won't hold that against us for the security positions."

"No, that has very little to do with it, fellows. Gracia and I are highly trained fighters. Oops, sorry Gracia. She was, that is, until she was changed a few days ago. We are good judges of your skills."

"You really got changed into a mermaid? I mean a Daughter of the Seas?" asked Renata, wide-eyed.

"Yes, I was just like my brother here, a good swords woman. Of course, now I can't even hold my ale mug. God, I hope that changes soon," Gracia admitted.

"Changed or not, Señorita Gracia, you are one fine looking woman," Diego replied. Both Andres and Gracia sensed telepathically he was being totally sincere.

Renata spoke up. "Well, if you were like us and got changed, then I can be changed too. Please, can you change me into a Daughter of the Seas like Juana? We all thought you had to be born this way. It was so with Juana and Alicia." Emilio gave her a nasty look.

She pouted, “Look, if you can be a security man, then I can be what I want to be, a Daughter of the Seas, just like Juana, and help people. I am not going to be a stupid barmaid or some man’s baby factory! Please, change me too so I can help.”

Gracia smiled, “We’ll see, Renata. First, all three of you need your tower training.” She watched three faces change from one of hopefulness to a drooping hopelessness. “Hey, don’t’ worry about that. Dad is forming up a new tower by our hacienda. In a while, Villa Del Rey will have its own tower. The training is free. Come on; we should take all three of you back to the hacienda now and introduce you to dad and see about getting you three trained pronto.”

“Señorita Gracia! How can we ever thank you enough?” Diego exclaimed. He rose to kiss her hand, in the polite manner of the Westerlings.

“Er, sorry, Diego, I don’t have my hands anymore, but I accept your kiss,” Gracia replied graciously. “Thanks for the ale; it’s been a long time since a handsome lad bought me a drink.” For some reason, Gracia really like this teen. Maybe it was the way that he carried himself, confident and sure. *I can’t quite put my finger on it. Shit, I don’t have a finger anymore!*

“Well we best get you all back to the hacienda. We were taking Gracia out to practice her hopping skills. Sis, we ought to do a few more blocks before we let Alicia and Juana jump us back. Practice, practice, practice,” he teased her.

I know, but it is so scary, Andres. Make sure that I don’t fall, not in front of Diego!

They rose and Diego noticed all three women did a little lunge movement that got them to their feet. While Alicia and Juana used their powers to move their chairs out of the way, Andres did so for Gracia. Then, they hopped and walked out of the pub. “Which way? We’re lost,” Andres said with a chuckle. “I can see we need to get out into the city lots more, Gracia.”

She laughed. Her fighter sense kicked in. “You are right. We simply must get familiar with the whole city and soon. Okay, I’ll practice walking more each day, even if I do fall.”

“That’s the spirit, sis.” They hopped along for another

six blocks. Gracia and Alicia noticed that Emilio hung back and walked alongside of Juana, while Renata walked close to Alicia. Diego continued watching Gracia from the corner of his eyes, as he led the way through the crowded streets, ignoring wholly the constant stares the three women received. At last, Alicia and Juana jumped them to the hacienda.

"My goodness, this is a noble's mansion!" Diego exclaimed as he walked through the black iron gates into the gardens.

"You live here?" Emilio asked, totally awed with the rich, lavish surroundings. "Juana, this is even better than I imagined! No wonder we couldn't find you. You are living with the nobles." While they chatted, Andres left Gracia to talk to Diego, while he headed off to find his father.

"Look, dad. There are many, many *mentales* gifted here in Villa del Rey who simply couldn't afford to get to Valen Tower for their training. Your new tower could gain tremendous allies and goodwill by training them right here," Andres suggested to Fons.

"My god son! I had no idea. Yes, yes, this is the answer to our prayers. Help. Terrific, son." Fons was visibly please and, Andres thought, rather relieved as well.

"I've got three that need it right now. There's a good chance we might be able to use one or more to help our group. Should I call you Venerado or not?"

"Let's. It's time that Villa del Rey starts to know that they have a tower here. We need to build up local support quickly," he replied. The two began their slow walk to the gardens.

Gracia hops faster than dad walks, Andres noted.

While Andres was gone, Gracia began chatting with Diego. She was used to taking charge of conversations with her fellow fighters. "Do you know the Salvadore move? That was my favorite parry-counterstrike."

"Why yes, it took me weeks to get that one down, but to be honest, I've not have any opportunity to use it in a real fight. Now the Cornish maneuver, that works best in street fights."

"What's that one look like? Don't think I've heard of it,"

she asked, intrigued by a new sword maneuver. He demonstrated with his sword. "Oh, we call that one the del Arte move. Same thing, different names. How about the Ortego parry?"

"What's that one?" he asked. "I've not heard of that move. Would it be good in a street fight? That's what we have mostly around here."

"Like this," she replied without thinking. She tried to make her arms and legs demonstrate the maneuver and her face flushed. They were not there. Her face flushed bright for a second, and then her eyes watered. "I can't show you anymore. That's all gone. I've lost all my fighter abilities." She broke down and cried over the sudden, stark realization that the part of her life which had meant everything to her was now gone utterly.

"There, there, Gracia. This change you've had, it must be horrible for you," he said sympathetically.

"It is, truly it is. It's all gone for me, all that I was so good at doing. I can't do any of it anymore and I haven't gotten the powers Alicia has yet. I'm so helpless right now," she admitted. It was hard for her to say this; she was used to being in control of situations and men. Now she couldn't wipe her own eyes.

"I know, you direct me; tell me each step, and I can see the move that way," Diego suggested. Gracia sniffled and tried to walk him through it by describing and telling him each step. "Oh, yes, I know this one; we call it the Pedro Stop. I guess we've both been similarly trained, only we call them by different names."

Just then, Andres returned with his father. "Diego Rique, this is Venerado Fons Valen. Emilio Cuelo and his sister Renata." After the introductions, Fons rapidly tested the three and found them acceptable for training.

"I and my staff will get you three trained at once and see you get your germanium crystals of power. It will be best if you move in here and plan to stay with us for a couple of weeks," Fons declared. All three were exuberant; they would get their training against all odds.

"Venerado," Diego spoke up after thanking him

profusely, "we know of at least fifty more of us poor folk who cannot get to Valen Tower and who need the training! Our choices are limited to only joining the Lord's Guards. Those men our lord sends to Valen Tower, though of course all the noble's children and the lord's get to go. Around here, only the rich or well-connected get the training."

"Son, as soon as we get a bit more organized here, please spread the word. All untrained gifted can be trained here at no charge. This is one of the tower's responsibilities, son, to train the young *mentales* gifts. An untrained telepath is both a danger to others and to himself," Fons replied.

"Venerado! We will, we will! So many will owe you so very much!" Diego gushed out heartfelt admiration.

He wanted to say I certainly hope so, but replied, "Good. You three go get your things and be back by supper. Your training will start after dinner. Go, go. Time is wasting." The three hastily said good bye and dashed off with youthful enthusiasm. "I'll tell Esmeralda to expect three more in the guest rooms." He then moved off slowly to inform the others of this remarkable turn in their fortunes. They had a ready-made supply of *mentales* gifted! He began to realize there were likely far more of them in the other coastal cities far from Valen Tower. *We have an untapped goldmine here!*

Around four, the three companions returned; each carried a small sack with a few clothes and personal items. In fact, the three hardly had more than the clothes on their backs, if they were honest about it. When they walked in the gates and entered the courtyard, Andres and Alicia were at the far end, passionately kissing. Juana was sitting closer to the gates by the pond, and Gracia was sitting rather in the middle among the grove of orchids. Glancing at her brother, she rose to act as hostess, hopping toward them.

"Welcome back. Your rooms are this way. I'll take you. After you put your things inside, come out in the gardens here and chat. Supper is in about a half hour or so," she said. She carefully did her hopping turn, wiggling slightly, and then led the three down to the western side's guest rooms. They passed by Andres and Alicia, who were making out in a rather concealed shade beneath a flowering bush, ignoring the arrivals. “Sorry, I can’t open doors. This one,” she nodded with her head slightly, “is for you fellows. Renata, yours is the next one down.”

The three headed inside and she hopped back to her seat. Carefully, she did her hopping turn, and then tossed her hair to her front and carefully sat down. She knew she was physically attracted to the handsome Diego. Before she had been changed, she’d have pursued him some; she was a take-charge woman then, but now she felt more like a freak than anything else. A bit later, Diego came out and sat beside her. Her heart skipped a beat.

“Boy, the venerado has the same ornaments and boots as does our lord and many in his court. I still say they look weird, but don’t tell him that,” Diego admitted.

“You might let Venerado Fons know about the lords and his court. I think that he will appreciate knowing there are others as hobbled as he and the other twenty here are,” she replied.

“Say, what’s with his strange looking hands?” Diego asked.

“All twenty-one of them lost their hands. There was this infectious virus that swept the Midlands last year, and the only cure was to remove their hands, replacing them with those alien prosthetic hands.” She left it at that, uncertain whether or not to tell him it was a hoax and they all did it to help further the late Lord Valen’s plans. Right now, Paco Valen was very poorly thought of around here. Too many young men had been conscripted into his army and had died.

“That must be terrible for them. Say, I couldn’t help see Andres and Alicia there. Is it permitted for you Daughters of the Sea to have boyfriends?”

“Oh sure. I think my brother has fallen for Alicia in a big way. I wouldn’t be surprised if soon they announce that they are engaged,” she replied with a wry smile.

“That is most encouraging. Will you permit me to court you, Señorita Gracia? Never have I seen such a charming, beautiful young woman with so many talents,” Diego asked. Her heart fluttered a little.

“Yes, you may. I would really like to get to know you,

Diego, but I am so physically not myself anymore. I can't see what you can possibly see in me like I am now," she attempted to give him a way to back out graciously.

"Your body is so unusual, but no matter, I see only your face, your eyes," he replied charmingly.

Meanwhile, Renata and Emilio headed down to chat with Juana. Both had walked past the embracing couple partially hidden in the flowering bushes. "Go on. Ask her, silly. Andres is, so try, brother. Tell her. I bet she doesn't know how you feel about her. If you don't, then I will," Renata whispered animatedly to her brother, who flushed at her threat to bypass him.

"Hello again, Juana," he said, taking a seat close to her. "I couldn't help noticing Andres and Alicia down there. Is such permitted? Are you Daughters of the Sea allowed to have boyfriends?"

"Oh sure, Emilio, but until now, we never expected to ever have one, not like we are, the freaks of the beach, the mermaids. But Andres — he's really smitten with Alicia, and she really likes him. I can tell," Juana replied honestly.

"But I don't think you are a freak, not really, unusual, very pretty, but not a freak. I, I've always admired you, Juana, but I thought it wasn't permitted for you to have boyfriends."

"Really?" Juana asked.

"Juana, for years I dream about you every night. You are in my mind always, but I feared to say anything because I thought you were not allowed to have boyfriends."

"You have? I've often thought about you, too, Emilio, but I never wanted to say anything because everyone thinks we are freaks, but we aren't, not really, just different," Juana admitted.

"Juana, please, can I be your boyfriend, please? I will always treat you right, with honor and respect," he pleased.

A smile appeared on her face that only grew by the second. "I would love that, Emilio, really that means a whole lot to me."

Renata just couldn't resist speaking up, "Juana, Emilio really is in *love* with you! You are *all* that he talks about! Kiss her, Emilio, go on. I won't look." Both Emilio and Juana turned slightly crimson, but seeing her not objecting, he gave her a short, passionate kiss. She used her psi powers to pull him up against her, returning his kiss, sending waves of emotion and excitement through both of their bodies, releasing passions long hidden in both of them. However, Renata did peek and grinned broadly.

At supper, the three new arrivals were introduced to all the others. All three were very much impressed with them primarily because the lords, ladies, and nobles of Villa del Ray also wore toe shoes and lip plates, while the women also wore pipe corsets. In their minds, they were now dining at some very rich nobles' table and staying in their lavish hacienda. Countering this was the terrible time the twenty-one had using their artificial hands while attempting to dine. Still they knew hands, for the most part, were not needed for their mental training.

The two weeks of their basic *mentales* training passed rapidly, culminating in their receipt of their own amplifying crystals. Andres and Gracia monitored their progress and got daily updates on what Fons discovered about their natures as people, as well as the nature of their gifts. When their training was finished, Gracia took Renata aside.

"Congratulations, Renata. Now then, you once told me you really wanted to become one of us, a Daughter of the Seas. You have all the right qualifications to be one, so if you still desire it, I will accept you as one and get your body changed into that of a Priestess Daughter of the Seas."

"Oh, yes, yes, I want to more than anything. I want to help others," she gushed.

"But look at what has happened to our bodies. Are you really sure, Renata? Once done, there can be no undoing this, no going back."

"Yes, it must be so terribly hard, but Juana manages very well. I so want to be like her, please," Renata begged.

That night, she ate her first meal of the diablo rojo fish. To be safe, Gracia had Renata sleeping in her bed with her. Gracia realized she knew from her own experiences what was likely to happen with Renata as the huge transformation changed her body so dramatically. She would be there to help her all the way.

Meanwhile, Andres offered both Diego and Emilio positions as Guardians of the Daughters of the Seas, pleasing both men. "We need to get ourselves some distinctive uniforms," Andres suggested. In a few days, they wore uniforms whose color matched that of the women. That they and the mermaids were joined was now quite visible at a glance.

For the last two weeks, Diego spent all his free time at the side of Gracia, giving Andres time to be with Alicia. Likewise, Emilio and Juana were definitely romantically engaged as well. Andres began to believe they were actually making substantial progress along the route defined by Calder. Now they needed their own space.

As far as Diego was concerned, things could not have worked out better. His dad had returned last week with a record catch of fish and a wild story about their phenomenal luck in avoiding a disastrous storm at sea. His father now began to sing the praises of the Daughters of the Sea, adding his to those of many others who Alicia and Juana had been blessing for some years now.

Chapter 3 Expansion Begins

The transformation of Renata went far better than anyone expected, especially Gracia. When she awoke to find her legs had been modified and her upper legs merged into one at her knee with one lower leg, she was a little scared, a little nervous, but very proud of the changes she was undergoing. When her arms withered and fell off, for a short while she experienced the same frights Gracia had, but she soon overcame them. Now Gracia saw why. Renata had really wanted to be like her friend Juana for so long that when it occurred, her relief and happiness overcame her feelings of helplessness and the frightening experiences of learning to get around on her own by hopping. Gracia had not wanted the changes, but had accepted them because of the awe-inspiring visitation of the god Calder. The difference in outlooks Gracia took notice of, promising to use this as part of her selection criteria for future Daughters of the Seas.

As Renata's transformation began, Gracia finally began to receive her additional psi powers. Within days, her telekinetic abilities equaled those of Alicia and Juana. Her teleportation ability appeared next and was at least double the power of Alicia's. After much testing, they discovered that while Anita and Juana could teleport the weight of three other people, Gracia could bring ten with her, an amazing amount. Instinctively she knew she could bless a ship, and it would actually safeguard and assist those she blessed. Before she only had the rudimentary psi skill to heal partially her own body. Now she discovered she possessed the full powers of ordinary healers, a great gift in its own right. Only later did she discover she had immense powers over waters.

While Gracia had to wait for a lengthy time before her special psi skills manifested themselves, Renata's appeared within a few days of her complete transformation. Once more Gracia realized she had needed a whole lot longer to adapt and get accustomed to her new physical form and limitations than had Renata, who'd been studying Juana and watching her for years. Again, she filed that observation away for future use. Now she and Renata had to practice their new skills, especially their jumping or teleporting.

Alicia stated, “First, you two, you have to learn how to get yourselves up when you are lying flat on the ground. You see, sometimes we use too much of our energies. When they are gone for the day, we sometimes take nasty spills. We also sometimes fall when going up hills or down them or are on rough ground, where we lose our balance completely. Sometimes we get bumped unexpectedly in the streets and fall down. You have to know how to get back up on your own and then how to fall without getting hurt. Juana sprained her foot once and then she was so laid up it wasn’t funny.”

She demonstrated their techniques for getting up. Their single lower leg only moved a slight amount to either side, quite unlike normal lower legs. Thus, they were highly constrained in what they could realistically do with their leg. Really, the only major movement of their leg was their easy ability to touch their nose with their knee, which everyone could do, plus a very unique motion. That is, their upper legs could move backwards to touch their backs, which allowed their heel to touch the back of their head. (Later they would see the need for this when giving birth.) Alicia first rolled over onto her stomach. Next, using her chin and leg, she got her knee up under her chest. That was the difficult part. By throwing her head back, she was able to sit up on her lower leg, but only for the briefest of moments. With nothing to support them, their bodies would quickly roll over either to their left or right side. Thus from this brief position, she leaned back and rather rolled up onto her foot, pushing upwards with her leg muscles, wobbling a little as she got her balance on her foot once more. If they were too slow in lurching up onto their foot, they rolled over onto their side and had to start the whole procedure over once more. Both Gracia and Renata practiced this until Alicia felt they had it down, which took an awful lot of practice and failures.

That learned, accompanied by their three guardians, Andres, Diego, and Emilio, the four headed off to practice jumping, as Alicia and Juana continued to call their teleportation skill. At once the two knew why Alicia had them practicing getting up from the floor. Landing was tricky. More than once, Gracia and Renata lost their balance and fell, before they could use their telekinetic skills to steady their bodies. Once they were fairly accomplished at landing on level ground, they experimented hopping onto rough ground and found that almost too difficult to manage. Likewise going up or down a steep hill was so formidable that jumping to their destination was vastly more preferable.

As August came, Alicia pronounced Gracia and Renata up to speed, and both women felt confident they could manage life now. With his sister back to battery, as he put it, Andres now felt he could ask Alicia to marry him. One evening in the fragrant gardens, he got down on one knee and asked her. So overcome with joy and happiness, Alicia could only cry for a couple of minutes. "Yes, oh yes, a thousand times yes, Andres. I never, ever expected anyone would ever love me, let alone want to marry me, the freak of Villa del Rey."

When the two announced their plans to the others, after a loud round of congratulations, Emilio finally found his courage to ask Juana the same thing. Her reaction was similar to Alicia's. The two sisters had years ago realized being freaks, love and marriage and families of their own would be forever denied to them. Now their strongest desires in life materialized and they were both overcome with emotion.

During these weeks, the blossoming love between Diego and Gracia continued to grow. He seldom left her side, much to the relief of Andres, who wanted to be with Alicia as much as possible. With the other two's announcements, Diego took the plunge and asked Gracia for her foot in marriage. After a hearty laugh, she consented as well. Mid-August, the three couples were married in a simple, triple ceremony. Renata cried throughout the whole ceremony; her dear friends from childhood had finally found the happiness they deserved, she thought. On the other hand, Fons was extremely pleased with the three marriages. Now he would finally get his questions answered. Could they breed? If so, would their children also be born like Alicia and Juana were, that is, already transformed into Daughters of the Sea? Would these children also possess these immense psi powers? If so, he had many plans for them.

The last week of August, their simple single story tower was finished. At this time, Venerado Fons and his team began setting up their crystal networks. However, they wisely decided not to activate the comm network. Once that was up, every other tower on Tierra would instantly know of their presence. Retribution would surely follow, and they were not yet strong enough to withstand the anticipated backlash. Rather, they were pathetically weak.

That began to change in August. Diego, Emilio, and to a lesser extent Renata, began to spread the word through Villa del Rey that a new tower had come to the city and that they were providing tower training and the crystals of power to those who needed them. Slowly at first, desperate *mentales* gifted men and women made their way to the hacienda, not truly believing here was a real *Círculo de la Torres*. It didn't look like what they imagined a mighty tower should look like nor did it match the descriptions some had heard of Valen Tower far north of here.

Nevertheless, the toe boots and shoes along with the lip plates of the venerado, capo, and tower members quickly changed their views. They looked like the city lords and nobles. As each one finished their training and received their crystal, Venerado Fons asked them to come and help defend the tower, should the need arise. All swore to do so.

By the end of August, each day brought three or four more begging for the training and crystals. Their entire circle was now constantly busy with training so many who needed it. Even more interesting, as word of mouth spread of a real *Círculo de la Torres* here in Villa del Ray, the sick and injured began making their way to the hacienda, begging for healing. Now Venerado Fons had a new problem. While many of his twenty-one had at one time possessed some healing skills, these forms depended upon their hands, moving them just above the injured part or over the ill. Now wholly unable to do this, their entire healing lay in the hands of Donato de la Portales' youngest daughter, Anita, who was only fourteen and unmodified. With so many coming in need of healing, Fons asked Gracia for help. She agreed, if Anita could be assigned to help them, and Fons agreed.

She and her three Daughters of the Seas, assisted by Anita, began handling the sick and injured who came. Renata soon excelled at this, for she'd been wanting to do this all her life. Within a week, Gracia came to depend upon Renata as her best healer, though Anita was a close second. With the hacienda now routinely filled to capacity during the daytime with so many visitors, Gracia knew her group needed their own facilities, perhaps some kind of temple structure as opposed to a sterile tower. Further, Alicia and Juana were often kept busy blessing ships about to set sail. Hardly a day went by when one or both were summoned to the docks to do this. Word was slowly spreading of the miraculous blessings of their mermaids.

Gracia faced two problems now. She needed her own space, her own temple as it were. She needed to recruit more women to become Daughters of the Sea. The four were now being kept constantly busy. She talked the space problem over with her father and Fons agreed to finance a new building for their use. Unresolved was just where it would be built. She felt partially satisfied knowing it could be built, once she found the space for it. She considered building it further up the hill behind their hacienda, but that would make it even more inaccessible for the sailors and the injured townsfolk. For now, she put this one on hold and attempted to solve the second one, more recruits.

This was a tough one, she knew. Who in their right mind would want to undergo the enormous physical transformations she and Renata had? This, she thought about for some time. True, she was now using her telekinetic skills where she'd used her arms before, but walking was really gone; hopping was her only means of movement, short of "jumping." She knew if Calder had not appeared and specifically chosen her to be his High Priestess, she would never had consented to this horrific change, except to help her father in his tests. Even then, she'd not thought it would really happen, not like this.

No, finding other women to become like her would be challenging. Already, Andres and Diego had recruited five more young men to be guardians, protecting the Daughters of the Seas. At least one always accompanied them wherever they went, particularly so when they went to the docks to bless a ship. For a time she wondered if they had to already have the *mentales* gifts? Could the head blind be chosen? If so, would their transformation only go as far as it had with Dorita, a loss of arms? Her intuition told her even the head blind, if found worthy, would be fully transformed. If they couldn't be used, surely Calder would have told her so.

She took another look at her transformation and that of Renata's. She was eighteen and fully a woman when hers came. She still recalled the fear and terror she'd felt when she stood for the first time on her leg and with no arms at all to help her. Renata was just fourteen, barely past puberty, her body still growing and maturing. She adapted extremely well. Besides, she wanted the transformation badly. Gracia concluded the new recruits ought to be young teens. If nothing else, they might adapt more readily. But how to get them?

Her husband, Diego, offered her a suggestion. "Honey, why don't you advertise some? Most all down at the docks now think highly of you mermaids. You ought to become more visible. Perhaps that will help."

"You don't mean I should put up posters around the city saying: wanted young women who want to lose their arms and a leg to become mermaids?" she said jokingly. Both laughed.

"While that may well be the truth of it — these gods of ours sure do demand a heavy price for their aid — no, I mean make yourselves visible on the beaches. Show the other young women you are alive and doing well, even as altered as you are. Your healing and blessing skills are now becoming more widely known. With increased visibility, perhaps others will come up to you and want to join up," Diego suggested.

"So you would walk up to me and say I want to lose my arms and a leg so I can heal too?" she asked pointedly.

"Renata did just that, didn't she," Diego countered, recalling how Renata had pleaded to join, to be like her friend Juana. "Make friends. Show them you are a real person, like I know you, a beautiful woman still."

"You think that will work?"

"Can't hurt to try." The next day, Gracia told the other three of Diego's plan.

"Great! I've not been swimming for days. I miss it, come on," Alicia was more than willing to hit the beaches daily.

Accompanied by their guardians, the four jumped to the beach. "Oh god, Diego! I've never been to the beach like this. I'll have to be naked and show my distorted body to everyone! I can't swim!"

"Be brave. You are advertising you can live life as a Daughter of the Seas. Show them you can. I'm with you. I'm a good swimmer," Diego replied, helping her off with her dress so that she didn't have to waste psi energies on it. Beside them, Andres was doing the same for Alicia, while Emilio took off both his sister's dress and his new wife's, Juana's. The men spread out their towels.

"Oh, sorry, guys, I don't know how to swim," Andres admitted growing embarrassed about it again.

"I wonder if I can still swim — like this, I mean," Renata added hesitatingly. She'd been swimming countless times, but not armless and with only one leg as a mermaid.

"Sure, it's easy. You've seen me do it a hundred times," Juana pointed out.

"Okay, you're right. If you can do it, so can I. Come on. I feel really pulled to the water, don't you?" Renata asked.

"Hum, you're right, I do feel really pulled to it," Gracia admitted the growing feeling she had. The four hopped to the water's edge and then jumped further out into the deeper blue waters, far from the white sandy beach. Hundreds of the younger set were there, swimming or lying on the sand or playing games. Nearly all stopped to stare at the four strange looking women hopping across the sands and then miraculously appearing out in the water. To Gracia's utter amazement, she knew how to swim and swim well! *Must be Calder's doing. This is really fun!*

In her head, she heard, *Yes, it is, my High Priestess. Come more often unto me.* That surprised her, and she realized if she ever wanted to talk to him, all she needed to do was to go for a swim. She looked about and saw Renata was also taking to the water like a fish, emulating Juana's moves like a natural. All four were fast swimmers; their leg was thicker than a normal leg and their kick and undulating motions more powerful. She loved the feeling of her hair flowing behind her back. Then she thought of Andres and went to check on him. Diego and Emilio were doing their best to teach him, but he was struggling at it. Diego saw her and sent, *Give him time, honey.*

After a long swim, the four mermaids jumped to the beach and let the water drain off their bodies for a bit, before hopping over to their towels. As they approached their beach towels, a couple of giggling teens came up to them. One said, "Are you the mermaids who blessed my dad's boats?"

"You bet. That's us," Gracia replied, a little embarrassed of her nakedness.

"Way cool! I heard you healed Chico's broken arm last week. Is that really true? Can you really heal and cure people?" she asked, wide-eyed. Gracia realized, while they still thought of them as "freaks," the mermaids were talking to them was really somehow significant.

"Yes, I forgot his name, but it was a young lad, right arm," Juana answered.

"Even cooler. So who are those boys that came with you? One can't even swim," the first girl asked.

Gracia laughed, "Our husbands. Sorry, Diego, Andres, and Emilio are already taken."

The first one giggled. "We didn't know you could be married. So who has that really handsome one with the moustache?" she asked.

"That's Diego. He's mine. You keep your hands off him," Gracia teased her and she giggled even more.

The second girl asked, "Can anyone become one of you?"

Gracia saw both were head blind, but intensely curious about them. "Sure anyone can who really wants to become one of Calder's Daughters of the Seas and help bless the ships and heal and cure others. It takes a lot of dedication to really wanting to help others. It's pretty hard living like we are, physically, so you really do have to want to help others."

"We would like to heal people and cure them, really we

would, but we don't know how. So I don't suppose we could become Daughters of the Seas like you four are," the second replied, sadly.

Renata butted in, "Oh that's not a problem. When your body changes into our forms, you also get the skill to heal and cure. You just know how to do it. Before I changed, I didn't know anything about healing, not much anyway. Now I know lots. Plus, you get all sorts of other powers to help you do things you can't do without arms."

"Oh!" the first said. Both girls brightened up. "Can we join up? Who do we see about becoming a mermaid like you all are?"

"Me," Gracia smiled. "What will your parents say about this? It's a pretty drastic change, and once you do it, you can't undo it. My arms are gone and I can't ever get them back." She thought ought to dissuade them a little. It didn't."

"My dad is a fisherman and is gone all the time. Our moms are dead and we're staying with her elderly aunt. Her dad was a soldier and never came back. He's probably dead too. So it's just us two," the first replied. "Please, we'd like to become mermaids too."

"What are your names?"

"Gabriela and she's Francisca."

"And you both want to bless ships and help cure the sick and heal the injured? There's no going back once you become a mermaid," Gracia again cautioned them.

"Why would we want to? You have the cutest husband. We were worried you couldn't have boyfriends and get married and all that, cause, well you know," Gabriela said, becoming too embarrassed to finish her thought.

"Thanks, I think Diego is really handsome. We want to have a large family. The only problem is finding boyfriends. Most think of us as freaks or something," Gracia added another caution.

"Well, you have to admit you look really strange, but we've seen what you can do, though we don't know how you do them. We do want to help people somehow," Gabriela admitted.

"Okay then. First, we have to have your dad's

permission and your aunt's I suppose. When he gets into port, bring them around to our hacienda, and we'll see if they agree."

"Yahoo! You bet. Thank you, thank you, thank you!" Gabriela gushed.

The more reserved Francisca said, "You know there are others like us who want to become mermaids too. Can we tell them to come and see you about it?"

"There are? Why sure, Francisca. We're planning to come for a swim each day, if we can. If you don't see us one day, we're probably tied up curing or healing someone. Just come the next day. Just tell them what I've told you. Once your body changes, you can't go back." Gracia watched the two dash off and immediately start chatting with several other girls, who kept glancing over at them. "I wish there was some way to sit down on the towel without having to use our psi powers or just falling down." Alicia laughed. All four lowered their bodies to the towels, while holding their wet hair up and out of the way. As they sat, they lowered their hair out across their leg to dry in the sun.

Before long, several more groups of young teen girls walked up to chat as well. "Gabriela said we should see you about becoming a mermaid like you?" a tall, thin fifteen year old girl asked. "I'm Blanca. She's Dominga, and she's Carmela." They asked similar questions as the others had and Gracia answered them with nearly the same cautions.

"Can you really have babies? I mean, like us?" Dominga asked. "We don't see how you can, but. . ." She didn't finish her sentence, too embarrassed to continue.

"I certainly hope so. I'm pregnant now," Gracia admitted.

"So am I," Alicia added.

"But how can it come out?" Dominga continue to muddle her way through what she wanted to know. "You can't spread your legs wide open."

"Nope, that we can't, but we can drop our upper legs way down. That will be enough, we think." Gracia tried to explain her newfound flexibility in her hips. She could drop her upper legs behind her torso and touch her back with them.

Dominga giggled nervously.

"Then you really are just like us only with weird legs and no arms," Blanca summarized.

"Put that way, Blanca, yes we are just like any other woman in all ways, except we don't have arms now and our legs are definitely strange. Still, we Daughters of the Seas gain other mental skills to help us do the things we have to do," Gracia explained. The three chatted for a while, and she invited them to bring their relatives and come and see her about joining up.

When they finally headed for the hacienda, they had five more recruits, if their parents or guardians agreed to allow them to join. "Wow, I had no idea this would work. Diego, thanks. Your idea is working far better than I thought." She gave him a loving kiss before they joined for the "jump" back to the hacienda.

Gracia did notice several girls watching them kissing and realized many would have similar hesitations about joining. None wanted to give up boyfriends, marriage, and having a family. She resolved to make this clear to anyone else that approached her about joining. Two days later, Dorita again began preparing diablo rojo fish, this time for five head blind teens between fourteen and fifteen years of age.

While Gracia would have preferred to do only one, just in case the transformation only went as far as it had with Dorita, they all showed up at the same time, ready and eager to become mermaids. She had no choice but to do them all at once, hoping for the best. She took Gabriela and Francisca into her bedroom to stay with them for the transformations, while the other three took Blanca, Dominga, and Carmela into their bedrooms to watch over them.

A day later, Gracia's worries were over. All five's first modification was the same as hers and Renata's had been, the fusing of their upper legs. Now they only had the one leg, just like the four. As expected, this was the hardest part, as their fears grew while trying to stand on their single leg. A day later, their arms were lost and their fears grew even greater. Only their desire to be like the mermaids and help heal others kept it at bay.

Presenting them with their official light blue matching dresses greatly bolstered their morale and helped them conquer their fears. As Gracia anticipated, after a period of four more days to allow them to adjust to their new limitations and to learn to hop properly, their eyes changed to yellow and their gifts began appearing. Now they had to be trained as *mentales* gifted and given their own crystals of power. Two weeks later, the five were ecstatic and very much ready to start blessing ships, curing the sick, healing the injured, lightening the load on the four.

Andres added more guardians, insisting that each mermaid had her own body guard. Several of the new guards began to express more than just a desire to protect these valuable women. In time, he hoped, some would become romantically involved. However, space was now at a premium. Gracia had to do something soon. While the nine made quite a sight at the beach, more women were coming up asking about them and a few expressing an interest in also joining. For now, there was no more room for more.

That all changed when a courier arrived the next morning with an official summons to the Royal Court of Villa del Rey.

Chapter 4 Social Impact

"I think we've finally been noticed," Venerado Fons pointed out to the large group and Gracia. Everyone saw the fancy gilded carriage arrive and wanted to know what the message said. It was plain and simple:

Fons Valen, you and your group and the mermaid Daughters of the Seas are hereby ordered to attend a special meeting tomorrow at 1 p.m. After which you are requested to attend the Fall Formal Ball at the Royal Palace.

Lord Gabino Rosa

Fons finished reading it to everyone. "It does have an official seal, presumably the lord's."

"This could be very bad for us," cautioned a worried Donato. "On the other hand, it might be well for us to meet the lord of the city." A quick check of all the guardians yielded no further information on the lord, except he looked like Fons and his group. That is, they wore the toe boots and lip plates and their wives wore the restrictive pipe corsets as well.

"Okay then, Andres, you have your guardians ready to protect the mermaids, and we'll take care of ourselves," Fons ordered. "Expect trouble; be ready for anything. Let me do most of the talking."

"Oh no, Diego! I've not been in a carriage since I changed. I don't know how I am to get in it!" Gracia felt the sting of uncertainty and panic she'd not felt for quite some time.

"I can lift you, love. Don't worry. It'll be just fine. No one can expect you to hop into a carriage or even out of one," Diego put her at ease once more. "You look stunning. Shall we?" He offered her his arm, causing her to grin.

"Noble gesture, dear, but what am I to do with your arm?" she teased him. She, like the other mermaids, wore their light blue satin dresses and their flat shoe. The guardians wore their matching satin uniforms, with black belts and boots, their sword scabbards hanging at their sides. Gracia had her hair very nicely brushed out, falling to the edge of her dress, just at her knee. Of course, her hair bobbed up and down a little as she hopped out of their suite, joining the other somewhat nervous Daughters of the Seas. They looked very much like she did, with perhaps the greatest difference being the length of their hair. Alicia's was the longest, nearly touching her ankle.

"Gracia, how are we to get into the carriages?" asked Blanca.

"I believe we will have to let our guardians lift us in and out. I can see no other way that we can do it. I am so proud of you all. You all look very pretty." The younger teens grinned, pleased with the compliment.

They hopped on out to the waiting carriages, and their guardians experimented with lifting them into the carriages, working out how best to do it. Then they waited for the very slow moving others in their toe boots and shoes. The tower women wore their fanciest gowns, but shunned the fetter style and the arm binding ones. Their many golden lip plates flashed in the noon sunlight, casting rays about the world outside the hacienda. Gracia also noted they needed help getting into the carriages as well and relaxed a little.

"You know we still haven't actually visited all the city yet. I keep meaning to, but there just never seems to be time for it," Gracia admitted to Diego.

"True, sis, we really ought to make a point of doing it soon," Andres overheard, agreed, and suggested.

They looked out at the city as they rode swiftly along the main streets. The Royal Palace was located near the heart of the city. Fons described it well by saying, if you took four haciendas of theirs and connected them in a square, you'd have the palace. Like all other constructions here, the palace was built of grey stone with red tiled roofs. In the very center of the enormous square was the Formal Gardens where the dance would be held. It could easily accommodate several hundred guests in a luxurious and fragrant setting.

As they approached the main entrance out front on Main Street, two guards and a doorman in very elegant uniforms were there to greet them. The guards watched the group closely, especially when the mermaids were lifted down. They'd heard of these one legged women, but never seen them. Gracia picked up one guard's thought: *Boy will I have something to tell the wife and kids tonight!*

After everyone was out and more or less together in the two groups, one guard asked them to follow him. Fons and Delfina led the procession, followed by Roberto and Natalia, and then the two advisors and their wives. The many children fell in behind them. Husbands held onto the arms of their wives for additional walking support, as they took their always precarious tiny steps in their toe boots and toe shoes. Gracia and Diego led her band behind them, taking very small hopping steps every so often, while waiting for the others to advance enough for her to hop.

They were led down a long hallway and into the lord's Great Hall, which was approximately the size of three of Fons' main suites. Many tables were arranged in a large square and a lot of people were present at the far end. All were standing in a long line waiting the formal introduction process. As Fons reached the head of the line, he said formally, "Venerado Fons Valen, my wife, Delfina. Best not to shake hands; these alien hands slip off far too easily."

"Lord Gabino Rosa, my wife Margaretta, our widowed daughter, Maria, our son, Gilberto." Gabino looked to be perhaps forty-seven, his wife a couple of years younger. She wore a gown quite similar to that of Delfina, putting Delfina instantly at ease. She was terribly worried about how to dress for this meeting. Both the lord and lady had the five inch lip plates. He wore toe boots, while she wore toe shoes. Her black nylons were clearly visible below the hem of her dress as were Delfina's. His eyes had a shrewd look to them, Fons noted, clearly a man of power. all the women wore the extremely long dangling earrings whose ends rested upon their chests.

Next in line was his advisor. "Alvero Rossi, my wife Ria, my son Gervasi and his wife Luisa." He was fifty, spots of grey lined his otherwise black hair. She was several years younger, though age lines did show beneath her eyes. Gervasi was twenty-five, the obvious heir to the throne of the city, but he looked perfectly miserable, though he tried not to show it. He hated the toe boots he was forced to wear, that was quite clear. Luisa was trying not to gasp for air; her nerves didn't agree with her pipe corset's restrictive nature. She, too, was uncomfortable and wanted to sit down soon.

The next group was nobleman Antonio del Rey and his wife Marcelina. He was fifty and she forty-six. They wore a very expensive suit and gown respectively, though she also had quite a bit of jewelry adorning her. "My son, Gil and his wife Anita. My son Lalo and his wife Angelita." Gil was twenty-five, Lalo three years younger. All four likewise wore very expensive outfits. He added, "My wayward daughter who still defies me, Marcela." She was twenty. Unlike the other women, she did not have any ornamentation nor did she wear a gown. Rather she was dressed much as a male guard, a short sword strapped to her waist. Still, her hair was quite long, flowing to the middle of her back, held in place by the usual bluebird clasp. Marcela had a defiant look about her. Her arms looked strong, as were her legs, what could be seen of them.

Last in line was Antonio's brother, Julio and his wife Agata. He was the youngest of the leaders at thirty-five and Agata was thirty-three. "My son Leandro, my daughter Natalia." He was fifteen and she a year younger. Remarkably, both had no body modifications and worn normal clothing, though Natalia wore the usual black patent heels with their six-inch steel stiletto.

As Fons bowed to Natalia and Delfina attempted the best curtsy that she could, Natalia said, "You are supposed to take seats starting along that side there, my lord." Her eyes kept darting to the end of the line; she could not quite see yet the mermaids. Fons sensed she was eager to see what they looked like.

"Lord Gabino Rosa, my wife Margaretta, our widowed daughter, Maria, our son, Gilberto," he repeated staring at Gracia, uncertain how to acknowledge her formally.

"We can nod, my lord, not much else," she said defusing the momentary awkwardness he felt. "High Priestess Gracia Rique, my husband and guardian, Diego," she said formally, then hopped a little more and repeated it to their daughter and son.

Behind her, Alicia said very proudly, “Priestess Alicia Valen and my guardian husband, Andres Valen.” Gracia could not help but smile. Alicia’s pride was infectious. So were all her other mermaids as they proudly gave their title and names to the lord of the city and the others down the long line.

After nodding to Natalia, she saw she now had to walk nearly all around the square of the tables to get to the next empty seat. With Diego at her side, she hopped along at a pace that matched his walking gait, consciously aware all eyes were staring at her and her other mermaids, as they took the long walk around the tables to get to their seats. As she got to hers, she bent forward a little and tossed her head to get her long hair to slip over her shoulder before sitting down. As always, it draped over the front of her left side. Diego loved seeing her hair this way, and she flashed him a knowing smile as he took his seat at her side.

Once Dominga took her seat, the hosts moved slowly to theirs and sat down as well. Lord Gabino spoke first. “I will be up front with all of you. When I learned the Valens from Castle Valen had moved down to Villa del Rey, I was very concerned and worried you would be bringing that traitor’s methods and ideas with you. Here we fully support our new Lord Pedro Valen. Indeed, it was suggested to me I simply run you all out of our city, but I decided to watch and see. Frankly I don’t know what to make of all of you, which is why I called for this meeting before our big dance.”

“Is it true, the rumors are saying you are making a new *Círculo de la Torres* here in Villa del Ray?”

“That is true, my lord. We have not yet gone online with the comm network. The official towers do not yet know of our intentions to do so.”

“I see. Would it be safe to say then your tower is not sanctioned by the official Valen Tower?”

“That is correct. We do not recognize the authority of the existing towers to dictate to us whether or not we can form our own tower, my lord. However, at this time, we have no intention of building massive tall towers like Valen Tower. We can’t easily deal with stairs. Our tower does not rise over my hacienda; it is only one story. We have no intention of building a castle or any other fortifications around our tower either, for that matter," Fons replied, suspecting one or more here could tell if he was lying.

"Well, that is most interesting. A renegade tower. Yes, you would most certainly need my permission to erect such a tall tower let alone a castle. That is all in your favor, so I am to call you Venerado Fons Valen then?"

"That would be appropriate, my lord."

"I see. Let me then ask, Venerado Valen, is it also true your tower has been providing basic *mentales* training to some of our men and women? Even giving them their germanium crystals?"

"That is also true, my lord. To date, we have fully trained and given crystals to fifty-five young men and women of Villa del Rey. We have charged them nothing for our services. None of these had the means to get to Valen Tower for their critical training. An untrained telepath is both a danger to others and to himself, as you are well aware, my lord. It is a pity Valen Tower deigns not to come here periodically and train all the worthy *mentales* gifted, who have not the means to visit them." Sensing this might be a critical point, Fons punched it home forcefully.

"Will the records of those who were trained and their skills be available for our review?" he asked.

"Of course, my lord. Anytime you wish to see them, we will make them available."

At last, Lord Gabino smiled. "Then I commend you and your tower's efforts. Let it be known this renegade tower is providing the service we all were led to believe a tower was obligated to fulfill." Fons knew now he had scored a small victory. Helping the people of Villa del Rey was the route to success.

"A tower also provides other services, per the original contracts," Lord Gabino stated dryly.

"Yes, it does. However, with twenty-one of us lacking our hands, our ability to heal is virtually nil. These alien prosthetic hands, which we were so kindly given, only barely function. Eating is most challenging, as we can only with difficulty pick up a fork, for example. Yet, if Villa del Rey should be attacked, you may count on the full and complete support of the Renegade Tower, in whatever manner we can be of assistance." He was referring to the defense pact, which stated the tower had to come to the aid of the city and territory when they were threatened. However, if they went on the offensive, the pact did not specifically say the tower needed to aid them. Fons purposely avoided this angle.

"Ah, that is most gratifying to hear, Venerado Valen. Then I can find no fault with them. Do either of you wish anything else to be clarified regarding the tower?" he asked looking at Alvaro first, then the two noblemen. None had.

"Good. Moving on to the most intriguing aspect, the strange mermaids. To be truthful, I thought the descriptions we were given of your young women were highly exaggerated. Yet I see with my own eyes they are not. You do not have any arms at all and only one strange leg. Yet, you are married like ordinary women? Please, what exactly are you? Where do you come from?"

"I am Gracia Valen, recently married to Diego Rique who was born and raised here in Villa del Rey." That brought several involuntary gasps. "I was a highly skilled fighter before my transformation into the High Priestess of the Daughters of the Seas. It is a strange tale. It began with a visit from the ancient god called Calder, God of the Seas and Waters of Tierra. Yes, he appeared to us and chose me to become his High Priestess. Through his power, I and my other priestesses were somehow transformed into what we are today. True, we have no arms and only the one leg. Yet, Calder has given us great powers, far beyond those of normal *mentales* gifted."

"In order for us to even survive, he has given us enormous telekinetic skills so we may move what we used to with our hands, for example. Since we now hop instead of walk, he also gave us the ability to teleport ourselves and others. That, I might add, has been a godsend. Just try hopping a long way. Tough. So yes, we are able to survive well with our god given powers."

"Calder charged us with blessing ships and healing the sick and injured. We are able to bless ships and their crew. Already we have healed or cured a number of your city folk who've come to us. We do not charge for any of this. It is the blessing of Calder that we freely bestow on those who ask for it and need it."

Lord Gabino spoke up, "Then it is true – the wild stories that we've heard of fishermen who have been blessed, returning with record cargos of fish?"

"Yes, indeed. And some have said our blessings brought them great luck on the seas when storms struck them," Gracia added.

"Yes, we have heard such tales as well. We have also heard of your healing skills, most impressive, High Priestess. Say, do you wish to be called mermaids or Daughters of the Seas?" he asked for clarification to avoid any potential goofs on his part.

"Officially we are Daughters of the Seas. However, most of the locals who we know simply call us mermaids, because of our one leg and the fact that we are strong swimmers," Gracia replied. "We are still normal women. I'm married now and pregnant with our first child. Yet I will admit, sometimes I regret having lost all my skills as a fighter."

"Admirable, High Priestess. We thank you for your blessings of our ships and the healing. Again, Valen Tower has always refused to bring their healers here to Villa del Ray to heal our sick and injured. We desperately need your services. Is there anything we can do to assist you? Can all nine of you heal?"

"Oh yes, all of us are healers. Well, there is one big problem I've not yet solved, my lord. We are totally out of space at dad's hacienda. We need our own space, but we would like to be closer to the docks and more readily available to the sick and injured of the city. Right now, they have to get way up the hill to us, which can be sometimes difficult for them. Dad's offered to help pay for a building, but I have to admit, we've been so busy since we moved here we've not had the opportunity to visit the whole city and see if there might be someplace we could move to which would better serve the people of Villa del Rey." If Gracia had fingers, she would have crossed them, hoping he would think enough of their service to lend a hand.

Lord Gabino nodded to Alvero who spoke up. “Well, there is an unused warehouse close to the beach and docks. It is straight down Main Street from here. With some renovations, it might serve your needs, High Priestess. Tomorrow if you would accompany me, I can show it to you. If it is suitable, the city will donate the land and building to you, and let your father handle any needed repairs or modifications you deem appropriate. Will that be satisfactory?”

“Oh thank you. Yes, most satisfactory, sir.”

Lord Gabino asked, “And you don’t mind healing the poor or the rich?”

“Illness does not differentiate nor does an injury. We will heal any who come and asked for help,” Gracia replied.

Gabino looked at his wife, Margaretta. She spoke up, “Thus far, there have been no lies on their part.” Fons realized Lord Gabino was using his wife to make a point. If nothing else, Gabino was shred and knew his job well.

Julio took the lull in the conversation to speak up. “It is such a pleasure to finally see more of us who have adopted the latest fashions, these elegant lip plates and toe boots. We are so pleased to see your women also wearing the enticing pipe corsets as well. We will be most pleased to have you attend our ball this evening. I must apologize for my son and daughter though. They were too young to undergo the body modifications at our local Elegant Fashions Inc. Now they are of age and ready to join us in high society, but alas, Elegant Fashions Inc now refuses to perform any more of these exquisite body modifications!”

Fons had another idea. “I take it they both wish to have them done?”

“Yes, as befitting our positions,” he replied. Leandro shook his head yes, while Natalia shook her head no.”

The elder Antonio added, “Alas, forgive my wayward daughter, Marcela. Time and time again, I had asked her to stop behaving as if she were a man and to have the feminine modifications done. Always she refused. Now when I have finally ordered her to get them done, we find they will not perform them any longer! Idiots.”

“If I may make a suggestion, my lord,” Fons said

quietly. "We have brought with us some of the very medical machines that make these modifications. We know how to operate them, and we have a goodly supply of the lip plates, toe shoes and boots as well as the fancy earrings. And oh yes, the pipe corsets for the women too. We thought to bring them along with us, though we didn't really see any use for them. They are still in storage at the hacienda. We would be honored to perform these required body modifications on those who wish to get them so they may look as elegant as we all do."

"Heavens! A miracle! Yes, yes, we would dearly love to make use of your services!" Antonio replied enthusiastically. "And there are other nobles who would also like to make use of such a service." He turned to Marcela. "I order you to get your corset and either get your lip plates and look like a noblewoman of the del Rey house or get the toe boots. One or the other. Not another word out of you!" Turning to Fons, he said, "Please send word when you have them up and ready to go!"

Advisor Alvero then said, "I'd like to return to this god Calder. He is one of the ancient gods, if I am not mistaken. Why has he chosen to return now? Has he said anything else to you?" He looked first at Gracia and then Fons.

Gracia looked over at her father. He smiled at her and answered, "Well, sir, as a matter of fact, he did say something I consider vitally important, though he said nothing of why he chose this date return. He suggested the time was right for the coastal cities to flourish and prosper beyond their wildest imaginations, eventually to rule all Tierra. He told us to get a large fleet of sailing ships built and to establish trade routes to all the other ports of Tierra. With his blessing of their safe passages and via the extensive trading, the coastal cities would gain enormous economic and thus political power over all Tierra. I think that is his idea, if I am not misinterpreting what he said. He would like his High Priestess to build a temple in every coastal port so that her priests may bless every ship that sails there, along with healing all their sick and injured as well. To me, it seems an enormous undertaking, far beyond my means. Yet I do see wisdom in such a venture, especially with the priesthood backing the ships while at sea. In truth I know neither of ship building nor its cost. Nor do I know how my daughter can possibly find enough women to become priestesses to fulfill such a large order."

Lord Gabino immediately asked, "High Priestess, are you saying you can take other young women and somehow turn them into mermaids who have the powers of you nine?"

"Absolutely my lord. That is how we three became nine. All six not only volunteered, but also greatly desired to become a priestess so they could help others and heal the sick and injured. It takes a special young woman. I was eighteen when I was changed and I had a rough time with adapting to the transformation. The ones I've recently done were fourteen or fifteen, and they had a much easier time adapting. Honestly, my lord, there is a great deal of adapting, as you can well imagine!"

As she was speaking, she picked up Natalia's thoughts. She hated being ordered to undergo the body modifications of her parents. She had images of how her mother often couldn't breathe properly, how difficult her walking was. She hated the lip plates entirely. Worse, she knew as soon as she was modified properly, her father was going to marry her to someone that she detested. *Maybe this is my way out,* Natalia thought. As soon as Gracia finished, Natalia spoke up rapidly. "Dad, I want to become a priestess, a Daughter of the Seas. Please, dad." She was begging.

Julio grasped the situation instantly. With one of his own daughters being one of these special priestesses, he'd gain fame, a family healer, and a way to keep tabs on this priesthood. "Natalia, are you sure? They don't even have arms. You'll be more helpless than your mother is."

"Dad, you heard her, they are given special powers to offset that. Please, dad, please."

"Okay then, Natalia. I consent. High Priestess, please consider doing what you do so Natalia can become one of your priestesses. If you do so, I'll pay your renovation costs of the warehouse or whatever building you do choose as your new space. Natalia already has had her training and has some healing skills."

Gracia knew she was in the cross hairs. She dare not

outright refuse the nobleman. "My lord, I will speak with Natalia and, if she is truly desirous of this, then I will accept her as one of our priestesses."

"Excellent, excellent!" Julio was exceedingly pleased. Even Natalia greatly relaxed.

"Can we get back to the important items? This fleet of ships and extensive trading has me greatly intrigued," Antonio interrupted. "In the past, we have rather wanted to open up extensive trading, but always the seas are unpredictable. Whole ships can be lost with all its cargo and hands. While the hands are replaceable, the cargo and ship cannot easily be replaced. Merchants suffer terrible losses. Now we are being presented with the solution to that, Calder-blessed ships. Indeed, if the High Priestess can build her temples in the trading cities and truly bless these ships, then cargos would not be lost. This could well be the most profitable venture in centuries."

"Let us test this plan of Calder's. I will see to the construction of say four large sailing ships. It will take at least a year to get one ready to sail. Meanwhile High Priestess, you get one of your temples built in, let's say, Arabella. Then we can begin to test this theory. The ship will be blessed here when it leaves Villa del Rey and blessed again when it sails home from Arabella. If that proves successful and no cargos are lost, we can then add Benito to the trade cities, assuming you can get a temple built there as well. If both of these work out and cargos are not lost, then we can continue to expand to other coastal cities. Imagine the vast amount of trade that can be done between here and all the way across the southern coasts of Tierra into the Easterlings. If cargos are not lost, the profits are almost incalculable!"

Gracia replied, "It will take us time to find women willing to become our priestesses, my lord. Yet I will do my best to help fulfill Calder's dream."

"Surely within a year you will be able to have at least one priestess in Arabella for the test runs. You could even send one of your eight priestess you have just for the test," Antonio argued.

Gracia smiled. Antonio most definitely wanted this to

pan out. If it did, Villa del Rey may well become the capital of the world!

"My, it is getting late. Please, would you all care to join us for dinner? The dance begins shortly after that. We can eat here and then the women can freshen up before the ball begins," Lord Gabino offered. Fons accepted and soon servants began bringing in plates, silverware, and mugs. Then the chefs wheeled in carts steaming with expensive and delicious dishes.

Many eyes covertly glanced over at the mermaids to see how they could possibly eat. All were somewhat awed and amazed to see the forks and spoons rising and falling seemingly being used by unseen hands. The nine definitely made an impression on their hosts.

The ball turned out to be quite an experience for the group. Fons and his group made numerous connections and the acquaintance of various key leaders and opinion leaders of the city. As word slowly spread they could provide the body modifications so many desired, Fons found many chatting privately with him about such things. A few wanted to get their young children tower trained here, avoiding the costly trip to Valen Tower. For the first time since they arrived, the twenty-one body-modified felt like they belonged in society again. While there were several hundred in attendance, at least eighty had some of the modifications and many more were desirous of obtaining them.

Of course, hundreds of eyes fell on the nine mermaids, who found themselves often the center of attention. Diego tried to see if there was any way for Gracia to dance with him. All she could do was take tiny hopping steps, which didn't look elegant at all, and the nine soon gave that up, spending their time answering many questions put to them. At a quiet point, Gracia whispered to Diego, "Dear, it's all right. I never was very good at dancing. My sister is, as you can see."

All of the guardians were not taking any chances their wives or charges could accidentally get bumped by the crowd. They kept one arm around their waists at all times, often moving in synch with their hopping, as they mingled with the crowd. While the nine were glad when the dance was over, the tower folk were not.

The next day Diego, Gracia, Andres, and Alicia toured the empty warehouse and found that it would work well, but only with major renovations that would turn it into a hacienda proper. Gracia got her money's worth out of Julio on this one. On the return trip, Natalia joined them. Gracia did her best to dissuade her from making the choice to become a Daughter of the Seas.

"Look, I would rather be like you are, than horribly modified and married off to that pig. Please, I will do my best to heal others. I am a healer now," Natalia insisted. Gracia had no choice but to accept her, having her returning home with them. At supper, Natalia was fed diablo rojo fish and her transformation was set into motion.

The next day Fons summoned Gracia to him. He'd setup the medical machine in the last small suit, moving some of the other equipment into his own room for now. As Gracia hopped into the room, she saw Marcela lying on the machine unconscious. *Poor woman,* she thought, *what a waste of a good fighter. Men!*

As if reading her thoughts, Fons said. "Yes it is a pity." He actually knew his own daughter well, for she'd been much as Marcela was. "I'm caught between the rock and the hammer on this one. Marcela came here expecting to have lip plates and earrings put in and nothing else. She agreed to them but not the toe shoes, if you remember from the meeting. My problem is this. He struggled to pick up a paper lying on the machine with his poorly working hands. After three failed attempts he said, "Crap, you pick it up and read it."

She obliged using her telekinetic skills. "He's ordering me to perform all the modifications on her, pipe corset, earrings, toe shoes, the works. She went under only agreeing to the lip plates and earrings, since she believes she will still be able to fight with them. Lesser of two evils, as she put it. So here I am ordered to do all these things, and she doesn't want them. What the devil do I do, Gracia? If I do them, she'll never fight again. I can't imagine how depressed she will be. Suicide perhaps?"

"Dad, you *are* in a bind. Let me think. He was most adamant about the lip plates. That seems to be one of the key ornaments that distinguish the high nobility here. I know, go ahead with the lip plates and earrings, because that's what she and he agreed to at the meeting. When she wakes up, show her this order from her dad. Then send her to me. I think I have a way to salvage her."

"Your mind is sometimes a mystery to me. Thanks for saving my butt on this one." She smiled and hopped out and headed off to find Andres.

A half hour later and in misery, Marcela awoke, feeling the awful tension in her split lips and soon after that how difficult her speech had become. As she sat up, her ears felt like they were being pulled off. As Gracia had requested, Fons said, "Marcela, it is worse than you think. I can't pick up that paper there, please do so for me. It is an order I received from your dad just after I put you under to get your lips done."

She did so, but annoyed at having to lift it higher up than she normally had to do so just to be able to read it over her lip plates that now blocked part of her vision. Without lips, as she looked downwards, she began to drool a little, and Fons hastily explained how to avoid that. "My god! Dad wanted me turned into a useless cripple like mom!" She let lose a tirade of cussing and violent anger. When she calmed down a bit, Fons merely pointed to her waist and feet. "Oh, Venerado, you didn't follow dad's orders?"

"No I didn't."

"But he'll take revenge on you for disobeying him. He has a violent temper!"

"We will see. I am to take you to see Gracia now. She wants to talk to you about a way out of this mess." He started to make his pitifully slow way out of the room to take her to see Gracia. Annoyed with his slowness that could well have been her now, she said, "Oh just tell me which is her room. God, I can't stop drooling!" He did so, relieved he didn't have to make that long walk.

She knocked and Gracia had her come in. "Natalia is undergoing the changes and I have to stay here with her. It is very scary for us at first. We are so helpless, until we get used to it and our powers come. Now then, as you can see dad directly defied your dad. I asked him to do that, Marcela. I was once a fighter like yourself, and I know how horrid it would be for you to have woken up to find yourself hobbled up like your dad ordered. Your life would be ruined utterly."

Slobbering a good deal, she replied, "Duh, no kidding. I'd probably go drown myself if I could even walk that far! Sorry for the drool. I can figure out how not to yet. Even these are awful. Earrings are just annoying."

"I can imagine. I have an idea. How would you like to become one of our Guardians? You would live with us, protect us, and help us when needed. You'd be out from underneath your father forever."

"Really? Oops, sorry. Slobbered on you. Damn these anyway."

"Yes, when your father sees you at least have the lip plates and earrings as you both agreed and you are now a Guardian, he ought to be appeased sufficiently. What say you?"

"You bet I will take your offer!" Marcela exclaimed, shooting more drool out of her mouth. "Crap, I don't have lips to keep my saliva inside my mouth. This is so embarrassing. Sorry Gracia."

"That's okay. When you need to fight, you can take them out. I wish it could be undone, but it can't. There is one side benefit my family has told me about. When you take them out, your lip loops will be hypersensitive to the touch. Hermina, my sister, tells me that, if her husband licks her loops, it drives her mad with lust. She claims that they have given them the best sex ever, but perhaps she is exaggerating it."

"Hell, I can't even smile anymore. I'll remember that. Thanks. I suppose that I can be Natalia's guardian. She knows me and trusts me. Please, let me be Natalia's guardian; we've been close friends since she was a child."

"I was hoping you would say that. Thanks, you will be her guardian always. I will send word to your father about this. Go see Andres. He's going to get your uniform ready for you. Later he and Diego will accompany you back to your place so you can get your things and move in here yet today. This way, he'll see your lip plates and your uniform and have proof I'm not lying about it. When you get back, you can help me with Natalia."

"Thank you, thank you," she gushed, though splattering more drool. She tried to wipe her mouth and bumped the plates awkwardly. She cursed them again, then left to find Andres.

Well, I've salvaged two lives today. That's something. Best get back to Natalia. She's lost her leg now and ought to be rousing soon.

Dressed smartly in her new guardian's uniform of sky blue with her black boots and matching belt, Marcela strapped on her sword scabbard and adjusted her hair once more. "Okay, Andres, I'm ready to face dad now. God, these plates are annoying!"

"You fit in with the nobility around here. At least the earrings and rubies don't clash with your hair," Andres commented. He, Diego, and Marcela headed out to the stables and mounted three horses. She led them directly to her parent's home not far from the palace. Here was another huge estate, a trio of haciendas in a U shape. Tying up their horses at the hitching rail, Marcela, head held tall, marched in past the staring guards, ignoring their smirking looks at her lips and earrings. *Damn them anyway! They always wanted me out of dad's guards! Well, they got their wish! I'm never coming back here.* Andres and Diego followed her, walking fast to keep up with her.

"There you are dad!" Marcela shouted angrily. Her speech sounded strange to her, but in fact it was now similar to her parents.

"I see that you have your lips done and earrings. Now you look like a proper del Rey. Wait!" Antonio first smiled appreciatively, though it wasn't visible. Then his face changed to open hostility, as he saw she was walking normally and didn't have the tiny waist as he'd ordered.

"This is all you get! I am now the Guardian of Natalia. I work for the High Priestess from now on. If you ever try to run my life again or have me mutilated like yourself and mom, I swear I will kill you. I am packing and leaving now. These Guardians will explain." She turned and marched out of the room, leaving her father staring at her, his lip plates opened wider than normal.

"I'm sorry my lord," Andres hastily spoke up, trying to defuse the hostile air. "She was most insistent about joining Calder's Guardians of the Daughters of the Seas. She has been accepted and now wears our uniform. Perhaps, this is a good thing," he suggested.

Antonio had not become the wealthiest man in Villa del Rey without having the ability to adjust to rapidly changing situations. No indeed. When Lord Paco Valen had insisted lords get the body modifications, he was quick to see the keen advantage in that. Wherever he or his family went, their lavish ornaments separated them instantly from the crowd of humanity around them. Everyone had no doubt about just who they were; introductions were never necessary.

"I see. Strong headed, pig headed. That's my Marcela. Well I accept her decision to join the Guardians. In fact, this is probably for the best. She will get to do what she always wanted to do, fight and protect, but she will always carry her noble birth along with her. Everyone will see she is a del Rey from her lips and earrings, in spite of the uniform she wears. When you see her, tell her that I approve of her decision. He will show you to her room," Antonio replied. From his tone, Andres knew the brief meeting was at an end. Antonio would have nothing more to say to him. He and Diego turned and followed the guard.

An hour later, the three returned to their hacienda. Marcela had one large bag containing the few possessions she still wanted, along with a few things of Natalia's as well. "Thanks guys, for coming with me. You saw his temper."

Andres chuckled, "Quick to anger, but quick to mellow. I think he is one shrewd business man."

Marcela chuckled, "Aye, that he is, so is his brother, Julio. At least Julio is more understanding. God, how am I going to live with these stupid plates? I've already slobbered all over my top."

"I think you are supposed to keep your mouth kind of upwards. The others here always keep their heads elevated a little. I've noticed when they lower their heads, drool comes out too," Andres suggested, pitying her a little, but knowing there was nothing now anyone could do for her. She was stuck with them.

Diego spoke up, "Marcela, bring your bag. Since you are Natalia's Guardian, you will be bunking with her. We're out of rooms and are doubling up in the suites. You will be in our suite, with Gracia and me. You and Natalia will have our bedroom for now, Gracia and I are making do in the living room." He and Marcela headed off to the suite, while Andres made sure the stable lad took care of their horses, before heading inside to find Alicia.

"Ah, good. How did it go? Natalia is starting to stir," Gracia said as Marcela walked in, tossing her bag in a corner out of the way.

"He nearly burst a gut, but he did accept my few ornaments as meeting his criteria for a noblewoman. He's okay with my being a Guardian. I think he now believes he has an inside line here. Well, he's got another think coming, if he imagines I'm going to spy for him, the bastard. How's dear Natalia? This has got to be so awful for her." Her hostility melted into a deep sympathy for Natalia, as she looked at the young teen lying on the light blue satin sheets. She was starting to stir.

Marcela leaned over and looked under the sheet. "It's happening isn't it. So different looking," she whispered to Gracia. Her upper legs were bowed slightly and now fused together just above her knees. A single leg, larger than normal extended on down to her single foot. Marcela covered her back up and wiped Natalia's forehead. She stirred and opened her eyes.

"Marcela? Oh, I feel so weird. You did it! Your lips, earrings. You look really good, Marcela. My legs feel funny." She moved her arms a little, noticing that she still had them. Natalia lifted the sheet and sighed. "It's happening, isn't it? Marcela, can you stay with me? I am getting a little afraid."

"Natalia, I won't ever leave you now. Not ever!" Leaning over her, she again drooled slightly and tried to wipe it, once more banging her plates. "I'm your Guardian now. We are joined at the hips forever! You and I, we will never be parted now. It's a miracle, but we are together now and free of our fathers."

"Really? Forever? My Guardian? Oh Marcela, I do so love you! Thank you, thank you." Natalia showed a rush of happiness. Then concern replaced that look. "But how?"

"Dad tried to order Venerado Fons to totally modify me while I was unconscious, pipe corset and toe boots, the whole thing. He issued Fons a direct order to do it to me. Thank god Venerado Fons didn't. Gracia gave me the job of being your Guardian. Now we will never, ever be parted again. I will be here for you always, my love," Marcela whispered.

"So we really are free of them at last? I never thought we ever could be. Oh, Marcela I want to get lip plates and earrings just like you. I have to, please, tell Gracia I have to have them too."

"Tell me what?" Gracia hopped over to the bed.

"Please, Gracia, I want lip plates and earrings, just like Marcela has, identical ones. Please, I must have them too," Natalia begged.

"Natalia, I wouldn't do that. It's dangerous for us. We sometimes fall down. You could really hurt yourself," Gracia pointed out the obvious.

"I don't care about that. Marcela will always be with me. Please, this means everything to me. I have to look like her, I just have to, we promised each other we would get them, if one of us had to get them. I can't live with a broken promise, not to Marcela, please, I have to do this small thing, please."

Gracia sensed there was no way to talk her out of it. Natalia could not see the risk she was taking. Further Gracia saw no matter what she said, Natalia would just find a way around that argument. She took a different approach. "Natalia, you must wait until the transformation into a Daughter of the Seas is finished. Then, if you still want them, you can have them, but only if you hop to the room where dad's doing them all by yourself."

"Thank you. Thank you. I will. I promise I will. Marcela, I promise I will. I won't let you down. I have to go to the bathroom, but I feel kind of dizzy and dopey," Natalia replied.

Marcela helped her sit up and get to the edge of the bed,

with her single leg upon the floor. "Okay, up you go, Natalia. I've got you."

Carefully Natalia stood up, wiggling a little. "This is kind of frightening, Marcela. I can't walk."

Her arms around Natalia, Marcela said, "I've got you. You have to hop over to the commode there. Come on; you can do it. Hop like Gracia does."

A while later Marcela fed her some more of the fish and helped Natalia lay back. Soon she fell asleep again. Gracia took the quiet time to asked, "Marcela, why is she so insistent about the lip plates and earrings? What promise?"

"Gracia, we have been like sisters. I've always been protecting her from her father's sometimes scheming ideas. Our fathers have been threatening to make us totally modified women for years now. We've only escaped because, for some reason, Elegant Fashions Inc has stopped doing them. We both pledged if one of us got screwed and ended up with them, the other would have it done too so we would look the same. This means a whole lot to her. Her father rarely lets her live up to the promises she's made in her fourteen years. I know it's not wise for her to have them, but she truly needs to be finally able to make a decision for herself and not have adults totally overrule her. She's not like me. I can stand up to our fathers. I'm the bitch in the family, according to dad anyway." She jested a little.

"Okay. I rather guessed it was something important like this. If she can make the walk on her own to the room, she can have them done."

"Oh! I see what you are doing now! When the changes are done, she's going to be even more helpless. You are going to get her to see she can still do things right away. You are the clever one!" Marcela grinned, though now it was no longer visible. Still, Gracia saw the enlightened smile in her eyes.

"I'm devious sometimes. Yes, it's always hard when they awake fully changed and have not yet gotten their powers from Calder. I found it damn scary. I was terrified when I first tried to hop. Now she has a driving need to hop and fend for herself a little. I'm hoping that will raise her confidence really quickly," Gracia explained her rationale.

Marcela sat with Natalia all that day and slept beside her during the night, feeding her twice more during that time. Around noon the next day, the dried husks that had been her arms finally detached from her shoulders and Marcela disposed of them. Now she waited for Natalia to finally wake again. Early afternoon her eyes flickered and Natalia awoke as a Daughter of the Seas.

"I've got to pee again. Oh, Marcela! This is really scary now! Hold me!"

"I'm right here, Natalia. Come on, to the commode we go."

Gracia hopped in carrying a new light blue dress for Natalia. After getting her dressed, Marcela again headed off to get her some more fish to eat. Natalia was craving it now. With Marcela temporarily gone, Gracia again attempted to convince Natalia to not get the lip plates.

"No, I must do this, Gracia. I promised. What good am I, if always I can't live up to my own promises?" Gracia sighed, realizing there was no way to talk her out of this. She could simply refuse to let her do it, but that would cause more damage to her, especially now in her fragile mental state. She would have to adapt rapidly to her altered physical form.

"Eat and when you are strong enough, Marcela can accompany you to dad's room to get it done," Gracia promised her, bringing a huge sigh of relief to her face.

"Thank you. No one's let me keep my word before, except Marcela."

After feeding her more fish, bread laced with honey, and some tea, Natalia finally felt stronger and human again. The dopey feeling was gone. "Okay, I am ready to get my lip plates and earrings now, Marcela. I hope I can somehow get to that room. This is really frightening, love."

"I know. It must be really awful for you, but I'm your Guardian now. I will be at your side always. Remember that. Gracia, she's ready. Is Venerado Fons ready for her?" Marcela asked.

"He's waiting. Last chance to back out, Natalia," Gracia said, but knew the teen would not back down. However, would she make it on her own that far this soon?

Marcela helped her to her foot. “Marcela, this is so scary!”

“Be brave, like we always pledged we would. You can do it. I’m here.”

Natalia began taking her first real hops as a mermaid, wiggling her torso after each hop, keeping her balance. Soon, though, she began doing better at it. By the time they’d traveled the length of the long garden to the storeroom, Natalia was doing fairly well, far better than Gracia had done on her first attempts. As Gracia watched them enter the room, she saw if nothing else, this had gotten Natalia up and hopping far sooner than any of the others had. That was something at least.

An hour later, Natalia sported identical five-inch lip plates and earrings. She was all smiles, but those were unseen, except in her eyes. With Marcela hovering at her side, Natalia hopped over to the chairs in the middle of the garden and sat down. “We talk so strange, Marcela. Do your ears feel like they are being pulled off? Mine do, especially when I hop.”

“Yes, we sound really strange, just like our folks and many here in the tower. You look gorgeous, my love. Thank you for honoring our pledge to each other,” Marcela replied, her arm over Natalia’s shoulders. “Now we look the same again.”

“I’m drooling some.”

“Me too. I haven’t figured out how to avoid it totally.” She wiped off Natalia as gently as she could. “We’re going to love it here, don’t you think?”

“Yes, and we’re free from our fathers at long last. Now we can be together, always. I can’t tell you how much it meant to me to wake up and find that you are to be my Guardian and not some strange man.”

“Me too. Somehow, we made it all work out. Now you must be braver than I *ever* was, Natalia. I am so proud of you, my love. You put me to shame. You are so much braver than I was.”

“But I am a little scared too, Marcela. Right now, I feel completely helpless. Can you scratch my nose? It itches. I will be brave for you, I promise,” Natalia declared.

"I know you will be. Already you are so much braver than me. Come on. Gracia told us the sooner you practice hopping, the easier this will become for you. I will be right beside you, always, my brave honeybee." Natalia grinned, hearing Marcela's private nickname for her. As a little girl, they used to walk the meadows at the edge of the city, and the honeybees always seemed to be around Natalia, prompting the nickname. They only used it in private.

Natalia lunged forward and got to her foot, again wobbling and wiggling throwing her arms about only to have the reality of her physical form come crashing in on her again. She barely kept it together. "I'm scared, Marcela, *really* scared. What if I can't *do* this?"

"Sure you can, my love. The other nine can and I just know that you can do it too. Be brave. You are up now. Let's walk to the other end of the garden."

"You mean hop, silly," Natalia corrected her, trying to make light of her own fears. She bent her leg and began to hop once more. Her long hair that nearly touched her ankles bobbed up and down as did her new earrings and breasts. Even her lip plates bounced a little, but the dowels held them from slipping. She almost fell when she tried to turn, but with wild gyrations of her torso, she kept from falling. They hopped back to the center of the gardens safely and took another rest.

The rest of the afternoon, Marcela kept Natalia at it and by supper, she was starting to feel more comfortable moving around on her own. At supper, Marcela fed her more of the special fish along with other vegetables and berries. After that, they again walked around the gardens several times. The other mermaids kept dropping by offering her encouraging words and praising her for doing so well on her first day at it. They also complimented them both on their fancy ornaments. This last made Marcela feel slightly better about having them.

Later in Gracia's bedroom, Marcela brushed out Natalia's hair, first slipping off her dress. While Natalia sat on the edge of their new bed quite naked and waiting on Marcela to undress and brush her own hair, Natalia got a good look at her new form, though the lip plates tended to block her lower vision some. "It is so weird, isn't it? But I am still a woman, see."

"Oh you are very much a woman, a very beautiful one too. I agree, it is weird, so different. There I'm done, now we are supposed to take the plates out." She took hers out and Natalia's next. They looked at each other's drooping lip loops and they both giggled. After helping Natalia lay down, she slipped into bed beside her. At last, wholly alone, Marcela began passionately kissing Natalia, who just as passionately kissed Marcela. Then their hypersensitive lips activated, and before long they were both ecstatically pleasured. Almost panting from their frantic love making, Natalia whispered, "We can still have our babies and family as we planned."

"I know. We will just find some guys to knock us up when we are ready to have our children, my love. First, though, we have to get you doing really well. We'll keep our eyes open for the right guy for us. I so love you, my honeybee." She kissed Natalia once more before pulling the sheets over them.

In the next room, Gracia could not help but sense the two and finally realized that they were lovers. She grinned; now their behavior made sense to her. Diego merely grinned and massaged her abdomen. "It's a girl, by the way," Gracia whispered. "What are we going to name her?"

"How about Teresa?" Diego whispered back. Gracia smiled, she liked that name.

Chapter 5 Establishment

Late December 1245, the extensive renovations were finished. The first Temple of Calder stood beckoning all. The temple was U-shaped, with an iron fence across the two hundred foot open front that led to the huge central gardens and pond. Hacienda style, the three other sides held small suites, many of which were living quarters. One held the kitchen and pantry, and one held their communal dining room. Others were reserved for their work, a place for the sick and injured to rest while the Daughters of the Seas worked their magic. Behind the back of the north set of suites was their small stable where the guardians kept horses and a few carriages.

True to his word, Julio spent lavishly. They were now living in luxury. Further, Gracia hired a small staff. Dorita and Geraldo also had a suite here so that they could still live close to their daughters. Both were waiting anxiously to become grandparents. What surprised them all the most was Antonio's unexpected bequeathment. He and Julio were so impressed their daughters were now a part of the group that they paid for all their operating expenses. "Look, you are healing our city's sick and injured and not charging them. You have to eat too, so we'll cover your operating expenses from the city taxes."

With no financial matters complicating things, Gracia again decided to bring in more women to become mermaids. Despite the lip plates, Natalia adapted well and was now doing her part, healing others as well. Alicia made sure that both Natalia and Marcela had the trauma of their lip plate surgery vanquished, and the two women were now inseparable. Gracia's team had ten mermaids, counting herself. She had space here to house at least twenty more along with their guardians. Again, she took the approach of making themselves visible, and all ten visited the beach daily, swimming and chatting with those on the beach, who were predominately the younger generation.

With the mermaids gone, Venerado Fons had space available in his hacienda once more. While he didn't like

Gracia and Andres being so far from them, it being almost two miles from his hacienda to their new temple, he desperately needed the suites the mermaids had been using. Now he began performing more of the body modifications, which many lesser noble families desired. In order to support the apparel needed by these modified men and women, Venerado Fons visited their Elegant Fashions Inc. After a lengthy discussion, the young manager, Ria Rosita, agreed to have all the unused stock of pipe corsets, fitted gowns, and toe shoes and boots from all the other stores sent here. Soon, her business in these extreme styles was once more booming. She was selling more of these types than any other of the currently popular fashions being sold in the Midlands. Ria simply could not understand this and sent off messages to her boss back in Exchange City, Inez (Valen) Franks.

Inez had been victimized by these very same body modifications. Her hatred for what had been done to her in the name of fashion still haunted her. While her life had been salvaged by Benjamina Blackwater of the Underground, she thought long and hard about what she was hearing from her Villa del Rey branch office. She had disowned her Valen heritage and even that of the Westerlings, who had now voluntarily isolated themselves from the Midlands, where she lived and did most of her business. Rather than bother Benjamina about this anomaly, Inez decided to send two of the old body modification machines and all their many store's supplies of those severe styles of apparel down to her store in Villa del Rey. "If they want to hobble themselves, let them! Serves them right for the wicked harm they inflicted on me and hundreds of us here in the Midlands."

Thus, in January of 1246, the Elegant Fashions Inc in Villa del Rey once more began to market extensively these severe apparel items and offered free body modifications, much to the relief of Venerado Fons. He'd already pumped this aspect for all the points he could with the nobles, who saw his efforts as being the sole reason Elegant Fashions Inc got back in operation again, serving their perceived needs. Besides, handling the seemingly never ending requests for more modifications, he had far less time to spend on getting his

Renegade Tower in better shape.

As before with the ten mermaids going for daily swims in the warm blue waters, they attracted even more attention. Gracia also noted Natalia's lip plates drew lots of attention, not only because they were highly unusual, but also because they were widely recognized as identifying nobles. Seeing noblewomen as mermaids began to draw even more inquiries from other young teens. It was as if the nobles were now part of and backing them. Further, that her own pregnancy and that of Alicia and Juana were now quite noticeable also aided, vanishing any notions the mermaids could not have children, but were real women, albeit with very unusual bodies. Within a week, she had another dozen volunteers, having discarded almost that many who wanted to join for the wrong reasons.

She decided to take the plunge and do all dozen at the same time. Why? Gracia was worried that as her pregnancy moved further along, she might not be able to deal with a high level of action, as she still was able to do at this moment. A pregnant mermaid was uncharted grounds for all of them. In addition, she still had to setup a location in Arabella for Antonio's big test. She needed time to deal with this as well. Thus, Andres and Diego quickly rounded up another dozen young men who wanted to join the Guardians of the Daughters of the Seas. More than a few were the boyfriends of the teens. This, the largest conversion yet, began the second week of January.

Figuratively, they had their hands full the third week of January, as twelve young women began to confront their vastly altered conditions. Somehow, Gracia and her team got the twelve over their bout of terror and shock. By the end of January, the dozen were hopping successfully and their vast psi powers began appearing. For the next three weeks, the new recruits were trained to use their newly gained *mentales* gifts and powers. As always, the telekinesis and teleport skills were essential to the twelve, who finally lost their awful feelings of utter helplessness.

Towards the middle of February 1246, she faced an unexpected development. Many of these new recruits now wanted ornaments like those that Natalia wore and her guardian, Marcela. For days, Gracia just couldn't figure out why eight of the dozen wanted them. While dining, she glanced at Natalia. In a flash, it came to her and realized why. With the ornaments, they would be seen by others as now belonging to the noble class! Further, the reports from Natalia about the greatly enhanced sexual stimulus also played a major role in their desires for the fancy ornamentations. She decided to hold a group meeting to discuss this.

In their formal garden, Diego and Andres arranged twenty-two chairs in a semi-circle. It was quite a sight seeing the nearly two dozen women in their light blue satin dresses all hopping into the area at one time. Gracia felt a huge surge of pride in these women, who were giving their all to help the sea faring men and to heal the sick and injured of Villa del Rey. "Wow, what a powerful group we are, ladies," she said as they all adjusted their long hair over a shoulder and out in front of themselves before they sat down. Many cast glances at Natalia, admiring her ornaments.

"I called us all together to discuss the request by eight of you who want to have similar lip plates and the very long, dangling earrings that Natalia has. As I have told you individually before, they can be dangerous. If you should take a fall and land on them, you could accidentally kill yourself. Still since we are a group, we should discuss this fully, before I make my decision."

Blanca spoke up, "I think we all should wear them. They make us look good and show we are respected nobles, even if not by birth. We are now very special and I think anyone who sees us ought instantly to know that. The fancy ornaments will do just that. They can't be missed."

"But some of us aren't interested in having others think of us as nobles," Alicia pointed out.

Adora, one of the new recruits spoke up, "Hey, if say eight more are allowed to get them, then when we're all seen at the same time, anyone out there, including the lowest dock hand, will know that Natalia's a noblewoman, while the rest of us who don't have them will just be commoners. We *are* special. I don't want others to be thinking less of me because I don't have the identifying ornaments of the nobles."

"She's got a point, Gracia. When we go swimming, they see me," Gabriela spoke up, "and they see Natalia. At once, they know she is more special than I am, because she wears the noble's fancy ornaments and I don't. I don't like that. It's like Adora says, we are all special."

Blanca added, "We can use our katalyein skills to remove the small amount of trauma that we suffer getting them, just like we have been doing for all the other noble men and women."

"But I don't mean to discriminate against all of you. I love and respect all of you," Natalia gushed. She was fighting back tears.

"We know that, Natalia. Please don't cry. We're just making a point," Blanca said kindly. Others agreed and Natalia felt a little better.

Francisca spoke up, "Hey, as long as we are being frank about this, can I ask Natalia a question about her lips?" Gracia knew where this was headed, but allowed it anyway and nodded. "Is it true that sex is really better with them?"

"Yes," Natalia blushed. "The lip loops are hypersensitive to touch. When Marcela licks mine with her tongue, I have the most powerful orgasms ever. It's indescribable."

"See, another benefit," Francisca added. Others were awfully silent, but Gracia knew they too wanted such experiences.

Alicia said, "Perhaps some of us want them and some don't. That's one point of view. The other point is we all ought to look the same. Consistency among the priestesses. If we don't, then we may get sea men insisting only on having a priestess who has the ornaments bless their ships, figuring she's more powerful because she is a noblewoman."

Blanca pointed out, "She has a point there, Gracia. We all look alike, no arms, one leg. We dress in identical light blue satin dresses. We all have long black hair, but so does all Westerlings women for that matter. Still my point is Natalia looks different from the rest of us. None of us are more special than the others, excepting you, of course. We all know why Natalia got hers, and we respect her for doing that; we admire her courage and that of her lover. Still we ought to all look the same."

After more discussion, the priestesses agreed they all should look the same, that their group image was more important than one member's desire not have them. At last, Gracia saw really she had no choice but to request they all get the ornaments. When she suggested this, no one objected. They were a group of very special priestesses, and they wanted to look similar; none wanted any discrimination by others based solely on ornamentations. The last week of February, all the mermaids underwent the two modifications, sporting the five-inch lip plates and extremely long, dangling earrings. Accidental drool became rather commonplace after that for quite some time.

Now Gracia face the problem of how to expand to Arabella. At least one mermaid had to be stationed there to bless the returning ships in order to test Antonio's theories. Everything depended upon that test being successful. No ship could be lost at sea or the whole project might end before it ever got going. Knowing how the average person had reacted to Alicia and Juana before she arrived, she knew sending only one would not work; she needed to send at least three there, maybe more. One or two weird looking mermaids would only be seen as a couple of freaks, ornaments or no ornaments. She recalled how all that changed as their numbers grew on the beach. She decided to send six, along with their guardians. The unanswered question was: should she go and try to help find a suitable place for them to stay and from which to conduct their work or not? Wherever they would locate, the ship's captain would need to be able to easily find them.

"Diego, we are going to need to visit with Antonio. Whatever we do, it has to be coordinated with him so that he can relay it to the ship's captain and crew. Shall we take a short trip?" she asked.

"Shall I bring the carriage round?" he asked.

"No, let's go on foot. Fresh air will do me some good. Damn drool anyway. I keep forgetting to keep my head up."

He smiled, "But you look stellar. Come on; let's go see Antonio." She smiled, but he could only see it in her eyes now. He opened the front gates and Gracia hopped on through, while he moved quickly to her side as they headed up Main Street.

She hopped along at an easy pace for Diego to keep stride. He admired how her hair bobbed up and down. She noticed, “Yes, and now with each hop I feel it in my ears and lips too. Good thing that my leg is far more muscular than either of mine were before I changed.” As usual, she ignored the many stares she got from the passersby on the crowded streets. “Still, Diego, this is hard work. You should try hopping a distance on one leg sometime.”

“Yes, but there is no one who hops who is sexier than you, my love,” he teased her, a big grin on his face. “Still I can’t stop thanking Calder for the gifts he gave you. Sometimes I wonder what it would be like if you lost those gifts. Utter hell, I imagine.”

“What makes you think we might lose these gifts, honey?” she asked. That idea had never struck her. Did he know something she didn’t?

“Well, if all the wild rumors I heard about the war god Wystan going to sleep are true, what’s going to happen to all of you, if this Calder god should suddenly go to sleep too? If he is the source of your powers and if he goes to sleep, will the powers disappear? I get strange thoughts sometimes. Don’t worry. I’ll always be here for you no matter what,” Diego explained and tried to reassure her.

That was a chilling thought, one Gracia hastily buried immediately. “It is such a nice day, Diego. I just don’t get outside nearly enough. When I was a fighter, I spent most all my time out of doors. Now I’m cooped up and have mostly a garden to look at. Mind you, it’s a very nice one, but it’s not the same. Oops.” A man in the crowded street accidentally bumped into her. She had to use a bit of her telekinetic psi power to keep from being accidentally knocked over.

“Are you going to jump now?” Diego asked, glancing defensively back over his shoulder at the man, always wary about attacks on his mermaid charge.

“No, I want the fresh air for a while. I know, hopping this far is tiring, but I’m tired of being cooped up.” She was breathing heavier than normal and it felt good for a change. A half hour they arrived at the del Rey haciendas. “That was a good walk,” she said taking deep breaths.

“Here to see Lord Antonio,” Diego said to the uniformed guard at the main door. He evidently was expecting them. He opened the door for them, curtly giving them directions to follow. She hopped inside and turned right down a red-carpeted hallway, Diego was right beside her. As they approached, a side door opened and the elegantly dressed Antonio stepped out. His suit was immaculately pressed, his lip plates glistened.

“In here, High Priestess, Guardian,” he said. “You may close the door,” he indicated to Diego, as he turned and made his very slow way back to his desk, measuring each step carefully, his highly polished toe boots moving only a couple inches with each step. Gracia leaned forward a little, used a head bob to toss her hair over her shoulder, and sat down long before Antonio reached his.

“What do I owe the pleasure of this visit, High Priestess?” he said pleasantly.

“It’s about setting up in Arabella, my lord,” Gracia began. “I am ready to send some of my priestesses there.”

“Ah, logistics time. Yes, I’ve been expecting this. I’ve a contact in Arabella. I’ve asked him to make some arrangements for your priestesses. There is a small hacienda close to the docks. It used to be an inn, but the owner has built a much larger one two blocks further into the city. Currently it is empty. I’ve arranged to purchase it on your behalf. It will be ready when your priestesses arrive. I wonder, will you be going there as well?”

“That’s what I’ve not yet decided, my lord. I’m responsible for my priestesses, so I ought to go and help them get settled. However if you have the hacienda all ready for them, perhaps I don’t need to go,” Gracia answered.

“I can understand your position. You are like the general who feels he must lead his troops into the battle.”

She grinned, but it wasn’t visible. “Astute observation, my lord. Yes, that’s it precisely.”

“Hum, might I offer another possibility? You see, the more I’ve thought about this grand plan of Calder’s, the more I can see it working. Hence, I've hastened the ship building program. It's amazing what offering monetary incentives can do to work crews and craftsmen. The first of these new ships will be ready to set sail in late May. However, by December, three more will be finished. Might I suggest you continue recruiting more priestesses? By December, it would be ideal if you could have another six ready to go up in Benito and another six in the Midlands coastal city of Nasik. That should be enough for the test runs."

He continued, "If all goes well, then during the next year, we'll need your priestesses operating out of a dozen smaller coastal towns here in the Westerlings as well as in Karnatalka, Madya, and Turda in the Easterlings. Assuming that works well, then the following year, add another dozen smaller coastal towns along the southern Midlands and around Alba, Easterlings, plus the other two large Easterlings coastal cities of Tecuci and Teraspoli. A year later, add another dozen smaller towns along the Easterlings eastern coastline and then two dozen smaller ones here in the Westerlings. And the following year, another two dozen split between the Midlands and the Easterlings."

Gracia laughed. "So you now have a five-year plan?"

Antonio smiled mischievously, but it wasn't visible. So many usual facial expressions were now absent from the lip plate wearers, and he often used this to his advantage. "Yes, a five-year plan. I think you are wise in sending six priestesses to each of these new cities and towns. As we all know, the official towers simply are not ever spending time in them healing and tending to the people's needs there. With your priestesses, we can change that for the better and turn a tidy profit as well. Can you handle the creation of that many priestesses?"

"Damn, I can't write any more. Diego, write down his estimates, year by year for me. This year I need three times six or eighteen priestesses."

Shortly, Diego called out, "Okay then. In 1247, you need to service three more cities, that's eighteen priestesses. In 1248, you will need to handle fifteen cities with ninety priestesses. In 1249, you add another fourteen cities and another eighty-four priestesses. In 1250, another twenty-four cities will require a whopping one hundred forty-four priestesses! Let's see, starting now we have to get three hundred fifty-four priestesses! Unreal! Wherever are we going to get that many volunteers?"

"Ah, I can see this will become a problem. I suspected as much, High Priestess," Antonio stated dryly. Gracia suspected he'd already given this considerable thought.

"I don't know if we can find anywhere near that number of young women who want to truly dedicate their lives to healing and helping others," Gracia admitted. "I need to hand-pick each young woman. As you can see, the alterations to our bodies are horrific, to be perfectly blunt about it. We need to choose the priestesses carefully."

"Yes, indeed you must. Please continue to do your very best, as I know you will. Still as the years progress, if you cannot meet the needed numbers, please allow me to lend a hand with this. After all, by then I and several other nobles here in Villa del Rey will have invested substantial fortunes into this venture. We all want it to succeed. Hence, if the time comes when you need more help, please let me know," Antonio suggested.

"Thank you, my lord. That is very kind of you. I certainly will need the help with this many priestesses," Gracia replied. In the back of her mind, a warning flag appeared, but she failed to recognize it. In later years reflecting back on all this, she would return to this pivotal conversation. "I think it best then, if I stay here and work diligently on recruiting more priestesses."

"Probably that is wise of you, High Priestess," Antonio replied with a wry grin, wholly invisible. Again, he was pleased he could make the gesture and have it be invisible to those sitting before him. They chatted more, but little of consequence was discussed. At last, Gracia and Diego bid him good day and left.

"Let's hop home. I need the exercise and time to think, Diego." She began the long hop home, nearly two miles. At her side, Diego was also pondering the sheer numbers, but he knew his duty and kept a constant guard over his wife, as she continued her awkward hopping down the still crowded Main

Street.

That evening, Gracia made her decision on who to send to Arabella. She chose Gabriela, Francisca, and four of the recent recruits. Antonio provided a small coastal dhow with its double lateen sails to ferry them from Villa del Rey the thousand miles eastward along their southern coast to Arabella in the old kingdom of Almendia. They intended to set sail on the first of March, arriving by April. She then held another group meeting and outlined her choices and the arrangements that Antonio had made for them.

"Now we also know Antonio's five-year plan," she explained further, ending with, "That means we need to have a total of three hundred fifty-four priestesses, and we number what? Twenty-two? Ideas?"

"We as a group ought to continue to go swimming and see if we can recruit more," Alicia suggested.

"We could put up help wanted posters around the city," Blanca suggested. Beyond these two ideas, no one could come up with any viable other alternatives. Diego agreed to make and post the help wanted posters, and the mermaids once more began to visit the beach on a daily basis. With so many of them there now, Gracia found the attitudes of the locals were changing to a very positive one. In just a year, she'd gone from being called a freak to being well respected. This she took as a very hopeful sign, but still she needed so many more volunteer women.

Their extensive recruiting yielded another twenty volunteers and their conversion went during the month of April, 1246. This brought her total to forty-two mermaids. In May, she fired Blanca and Carmela along with four others to Benito in the old kingdom of Trujillo. In June, she sent Dominga and five others to Nasik in the Midlands. Counting herself, twenty-four mermaids remained in Villa del Rey. If worst came to worst, she could just barely cover the eighteen that Antonio needed for his proposed expansion in 1247.

Recruiting then rather dried up. Besides, the pregnancies of Gracia, Alicia, and Juana slowed them down greatly in late April. By May hopping was painful to themselves and their unborn girls. During the first couple of weeks in June, the three had their daughters. Anita de Portales of the Renegade Tower, their healer, delivered all three new little mermaids. Yes, their three daughters looked just like their proud mothers. Gracia and Diego named theirs Teresa; Alicia and Andres named theirs Inez; Juana and Emilio named theirs Izabelle. Later in August, Renata, Emilio's sister, and Carlos Hernandez named their daughter Elmira.

With the birth of the children, the many mermaids were quite relieved. Any lingering doubts they could not become mothers and raise a family were dispelled. Many more of the newer mermaids then were married, often to their personal guardian, for which Gracia was grateful. Dealing with her new child, running the many priestesses in Villa del Rey, and coordinating daily with her dozen in the other two cities, kept her totally occupied from dawn to dusk. With almost no more new recruits volunteering, Gracia finally had to let Antonio know she could use his help in obtaining more mermaids. By the middle of 1247, she would run out of priestesses.

Antonio was delighted to lend a hand, but he asked that Gracia assign Natalia and Marcela to his newly formed Daughters of the Seas Creation Organization, the DSCO, as it became known. "Look, you leave the recruitment and their transformations to the DSCO, and we will send you the new mermaids, once they have their powers and are hopping well. You then train them as you wish your priestesses trained," Antonio told her. Gracia had little choice but to accept his help with this.

As far as Gracia was concerned 1246 through 1247 were idyllic years. Her priestesses were handling large volumes of ship blessings, healing, and curing hundreds of injured and sick townsfolk, removing the trauma of over a hundred's body modification surgeries, and for the Renegade Tower, even removing a half dozen *mentales* gifted's mental blocks. Similar results were now also occurring in the other four cities; though the mermaids there continued to beg for more help, they were swamped with work. By the end of 1247, Calder's Daughters of the Sea were well established in the five cities. As Antonio anticipated, the demand for more was going to be tremendous. He fully intended to fulfill that need.

Chapter 6 Change Comes

Benito, Trujillo was far from Exchange City and Castle Valen, nearly three thousand miles, in fact. The only way Nita Valen could get further from the now despised castle and tower was to go to the frozen northern coastal towns. She knew she could not survive up there at all, not in the horrific condition she was in. The alien prosthetic hands were dismal, when they actually worked and stayed on her aesthetic arm stumps where her gorgeous hands had been. Lord Valen's grand plan was ashes, just as he was. Constrained by her immoveable neck rings, her steel encased pipe corset around her twelve-inch waist, and her almost impossible-to-walk-in toe shoes, Nita was beyond miserable. Her five-inch lip plates only added to her misery, though she still loved her long dangling earrings whose ends rested above her massive breasts.

Once the epitome of grace and elegance worldwide and owner of Elegant Fashions Inc, Nita now was merely a pathetic, helpless twenty-five year old woman, who was noticeably pregnant and nearly broke. Actually, she was fifty-eight now, but she had made use of the alien rejuvenation machine. She'd given the nearly bankrupt business to her daughter Inez and fled Exchange City to Valen. There, she'd stolen an air car of Lord Valen's and gone to Benito, the last large city on their southwestern sea coast that had a decent climate. Though there was a little light snow in their winters, it melted in the morning sunlight.

There was a branch office of Elegant Fashions Inc in Benito, and it was here she decided to land her air ship. Adopting the last name of a grandmother, she chose to call herself Nita del Gato and via the store manager, made arrangements to sell the air car to the city lords. Again, via the store manager, she purchased a small home on the southern edge of the city close to the beach and the docks. With the little funds she had left, she hired a domestic maid to help her get her home established. After the maid got her kitchen equipped, food supplies purchased, her meager furniture bought and arranged, she had to let the maid go. She only had enough funds left to purchase food for herself and no conceivable prospects for making money. Besides, her pregnancy was now well advanced, only adding to her misery.

Alone without a friend in the world, nearly financially destitute, and almost completely helpless, Nita struggled to stay alive. Putting in her lip plates and dressing in the morning took her nearly three hours. She had no mobility above her waist and her prosthetic hands almost didn't work. Another two hours were spent cooking and eating her first meal of the day. From noon until four were the only hours she had to accomplish anything constructive, before spending another two hours dealing with supper and then another three hours getting ready for and into bed.

As May came, she was so pregnant that even doing these minor things were becoming almost impossible to do for herself. Then she got her first break. Her neighbor was able to get the debilitating neck rings off her. He'd taken pity on his neighbor and had asked her if she really had to wear them. She didn't, but could not get them off herself, and he'd kindly done it for her. That alone made her life easier to bear.

In June, she gave birth to her son, Felipe. Alone, she'd delivered him by herself, somehow managing it. It had been an easy, uncomplicated birth; otherwise she might have died then. She really didn't care whether she lived or not, but with the birth of Felipe, her mother instincts grew stronger, and she began to devote her life to her new baby.

Once a week, she had to venture out to the markets three blocks away. It took her an hour to make her slow, careful way there, taking only measured two-inch steps in her toe shoes. She had to be exceedingly careful. More than once, she'd pulled her pathetic hands off her stumps, while trying to lift a melon that weighted more than a pound. Long ago she'd given up trying to open her money pouch to hand the sellers their silver or copper coins. Trying to get the fingers to get inside the pouch and grab a coin took forever. Now she just handed the ever-shrinking pouch to the vendors, hoping they would not cheat her. Usually she'd have to spend an additional silver to have a young lad carry her few purchases back to her house for her.

Early on her arrival in Benito, she learned some of the noblewomen also wore pipe corsets and toe shoes as well as elegant gowns. However, Nita steered clear of these nobles out of fear they would possibly recognize her. If they held a grudge against her, which they had every right to do since she had been the one person who had sold everyone on this debilitating apparel, they might well attack her. She now had little Felipe to consider, the true heir to the throne at Valen Castle. In her mind, one day he would rise to reclaim his birthright. For months, that was her sole consideration, raising Felipe that he one day could claim the throne that was rightfully his as Paco's heir. That Paco had other heirs, she wholly ignored.

Beginning in August 1246, she began taking little Felipe to the beach during the afternoons, when she actually had her only free hours of the day. It took her nearly an hour to walk the short distance to the grey sandy beach filled with the younger set out swimming, sunning themselves, or just playing in the sand. Of course, walking on the soft sand in her toe shoes was extremely challenging. Therefore, she always stayed near the edge of the beach, far from the summer-warmed waters. In time other young mothers, who brought their babies to the beach, began to befriend her, assisting her with little Felipe. Slowly Nita began to make friends with these women and her hideous life began to get slightly more bearable.

In September, everything changed with the arrival of six of the strangest women that anyone had ever seen! Shouts of "Look there!" echoed around the packed beach. Nita and several of her new friends turned to look at the source of the commotion. She blinked not believing her eyes. Six women were hopping along the beach! She saw that each only had one leg! That they had no arms was quite obvious from their light blue satin dresses. Sunlight reflected off their lip plates and huge earrings. One of her friends commented, "They have lip plates and earrings just like you do, Nita!" They also saw six fighters with short swords at their waists accompanying the six freakish looking women. The men also wore identically colored satin uniforms, obviously watching over and guarding these strange women.

Wherever the six hopped, some of the braver teens came up to them to chat, but from where she sat, Nita and the other young mothers couldn't hear what was said. Nevertheless, she and the mothers chatted about these weird women constantly. Each day in the afternoon, the six came hopping out onto the sands. Several times, they even went swimming in the waters, though it was getting a bit too chilly to stay in the waters for long.

One afternoon when Nita and little Felipe were sitting alone on their beach towels, one of these strange women came hopping up to her. "Hello. I do like your fancy ornaments. I'm Blanca, by the way. You have a cute son there. What's his name?"

"Nita del Gato. Thanks, he's Felipe. What are you? What happened to you six women? It must have been dreadful. How can you survive? Your men?" she asked. A million other questions flooded her mind, but she stopped after these.

The young woman laughed, tossed her hair to her front side, and then carefully sat down in the sand next to her. "We are Calder's Priestesses, Daughters of the Seas. We bless ships so they have safe voyages and can catch a bountiful harvest of fish. We are healers. We cure the sick and injured. We also are able to remove those awful traumatic mental blocks women like yourself have from all the body modifications you've had. If you like, I can remove your blocks for you."

"Who's Calder?" Nita asked, never having heard of him.

"One of the ancient gods of Tierra. He's awakened now and given us, his priestesses, great powers to heal and bless sea going ships."

"Oh. I see. Well, thank you, but I don't have any trauma from the body modifications. They were painless. Usually I was unconscious the whole time and didn't feel anything," Nita explained.

"Actually though you were unconscious, your body still felt the terrible pains from the operations. Let me show you, all right? We've done this for many of you who have had the modifications," Blanca was most insistent.

"Well, all right." An hour later, Nita had re-experienced having her hands removed. At first, she had no pain, but on further passes through the incident, she re-experienced the tremendous pain that had occurred. That these operations had been painless was now gone. She knew firsthand they were anything but painless!"

"That was incredible, Blanca. Thank you ever so much! I had no idea there was all that pain there."

Smiling, Blanca said, "Of course, you yourself were unconscious at the time. Yet the pain was there. If you are here tomorrow, I will get all the other painful incidents erased for you as well."

"You have a deal!" Nita responded. She felt so much better, but didn't truly know why. The next afternoon, Blanca was there ahead of her, awaiting her arrival. Her Guardian took Felipe from her and promised to watch over him. Blanca started in on Nita right away. It took her the rest of the afternoon to erase the painful lip slitting, the break and reformation of her feet, and the really painful extraction of her ribs and reforming of her organs. Yet, when she finished, Nita felt more alive and happier than she could remember.

The next day at the beach, Blanca checked on how she was doing to make sure nothing else needed to be handled. "Blanca, how can I ever thank you for what you've done for me? May I ask you how you can possibly survive? I am having a dismal time of it really. I can't imagine how you can, what with no arms at all and only one leg."

Blanca laughed. "Calder's doing. When he transformed us into this form, his mermaids many call us, he gave us immense psi powers. We use telekinesis to move those things we need, such as our forks and spoons. We use it to help keep our balance if we get bumped. Normally we hop everywhere, but we also can teleport at will when we have too far to go. So Calder has given us huge mental powers we use in place of our arms and missing leg. But we are still women. Several have married and given birth already, like our High Priestess Gracia."

She chatted on, "Most importantly Calder has given us

the ability to bless a ship and its men. We have the katalyein gift as well as immense healing powers. Our job here in Benito is to help cure all the sick and injured, as well as bless all the ships. So we have our hands full. That's a joke, by the way." She grinned, but it wasn't visible because of her plates, which is why she often explained something was a joke, so that others could have a way to tell.

"Incredible, Blanca. Say, how does Calder obtain his priestesses? Can anyone become one?" Nita asked.

"Oh we are always looking for volunteers, women who want to become a Daughter of the Seas and help cure others, heal them, and bless the ships and crew. They have to really want to help others, you see," Blanca replied. "Well, if you'll excuse me, I've got a fishing boat to have to bless. Perhaps I'll see you tomorrow?"

"Yes, please stop by and chat, please," Nita replied. She watched the woman hopping away, accompanied by her light blue uniformed guard. Partway down the beach, the two simply vanished, but Nita knew that Blanca had just teleported them to the docks.

That night after spending three hours getting herself and Felipe into bed, she lay there and thought. *As I am, I can't do much of anything, but Blanca has all these powers to help her. My arms are darn well useless, three hours to get us up and dressed! Telekinesis and teleportation? Incredible. If I had those, I would no longer be helpless like I am now. Besides, I could help Felipe more when he grows up.*

The idea began to appeal to her. Then she thought about what Blanca and her mermaids were actually doing. *I could heal and cure others. I could really help others. Would that somehow make up for the hideous amount of damage that I've done? If I looked like Blanca, no one would ever recognize me, that's for sure.* She felt guilty and this seemed the only possible way she could both survive and make amends for what she'd done.

The next day she again examined her money pouch. Three silvers were all that remained, barely enough for her to purchase the week's groceries. She had to do something and headed to the beach, determined.

As always, the six mermaids made their appearance during the afternoon, and Nita hailed Blanca, who came hopping over to her, seemingly effortlessly she noted. After Blanca had gotten seated on a corner of Nita's towel, Nita said, "Blanca, I desperately want to become one of your priestesses, Daughters of the Seas. How can I become one of you? I want to heal and cure others, to help them. Please, can I become a mermaid like you? I am out of money now, and I don't know what I can do for Felipe next week. Please, I am desperate. What do I have to do to get Calder's blessings and gifts?"

"We are always looking for more volunteers. Are you sure that you want to do this?" Blanca asked. "It is really scary at first, before Calder gives you your powers."

"I don't care about that. I'll do anything to become one of your priestesses, please, Blanca, please," Nita was actually begging for the first time in her life.

"Okay then. You'll be my first volunteer. Each of us is given a Guardian when we become a priestess. He will always be at your side to help you if you need it and to protect you. Oscar here is mine. Oscar, will you go with us to Nita's house so we can get her things and bring them back to our place? She's volunteering to become one of us."

"Absolutely, Blanca. Let's go now." He picked up Felipe. Blanca got to her foot and asked them both to put their arm over her shoulders. She took a jump, arriving near Nita's front door. "Boy you sure do have a tiny house."

Nita had only a few personal items to bring along, such as her hair brush, plus a pile of baby clothes and blankets for Felipe, which Oscar quickly gathered up for her. Both saw how terribly slowly Nita moved in her awful toe shoes and he did this for her to speed things along. Once ready, Blanca jumped them to their large hacienda, plush and elegant compared to the tiny home Nita had been living in. Blanca ordered her cook to whip up a batch of the special fish and hopped Nita to what would be her room, leaving her to get herself and Felipe settled in.

Later Blanca returned with a twenty year old fighter named Gael. "He will be your guardian, Nita. Let's get you fed your first batch of the transformation fish, and then Gael can help get you into bed where the transformations will occur. He'll look after Felipe for you until you are able once more."

Nita began to make her slow way to their dining room. Impatient, Blanca decided that she'd jump Nita around to speed things along. The fish was delicious and Nita ate all that she was given. Later back in her room, Blanca insisted she remove all her clothing so they would not interfere in the massive changes to her body, which were soon to come. Gael's strong hands quickly got her fully undressed, including her pipe corset, which had not come off her for months. He then gave her a quick bath, long overdue, and put her beneath the light blue satin sheets. By now, Nita felt exhausted and quickly fell asleep.

Much later, she awoke rather groggy, but Gael was there to feed her more of the fish. Afterwards, she fell back asleep again; the transformation had begun. She awoke around noon, starving and desperately in need of the commode. She used her arm stumps to pull the sheet off her and she gasped. Her legs had been transformed. Her upper legs were now bowed a little and had somehow merged together above her knee. She now had only one leg, but to her immense pleasure, the mal-formed foot was now perfectly normal! No more toe shoes.

Blanca was there with Gael. "It is okay to be scared as you first stand. I know I sure was. Just see if you can hop over to the commode, Nita."

"Oh, this is so wonderful! I can stand on my foot again!" Instead of being utterly frightened, Nita was jubilant. Gone forever were the impossible toe shoes that had so hobbled her these past years. Still she used her arms to help herself keep her balance as she hopped. Once done Gael fed her more fish and when done, she fell back asleep. The next day, Nita awoke a full Daughter of the Seas. What was left of her arms had withered and fallen off. Only now when she stood did she become scared, as Blanca had warned her. *Be brave. You can do this. You have to do this,* Nita told herself, as she struggled to hop to the commode without falling down.

"Okay, after Gael dresses you, let's hop to the dining room and get you fed. After that, Gael will help you practice your hopping. You have to get really good at it. In a week or so, Calder will be giving you your immense powers, but first you have to get adapted to hopping," Blanca explained, just as Gracia had done for her.

Later as a very scared Nita began hopping about the gardens of the hacienda, she thought, *Now you've done it! You are more helpless now than before! Whatever came over you to do this?* "Gael, I'm scared out of my wits!"

"It's perfectly natural, Nita. Every priestess experiences this, just as you are. Get used to hopping, and soon the great Calder will give you your immense powers. For now, just focus on hopping," he said reassuringly. "In a bit we'll take a break so you can nurse Felipe again. You are doing fine. Keep it up. Let's see if you can get to the other end of the garden this time."

This is beyond horrid! All I am now capable of is this hopping! God, what kind of a stupid fool am I anyway? I can't even keep from falling. Nita continued to try to hop to the other end of the garden, then sat down on her hair, but didn't care. *I don't dare start crying on him. Oh god help me now!*

"You are doing fine, Nita. Now let's hop back to your room and feed little Felipe, shall we?" Gael suggested. She knew she had to feed him and rather threw her body upwards. She lost her balance and would have fallen had Gael not caught her and steadied her. *Why doesn't he just carry me back to my room?* "Come on, hop Nita. That's the way." She hopped. *Stay alive to feed Felipe. Have to. Why? They could just find some midwife to substitute for me.*

Gael drove her relentlessly during the next two days. Then he shocked her. "Okay, enough of this inside hopping. Let's take a walk on the street. I bet you could do with some fresh air."

She wanted to scream, "No!" Instead, she found herself obeying him, hopping towards the gate. As he opened it for her, motioning for her to step outside, Nita again panicked! Out among normal people, she'd be a real freak now, utterly helpless. "Come on, slow poke. Let's get going." Nita had no choice but to hop out among the others in the street. Yes, they stared and gawked at her, only adding to her misery. She managed to not fall down, though having to look down caused her to drool considerably, covering her lip plates, but she could do nothing about it.

Each day, he forced her to hop farther and then faster. After the terror-filled week had passed, Nita at least felt somewhat confident of her meager ability to move around on her own. At this point, her new Calder gifts began materializing. Two weeks later after her training was finished, she blessed her first fishing boat and then was able to heal a boy's broken arm. At long last, Nita felt serenely happy. With the gifts she now had, life became livable for her. She no longer hated her choice to become a mermaid. She could do far more now than before, and she was truly helping people in need. Nita began her career of making amends for the evil that she'd done.

Gabriela acquired several more volunteers, and Nita began helping them with their intense periods of adjustment. She had a good reality on what they were facing and feeling. For the first time since she got body modified, she felt wholly alive and she was doing well.

In December, the first of the new large caravels docked for the first time in Benito, causing quite a stir. It could carry over four times the cargo of the old dhows and twice as fast. all the mariners took note of the fact the caravels never sailed without first being blessed by one of these strange mermaid-looking priestesses. By January of 1247, the services of the priestesses were in great demand both for ship blessing and for their unfailing ability to heal. In fact, Gabriela and her team were swamped with work. She needed many more priestesses but had only made six more herself, including Nita.

As far as Antonio and Julio were concerned, this test venture with their new caravels was a smashing success! In January 1247, many other lesser nobles of Villa del Rey wanted in on the action, promising to help finance the caravel fleet. Ten more were scheduled to be launched during the year with ten more during each of the next four years.

However, Antonio knew he had to take positive steps to "make" more of these priestesses. Gracia simply couldn't make enough. She'd used up her pool of possible volunteers. *Hell,* he thought, *what woman in her right mind would volunteer to lose her arms and one leg? No, while volunteers may be nice, it doesn't handle the business or the true needs for these priestesses. It's up to me to secure the hundreds of new priestesses and I know just how to do it.*

After arranging for continued large shipments of diablo rojo fish and ice to keep them for days, he purchased a large hacienda on the edge of Benito that was just beyond the northern edge of the city, rather isolated. Here he setup his priestess manufacturing plant, the PMP, as it was known within his inner circle. Next, he chose the least bright of Blanca's mermaids and her Guardian to become his matron of the PMP and the Guardian Acquirer. She would assist and train the priestesses, while he would round up young fighters to become their Guardians. Offer the men enough pay, and they would sign up for duty. Antonio chose one of his Elite Guard squads to carry out his orders to "acquire" more young maidens to be turned into his new army of priestesses. In June of 1247, under the control of Captain Juarez, they began their operation in earnest.

Early Monday morning, the giggling fourteen year old Adalina de Scala was walking down a side street in Benito heading towards the millers to purchase more flower. She was a baker's apprentice, planning one day to open her own bakery, if only she could either find a financial backer or save up enough money to get started herself. The youngest daughter of the de Scala family, she could not hope for more. Whistling a dance tune, she skipped along in the orange-red morning sunlight. The streets were already starting to fill, and she was just a little behind schedule, having stopped to chat with one of her girlfriends.

Captain Juarez spotted her and smiled. He'd already found out who she was and had sent six men to her parent's home. They ought to be there about now, he thought. Time for action. He brought his hand down sharply. Spotting his signal, his men rode out of the alleyways surrounding the teen forcing her to stop. She tried to move this way and that to allow these soldiers to pass her. Captain Juarez rode up, leaned over, and placed a rag over her face. She tried to protest, but her legs gave out. She blacked out from the odor. Strong arms lifted her up onto the lap of a soldier and they rode off.

When Adalina came to, she was lying in a bed with satin sheets. At first, she marveled over them, but soon discovered she was completely naked between the sheets. Fear swept over her, but she didn't feel like she'd been raped by the soldiers. Just then, Captain Juarez entered, she flinched, recognizing him as having kidnaped her. "What do you want with me? Please don't rape me? I've done nothing wrong," she cried out, fighting back tears and fearing the worst.

"Adalina, no one is going to rape you. You have been chosen to become a priestess of Calder, a Daughter of the Seas. You will be healing the injured and curing the sick along with blessing of sea going ships."

"But I don't want to do that. I am a baker's apprentice. I want to open my own bakery shop. Please, give me my clothes and let me go. I was supposed to be going to the millers to get more flower."

"Sorry, you will be a priestess. You have no choice in the matter. The conversion process has already begun. So lie back and get some sleep. You look tired to me."

"But I don't want to be some priestess. I don't know anything about all those things. Let me go."

"Sorry, you will be a priestess and that's all there is to say on the matter. If you don't cooperate, your parents will suffer great harm. You want us to kill you mother?"

"No!"

"Then lie back and become a priestess like a good girl. You don't have any choice."

Adalina laid back down. She did feel awfully tired, even though it was early morning. She felt stuffed. Had they fed her something while she was unconscious? *They'll kill mom.* That was her last thought as she drifted into a sweaty, ill sleep.

Sometime later, she awoke very groggy. Someone kept stuffing fish into her mouth. Mechanically she ate it, while it was quite tasty, she found herself craving it. How queer, she thought. As soon as she finished, she lay back and slept again.

She didn't see another young teen being carried in and placed in the bed next to hers.

In the small village of Palo Fallo, just north of Benito, the soldiers barged into the Fina family's home. "Where's Lola," one soldier asked harshly. Hiding behind her mother, Lola peered out at these men with drawn swords.

"What's she done?" her father attempted to intercede.

"Nothing. She has been selected to become a priestess of Calder, a Daughter of the Seas. She will be highly honored in that role; she will heal the injured, cure the sick, and bless sea going ships," the soldier replied.

"But she doesn't want to be a priestess. We've never heard of this Calder. Leave us alone. You can't come in here and just take away our daughter," he protested.

"Either she comes peacefully or we take her by force. If you resist, we will not hesitate to kill you both and your other children. Now you come with us, Lola."

She screamed and kicked, as another soldier grabbed her and carried her out of her home. Her father tried to protest, but a soldier held his blade at the man's throat. "If you ever tell anyone about this abduction, we will come back here and execute you and your whole family. Do you understand me? One word, and we'll be back here. She will be a priestess. You should be honored she has been chosen for such an important position. Remember, one word and we'll be back." The soldiers left, slamming the door.

Outside, the soldier carrying her barked, "One more outburst from you and I will have the men kill your mom, dad, and everyone inside. You want us to kill them?"

Sobbing, she muttered, "No, please don't kill them. We haven't done anything wrong."

"If you ever tell anyone we've taken you like this, I promise you we will come back here and kill everyone your house and burn it to the ground. Got that, Lola. One peep out of you and your whole family will be dead." She shut up What choice did she have? She was taken to a fancy hacienda on the edge of Benito. There, someone stuffed her full of fish. *At least,* she thought, *they are feeding me and it is good.* After that, she felt sleepy, and they took her into a large bedroom with many beds. She vaguely remembered later seeing other sleeping young women. Someone took off all her clothes and put her into the bed. She sensed elegant satin sheets, but no more. She fell into an ill sleep.

She awoke quite groggy and someone stuffed more fish into her mouth. Somehow she ate it, for some reason she seemed to crave more of the fish. As soon as she'd eaten, she fell back asleep. How many times did this happen? She couldn't remember, one, two, maybe three times?

Adalina finally awoke. She opened her eyes and looked around. Other sleeping young girls her own age lay much like she was between satin sheets. She suddenly had to pee badly and sat up. She tried to get out of bed and moved the top sheet back. She saw her leg and stared uncomprehendingly at herself. Her upper legs were bowed slightly and seemed to have melted together into one just at her knee. One single leg extended down from her knee ending in one foot. She began screaming wildly. Shortly a matronly woman came bustling into the room.

Her wild screaming roused Lola, who was sleeping in the next bed. She woke up and also had to urinate. She saw Adalina screaming next to her and her legs felt funny. She pulled the sheets back and saw her own transformed upper legs and single lower leg and foot. Lola too began screaming, quite terrified.

The older woman ignored their screams. "Get up. You have to hop over to the commode, Adalina. Come on stand up. I'll catch you if you fall." She pulled the screaming woman to her foot and gave her a slight push in the direction of the commode. Adalina tried to walk as she always had and began to fall over forward. The woman caught her. "Hop, Adalina, hop. Jump, come on, Lola's got to use it too. Hop." Adalina tried to hop but the woman had constantly to catch her as she misjudged each hop. After using the commode, she was forced to hop back to her bed. By then, she was sobbing wildly, but her high pitched shrieks had ended.

Now the woman walked over to Lola, who now was sobbing too. She told Lola the same thing, hop. She had to pee so badly that she did as asked, but again, she could not keep her balance at all either. The matronly woman got a work out with the two. That handled, someone brought in more plates of fish.

"Here, you are hungry," the woman said.

"What's happening to me? What's happened to my legs?" wailed Adalina.

"Me too, what's happened to them?" Lola called out.

"Here, hold the plate and eat the fish." Adalina took the plate. For unknown reasons, her body craved the fish. She temporarily shut up and ate it as fast as she could. Nearby, Lola, too, was quiet, stuffing more fish into her mouth. When Adalina finished, the woman said, "You are being transformed into a priestess Daughter of the Seas. Now sleep."

Adalina had no idea what the woman meant. Suddenly she felt exceedingly tired again and struggled to lay back down and cover up. Lola did the same, but was asleep before she could cover up. The older woman kindly pulled her sheet up for her and left. Soon others would be waking and she needed more fish.

A day later, though neither young teen knew the day, both Lola and Adalina awoke at the same time. Once more, both women were shocked and then shrieked in terror as loudly as they could. Neither now had their arms. The dried, withered husks, which had been their arms, had fallen off their shoulders while they slept, leaving them almost totally helpless. They shrieked at the top of their lungs.

Shortly the matronly woman entered carrying two light blue dresses. Two older men, perhaps in their early twenties, followed her. "Adalina, stop that shrieking. You are now fully transformed into a priestess. Here is your new priestess dress. This man here will be your Guardian and help you with your needs and guard you with his life. Now let's get your new dress on you, and he can help you to the commode. Then you hop down to the next room where you will get your ornaments. Hop, hop, hop."

She walked over to Lola's bed and quickly put the new dress on her, repeating the same words, but pointing to the second man. "Okay, up you go, hop, hop, hop." Just then another young woman who still had her arms awoke and began screaming. Her legs had transformed, and the older woman headed over there to help her to the commode.

The man said, “Adalina, start hopping to the commode. Hop. How else are you going to move about, except by hopping? I’ll catch you if you start to fall.” He gave her a push’ she had no choice but to make the attempt to hop. Both women were wildly overcorrecting, forcing the two men constantly to keep them upright. At last, they sat down on the commodes, catching their breaths while still crying.

As soon as they finished, the men forced them upright again. “Come on, hop. We have to get you your fancy ornaments, the kind that the nobles wear. You are a noble now. Hop, hop. Come on. I’m not carrying you.” Sobbing continuously, Adalina began hopping once more; Lola and her guardian were right behind her.

“How far? I can’t hop anymore,” Adalina complained. Her guardian just gave her a gentle push, she had no choice but to hop or fall down. They entered another room where another woman sat with the medical machine. At least the man allowed her finally to sit down on the seat of the machine. He pulled her long black hair back and out of the way, and the woman pushed part of the machine around the front of her head. At least her eyes were above the machine’s part that touched the rest of her face. She had no idea what was happening. “You will feel a little pair of pin pricks, that’s all. Here we go. A half hour later, the woman slipped the two five inch lip plates into the four holes on the top of her gums and the four on the bottom. Then she fastened the huge earrings onto the golden disks in her ear lobes.

“What’s happening to me? I can’t talk well. Why are you doing this to me?” Adalina asked.

“All priestesses wear these fine pieces of jewelry and earrings. Now you look just like you are supposed to look, a fine young priestess of Calder, a Daughter of the Seas. Now up you go, Adalina. We have to get you practicing your hopping,” her guardian explained.

“But I can’t talk well and my ears are falling off and I’m slobbering all over,” she complained.

"Doesn't matter, up you go," he forced her up and gave her a push. It was either hop or fall down. At first she reacted by wildly moving her arms that weren't there. He caught her just in time and gave her another push to get her started hopping.

"They're going to pull my ears off and rip my lips," she complained, but he ignored her.

"Just hop. That way, we are going to walk around the garden."

"That's too far. I can't make it. Why are you torturing me?"

"To get you used to hopping. After all, you priestesses have to hop everywhere you go. So you have to be able to do this well on your own. Now continue hopping."

Behind her, Lola tried to protest that she didn't want the lip plates, but she was utterly helpless to prevent having them. Soon she too was being forced to hop around the gardens. She saw Adalina hopping far ahead of her and knew she had no choice but to hop. She too was utterly and completely helpless. Hopping was the only thing she could do and only just barely.

Later utterly exhausted from all that exercise, their guardians again fed them a huge helping of the fish. Then they left the two sitting on their beds, saying that it was time for them to eat too.

"What's happened to us? I can't do anything at all. I'm completely helpless. I'm Adalina."

"Lola. I don't know. I'm completely helpless too. All we can do is hop, just barely too. I almost fell dozens of times. Why are they torturing us like this? Why don't they just kill us, like they promised to kill my parents when they took me?"

"I don't know. I can just barely understand you. Can you understand what I'm saying? Are you drooling all over yourself too?" Adalina asked.

"Yes, it stops if I hold my head up, but then I can't see to hop. The front of my dress is soaking wet. This is a nightmare. How can we even live like this?" Lola complained bitterly, trying to keep from another bout of crying.

"I don't think we can live like this. We can't do anything

at all except hop, not even feed ourselves. My lips feel stretched. Do yours? My ears feel like they are being pulled off. I can sort of scratch my shoulders by wiggling the earrings though. Do you suppose that's why we have them?" Adalina asked.

"Mine are throbbing too. Maybe so we can scratch a little. I've seen some noble women wearing these things once. Maybe we are now nobles too?" Lola replied. "Even so, we can't live like this, completely unable to do anything at all for ourselves. I wish they had just killed me." Lola sighed and began crying again.

"Me too. We can't even run away now. How could we possibly open the doors? We are their prisoners now, but look at all the other here. How many have they kidnaped? Are they all going to end up like us?" Adalina asked.

Just then, another woman woke up and sat up armless. She shrieked madly, terrified beyond all reason. The matronly woman again entered with a light blue dress along with another strange man. The two sat watching the same thing happening to her as had happened to them. The terrified girl was dressed and forced to hop to the commode, the man catching her with each step, as she wildly tried to hop on one foot. A bit later, over her screaming protests, the man forced her to hop out of the room to get her ornaments as well. Both Adalina and Lola sat there stunned. all these teens were obviously facing the same hideous nightmare, and there wasn't anything any of them could do about it; they were all becoming utterly helpless women, forced to do whatever was asked of them!

Later the teen returned as exhausted as the two had been. She too now wore the fancy ornaments. He guardian fed her some fish and then left, just as their two men returned. They brought along more fish in case the two were hungry. Each ate a little more and then the men brushed their hair and took out the awful lip plates. They tucked the two into their beds and bid good night. Sleep overcame both women, but they were awakened twice during the night by the terrified screams of other women, who were waking up to the hideous nightmare.

The next morning, six men returned with plates of fish. After dressing their charges, they were made to hop to the commode and then back to their beds, where they were fed. That done, the six were forced to begin hopping around and around the huge gardens. The small group of terrified women had little choice but to attempt to hop. When they halted, their guardians gave them a push. Again, it was hop or fall down, but the men always kept them from falling. Adalina and Lola rapidly tired and again became exhausted. Their continuous drool from their mouths soaked the fronts of their dresses. They no longer had any way to keep their saliva inside their mouths. Begging for a break and at long last, they were allowed to return to their beds and sit. There, they watched helplessly as another six women awoke to the same terror they'd been enduring.

When her guardian returned with her fish lunch, Adalina protested, "How can we be priestesses? We don't know anything about it and we can't do anything."

"That, I don't know, but in time, we will find out. Eat up. When you are done, it is back to practicing your hopping. You have to be able to hop all over this hacienda on your own without my helping you in the slightest. We have a whole lot of work to do, Adalina." She moaned and again wished she could either wake up from this nightmare or die.

One day merged into the next, broken only by more and more women joining them in the torturous hopping around the gardens. By the end of the week, both Adalina and Lola were hopping well and no longer needed their guardians so close at hand. Several others were getting almost as good as they were. Next, their men shocked them further. "Today, we hop around the city and back."

Once out of the gates of the hacienda and into the crowded streets, they faced utter humiliation, as nearly everyone stopped to stare at them as they valiantly tried to hop on down the packed streets. They were just about to cave in utterly and fall down waiting to die, when they finally returned back to their gates. Now they did break down. All began bawling again, humiliated beyond words.

"Tomorrow we go for an even longer walk in the city,"

her guardian said. She just bawled harder.

Six of them were scheduled to take the long walk that morning. Again, the men dressed them and let them use the commode before feeding them. That done, they brushed out their long black hair and packed their brushes into a small sack. "Okay, time to go hopping," her guardian said with a smile. "This time, you have to go three miles." All six women moaned.

"We can't go that far. Please, take your sword and cut my throat now. I can't go on like this," Adalina declared and held her head to one side, waiting for his chop. Instead, he laughed and pushed her to her foot.

"Hop." He pushed her. Again, it was hop or fall. With her lip plates protruding, she dare not fall and began hopping, most unwillingly. The other six fell in behind her. Soon they left the security of their hacienda, again heading out into the crowded streets. Vendors hawking their wares ceased yelling and stared at the passing half-dozen, weird-looking women and six men, all wearing the same light blue satin. It was all the women could do to keep from sobbing. Slobber covered the fronts of their dresses in no time, further humiliating them. Relentlessly, their guardians kept them hopping along the streets. None had any idea where they were going or why.

Adalina spotted one of her girlfriends in the crowd. For a moment, she wanted to call out to her for help, but then realized she would not understand her nor would she likely recognize her. She focused on hopping onwards. Soon they all did the same, focus on the ground before them and hop. An eternity later, Adalina realized they were heading for the docks and wondered why. Before long a hacienda appeared ahead of them, and to their surprise the guardians led them to it. At the gates was another young woman identical to themselves. The gate opened as if by magic.

"Welcome my new priestesses, my fellow Daughters of the Seas. I am Blanca and soon you will be getting your immense powers. I am your leader for now, until our High Priestess comes, that is. Come on in. I have suites ready for you, but you're going to have to double up, I'm afraid. They have lunch ready for us. I bet you are all tired from your long walk. Follow me, please. I'll try to answer your questions over lunch."

At least Lola and Adalina got to room together. After listening and watching Blanca and her small group, these six began to realize soon they would be getting huge mental powers from some god called Calder, powers that would allow them to live easily and to perform their priestess duties.

Every few days, another group of women arrived. In six weeks, there were ninety of the new mermaids crowded into the large hacienda. Next, they were given their assigned cities and towns, where they would be taken and where they would begin to work their many miracles. Once more, they had no choice but to do as asked. On their own, they could only barely survive. At least Blanca allowed Adalina and Lola to stay together.

Antonio smiled as he got the final reports back. He had his 1248 tally of needed priestesses. He decided to wait a while before working up his 1249 supply. He was totally confident he'd have all the priestesses he needed for his global shipping expansion. Back in Villa del Rey, Gracia could only marvel and wonder how Antonio had been so stellarly successful in his recruitment. She had no idea these women were being abducted and turned into her priestesses without their consent: either they did it or they watched their families being murdered.

She also didn't know at least ten percent of the abducted women died during the transformation phase. Antonio merely replaced them with newly kidnaped women, but he knew he'd have to spread the kidnaping around to other towns and villages. Otherwise, the local lords might get wise to what he was doing.

By 1250, Villa del Rey's large fleet of the new caravels dominated all trade along the entire southern coastline of the continent. Trade was booming, expanding tenfold over all previous record years. The nobles who backed this venture were making vast fortunes.

Part II Renegade Tower Recognized

Chapter 7 Challenge

Venerado Fons replied to Capo Roberto, "Excellent. All the tower's defensive networks are up and running. I've got forty of the local gifted sworn to help protect us, should they try to attack us."

"Good to hear. With our six blasters, the playing field ought to be more than level. I doubt Lord Pedro is going to give any supply of blasters he might have to Valen Tower. He dislikes all *mentales* gifted. The Comm Network is ready to go. When are we going online and letting all the other towers know of our existence?"

It was late February 1247. Here in Villa del Rey, the days were still balmy thanks to the ocean winds. Farther north, however, the lands were deep in snow. Fons had already given this some thought. "We ought to wait until spring comes to the north."

"Why? They probably can't take any effective actions against us until the snow melts," Roberto replied.

"True, but they would have several months to plan out what actions to take against us. When the thaw comes, they would likely have their plans ready to execute. If we wait until spring, then they have little time to plan. Hasty actions often lead to disasters. Let's bring us online on May Day," Venerado Fons suggested, though Capo Roberto took it as an order.

May Day, Capo Roberto ceremoniously installed the final germanium crystal in their Comm Network, activating it. His twelve circle members were already sitting and in rapport. His two Regulators were also at work monitoring the physical bodies of the dozen and himself, keeping breathing regular, heart beats uniform, and kinks out of muscles. He activated the Comm Network and sent his first message.

Capo Roberto Valen and Venerado Fons Valen are pleased to announce the activation of the Renegade Tower. Venerado Fons wishes to speak to all the tower's venerada at ten. Please have them standing by at that time. He broke the connection and grinned. One by one, his team slipped out of rapport. "It's done. I wish we could have seen their faces when a new tower suddenly appeared in their Comm Network! There hasn't been a true new tower in centuries."

Watching from the sidelines, Venerado Fons praised them, "Well done, all of you. We've just shaken the very fabric of the established towers. Empress Amy forced all the men out of their traditional roles as capo and venerado, putting women in those positions. Now we have reclaimed our birthrights! This will give all those women something to chew on!" Many laughed.

At ten, they resumed their positions at the Comm Network that lit up like the night sky! All eight towers were online, chatting furiously. The ninth at the Imperial Castle had been abandoned when the Council of the Lords effectively made the position of emperor and empress a thing of the past.

Venerado Fons Valen of Renegade Tower. I see none of you are welcoming us, so I will do it myself. Welcome Renegade Tower.

Venerada Marisol here. You are in direct violation of the Blackwater Ultimatum. Men are specifically prohibited from the positions of capo and venerado.

Ha! We do not recognize that ultimatum, not in the slightest. Next question. Fons replied. He sensed Marisol was fuming as were many others, but the questions then came faster than he could recognize the senders.

Where is your tower?

Villa del Rey, Trujillo, Westerlings.

Are you a branch of Valen Tower?

We have nothing to do with that despicable tower. We are independent of them and want nothing to do with those traitors.

What territory are you claiming as your dominion? Are you seceding from Valen Tower's territory?

We have nothing to do with Valen Tower and never will. We claim only our city-state of Villa del Rey. Look, Valen Tower has failed utterly to fulfill its duties as a tower to the territory they claim to hold: all the Westerlings. They are nearly in the mountains. How can they handle what is needed in a land that is roughly three thousand miles square? They have neglected the major cities long enough. We aren't.

Who gives you the right to make your own tower?

The ancient god Calder is backing us with his High Priestess and his Daughters of the Seas. We have over twenty katalyein supporting us. Do not mess with us or we will bring the wrath of Calder down upon you! Soon, we will have hundreds of katalyein priestesses. Their wrath can be devastating.

So you are operating only in Villa del Rey?

Hardly. We now have our priestesses in Benito, Arabella, Nasik, and other coastal cities. They are doing what your towers were called upon to do when they were set up. Heal the injured, cure the sick, handle mentales blockages, train all local mentales gifted, not just the ones in your cities.

But you can't do this! Nasik is the responsibility of Rusden Tower.

But you haven't even been there in years. We are and we are doing what you should have been doing. Too late for you, stick with your cornfields.

What does the Lord of Villa del Rey have to say about this? Does he know?

We have his full and complete backing.

Will you then be demanding to attend the Council of the Lords later this month?

Not unless you invite Lord Gabino Rosa and he asks us to come with him.

Will you be attending the Valen's Lords' Council in May.

Hardly. You are all traitors, stealers of the throne. May you rot in hell.

Just then, the *Círculo de mentes* at Valen Tower attempted a psi attack on Venerado Fons. It failed, their circle had nine, the usual number, but the Renegade Tower had a dozen. Capo Roberto deflected the attack and countered with a huge blast of psi energies, temporarily stunning the *Círculo de mentes* at Valen Tower, taking them off line temporarily.

Do not try to attack us. Such foolishness. Capo Roberto could have acted to kill. Instead, he chose merely to stun. Do not mess with the Renegade Tower. We don't want to fight any other tower, but if you attack us, we will be merciless in our counterstrike!

You haven't heard the end of this!

I expect not. Rather than wasting your time with us, why don't you try and fulfill your own obligations to your lands, eh? We are doing our job and doing it superbly well. Not one of your towers can claim that! Clean your own house before you attempt to clean another's house.

This is highly illegal and is in defiance of all the towers. There is no precedence for this.

We are setting the precedence. It is done. We are in full operation now. Live with it.

So you also have a Renegade Castle?

Who needs a castle? Only those who do not have the full and complete support of those whom they are there to serve have to live behind castle walls. We don't have a castle and we don't want one either.

Does that mean that you don't have an army or are planning to form one? asked Venerada Marisol.

We neither need nor want an army. Throughout the Westerlings, Valen Castle is now synonymous with deceit, treachery, and treason to the people of the Westerlings. We will not make that mistake. If push comes to shove, Calder and his Daughters of the Seas will protect us. Their wrath shall be most profound. I advise you not to anger them or the god Calder!

But many say that Calder sleeps.

Not any longer, not for some time, in fact.

Wait, if you are not bound by the Blackwater Ultimatum, what are you obeying?

Our own rules.

And what are those?

Whatever we decide they are.

You fools!

Look who is talking. I believe you've run out of serious questions. This communication is now over. Good day, veneradas. He broke the connection and the circle dropped out of rapport as well.

All cheered and/or laughed. Capo Roberto exclaimed, "Well, that sure shook those women up!" All roared with laughter. The Renegade Tower was now a force to be reckoned with throughout Tierra.

Fons added, "About now, the venerada are all talking to their castle lords, ranting and raving about this. I'd give anything to see all the lord's reactions." He roared again.

This was precisely what was happening at all eight towers! The venerada at Rusden Tower and Lord Rusden soon agreed. He exclaimed, "We'll send a party down to Nasik immediately and see what these Calder's Daughters of the Seas are all about. Damn, this could be really bad."

His venerada suggested, "Investigate, but take no actions yet. Valen Tower members got mind blasted after they tried to blast the Renegade Tower members. Let's let Valen Tower and Valen Castle take care of this renegade group. We will not have to dirty our hands with it. Besides, they are deep within the Westerlings." Lord Rusden agreed. Within a day, his investigatory group headed down to Nasik, some five hundred miles to the southwest of Rusden.

Venerada Marisol visited Lord Bolivar at Brom Castle. After relaying the terrible news, Lord Bolivar frowned. "Well, this Villa del Rey place is deep within the Westerlings. They have no army and claim that they are not forming one. I don't see how this materially impacts us. It is wholly a Westerlings problem. I have no sympathy whatsoever for those in Valen. This is all their doing. Let them handle their own mess."

"I tend to agree, Lord Bolivar. They are far from here. However, the Blackwater Ultimatum specifically prohibited men from the two key positions to help prevent wars and wanton destruction, which we experienced when the men were in power with their chemical bombs, acid bombs, and fire bombs. It is prudent we at least keep an eye on them."

"Surely they won't be making those again, will they?"

"Not likely. The technology to make them has been lost in time. Besides, all the giant crystal networks that were needed in order to make those hideous weapons were destroyed by Amy Blackwater almost a century ago."

"That's a relief, Venerada Marisol. Say, what do we

know of this ancient god, this Calder fellow?"

"Only that he had been sleeping for centuries and that he is the god of the seas. I can't see what Calder has to do with anything. Still, we'll check on it just to be on the safe side."

Throughout the Midlands and at Adelmira Tower in the Easterlings, the response was similar to that of Brom Tower and Brom Castle. Clearly, this was a Westerlings problem, and after their recent treasonous actions against the Midlands, both the Midlands and the Easterlings had permanently cut off all ties to the Westerlings. Only Rusden chose to at least see what was going on down in Nasik.

At Castle Valen, the Westerlings Lords' Council was held and Lord Gabino Rosa attended. Lord Pedro Valen demanded, "Lord Gabino, what the devil are you doing by supporting this Renegade Tower in your city. I demand you remove them."

"With all due respects, my lord, they are providing us the support that you promised us years ago. To date, not one of your tower members has ever set foot in Villa del Rey, nor has any of them healed our injured or cured our sick. Not one of our local *mentales* gifted has been trained or given their crystals. Only those who are wealthy enough to come to Valen Tower have been trained. Not one of our people, who has the Verge Sickness or who has their gifts blocked, have been cured by your tower people, as the Blackwater Ultimatum dictates. Our Renegade Tower has done all these things and more for us."

"So are you seceding from my territory? Are you going to stop paying your legal tithes to us?" Lord Valen asked what concerned him the most, the hell with these tower things. He didn't have that cursed gift and he didn't need it.

"I hadn't considered that, my lord, but now that you bring it up, why should we continue to send our money up here, when you don't give us back anything in return?" Lord Gabino countered.

"We protect you, if you are attacked," Lord Valen fumed.

"Ah, I see. And can you tell me when in our long history

have we or any Westerlings city been attacked, other than by Valen Tower and Valen Castle's armies?" Lord Gabino again countered, growing more irritated by this obnoxious, self-centered man, who was obviously ignorant all these important points.

"Damn you, Gabino! If you persist in this, I'll send my army down there and take over control of your city and throw these renegades out myself!" Lord Valen almost screamed. His neck veins bulged, his face red with anger.

"I would not do that if I were you, my lord. God Calder might not like that. His reaction, I'm sure, you would regret most painfully."

"Are you threatening me?" he raged.

"I'm not threatening you. Rather it seems to me that you are threatening me."

Lord Benito spoke up. "He has a valid point. Why should we on the coast have to pay you tithes, when you do absolutely nothing for us? At least the Renegade Tower and the Daughters of the Seas are contributing in a very large way and charging us nothing at all."

"I agree with Lord Benito," Lord Arabella spoke up. "You always ignore us, and yet you expect us to pay you handsomely each year. You wiped out our tower at Dureo and then did not provide the services that they were providing to us. I can see no reason why we should continue to pay you for no services at all. Seems pointless and a waste of our funds."

Several lords of smaller coastal towns agreed and Lord Gabino finally had enough. He stated that he would no longer send any yearly tithes to Valen Castle. The other coastal lords followed suit, and they promptly left the council for home.

Once back, Lord Gabino messaged Venerado Fons, *You'd better be on the alert. I suspect Lord Valen will be launching an attack on you soon. We coastal lords withdrew our yearly tithes to him and he was furious.*

Thanks for the tip. We'll be ready.

Venerado Fons had six of the deadly alien blasters. However, with his nearly useless alien prosthetic hands, he simply could not operate them. Hence, he carefully handed them out to those who still had their hands and who he could trust with them. He put Rafael Valen, the youngest son of the assassinated Lord Paco Valen, in charge of the other five men, who had the blasters. The five were the most trusted of the *mentales* gifted of Villa del Rey whom he'd trained.

Capo Roberto placed the tower on high alert. Someone was always monitoring the Comm Network and watching for some invading forces. Three days later, around midnight, Rafael was awakened telepathically by the night tower technician, his sister Lucinda. *We are sensing the approach of two air cars from Valen Tower!*

Rafael was fifteen and the leader of the Elite Guards of Renegade Tower. Hastily, he summoned his five fellow blaster bearers. All six headed for the observation deck of the small single story tower, taking up their positions. They scanned the sky and before long spotted the two incoming air cars. Rafael sensed the presence of several *mentales* gifted, likely tower technicians. Their intent was clear, blast the tower to rubble. As they drew closer, Rafael barked his orders. The six fired. Six disintegration beams stuck the air cars. Although it was night, the damage done was observable. Both air cars veered wildly and then crashed into the ocean waters about a half mile off shore. There were no survivors found by the fishermen the next day.

While the tower members were jubilant over the easy victory the night before, Venerado Fons cautioned them. "The tower failed in their attempt to get us, so be alert. Lord Valen will probably be sending an army down to Villa del Rey to get us and Lord Gabino. Stay alert."

Each day, the circle spent hours observing the lands around Valen Castle using their *mentales* gift that enabled one to see what another was seeing. Early June, they spotted a massive buildup of soldiers around Valen Castle. Now they watched even more closely. A week later a thousand soldiers embarked on a flotilla of barges. They would be floating down the mighty Alcantara River, which emptied into the ocean just east of Villa del Rey.

Fons then paid a visit to High Priestess Gracia. After explaining the situation to her, he asked, "Is there something that you can do to stop this army from getting here and running rampant through the city, harming one and all?" He suspected she might, since the men were on water, albeit not the ocean.

"Dad, you're kidding, right? Valen is sending an army down here to wipe us out?"

"No, I am deadly serious, Gracia. If you want, I can have Capo Roberto join you to their circle, and you can see them for yourself."

"Please do, dad. This is not right," Gracia replied, the fighter in her roused. He focused and sent a message to Roberto. Momentarily afterwards, Gracia felt the capo's mind touching hers, forming a link with his circle. Now she was seeing what the others were seeing. Some twenty barges were packed with fifty soldiers and their gear. All were in a tight formation, floating down the Alcantara River, much as she and the others had done when they fled Castle Valen.

"Damn, damn, damn," the High Priestess exclaimed, breaking off the contact. "Dad, leave them to me!"

"I was hoping that you'd say that! When will you act?"

"When they are just above the city a couple miles away. Have Roberto let me know when they are about five miles from the northern edge of the city. Leave them to me! Damn that murdering Lord Pedro! I'll show him. Never mess with Gracia!"

He agreed and left, making his slow way out of her hacienda and into his waiting carriage. Fons was smiling all the way, but it wasn't visible, blocked entirely by his lip plates.

Several days later, Gracia received the advance notice. She and Diego headed to the hacienda's gates. She hopped rapidly and used her psi skills to open the gates before her guardian and husband could even reach them. She hopped on outside. "Hey slow down, wait for me," Diego called out, shutting the gates. Gracia hopped in place until he joined her. "You are anxious, my love."

"Yeh, I know. Put your arm on my shoulders. I'm hopping just outside the city first," Gracia ordered. After she felt his arm, she hopped and teleported to a northern hill just barely visible from where she had been hopping. She lost her balance upon landing and quickly used a bit of her telekinetic powers to regain her balance. She looked up the Alcantara River, chose her next landing point, and jumped again. Within fifteen minutes, Gracia had the very spot that she wanted to use for her attack. Here the river was a half mile across.

"You stay well back on the shore, dear. I am going for a swim and take these barges out." Gracia hopped and jumped, landing in the middle of the river, but her strong leg kept her upper half out of the water so that she could see the oncoming barges. Before long, the string of twenty came drifting towards her. Now she used the special gift that Calder had given her, his High Priestess. The waters of the river flowed up into the sky before her, draining the river rapidly. Within a minute, all twenty barges rested on the muddy bottom of the empty Alcantara river. She had lowered the water for nearly a half mile. Then she let it all go. A wall of water descended upon the barges and the thousand soldiers they were carrying. They were buried beneath a massive mound of water that slopped up over the riverbanks, soaking Diego, who merely laughed. His wife was utterly impressive!

Gracia now jumped back on shore, her hair and dress soaked and quite muddy. Diego moved to her side and they watched for survivors. At last, seeing nothing but floating corpses, she jumped them back to their gates. "Dear, I am going to make you give me a bath and do my hair. I'm rather exhausted. That took more psi energies than I am accustomed to using at one time. My dress needs cleaning too."

"Good god! Did you see that?" exclaimed Roberto to Fons. They and the circle had been watching from Diego's eyes and saw the whole thing.

"My daughter is incredibly deadly! We must be careful never to cross her. Good god, those men never had a chance! Come on; time to send a message to Lord Pedro," Fons declared.

Shortly, Lord Pedro received, *Don't ever try attacking us again or we will come after you next time. Pedro-zero, Fons-one thousand.* He need not have sent it, via his own tower, Lord Pedro had watched his mighty army of a thousand perish in an instant. He also saw one strange looking woman somehow standing in the middle of the river, apparently causing all this. Paled and visibly shaken, he returned to his castle to brood.

Within a day, all Villa del Rey was talking about their miraculous deliverance from Valen's army. Thousands of corpses had floated past the city and on out into the ocean. The average person of Villa del Rey now knew beyond a doubt that Calder's Daughters of the Seas were really going to protect them. Lord Gabino merely smiled invisibly. He suspected as much. Now he and the other coastal lords were free to make their own alliances, based upon shipping and trade. Similarly, Lord Antonio smiled invisibly. With this kind of power being wielded by these priestesses, he redoubled his kidnaping efforts to create a hundred more of them!

What very few noticed was that Wystan had been awakened by the formation of this army of a thousand. He was watching, anticipating a fine battle, probably wholly one-sided. He was eagerly waiting the raping and pillaging these fine soldiers would soon be doing. When he saw them wiped out to the last man, he was furious, but recognized the hand of his old opponent, Calder. *Calder is awake. Okay, where are you, old man?* He looked around, spotted Calder, and appeared beside him to have a "friendly" chat.

"Welcome Lord Able and Amo Howard. I am Calder's Priestess and Daughter of the Seas, Dominga. Come on in. This is my guardian, who is here to help me with something I can't do, which is almost everything, and to protect me, which I probably won't ever need. I know. I look strange to you," Priestess Dominga said with a smile was also invisible. She talked slowly, hoping they would be able to understand her in spite of her lip plates.

Able and Howard, Rusden's two spies sent to see what was going on in Nasik, stared in total disbelief. Here was a woman, sort of. She had no arms and a single leg, centrally located, wearing a light blue satin dress, reminding them immediately of the ocean they'd just seen as they entered Nasik. She had the old lip plates and long dangling earrings that had gone out of style a year or so ago. They followed after her as she began hopping through the elegant gardens of her refurbished warehouse now turned into a hacienda, Westerlings style. Her long black hair that nearly reached the floor rose up and down as she hopped along in front of them, so did her massive earrings and breasts, though the latter they couldn't see.

As she approached a side room, the door seemed to open by itself, though Amo Howard detected the subtle use of psi energies and suspected Dominga had opened it. She was the logical choice, as the similarly dressed fighter at her side was not *mentales* gifted. Inside the meeting room, they saw five other priestesses. All looked exactly like Dominga, who hopped over to them, tossed her hair to her front side, and sat down. Her guardian joined five others standing behind the six seated women. Able and Howard took the two seats across the table from the women.

Able spoke first. "Well, you must admit we are more than a little surprised by what we are seeing, Priestess Dominga. More than a little."

"Most people are when they first see us."

"As you probably know, we are here at Lord Rusden's request. Nasik is part of his territory. We are charged with finding out just exactly what your intentions here are and what it is that you do," Able added.

"That's easy to answer," Dominga replied. She began relating what it was the six actually did.

"Hum, that is all that you do?" Howard asked, seemingly perplexed.

"What do you think we can do, fight? How? Butt into you with our heads? We have to hop everywhere, not particularly easy to do. No, we are here merely to help the common folk of Nasik and to bless the seamen's ships so they have safe and profitable voyages at sea."

They chatted a bit longer and then the two men bade her farewell. Their report to Lord Rusden was simple: they are nearly helpless women, who somehow can heal and bless. Certainly, they were not even remotely a threat to him. "Sire, they cannot even walk; they have to hop about on one leg." Lord Rusden accepted their findings and proceeded to ignore the ever increasing number of these really strange priestesses, who continued to arrive in the smaller coastal towns of the Midlands, his territory according to the Blackwater Ultimatum.

Chapter 8 The Underground

When Amy Blackwater and Jan Bellweather gave up their positions as empress and emperor, they formed the Underground, donating all their vast totally illegal machines and equipment to the cause. Each had a son and they were fully trained in the use and purpose of each piece. Ben and Tim carried on the monitoring work of their mothers, after their deaths. Spying on the aliens at the spaceport and all the towers and castles, these two men attempted to stay ahead of plots and to defuse them or nullify them whenever possible. Up until now, they'd done a brilliant job of it, preventing Lord Paco Valen from retaking lands in the Midlands, staring another all-out war with the Midlands, and thus reawakening Wystan, the God of War and Men.

With the war threat removed and the collapse of Castle Valen, three serious problems remained that threatened Tierra. These, the two had set out to solve by some means. Although they tried everything, they could think of, no solutions had appeared and Ben had finally decided to ask the Goddess of Life and of Death, Lysandra, for help. She was the women's goddess, but because of what Ben had just done, she appeared to him. When he agreed to submit to a sacrifice of her choosing, she answered him, giving him what he needed to solve these three huge problems.

One of these was the steadily dwindling number of new *mentales* gifted children to the tower and castle people. This was due, he discovered, to the constant breeding from among this group of individuals. Each tower-castle group married others from that same group. Now the centuries of relative inbreeding was taking its toll. The solution was to marry many of the isolated local *mentales* gifted, who chose to live a normal life in the smaller towns and villages and hamlets of the land.

Another of these problems was the slow decline of overall emotional tone of the telepaths and others. They had sunk from antagonism to anger to a covert hostility, which embraced all manner of sexual perversions, along with an irrational urge to have intercourse solely for pleasure and without any intention of creating children. With the loss of hands and the awful body modifications most had undergone, many began to sink even lower into grief. Just below that was apathy and death as a telepathic group. Lysandra again gave them the missing data that allowed them to reverse partially this societal decline.

Using their alien medical machines, the two set about undoing these body modifications, as far as possible. The lip plates could easily be undone. The pipe corsets could be removed, but most then needed extensive exercise to regain abdominal strength. Of course their missing ribs could not be "undone." Their pathetic and poor alien prosthetic hands were replaced with top of the line models that worked significantly better. Their debilitating toe shoes and toe boots could be partially undone. The bones in their feet had been broken and reformed so only the person's toes would touch the ground. The undo process partially remedied this, but the person then had to wear heels with six-inch stilettos. Their feet could not bend sufficiently to wear anything lower. Still these changes did wonders for the emotional tones of the modified individuals.

The third problem dealt with a startling discovery by the Brom katalyein, who found that a person was a spiritual being, apparently immortal, who lived life after life in these physical bodies. Lysandra charged Ben with developing a science of the mind and spirit, which he did, working in conjunction with a katalyein, Adriana Bolivar Hanks.

His sacrifice was wholly unexpected by all. Lysandra changed his body into that of a woman's, charging him to have four babies and to learn what it means to be a woman. She gave Benjamina, her new name and a head start by having her pregnant with her and his wife's daughter. Ben was married to one of the Madiera women, Elana, who was of the Earth kindred. She'd just discovered that she was pregnant with their son at the time that Lysandra changed her husband into a woman. This didn't bother her much, since Madiera women were used to being married to other women.

Benjamina certainly got a fast education on being a woman. She gave birth in March of 1246 to Luisa, while days after that, Elana gave birth to their son, Ken. Benjamina's biggest comment had been, "God, you have to pee every half hour!" She had other things to say after giving birth, not such pleasant things, that is.

In May of 1247, Benjamina was forty-one, as was Tim. Elana was thirty-five, and Tim's wife, Petrona, thirty-six. Petrona was now expecting within weeks. Luisa and Ken were fourteen months old now, a handful for the two who had no hands and had to use the alien prosthetic hands.

Originally, Benjamina and Adriana had worked out fifteen basic assumptions and one query for their budding science of the mind and spirit. During the past many months, while dealing with her pregnancy, Benjamina had been working diligently on proving these fifteen basic assumptions. The query had already been proven, namely a non-katalyein could remove the same mental masses and barriers that a katalyein could. Therapy was born. As of May, Benjamina had proven to her satisfaction that all fifteen were correct.

There were eight other members of the Underground, men and women that Ben and Tim had rescued. First were Andres and Rafaela Bolivar. They'd been captured by mercenaries of Lord Paco Valen, while they were on a mission to recover some ancient giant crystals of power. They'd had their arms pinned behind them during the cold winter for so long that their hands had frozen and most of their arms as well. They lost their arms, but their lives were saved. Now they worked for the Underground. While operating out of a room at the Brom branch of Elegant Fashions Inc for the last eighteen months, they'd been performing Benjamina's therapy on men and women. Their work greatly assisted Benjamina in proving the fifteen assumptions held true in all cases.

They had also rescued three of Lord Humberhills' children. Darcy and Dawn were identical twins, now seventeen. Their brother Eric was a year older and married to the lone person rescued at Retford Hills, Sally Retford.

They had also given sanctuary to Annie Wells, now married to Sam Hays; both were twenty-four. She had been the manager of Brom's Elegant Fashions Inc and had been duped into having her body fully modified and her hands removed to prevent her from getting the "virus." Likewise, Sam, a *mentales* gifted soldier, had been forced to undergo the body modifications due to his stature as a *mentales* gifted, and then he got the "virus" and had his hands removed. Neither could then survive on their own and had met, helping each other survive. They came to Ben for help and got it. Now there were active members of the Underground. She had to stay invisible, because she had run the medical machine that had removed the hands of the many "virus" victims at Brom. She feared for her life. Hatred ran high against all those who had played a role in the hideous hoax, whether knowingly or not.

These six primarily did all the monitoring, watching the feed from the alien's geosat satellite and listening in to the alien's communications, as well as those sent by the towers. Jan had installed an eavesdropping crystal network here and anything sent over the tower's Comm Network was echoed here.

All twelve had at one time or another been fully body modified. Those totally debilitating physical changes had been undone using their alien medical machine, at least as far as possible. All of them had to wear the old style women's six-inch stilettos, because their feet simply could not go any lower. All had the best alien prosthetic hands as well, but they were poor substitutes for real hands.

The location of the Underground was beneath the tiny home of Tim and Benjamina. Amy and Jan had hollowed out a huge set of rooms far below the surface of the city of Brom. Here they could work in total seclusion. Very few people knew of them.

The two who knew them best were Venerada Marisol Bolivar and *Mentales* Squad Leader, Henry Bolivar, who had given up his position as Lord Bolivar a couple of years ago. all the Midlands' lords and ladies had been *mentales* gifted and fully modified before they lost their hands to the "virus." Utterly helpless, they wisely followed Ben's advice and resigned, appointing non *mentales* gifted to fill their thrones.

Early morning on May Day, 1247, Tim yelled,

"Benjamina! Come quickly! You won't believe what is happening! Well, that was quick." Tim was the resident equipment expert. Soon he heard the telltale clicks of her spikes on the stone floor. Benjamina came as quickly as she could, carrying little Luisa with him.

"What's up?" she asked. "Just feeding Luisa."

"A new tower! That's what! Fons Valen and Roberto Valen have just surfaced. They've formed a new tower called the Renegade Tower. They are being venerado and capo respectively, violating your mother's ultimatum! He's called for a meeting of all eight veneradas at ten this morning. This is going to shake things up big time!"

"No kidding. We knew that sooner or later something like this might happen. At least we now know where those two Valen's have gone. Summon everyone. We should all hear what they say. Please get your recorder going, and record the entire conversations so we can study it with a fine tooth comb," she requested.

At ten, the entire Underground sat near the monitors. Soon they overheard the entire conversation among the nine leaders. When it finished, Benjamina said, "Now we have a whole new set of things to discover. Calder is awake. That doesn't sound promising. While we know he is one of the five ancient gods and goddesses, we know nothing more about him than he is the God of the Sea. No one knows when he was last awake, let alone what impact he had on our ancient ancestors."

"Well, he seems quite benign," Rafaela put in. "Healing and curing and, of course, blessing sea going ships. No harm in that, is there?"

None could find any fault there. Eric added, "Well, at least they seem to be wholly against Lord Pedro Valen and Valen Tower. That much is clear. No army. I like that point. Maybe they have changed?"

"They were totally body modified and lost their hands," Annie pointed out. "Since we have not given anyone in the Westerlings the new replacement high quality hands, they all must be getting by on those nearly useless ones Nita Valen provided everyone. Since we haven't used our medical machines to undo anyone's modifications from the

Westerlings, the odds are they are still wholly modified, which means that they are completely hobbled and barely able to even walk, let alone function or do anything with their prosthetic hands. Nita still hasn't surfaced yet, curse her. I'd like to get my stumps on her." Everyone laughed. They all would like that and so would hundreds of others who lost their hands to her and Lord Paco Valen's virus hoax.

Benjamina spoke up, "We are going to have to pay a visit to this High Priestess and see their priestesses firsthand. I guess I'll be making a trip to Villa del Rey."

"Like hell you will, Benjamina, you are a woman now. You know as well as I, women can't travel about on their own," Tim pointed out to her. She spat out a curse word, realizing he was right.

"Okay, you can't go Tim. The last time that you and I surfaced, we attracted the attention of Nita and Paco and look where that got us?" Benjamina commented. "We need you here monitoring the universe."

"I'll go with you," Eric volunteered.

"Hum, that isn't going to work too well, a young man with a forty year old woman," Benjamina pointed out, "unless you could be my son. Andres and Sam are both twenty-four and look old enough. Eric's gifts are with our feathered friends. Sorry, Eric, that's not going to be too useful on this trip. We're dealing with priestesses and the sea. Andres, while I can see by your eyes that you are dying to go, without your arms, it could be tough on you, though your attack spells might be useful, but fire and water don't mix well. Sam, you are our resident soldier. Annie, can I borrow Sam for this trip? I think we need a soldier's point of view of what is going on down in Villa del Rey."

"Sure, I'm not due until July. I can manage without Sam for a few days," Annie answered. She and Rafaela were due to give birth in early July. Both women were now showing it.

"Okay, we need a cover story, one that will get us in to see this High Priestess, whoever she may be," Benjamina then said, looking at the others for ideas.

"We are obviously from the Midlands. Only I can pass

for a Westerlings woman, and possibly Andres, but his shoes will cause problems, since the Westerlings have not had their toe shoes undone," Rafaela pointed out.

"You could pretend to be Midlands nobles on vacation to the sunny beaches," Tim pointed out.

"But Tim," Rafaela countered, "there are plenty of sunny beaches drastically closer to home. It's a far stretch to go fifteen hundred miles into the Westerlings to find a beach."

"Rats, sounded good," Tim grinned.

Several others tossed out even wilder ideas. Finally, Annie spoke up. "You know, you could play it straight and say that you are from the northern part of the Midlands. Say you heard of these priestesses and you want to find out if any could be sent inland to help heal and cure. That might get you in the door, so to speak. If these are strictly sea priestesses, as they likely are since Calder is behind them, the answer is likely no. Still, it might get you an audience with their High Priestess."

"Main thing is don't get caught," Tim pointed out. "I am going to have a locator beacon on each of you and monitor everything. At the first sign of trouble, I'm teleporting you both back here pronto, cover or no cover."

Rafaela added, "Since these are priestesses, you best not lie to them. I would imagine that detecting lies might be one of their gifts. That makes it tougher on you both."

The next morning, Elana helped Benjamina into her blue satin gown and brushed out her hair for her. "There, if these are water priestesses, you'll look better to them in blue. Knock them dead, dear," Elana teased her. "And don't worry about Luisa." Benjamina kissed her wife and headed towards the door, where Sam was already waiting for them. He wore a blue suit, but the black patent stilettos stuck out visibly. His sleeves helped hide his prosthetic hands from a casual glance. He carried no weapons and with his hands, he couldn't use one if he had one. Neither could any of the Underground now thanks to the virus hoax.

Sam put his arm through hers and she sent a telepathic okay to Tim, who activated their alien teleport machine. Last night he'd very carefully calibrated it to land them at the northern edge of the city. After the two disappeared from

Brom, Andres was already watching the geosat images. "Ah, there they are right on target," he called out to Tim. Now all they could do was wait and monitor the two, though Tim worked to reset the controls, ready to bring the two back on a moment's notice.

"The Underground should stay in the underground," Tim growled, glancing at his missing hands, the price he'd paid for briefly being above ground.

Sam's Westerlings was not very good, so Benjamina did all their talking. Arm in arm, they strolled into the city, noting it looked very much like a large version of Brom in many ways. People and shops appeared basically the same, only here, everyone had black hair, not brown. As they walked down the street, a few stared at them, mostly at Sam's heels. Before long, she spotted a city guard and they walked up to him. "Do you know where we can find the High Priestess of the Daughters of the Seas?"

"New to town, lousy accent. You must be from the Midlands. I doubt she'll see you, but it's down Main Street close to the docks." He gave them directions to get to Main Street and she thanked him.

As they neared the docks, Sam protested, "No one said we'd have to walk two miles in these heels. My feet are killing me." The smell of the ocean had grown much stronger; the gulls overhead seemed closer.

"Better than doing this in toe shoes," Benjamina countered. He flashed her a smile. Oh how true that was.

Around eleven, they spotted the hacienda and walked up to the gates, where a man in a light blue uniform with a short sword at his waist stood guard. "Hello. We are from the Midlands and have come to meet your High Priestess of the Daughters of the Seas, if she will see us, please," Benjamina spoke politely.

"Wait here. I will check and see." He turned crisply and walked into the gardens that opened up in the center of the U-shaped hacienda.

The guard returned after a few minutes and looked them both over. "No concealed weapons on you?"

"No, we have these alien prosthetic hands and cannot

possibly hold even a dagger. Sorry," Benjamina explained, holding out her hands so he could see them. Sam did likewise.

"Okay then, High Priestess Gracia Valen will see you. This way please." He opened the gates and let them in. *Another Valen!* Benjamina thought. Sam noted that these gates were purely ornamental in nature. Anyone who was determined to get in could easily break them. They had not gone but a few feet, when a door at the other end of the gardens opened and a man in a similar light blue uniform stepped out holding an infant. Right behind him came what appeared to be a woman. She was hopping, her hair bouncing up and down along with her large breasts and earrings. She had no arms and soon they both saw that she had only one leg and it was located strangely for a leg, centrally. Her hair reached her ankles and she had lip plates as well. Both Benjamina and Sam could not help but stare at her as the distance between them slowly closed.

"Hello there, I am High Priestess Gracia Valen, my husband, Diego Rica, and our daughter, Teresa; she's eleven months. He said that you are from the Midlands?"

"Yes, so very pleased that you will see us. I am Benjamina and my friend here, Sam. We are from the northern part of the Midlands. Oh, she's just adorable! Mine is now fourteen months old, Luisa. They grow up so fast, don't they?" Both noticed the young infant looked like her mother, no arms and with one leg sticking out of the blanket.

Gracia grinned, but it didn't show. "Please, come with us; we'll take you to our meeting room. Diego, send for tea and biscuits, if you will, dear." She did a hopping turn and began hopping back along the side of the gardens.

"What lovely garden you have here. The fragrances are intoxicating," Benjamina complimented her on what she was seeing.

"Thanks, we priestesses spend some time indoors, so it makes for a pleasant environment. However, we all love to go to the beach and go swimming. Here we go." The door opened by itself, but both Sam and Benjamina sensed psi powers in use causing it to open. Gracia hopped on inside and they followed. Just as they were about to follow her inside, a number of other doors opened and a dozen other women similarly dressed in light blue dresses hopped out to catch a quick glance of the newcomers. All looked like Gracia, causing Benjamina and Sam to involuntarily stare back at them, before walking into the room.

Gracia bent over and tossed her hair to her front side and then sat down. "Okay, Diego, I'll take her now." The infant seemed to float over to Gracia, settling gently on the table in front of her where she could keep an eye on her. Diego moved over and stood behind his wife.

"How should we address you?" Benjamina asked.

"Oh how about just Gracia. Now then, what did you want to see me about?" she asked.

"Well, we just heard you existed, and the many Daughters of the Seas, and of this god Calder. We are from the northern part of the Midlands, far from the ocean, but we do have the mighty Wyndl River nearby us. We heard all kinds of rumors about the skills your priestesses have, especially the healing parts. We thought we ought to at least see if these were true and if so, see if it would be possible in the future to have some priestesses come to our area and work their healing miracles. We doubt that will happen since we are so far from the sea, but we owe it to everyone to at least plead our case, that is, if your priestesses really do what all the rumors say," Benjamina stated. None of it was a lie. Healers were always desired in Brom, the city. She added, "I must admit we were both surprised at your, well, most unusual body. We've both lost our hands to the virus plague, but well, we were just surprised."

Gracia grinned invisibly, thinking their reactions were typical. "Yes, when Calder chose us, our bodies underwent a massive transformation, and we were given immense psi powers to compensate. All my priestesses have a vast capability of both telekinesis and teleportation. Obviously, we need that to compensate for our lack of arms. We have only the one leg and have to hop. But since sometimes we need to go a long distance, Calder has given us the ability to teleport at will. We call it jumping, not hopping. We are just ordinary women, who have been touched by the god Calder, and now work miracles on his behalf. Here. I'll show you what you really want to know." Using telekinesis, her dress rose up and the two could see she did have two bowed outward upper legs that somehow merged into one at her knee. A single muscular leg was attached to the knee. She added, "Our shape makes us powerful swimmers, right Diego?"

He grinned, "She beats me every time."

Just then, a cook brought in a tray of tea and biscuits. After serving everyone, she left. Gracia's spoon dipped into the tea and rose up and into her mouth. Benjamina and Sam struggled with their prosthetic hands, but managed fairly well. Gracia did notice how much trouble they were having with them.

Then she resumed, "Anyway, on to what we do. Each of us has the ability to heal injuries and cure illnesses in others. Daily we get dozens of such requests here at our hacienda. We turn no one away and charge nothing for our healing. We also bless ships and their crew. That way they have terrific luck at sea, often returning home with record catches of fish. Since you both are *mentales* gifted, I will tell you this too. Each of my priestesses has the katalyein gift, and we handle Verge Sicknesses, mental blocks to gifts, and even undoing the hidden trauma that the many body modifications caused."

"Simply incredible!" Benjamina exclaimed, thoroughly impressed. "You are indeed a wonderful gift to all mankind. There are only a few katalyein up in Brom, I believe."

"I am aware of that, painfully so. So very few of those here in Villa del Rey could ever afford to make such a trip to get their blocks undone, and the katalyein never leave their tower. Here, we help any and all who come to us and need our help. We've also handled many who had body modifications too. What I don't understand, Benjamina, is obviously you both have had most of those body modifications. I can see you both have fairly small waists. You've lost your hands. I think I see a red line where you used to have lip plates like mine, though you still wear even fancier earrings than I do. Yours are most impressive. Wait." She heard Calder's voice in her head. She then added, "Are those the goddess Lysandra's colors there — the middle strand of dangles?"

"Yes, Lysandra has touched me."

"Now that *is* interesting! Anyway, what is puzzling me is I see no signs of the many body traumas in your minds. They should be there, black masses."

"That's because I have found a way to erase them. No, I have no katalyein gifts, none whatsoever. I've been working on a mental therapy that is showing great promise. As you have pointed out, the Brom katalyein are so few and never leave their tower. There are so many of we gifted have these huge body modification traumas that something had to be done to help them. I've been asked by Lysandra to see if I can develop a science of the mind and spirit. It is showing great progress, but if we had a priestess Daughter of the Seas up north, she could greatly help so many who have these traumas. Hearing all these wild rumors flying about, I thought I ought to come and see if any were true. It is so wonderful to find out there is even more hope than before."

"So your therapy actually does remove the traumas?"

"Yes, I removed Sam's, that's why you find no trace of them in him or me, for that matter. I presume you also have none as well? I imagine you endured great trauma when your body was changed by Calder."

"No pain, but it certainly was scary, I'll admit that. Imagine waking up to find you only had the one leg and no arms. Now that's scary! Plus the leg can't go sideways. I used to be able to do the splits. Now that's impossible. Still we are able to bear children. Teresa here is proof of that."

Gracia then asked for more details about her therapy. Benjamina replied, "Well, I will let you know when it is finalized. While I have fifteen working assumptions at present, I don't want to give them to you right now and then later discover I've been wrong about one or more of them. When I do get it all worked out properly, I can tell you then, if you are really interested in them."

"Thanks that would be great. Now that we've met each other, we can use telepathy to chat. You don't mind if I talk with you once in a while? I'm terribly busy, but you intrigue me, Benjamina, though I can't say why. As far as sending one of my priestesses up north in the Midlands, while the river water would be perfect, just at the moment, I need them all down here at the many coastal towns. I promise you when things calm down here and I can spare one or more, I will get in touch with you and see about sending them. I always send six priestesses and their guardians to a town, never just one."

"Golly, how can you find so many women who are willing to undergo these changes and become a holy priestess?" Benjamina asked.

"We got a lot of them initially by just going swimming and talking with the young girls at the beach. I only take volunteers who really do want to become a priestess and help heal people. It is so hard to find as many as we need. However, since we need so many, recently, Lord Antonio is helping me out with the recruitment, and he is doing a much better job of it than I ever did. He must have quite a way with the young women. Anyway it's all I can do to train them properly, once they finally get Calder's gifts. You see, the gifts only come after the woman learns to adapt to being like we are and hopping about well."

"Oh my. So they don't get their gifts at the same time their bodies change," Benjamina summarized. "That must be incredibly frightening to them until the needed gifts come."

"Yes, it certainly is. Well, you must excuse me. I have another batch of new priestesses coming now, and I have to get them settled in and begin their training. Let's chat later by telepathy, shall we?"

"Certainly and thank you ever so much for seeing us. Goodbye for now," Benjamina and Sam rose and bowed to her, as Diego moved to open the door for them. He returned and picked up Teresa. Gracia rose and hopped out, passing the slower moving pair. When they reached the gates, they stood aside and stared at a dozen more young women, as they came hopping into the hacienda. Their eyes were looking around. It was obvious this was their first time here. Each had a guardian walking behind them. The amount of fear Benjamina sensed from the dozen women momentarily overwhelmed her. It passed as soon as Sam led her outside the hacienda.

"Are we going to have to walk back to the edge of the city?" Sam asked, leading Benjamina along.

Tim sent, *Take that side alley. There is no one there. Will teleport then.* Two minutes later, the pair was safely back at the underground teleport pad.

"Holy cow! Did you all see those priestesses?" Sam belted out the moment he had his balance back after landing.

"Yes, we all did, thanks to Tim's spy camera thingy," Rafaela replied. "Talk about body modifications, theirs are beyond wild!"

"Yes, we thought ours were bad, but theirs are beyond horrific!" Andres added, running out of ways to describe his feelings.

"Gang, that new bunch of priestesses who were arriving just as we were leaving, they were breathing heavily, like they had hopped a considerable distance. None had yellow eyes and none had any special gifts at all. They were just plain terrified! They were way beyond frightened!" Benjamina reported what the others could not tell from the video feed.

"So we know," she continued, "that ordinary women are being chosen to become priestesses. Independent of the way the massive body modifications are done, it is clear to me they are done some time before they are given the powers they need to survive."

"Hey, we have another name to study, this Antonio fellow. Too bad you couldn't get a last name," Tim added. "Probably a nobleman who has ways and means. I don't know if we really can find out anything about him, but I'll try."

Benjamina said, "I best relay what we've found out to Venerada Marisol. She needs to know that essentially Venerado Fons was telling the truth."

Andres broke in, "Look, I still don't trust this thing. Roberto and Fons were right there helping Paco Valen do his treasonous work. On the surface, it looks extremely positive, but I don't trust those men in the slightest. Besides, Gracia is Fons' daughter, isn't she? Like father, like daughter?"

"True, we need to very closely monitor them," Benjamina advised. Her crew volunteered somehow to get on it, and she returned to her room to nurse Luisa, who was about ready to be fed mostly solid food. Her monster breasts were more than ready to have that happen.

A few days later, Andres was reviewing some nighttime geosat images, watching them flick by at a rapid rate. Since their visit to Villa del Rey, they added that area to their daily watch program, as they had the area around Valen. Suddenly, Andres saw a streak of strange light, long and straight. He back up and ran the time-lapse sequence again and counted several of them. He called for Tim. "I found something but I don't know if it's anything."

A minute later, Tim exclaimed, "Damn, if those are not blaster shots, I'll eat my hat."

"You don't have a hat, only a winter parka," Andres pointed out. "So someone in Villa del Ray has blasters. Must be the Valens."

"My guess too. Makes them really dangerous. Wonder what they are shooting at? Can't tell in these nighttime images. Alas. Best go report this to Benjamina, Andres. Excellent job, by the way."

"Okay, will do, as Rafaela and I head over to Elegant Fashions Inc to give our therapy sessions."

Tim and his crew continued to monitor the Valen area. A few days later, Darcy noticed signs of a troop buildup and pointed it out to everyone. Now they all watched Valen like hawks. Before long, they estimated an army in the vicinity of a thousand men had gathered. Next, they apparently boarded some kind of river craft. The day that the small army began floating down the Alcantara River, Benjamina's earrings suddenly felt very funny. She realized Wystan had been roused from his slumber. She explained how she knew this way, "Look gang. I've been touched by Lysandra and wear her earrings. I think that is giving me the heads up notice her enemy god, Wystan, is now active again. We are in *big* trouble once more. Expect more wars, starting with a huge battle for Villa del Rey."

A few days later via the geosat images, the Underground witnessed Gracia's destruction of the entire Valen army. While the images were disconnected, separated by a minute or so between them, they still got a clear view of what had happened. Gracia was vastly more powerful than Benjamina had estimated!

Chapter 9 The Wars Begin

A vacuum was created when Lord Paco Valen's army of three thousand invaded and sacked Humberhills and Retford Hills killing all inhabitants of the two fortresses high in the foothills of the Goza Mountains. The surviving body-modified Humberhills teens, Darcy, Dawn, and Eric, had their hands cut off before the Underground could rescue them. All three were physically unable to claim their father's throne. Sally Retford was in a similar physical shape, ignoring the fact that she was female and unlikely to inherit her father's domain. Hence, distant relatives returned to claim the thrones and attempted to rebuild the fortresses. Obviously, both new rulers, Lord Robert Humberhills and Lord Felix Retford, had only a tenuous hold on their relatively small lands.

South of them lay Trent Hills, where Lord Harry Trent ruled his long narrow valley. He too had few soldiers. In the next valley south of his lay the ruins of Haverhills, only recently returning to life. It had been a dead-zone for over a half century. Valen Tower had dropped so many acid, fire, and chemical bombs on the city, tower, and castle there that all life, including plants, ceased. Hence the dead-zone. Much further south, the old city and tower of Oakham had also been a dead-zone. Only recently had life begun to return there. Just south of Haverhills lay the small kingdom of Wilde Hills, where Lord Billy Wilde ruled. Again, he was a weak leader. Derby Hills was the valley south of there, ruled by the strong fighter, Lord Francis Derby. Just south of that valley lay Yorkshire Hills, ruled by Lord Thomas Yorkshire.

With the rest of the Midlands rather quiet and Valen's small army destroyed by Calder's High Priestess, Wystan was furious. *How dare Calder interfere with me! I'll teach him another lesson!* Wystan looked over the Midlands and found little to his advantage. A relative peace filled the Midlands, though he saw intense hatred towards Valen Castle, but he saw no immediate prospects there that he could intervene and convince them to attack Castle Valen. At last, he turned his attention to the foothills, where he finally saw opportunities.

He visited each of the six ruling lords, subtly planting ideas into their minds. Into Lord Harry Trent's mind, he suggested this was his golden opportunity to expand his domain and take control of Retford Hills and Humberhills. After all, the valleys were ripe for the pickings. During the summer of 1247, Lord Harry assembled two hundred soldiers and began his attacks, first on Retford Hills and then Humberhills, subjugating the two new weak lords just as the winter set in.

Into Lord Francis' mind, he placed a similar idea that he had a rightful claim to Wilde Hills. His grandfather had once been heir to the lord, who was defeated by Valen's army years ago. He planted similar ideas into Lord Thomas Yorkshire and Lord Billy Wilde. During the summer and fall of 1247, these three lords battled each other. Men died, hamlets burned, but none of the three gained any substantial new territory.

Wystan enjoyed these minor skirmishes, but longed for *real* battles. He envisioned Calder sitting back out in his stupid ocean laughing at his pathetic attempts to foment wars. No, what Wystan truly wanted was a huge army to come sweeping down through the hills to Nasik first, wiping out Calder's pathetic attempts to play god. When winter came, Wystan knew these hill people would never be able to fulfill his goals of assaulting Calder's forces. He needed some other mighty army.

Again, he turned his attention to the Westerlings, beginning in the spring of 1248. With the coastal cities all declaring independence of his rule, Lord Pedro Valen once more began building up an army to enforce his will. Having lost all his blasters at the bottom of the Alcantara River during his failed attempt to take Villa del Rey, he now placed his emphasis upon holding onto as much of the Westerlings land that he could. He knew he dare not provoke these coastal, Calder-aligned towns. Yet, soon the inland towns and cities would also be rebelling. Hence, a strong show of force had to be made throughout the Westerlings, except for the coastal areas.

The problem was sheer size. The Westerlings was

roughly three thousand miles long and nearly that in width. To enforce his will throughout, he had either to field the largest army possible or to spread out what forces he could assemble. He chose the latter, unwilling to relinquish control of any more towns and villages. While Wystan enjoyed some of these relatively minor skirmishes, again these did not even remotely satisfy his war lust. Thus 1249 was wasted.

During the winter of 1249, he again took a look at the Easterlings, which had always been warlike, but always on a small scale. He found while they were fierce fighters, they were wholly unorganized and had really not advanced in three hundred years. At last, he moved back over the Midlands. Somehow, he had to turn their hatred of Valen into real action.

During the summer of 1250, Wystan attempted to turn the hatred of Valen Castle into action. Still Wystan was frustrated. He picked on Lord Rusden as the ideal candidate. If this lord would build up his army, he could directly assault the coastal strongholds of Calder a few hundred miles to the south. Repeatedly, Lord Rusden had the notion to expand his lands by sweeping down to Nasik and launching an attack on Valen coming at them from the south. Always he wondered why he would bother much with his southern coastal city? It was a major trade center for the grains his lands produced. Every time he thought about attacking Valen, he immediately rejected that idea. *God knows how many evil alien devices Valen has. Everyone knows they are in league with the aliens! No way. Got to control my anger.* Wystan grew more and more furious. At last, he turned his attention onto the aliens.

The tall, thin, gray skinned Sector ID Minister Emeryk Donat and his Valen wife, Adalina, had taken the news of the coup in Valen Castle in stride back then and now they took the loss of the thousand man army of Lord Pedro Valen with equal dispassion. “I’ll look into it, Lord Pedro,” Emeryk had promised the dim-witted ruler. Promptly, he filed this anomaly on the back burner. Strange things were happening on this planet, he was certain of that. Other matters now concerned him more.

It was spring, 1250, but he took no notice of the seasons

from his insulated office twenty stories above the flat Plateau Grado space port. Temperature and humidity controls of all Imperium buildings were identical, a perfect 78 degrees year round. Plus the lighting was uniform, quite unlike the dim orange-red of this godforsaken planet. He kept his jet black hair well-trimmed as he did is trademark moustache. His eyes were coal black and he cut a handsome figure, whose apparent age was now thirty-eight.

His wife was the gorgeous Adalina Valen, whose apparent age was the same. She had the extremely long, thick, and shiny black hair of the Westerlings. Her influence on him was pronounced. Unlike all the other personnel of the spaceport who wore the recyclable unisex cat suits, she had him dressed in the finest silk suits ever produced by Elegant Fashions Inc. Adalina Valen was wealthy and he enjoyed this aspect as well. She cut a stunning figure everywhere she went. Her tiny pipe corseted waist and form fitting gowns called everyone's attention to her enormous curves. Like all Tierra women, she possessed a huge bosom. She also wore golden lip plates with red rubies embedded in them, along with the enormously long dangling earrings, also ruby encrusted. Her feet had also been modified and she walked gracefully on her black patent toe shoes, with just enough of her black nylons showing to catch everyone's eyes. That she also walked incredibly slowly, he didn't mind, because all eyes followed her and thus him, when they saw the pair, much to the admiration of Emeryk, who puffed up in pride when he spotted them doing just that.

Their two children Antoni and Dorita were long from the coop, forty and thirty-seven respectively. A couple of times each year, they brought their families here for a brief visit. As a family, though, they were not close.

In truth, Adalina was miserable. Her massive body modifications effectively hobbled her, making everyday life challenging, though she continued to thank her lucky stars for not having her hands removed! All this was bad enough. All her plans for the future had died with the assassination of Lord Paco Valen. For years, she had spied on these aliens for him, even arranging valuable trades of illegal alien technology.

Now her head blind cousin ruled Valen. He was an ignorant, self-centered man, only interested in fighting. Adalina held firm to her earlier resolve not to spy for him. He never did find out she'd fed Paco key information. The only bright spot in her life continued to be at bedtime, when she took her lip plates out. Her hypersensitive lip loops drove her mad with lust, and Emeryk knew just how to use them to his advantage. As she rose each morning, she longed for the night once more. She had no more goals.

After Emeryk saw the geosat images of the loss of the Valen armies by some massively powerful and wholly unknown technology, he was determined to find out who and how. He sent out into the field the grandson of an ex-spacer, Pedro del Marco. He was a second generation half breed, the child of the child of one of Exchange City's many prostitutes and a spacer who had long ago left Ashford-5. The man was perfect for the spy mission, having no real loyalty to either side. His skin had a slight grey hue, but he easily looked like a native. Pedro had driven a hard bargain, twenty thousand credits in advance plus three thousand for expenses. If he discovered the who and how, he'd receive the other half, another twenty thousand.

Six months later, Pedro reported hearing rumors that a group called the Underground might have played a role in it. Back then, Emeryk felt finally they were getting somewhere. Then nothing was reported. Pedro, spurred on by the promise of doubling his newfound wealth, continued moving north through the Midlands. At each town, he made discrete inquiries, but few had even heard of the destruction of Valen's army in the foothills, let alone this mysterious Underground. Still, every now and then, someone would respond that the Underground might be further north.

In the summer of 1247, Pedro finally entered Brom and began making his oft repeated inquiries. Some here had indeed heard of the destruction of Valen's army. He found it unusual that Brom so far north would know of the seemingly isolated event over a thousand miles to the south. He persisted and finally got the break that he was looking for. Someone pointed him to Elegant Fashions Inc. "See Rafaela there."

"May I help you?" the elegantly dressed young woman asked, as the trail-grubby man entered the spotless store.

"Yes, I came to see a Rafaela," he replied.

"Have you an appointment?"

"Er no, do I need one?"

"Well, if it's therapy you desire, yes."

"Don't know nothing about no therapy. I just want a quick word with her."

"I see. She is conducting a therapy session right now. If you would care to wait, she can see you when she is finished." He agreed and took a seat off to one side and waited. *Now I am about to make my twenty thousand credits. With forty thousand, I can retire.*

An hour later and his heart beating swiftly, he was led into a small room with two chairs. "Rafaela, this man wishes a quick word with you." The office manager turned and left them. Pedro stared at this young woman. She had no arms at all, but was rather pretty in spite of this. Certainly, she was well-dressed.

"Please sit down. How may I help you?" Rafaela asked politely.

"I heard that you know about the Underground. I want to find out about them, miss."

Rafaela was surprised and acted accordingly. The man was head blind, yet was asking about highly secretive information. She stole a quick glance at his surface thoughts and picked up two concepts: credits and Emeryk. "Why yes, sir. You have come to the right person. I know all about the Underground." She paused, watching his eagerness, his greed, rising rapidly like a puppy being handed a tasty bone. "You want to drop by Leno's Bakery. He makes the Underground. It is an incredibly tasty pastry filled with chocolate on the inside. That's where it gets its name, Underground, the hidden chocolate. Around Brom, he's famous for his Underground. Everyone knows about him and his delicious treat. Tell him I sent you and he'll probably give you a free sample." She watched his face grimace, his anticipation evaporating. He rose, mumbled a thank you, and left.

As he left she planted a thought in his mind, *This is*

getting nowhere. Give it up. He did just that. He purchased more supplies and struck out for Southbend, Easterlings, there to retire, making plans to buy a small fortress and a harem of women to entertain him.

By the spring of 1250, Emeryk had forgotten all about Pedro and this illusive Underground. He had many far more pressing problems in this space sector to handled. However, he had agreed to meet with the dim wit, Lord Pedro Valen once more. He sent an aide to bring the lord to his office, where he and his wife met the man. "Be quick about it, Lord Valen, I am a very busy man at the moment."

"Sir, it's about these infernal Calder's priestesses, these Daughters of the Seas. They are slowly taking over all my southern coastal towns and cities. Have you found out how they wiped out my thousand-man army yet?"

"Oh that?" In fact he'd forgotten entirely about such trivial matters. "Well, frankly no. We have studied the situation and have no answers for what happened. Perhaps it was just one of those 'acts of God' that sometimes happen, over which we have no explanation. What are you talking about with these priestesses? I've forgotten. Far more pressing matters. I run this whole sector of space with hundreds of worlds." Emeryk was rapidly losing patience with the man.

"These priestesses. They are supposed to have god-like powers." He explained a bit more, but never having seen one himself, he mostly spouted rumors and hearsay.

"Okay, Lord Valen, I will look into the matter. Give me time."

"Thank you, thank you," Pedro groveled. Emeryk dismissed the man with a nod to his aide, who promptly escorted him out.

Priestesses with great powers? This intrigued Adalina, but not Emeryk. "So are you really going to investigate for him?" she asked.

"Hell no. Look, I have big problems. The rebels on Bellatrix-4 are threatening the Imperium miners. They may well attempt to sabotage our fuel mining colonies. Perhaps they might even come here. I have to stay on top of this. I've got no time or manpower to devote to silly priestesses.

Religion isn't my thing. You know that."

"Quite true, not mine either. Still you have to admit, it sounds intriguing."

"On the surface, all religious nuts sound intriguing. It's the same everywhere in the galaxy. Still I suppose we really ought to see if they do have some, as yet un-catalogued, mental powers. It's just that this infernal Bellatrix-4 mess is ten thousand times more important. I simply have to get a handle on them and put them out of business. It's causing me to get grey hairs!"

"Dear, I did see one or two grey hairs on your head last night. Worse, my love, I saw one long grey hair in mine too. I pulled it out! Perhaps we should use the rejuvenation machine again soon," she demurely suggested.

"God, two of them? Yes, yes we should. I'll make the arrangements down in Med. We'll get it done tonight after supper. Oh, to be twenty-one yet one more time. I need the vigor I once had if I am to put an end to this rebellion," he declared.

"Dear, that would be perfect!" she replied.

That evening their bodies were once again twenty-one years old. Adalina took Emeryk into rapport with her. Via her sensuous lip loops, the two shared a phenomenal round of sex, her reward to him for the gift of youth once more.

The next morning, more dispatches came to him marked Extreme Emergency, interrupting their quiet breakfast. "Crap, Adalina, I may well have to go off-planet a while to deal with this infernal rebellion thing."

"Say, while you are gone, why don't I take a quick trip down to one of these coastal cities and see what I can find out about these priestesses? It will give me something to do while you are gone."

"Say, I like that." *She could make a dynamite field agent. I'll see how she does with this one and go from there.* "Will you be able to manage it?"

"Yes, I can use the teleport pad. There and back in a day or so."

"You make sure they have the id marker implanted in your upper arm. That way the operator can pull you back here at any time. The transporter locks on to your id marker, dear."

"I will. I sure don't want to be trapped down there and have to travel back here by carriage." He grinned, knowing how difficult such a primitive trip that would be for her.

"We'll talk more about it tonight after I see if I really do have to go off-world."

That evening over supper, he said, "Looks like I am going to have to be gone for a few weeks, maybe a month. It will be more like July before I go." They chatted more, but he revealed little else.

Mid-July of 1250, Emeryk kissed Adalina goodbye and strode briskly to the waiting space shuttle craft that would ferry him to the battle cruiser orbiting far above the planet. These rebels were running rampant and had to be stopped by the use of ultimate force. As Sector ID Minister, this responsibility fell on him, and he took over control of the battle cruiser shortly after boarding the Star Shooter.

Adalina felt a surge of excitement. She'd been cooped up here in the spaceport for nearly a half century. Now she could get out and get some fresh air. Hobbled and constrained as she was, Adalina knew she would have a difficult time of it. Still just to taste the freedom of the open air once more led her on, that and the outside possibility of discovering what new powers these priestesses might have. She made her dismally slow way down to the teleport room.

The operator was bored, like so many of the others there at the space port. His cat suit smelled of plastic. She attempted to breathe as shallowly as possible. Even after all these years, she still detested that odor, sterile and inhuman. Mechanically, the operator checked on the id chip in her shoulder. "Okay, your marker is fully operational. Have you the location of where you wish to land?"

"Yes, let's visit Arabella. We have reports the priestesses are very active in that city. Since I don't know where they are located, let's land me somewhere close to the docks and ocean, but not too close. I hear docks can be a rough area. I have my blaster with me, so I should not be in any real danger." She petted her small handbag that contained the blaster and a small supply of silver coins in case she needed to make a donation to talk with the priestesses or if she got hungry and needed to dine. For a moment she relished the notion of eating real food once more.

The two examined the blown-up, geosat image of Arabella, looking for a reasonable location. They chose an alleyway where her sudden appearance would not draw undo attention. "Now how long will you be?" the technician asked her.

"That's a good question. It might take me some time to find these priestesses and to make arrangements for them to see me. Since I have telepathy, why don't I just contact you when I am ready to return? For safety's sake, if you don't hear from me in say a week or so, just bring me back anyway. A week ought to be enough time, don't you think?"

"Ma'am, I have no idea how much time you need. I am just a teleport pad operator." She smiled but it was invisible to him. "A week it is." He set the controls, and she stepped carefully onto the raised pad, about an inch above the floor. She watched him fiddle with the controls. She appeared in the alleyway a moment later.

Her senses were momentarily flooded. The smell of the nearby ocean, the call of many sea gulls, the low background noise of the not too distant docks and streets, the smell of many cooking fires and blacksmith shops — all vied for her attention. So much she'd missed for so very long! Distant memories returned to her of her life in Valen Castle. When was that? A lifetime ago? Rejuvenation had its price, she mused. She stood still for several minutes, taking in all of it with her senses, pleasure beyond pleasure. At last she stepped out into the crowded street and began looking around to get her bearings. A few noticed her, but paid her little attention beyond the fact of her good looks and noble appearance.

A band of Antonio's Recruitment Squad rode through the streets of Arabella. "We have to find us three more young women today. Keep your eyes open," the sergeant ordered. Slowly they rode through the crowded streets, looking at the passing people.

"How about that one?"

"Probably too young. We don't want to make that

mistake again. I got really chewed out last time," the sergeant replied, recalling the unfortunate incident. He'd later had to kill the kidnaped thirteen year old teen.

A bit later, one said, "Hey how about that one? She's already got the ornaments. Save them a little trouble. Good looking too."

"Okay, she looks old enough. Pedro, ready the ether. I'll distract her." They rode over to where Adalina was making her very slow way down the street, taking in all the long forgotten sights.

A uniformed soldier rode up to her and stopped. "Hello miss. Can we help you?"

"Why yes, perhaps you can. I am looking to find the priestesses. I believe they are called Daughters of the Seas or something like that. Could you tell me where I might find them?" Adalina asked politely. She was sensing something else, but could not quite place it. Although the soldiers were now all around her, she didn't think much of that. They were, after all, the city guards or perhaps city soldiers.

"Why yes we certainly can, Ama." The sergeant recognized her yellow eyes now and decided to opt to use the respectful title. "If you will permit us, we will take you to see the priestesses now." The use of the word "now" was his key word. The man behind her quickly put the rag over her face. Adalina began to act, realizing something was very wrong here. However, the ether was very fast acting. She felt her handbag slip from her grasp and then darkness fell. Another soldier leaned over and picked her up, holding her upright across his saddle. The sergeant neck reined and led the group rapidly away from the area. Few paid them any notice.

A small boy picked up the handbag. He confiscated the silver coins; this was his super-lucky day. He discarded the handbag and the strange metal object inside it. Smiling, he headed off down the street.

Adalina awoke. She felt satin sheets over her body and realized at once she was naked and in bed. Even her corset was gone; she breathed more easily than she had for several years now. Her head was quite groggy. Lying on her back, she struggled to a sitting position. *What happened? Where am I?*

Where are my clothes? A fuzzy memory of a rag over her face returned and the soldiers. She looked about and saw five other young women sleeping beneath satin sheets on small beds identical to hers. Several commodes were nearby. She saw no sign of her clothes.

"Ah, awake at last. Here, eat." A matronly older woman began stuffing fish into her mouth, carefully navigating the bite between her lip plates. For some strange reason, Adalina felt she had to eat. Once she tasted the fish, her body craved more of it.

"The priestesses. I came to see the priestesses. Where am I?" she asked between mouthfuls.

"You will see the priestesses soon enough. For now, you just eat. That's a good girl. Now lie back down. I can see you are very tired." Her voice was kindly. Adalina felt no malice coming from her and she did as asked. She did feel so very tired. Twice more, she awoke groggy and was fed more fish.

She awoke once more. I was dark outside, but a dim lantern illuminated the bedroom. She again felt groggy, but had to urinate. She pulled off the sheet to get herself up. The commode was nearby, and her mind slowly focused. Adalina then saw her legs and stared uncomprehending at them for almost a minute. *I must be in some kind of hideous dream.* The matronly woman came walking up carrying a plate of fish. "Ah you are awake again."

Adalina screamed louder than she ever imagined that she could scream. Her upper legs were slightly bowed outward, but merged into one at her knee. A single, somewhat larger leg than she had before was connected to her knee. "There, there, it will be all right. Now let's get you to the commode, miss. Up you go. You have to hop now, just like the priestesses."

The woman got Adalina up onto her foot, though she moved her arms wildly about, finally clinging for dear life to the woman. She gave her a slight push and said, "Hop, jump, hop." Either she hopped or she would fall down. Still screaming, she hopped, and then did a sort of hopping in place turn and sat down on the commode. Sobbing replaced her screams. When she was done, the matronly woman again forced her to stand up on her foot and hop back to her bed. Still sobbing, the woman stuffed her full of fish and tucked her back into bed.

Terrified beyond words and too groggy to focus, Adalina slipped back into a restless sleep. Again, she vaguely remembered briefly waking only to have more fish stuffed into her mouth. How many days later she finally awoke with no grogginess, she simply could not tell. As she tried to sit up, she began screaming hysterically. She had no arms now; two dried husks lay on her sheets, apparently what was left of her arms. Then they too simply vanished.

"There, there, it will be all right. Now up you go. To the commode." The matronly woman held a light blue dress in her hand. A strange man wearing a similar light blue uniform with a short sword at his waist stood patiently watching them. Adalina simply continued to scream hysterically. She was utterly helpless now, wobbling wildly on her single leg, no arms to latch onto the woman. "Hop. Come on hop." The woman pushed her. Again, terrified of falling and with no way to keep from smashing into the floor, she had no choice but to try to hop. At least the woman used an arm to continue to steady her.

Once she'd used the commode, the woman put the new satin dress on her, for which Adalina was thankful, but she was still hysterically crying, more terrified than she ever had been in her long life. What was happening to her? She had no idea at all. "Now this man will be your guardian. He will be helping you with your needs until you get your gifts from Calder and join the other priestesses. He will always be with you and will protect you with his life. Okay, Hernandez, she is all yours."

Just then, another woman woke up, discovered her horrid condition, and began hysterically screaming. Hernandez said, "Okay, up and at it. You have to learn to hop very well on your own. Off we go." He gave the hysterically crying Adalina a push. Again, she had no choice but to try to hop, losing her balance in the process, and wildly moving her head and torso to regain it. Often, he had to lend her a steadying hand, but he quickly took it away as soon as she was again stable.

Adalina continued to sob her heart out. She felt completely and wholly helpless now. Her strange leg could not move sideways. The only physical action she could do now was to hop on that leg, besides bending and turning her head, that is. There was no way that she could even touch her face. Relentlessly, the man in blue forced her to hop. Where were they going? Around and around some strange garden? Nothing made any sense to her any longer.

At last as her leg was about to give out, he let her sit down. Someone brought him a tray and he fed her more fish, finishing by spooning a cup of tea into her. "Why?" she finally said, though she was still crying.

"You have to eat and get stronger. You have to learn to hop very well without me always catching you. Soon you'll be given your immense powers and you have to be ready to get them. Now we're done eating, let's get you hopping again."

"Please, no more hopping. I can't live like this. Please, use your sword and kill me now. Please, have mercy on me. Kill me now," Adalina begged.

He only laughed at her, stood her up on her leg, and left her standing there, wiggling to stay balanced. "Now let's hop around the garden once more." She refused to budge, frozen, petrified to the spot. He pushed her. Again, it was either fall flat on her face or hop, she hopped. Then she saw the other woman, who had awakened with her own terrified screams, now hopping wildly to a side room. A while later she came hopping out now wearing long dangling earrings and lip plates like hers. She watched as the other man in blue began forcing that poor woman to start hopping around the garden as well.

After an endless eternity, she was allowed back into the bedroom, where another woman was hysterically screaming. While the matronly woman and another of the strange men began working with her, her man began to feed her more fish and then some tea. He said little. Then he took her dress off her. While she observed her body, he gently brushed out her hair, which was now rather a tangled mess. Then he tucked her in. "Tomorrow you must do better with your hopping."

Finally alone and semi-coherent, she tried to focus and make telepathic contact, but the technician was buried behind all this emotional trauma. She could not find him. Her precious germanium crystal was nowhere to be seen. In desperation, she searched for Emeryk. She could not sense him and suspected that he was still off-planet. At last feeling more hopeless than ever, Adalina fell into a deep sleep.

The next few days blurred into one hideous nightmare of screaming women, endless hopping until utter exhaustion overcame her, at which point she was fed more fish and forced to hop yet again. Her feelings of complete helplessness did not leave her, only growing stronger as she herself grew stronger and more alert. Each night, she tried to contact Emeryk, but he was off-planet. She realized she had no idea of when he might be back, perhaps months, he'd said. *Why did I ever come here to see these priestesses?*

Just when she finally began to feel somewhat comfortable hopping on her own around the garden, the man forced her out into the crowded streets. New nightmares flooded over her. Now the surface was rough, and she had to be observant of those around her. One bump would send her sprawling. Her terror only grew by leaps and bounds, but the man seemed not to care in the slightest. Twice and sometimes three times each day, she pleaded with him to end her life. He only laughed and made her hop some more.

"Today, we are going to meet the priestesses. You finally get your wish, Adalina," her man said. This sounded hopeful. Perhaps she could beg them to end her now pathetic existence. Again, they hopped out onto the streets of Arabella, crowded with folks going about their own business. Naturally everyone stopped to stare at her, but she ignored them, focusing all her attention on taking the next hop. It seemed endless. On and on they went until she was actually gasping for breath. "Just a little further," he kept saying endlessly.

At last, they entered the gates of some Westerlings hacienda. It too had a formal garden surrounded by many suites. As they entered, two young women, who looked like herself, came hopping towards her. "Welcome, welcome. I am Priestess Gabriela. This is Priestess Francisca. We are in charge here in Arabella. Soon you will receive your holy gifts from Calder. With them, you will be able to live a normal life, using telekinesis and teleportation. More importantly, you will be able to bless ocean going ships and their crew, heal the injured, cure the sick, and remove mental traumatic blocks like a katalyein. Oh! I see you still have your blocks. Well as soon as we get you to your new suite, I will help you get rid of them."

Several hours later, Adalina felt significantly better. She'd re-experienced the suppressed pains from her many body modifications — pains she never knew were there. Except for her horrid physical condition, she felt more alive than she had in a long time. Yet that simply could not overcome her terror of her current body's condition. Nothing short of death could do that, she knew.

The next morning, her gifts began appearing. Right on cue, Gabriela came and began working with her, training her in their usage. Soon she was able to use her new telekinesis skills to dress herself, brush her hair, feed herself, and most importantly, help her keep her fragile balance while hopping. Then came her new ability to teleport. She was a little dismayed to find she had to be able to see with her eyes where she was teleporting to. She had had the notion to just teleport back to the space port. Well, that was out.

When all her curing abilities appeared, she was put to work using them on the many who came to the gates in search of healing or curing. For once in her life, Adalina began doing things really helped others who were suffering. She began to like the feeling she had while doing it. Each night she tried to contact Emeryk, but had no luck. He was still off-world.

Soon she got accustomed to her new role as a priestess of Calder, healing and curing nearly every day. Although she began to find this was rewarding, she still had not told anyone who she really was, the wife of the alien Sector ID Minister. She imagined the retribution he would wreak on these people, when he found out what they had done to his wife. September 1250 passed by rather swiftly for her, then October and November. At last she forgot to continue to try to contact Emeryk.

In December, Wystan grew absolutely furious. Nowhere

could he get the lords fired up enough to field an army to go after Calder's bunch along the coast of the Westerlings. By now, they had expanded to the Midlands ports and even to the Easterlings ports. Wystan knew at the moment, he was losing his battle with Calder and wished he'd stayed asleep! At last, he sailed out over the southern ocean to confront his ancient nemesis.

How dare you take over my lands! Wystan sent.

I'm not. I'm reclaiming my rightful sea coasts, where we both know the real power lies, not in your petty inland empires, Calder sent back. *Besides, my people are being highly successful, whereas simply put, yours are not!*

None saw the amazing electrical bolts that illuminated the southern skies as Wystan took his anger out on Calder, who returned in like kind.

Far above them, twenty well-armed rebel frigates materialized. Tierra's two moons, the bright and white Echador and the pale blue Palidez, were visible along with the bluish planet below them, illuminated by the dim orange-red sun. A haze of dust rose from the refineries on the surface of Palidez. The rebel's goal was the destruction of the psi-crystal fuel refinery, crippling the Imperium's push into this sector of the outer rim.

Almost the instant they appeared, so did two heavy Imperium battle cruisers! Battle was joined almost instantly. Great energy cannons fired at the frigates, which returned their fire. Down below, both Wystan and Calder suddenly caught sight of this incredible battle. Both shot up and became a part of the combat, each urging one side on over the other. Several frigates were heavily damaged and began backing out of the combat. Then one of the battle cruisers took a devastating hit and it pulled away too.

Finally realizing they were being out-gunned and had no chance at getting to the refinery, the remaining frigates moved away too, retreating to fight another day. The undamaged battle cruiser headed off in hot pursuit. Both Calder and Wystan sailed off after them, highly impressed with the intensity of the battles and the high level of technology and its many more possibilities. At long last, those two ancient gods finally abandoned Tierra for good, seeking greener pastures, some said many years later. The actual truth would not appear for a very long time.

Chapter 10 Dealing with the Aftermath

With the relative quiet of the late forties, the Underground continued to raise their families. Elana and Benjamina had Alpha use the fertility methods the robot used with his Madiera women on them, and Elana had their daughter, Janice in 1248. On the other hand, Benjamina had been charged by Lysandra to have three more babies by men of her choosing. Around the same time as Elana had their daughter, she gave birth to Jake. Andres was the father. Then in 1250, she gave birth to Anita; Tim was her father. “Learning what it means to be a woman,” Benjamina certainly now had a very good idea.

Similarly Tim and Petrona had a son in 1249 they named Bart. Andres and Rafaela had Crystal in late 1247, and in late 1249, she gave birth to their son Henry. Annie and Sam had Jamie in 1247 and Misty in 1249. Eric and Sally had Thomas in 1249. Now Darcy and Dawn were getting desperate to find their own boyfriends and start their families. Venerada Marisol, recognizing that the twins offered new blood lines, began arranging dates for the twins. In 1250, both were now dating two lads their own age from Brom Tower.

Benjamina learned the difficulties of caring for infants and toddlers. With eleven youngsters to care for, each of the women took turns watching them. Darcy and Dawn lent a hand as well, so only one day in seven each woman had to care for the eleven, giving their mothers time to work on Underground business, handle laundry duties, go to the markets, and cook. By 1250, Benjamina fully understood the nurturing aspect, at least with toddlers through four year olds.

Tim and Benjamina kept a close watch on the minor conflicts that arose. If they had fingers, they would have kept them crossed. Wystan was awake and certainly doing his best to get new major wars started. So far, the armed conflicts were all minor, and they did not have to intervene. Then in 1250, they intercepted Emeryk’s communications about these alien rebels. Close monitoring suggested the rebels might well attack here, but Emeryk rightly concluded their target would be the refinery on the pale blue moon, Palidez. Still both were worried about what impact a battle between alien forces could mean to the people of Tiera. In war, there is always collateral damage. Neither wanted Tierra to fall into that category, but could see no way to avoid it. Both felt their mothers would have known what to do about this situation, but they did not. They could only worry.

Instead, they continued to focus on the shifting power base on Tierra. By using the hundreds of priestesses of Calder, the Shipping Barons, as Antonio and Julio were known, now wielded significant power. As anticipated with the newer caravels, new trade lines opened up. By 1250, nearly every town of a few thousand along the entire southern coastline of Tierra and even up the eastern and western sides had developed extensive trading. Dates and figs, for example, were commonplace in shops in Benito, Westerlings. Pod-silk was readily available at any of these coastal cities. Grains from the breadbasket flowed from Nasik in both directions. Profits were at an all-time high. The territories controlled by Rusden and Southbend became wealthy almost overnight, while the shipping barons rolled in their profits. Everywhere there was money to be made in shipping goods between the three major sections of Tierra. The power base had most definitely shifted by the end of 1250.

The damaged battle cruiser hovered over Tierra until a shuttle craft launched. Once clear, the huge ship activated its remaining engine and left the vicinity of Ashford-5 on its way to be repaired. Shortly after that, a tired, haggard looking Sector ID Minister, landed and strode briskly into the twenty-story administration building. Later he found a message on his screen. He stared at it in wonder.

Adalina Donat, deceased. This was followed by the Imperium Star Date. He showered, put on a clean suit, and headed down to the teleport room. “What the bloody hell happened to my wife?” he demanded angrily.

The technician, his hands shaking from nervousness, pointed to the dried husk remains of her left arm with the id marker still in it. "We don't know, but something awful, sir. Happened about a week after she left. This is all that is left of her. I am terribly sorry, sir."

"Transport failure?"

"I thought so at first and quadrupled checked everything. The equipment is in perfect working order. She told me she'd contact me when she was ready to be brought back, but I insisted if she didn't, I'd automatically bring her back in a week. After a week, I did so, and this is all that remained of her. She must have met some tragic accident down there. I've never seen anything like it. Medical folks verified it is her DNA."

"Damn! Well, get rid of it. Recycle what's left of her." Sadly, he walked out and took the elevator to his office. There as expected, he had reports piling up. One caught his eye. His technicians had at last captured an image of these priestesses. He stared in disbelief at the image of the young woman. Then he filed the report. Obviously, these priestesses were not worth further attention. They were merely some hideous freak of nature. He'd seen such things before on other planets. Well, not firsthand, mind you, just the reports and images.

That same evening, Benjamina sat bolt upright in her bed, waking Elana. "What's wrong, love?" she said sleepily.

"Wystan. I think that he's somehow gone from Tierra. I sensed it. I don't know how, but I am sure that we are rid of his constant meddling in our affairs."

"Well, that's good. Oh, Anita is waking. Need help feeding her?" Elana asked.

"No, you go back to sleep." She clumsily slipped into her hands and rose to the basinet where the three month old Anita was starting to fuss. "Mommy's coming," she whispered, pulling her long hair out of her way, as she leaned over to pick up her wiggling daughter.

Later after a long struggle with her hands, she had the diapers changed and was now lying down, Anita suckling hungrily. *Bonds between a mother and her child can be powerfully strong,* she mused, gently stroking the infant's thin hair with her arm, unwilling to trust her unfeeling hands.

Just then, a yellowish glow appeared in their bedroom, and Benjamina hastily woke Elana who sat up. The glow brightened until the shimmering form of Lysandra appeared before them. *Motherhood agrees with you, Benjamina. You have learned well. I release you from having to have more children unless you wish them.*

Thank you. I have learned a lot. We are making good progress on the science of the mind and spirit.

I am aware of your progress. Continue with that. I have come to seek your help and that of your friends. I know you know Wystan has abandoned Tierra.

Yes, I felt that a few minutes ago. I don't know why, though.

He found better battles out there among the stars. Calder went with him. She paused to let her analyze this simple statement.

My god! What's going to happen to all his Daughters of the Seas priestesses? I figured somehow he was directly giving them their special powers. I can see why he wanted them to sort of look like mermaids.

Her assessment of Benjamina was accurate. *That is why I have come to you. Yes, Calder was handling them directly himself. The process is called spanning of attention. Now that he's also abandoned Tierra, the connection to him is severed. Those women will no longer have any of the special powers he was funneling into them.*

They'll be almost completely helpless.

That is correct. It is so like a man to run off leaving women behind to suffer.

Some men, not all. We need somehow to help them, Lysandra.

Point taken. Soon I will hear hundreds of voices calling out to me, but I cannot undo what Calder did to their bodies. I simply do not know how he did what he did. I can only give them a kindly death, yet they most certainly do not deserve death. The sheer amount of healing they've done dictates I must help them.

What can we do to help?

Bring them and their families here with you. Work

with them and see if they can somehow be salvaged. I will continue to see if I can do anything for them physically. I am not hopeful. Will you do this for them?

Absolutely. But we are already cramped for space here in the Underground. It is winter here in Brom. They could not possibly even walk outside in the deep snow. It's incredibly tricky for us in our heels. However, I have an idea I want to check out in the morning.

I am seeing what you are thinking. If they will agree, I will create an underground tunnel for your travel discretely from your teleport pad to the existing tunnel beneath Brom Tower. That I can do.

I don't know how you can do that, but I think we have just the place where they might possibly be able to survive. If so, we can bring them here, house them, and care for them. How many are there?

Five hundred and six women, including their children. I anticipate some will not survive the sudden shock of the withdrawal of their Calder-given powers. Time will tell.

Boy are we ever going to have our hands full with this one! Okay, assuming we have the space, we can use our teleport pad to bring them here in small groups, but we need to know where they are located. I have it! The many branch offices of Elegant Fashions Inc each have a small teleport pod in them, illegally, I know. If they can somehow hop to their nearest branch office, we can teleport them from there. I'll get a hold of Inez Franks who runs them all from Exchange City. If you should answer some of their pleas for help, tell them to go to their nearest Elegant Fashions Inc store. We'll take it from there.

Thank you, Benjamina. There is one thing I can do for you and your Underground. You will see when you awake in the morning. I must go now and prepare your larger quarters.

Slowly the yellow form faded and then the afterglow vanished, leaving only the dim lantern light once more. "My god, those poor women," Elana whispered.

"We will have our alien hands full now. What a hideous disaster this has turned out to be." Anita was finished and asleep. Carefully she put her back in her bassinet, removed her hands again, and climbed into bed, snuggling up close to Elana.

In the morning, Elana was the first to rouse. "Oh my god! Benjamina, Benjamina! Wake up look! Look at my hands!" Benjamina opened her sleepy eyes. She looked and saw Elana had hands. She blinked. "Yes, they are real hands! Look at yours!" Benjamina looked at her own stumps to see hands there. She smiled. Lysandra knew how much they were really going to need hands if they were to handle so many women.

Soon they heard wild exclamations from their other Underground members. Before long, all gathered in their underground kitchen, all talking at once and waving their hands in front of each other. None was more pleased than Andres and Rafaela, whose entire arms had been restored by Lysandra.

Then Benjamina told them what had happened and why their hands were restored. After many curses and wild exclamations, Tim dashed off to see what Lysandra had done to his precious Underground. Others headed off to take care of the children, while Elana headed to the kitchen to fix breakfast. It was her turn to do so. Benjamina headed to the Comm Center and hailed the robot Alpha, outlining their situation and begged. Alpha agreed.

December 30, 1250, High Priestess Gracia woke up as usual at dawn. She used her telekinetic powers to push herself up as she had done every day for so many years now. Nothing happened. She still laid flat on her bed. She tried again, nothing. Slowly she realized power was completely gone! She began to panic, but forced herself to calm down. She focused and activated her crystal and examined herself. Only then did she panic and begin to scream, waking Diego who was sleeping soundly next to her.

"It's gone! All my powers are gone, Diego! I'm helpless! I can't even get myself up. I can't cure a thing now! No telekinetic skill! No teleport! No nothing! All that Calder gave me is gone utterly. Diego! I'm completely helpless again, just like I was that first week! Oh god! What's happening to me?"

Diego's face went white. He got up and quickly helped her up.

She rose to use their commode. "Oh god, Diego! I'm terrified all over again! I can't do anything anymore! What's happening to me?"

"I'm right here. Let's get you to the commode and then dressed. I'll fix breakfast and handle our daughters. You try to relax some. Why don't you check on the others here at our hacienda?"

After she was dressed, both heard more screaming coming from other suites in their large hacienda. Gracia rose to her foot and very carefully hopped to her door to go check on the others who were screaming. She went very carefully, acutely aware she no longer had any way to keep herself from taking a spill. Like all the priestesses of Calder, she had been wholly dependent upon her telekinetic powers for absolutely everything, except physically hopping. She reached the door and could not now open it! Diego saw her and ran over to open it for her and she hopped on out. The screams of utter panic and terror surrounded her, coming from all the occupied suites! Worse, she couldn't open any of their doors even to see them!

Just then the shocked, white face of Andres appeared, as he opened the suite door next to hers. "It's Alicia! She's lost her powers," he gushed. Seeing her fear-stricken face, he added, "You too?" She nodded. She could not even speak. If she did, she'd break down utterly. Somehow, she had to be strong.

Emilio opened his door to tell her that Juana had lost her powers. Renata, his sister, lost hers. The stark face of Marcela told her Natalia had lost hers too. Scared out of her wits, Gracia hopped very carefully on down the side of the gardens, as the guardian men continued to open their doors and call out for help. Marcela opened her door and begged for help. "It's Natalia,! She's lost everything. She can't get up. What's happening?" Again, Gracia couldn't speak; she dare not; she'd breakdown utterly. all these new recruits too, including Adalina Valen Donat, had completely lost their precious powers that enabled them at least somehow to live life. Finally, Gracia completed the long circle around the gardens and hopped back into her room.

Diego looked up at her. "All of them?" She could only nod yes. She slumped onto her bed, sitting on her hair, pulling it. She ignored the sharp pain. What was happening?

Before long Diego came over with a plate of breakfast. As he fed her, she finally broke down and began sobbing her heart out. With her stomach full and her sobbing ended, Gracia finally spoke. "Something awful has happened. I don't know what, but it is my responsibility, Diego, to find out what and help all of them. They are my priestesses."

"What can you do?" he asked. "Back shortly, I have to handle the kids." Teresa was now four and Hermina, two, and was just learning to hop. Teresa was unstoppable with her hopping now. She'd not gotten any powers as yet and needed help with most everything.

"What can I do? Maybe I can contact Calder and find out." She closed her eyes and focused her mind, searching for the unique touch of his mind she'd felt before when he'd visited them years ago setting this whole thing in motion. Nothing, nothing at all. Panic swept over her. *How could this be? It's like he's not here somehow.* As she sat there, suddenly she thought of Benjamina, the kind woman who made a big impression on her. An instant later, she had contact.

Benjamina, it's Gracia Valen Rique, the High Priestess from Villa del Rey.

Hi, I recognize you, Gracia. You are having terrible problems right now, right?

Yes, how did you know? We've all suddenly lost all our Calder-given powers. We are utterly helpless. We're all panicking. I can't contact Calder. I don't know why I am contacting you.

I do. Lysandra's doing. Last night, Calder and Wystan left Tierra, possibly for good. That has broken his connection to you and all your priestesses. Are all your powers all gone?

Yes. I can't move anything now. I'm helpless. I can't teleport either, but that's minor. Our healing skills have vanished utterly. It's all gone! Benjamina, I'm utterly helpless! What do I do?

Lysandra and I have come up with a plan. We're going

to rescue all your priestesses, if we can, and bring them here where I am at. Lysandra and I have a plan, a space to house all of you, but she doesn't think she can undo what Calder has done to your bodies. Still we are all going to try.

All of us? All of us are helpless? Dear god! We can't live like this!

Somehow, you can. Do you still have your original mentales gifts?

Yes or I couldn't have contacted you. I guess that's a little something.

Yes it is more than probably a lot of your priestesses will have. Start contacting your other leaders in their towns. Everyone is supposed to find a way to get to their nearest Elegant Fashions Inc store. Once there, we will be teleporting you here to our place, where we can help all of you. Inez Franks, who runs the outfit from her headquarters in Exchange City, is notifying all her branch managers this morning letting them know to expect your women. You are to bring all your families there.

Okay. Our powers aren't going to suddenly come back soon?

Calder is long gone. He's abandoned all of you.

Damn him to hell! Okay I'll get on it. I have to take responsibility for all my women and their families. I'll keep you posted. She broke the connection with her.

"Diego, go spread the word. We need a group meeting of everyone, except the kids. We'll hold it out by the gardens." She rose and followed him out of their suite. She took a central seat, but not before carefully tossing her hair out of the way before she sat down rather roughly. Gone was her ability gently to lower herself into a chair. Diego raced from door to door, announcing the meeting and then took his place, standing behind her. Gracia could not stop crying as she saw close to fifty women come sobbing out of their suites, taking extreme care with their hopping. All looked to her for guidance. She never had to deliver such crushing news, not ever. Gracia steeled herself. *I have to be strong for all of them, even if I am not strong at all!*

Once they were all assembled and seated, Gracia spoke

as clearly as she could with these cursed lip plates. "The god we call Calder has left Tierra, abandoning us all. His mental contact with us is severed and is not likely to be reconnected. That is why we've lost all our powers. The Goddess Lysandra is going to help us. She's arranged for a friend of mine, Benjamina, to get us to a place of safety Lysandra has already made for us. I don't know where that is though. What we are supposed to do is to contact all the others in all the cities. We are to make our way to the closest Elegant Fashions Inc. From there somehow Benjamina and Lysandra will teleport us and our families to this place of safety."

"A few of us have the *mentales* gifts. Those of you who do, please stay here. The rest of you, go and begin packing what you can take with you."

"Hey, we guardians didn't bargain for this. We've got our own families to worry about," Gael spoke up.

"I know. Please, help get your priestess to the store, then you can leave her there and return to your own families," Gracia replied, knowing soon, most of these women would be wholly on their own, more terrified than before! She hoped and prayed the men would at least help get their charge to the store.

Emilio and his sister Renata stayed along with Natalia, Marcela, Adalina, Diego, and Andres. None of the others had the *mentales* gifts. "Sis, I've already contacted dad," Andres spoke up. "Damn him! He said we're on our own. He knows of no way to help any of you. He suggested we be humane and kill you. I told him to go to hell, sis!" She grinned, but it wasn't visible.

Marcela spoke up, "Me too, I contacted dad and Julio. They were shocked at first, but they said our usefulness is at an end and we should be humane and kill you all. I didn't even answer that one!" Natalia began crying once more.

"Okay, this is it. Each of you, contact one of the leaders in each of our cities," Gracia began to issue orders again. Diego had the listing of their personnel, and from it she began doling out towns to the others. She took Gabriela in Arabella. When she made the telepathic communication like with Gabriela, Gracia was wholly unprepared for the almost overwhelming fear and terror that came back to her.

That morning Gabriela had arisen only to discover all her powers were gone, that she was almost entirely helpless. All she was now able to do was hop and even that was as terrifying as it had been those first few days after her transformation. With her guardian's arms around her, she'd hopped out into the gardens, surrounded by hideous screaming from all the other occupied suites. Gael opened his door and begged for help. "It's Nita; she's lost everything. She can't get up. What's happening?" Gabriela couldn't speak; she was completely stunned. Soon it was apparent all her priestesses had lost all their powers entirely. She sat down on a garden chair and simply bawled.

Then a miracle occurred, she felt the familiar touch of Gracia making telepathic contact with her. Her terror shot back down the line and nearly stunned Gracia. She recovered and told Gabriela what had happened, what she had learned, and most importantly, what Gabriela was to do now.

Gabriela then spoke up, "That was Gracia. We have all lost all our powers." She repeated what she was told. "So we are to have our guardians pack up our few things and get us to Elegant Fashions Inc and await our rescue there. We are to bring all our families too and once you guardians get us there, you can return to your own homes and families." She looked at her dearest friend, Francisca. Her eyes were black now, their original color. A quick glance revealed that only Nita still had the yellow eyes with brown spots. Of the other five who had originally come to Arabella with her, none now had any gifts at all. all her fellow priestesses that were still here in the city were sobbing to themselves. Nita was part of the latest new recruits, another dozen women doomed utterly. Reluctantly and extremely carefully, she rose and hopped back to their suite hoping the many guardians were packing their hairbrushes, dresses, and flats.

An hour later, in pairs the guardians and their charges came hopping out of their suites for the last time. All were still crying heavily. Gael had hung a large sack over Nita's five year old Felipe. "There you go. Felipe is carrying your stuff. I'm out of here. We didn't sign on for this mess. We aren't being paid enough for this." He turned and walked out of the gate, at least leaving it open. Gabriela's guardian hung her sack over her neck and split without a word. So did Francesca's. One by one, all the other guardians did the same. Soon, only Hernandez remained. He yelled, "We can't just leave them, guys. Come on! We have at least to make sure they get to the store. The other guardians ignored him. "Okay, I won't just leave you. Come on; we best get going. It's about two miles away from here. We'll go single file so we don't risk getting bumped. I'll lead the way. Gabriela, you and Francisca follow me. Nita, since you still have some powers, you and Felipe bring up the rear. If you see any of the others ahead of you in trouble, let me know, okay?"

"I'm scared out of my mind!" Nita cried out.

"You all are, but you have to be brave and hop to this store and your rescue. Okay, ladies, let's hop to it." Several managed a slight grin, though he couldn't see them.

"Thank you, Hernandez," Gabriela said, still sobbing quietly, as she began to hop behind him.

"We all aren't pigs, Gabriela. Besides, I really like you and Francisca. I always wanted to be your guardians. Well looks like I got my wish. Make way, priestesses coming," he called out, moving some of those on the street out of their way. He took it extra slow though. While still crying, the women were valiantly trying to hop, but they no longer had telekinesis to use to keep their balance and had to resort to throwing their heads and torsos around instead. This reminded them of their terror filled trip through the streets from the building, where they'd been originally transformed by the strange fish. Present and past merged for a dozen of these women, including Nita. The confusion of trauma only made things that much more difficult for the twelve. Several times a few of the women stumbled and fell, but managed to land on their knee, skinning them, before rolling helplessly over onto their sides. Hernandez always stopped and helped them back onto their feet, making sure they got going safely again. Never were twenty people so glad to enter a store before, even Felipe was tired from the long walk.

During that day, similar situations occurred throughout

dozens of towns and cities along the coastline of Tierra. As Lysandra anticipated, some of the mermaids didn't make it. Yet miraculously a little over four hundred women and their daughters made it, one way or another, to their nearest Elegant Fashions Inc. Additionally fifty of their husbands or guardians arrived with them. Per Inez Franks' orders, the store staff took care of the women's many needs until they could be safely teleported to the Underground.

Tim reported Lysandra had created a smooth tunnel that led to the tunnel beneath Brom Tower. That tunnel led into the hidden spaceship being run by the robots, Alpha and Beta. They continued to maintain their pseudo world of Madiera, just in case their women ever needed to leave Tierra. Their original spaceship had landed just north of Brom Tower in an abandoned rock quarry. It had then been covered up, hidden from sight. A tunnel led from the ship's cargo and docking bay to the basement of the tower. Now a side tunnel connected to that original tunnel, leading to the Underground's subterranean quarters. Tim reported back, "Benjamina! What a positively brilliant idea! There is room for all of them. With all the bots still operational and since the mermaids have a foot, they can operate the mechanical arms. Brilliant, positively brilliant!"

"Thanks. We've got to get all the medical machines fired up. As we bring them here, we have to remove their lip plates and heal their lips. That will give them the use of their mouth and teeth back. It'll help them a bit. Anything is better than nothing," Benjamina replied.

An hour later, they were ready to begin operations. Tim and Andres prepared to operate the teleport machine. Darcy, Dawn, Eric, and Sally would be there to catch them upon arrival and safely lead them into the next room, where Benjamina and Rafaela would heal two women's lips at a time. When each batch was finished, Annie and Sam would lead them to the ship and Madiera. Petrona and Elana were already in Madiera, ready to help Alpha get them into homes and to help them discover how to operate the bots. Additionally, the two women pulled in many others of their kind to help out.

Benjamina made contact with Gracia, who was about to leave for their store. *Just let me know when you are there and we'll begin rescuing you. I think we have everything worked out here. Let everyone know we will be removing their lip plates and healing your lips. That way you can use your mouth and teeth to help. I know that it's not much, but. . .*

That will be a huge help when you don't have anything else. Thank you, Benjamina. You are saving us all! Gracia sent her. Now everyone waited. Around noon, Gracia reported they were ready. Tim and Andres began bringing them from the Villa del Rey store to their pad, two at a time, beginning with Gracia and her four year old daughter, Teresa.

Darcy needed to catch Gracia as she landed, but Teresa didn't need any help. "My little princess here hops better than the rest of us," Gracia praised her little girl. "Thank you all."

"Follow me, Benjamina and Rafaela are in the next room waiting to fix you up," Dawn explained, leading the two. While Teresa hopped about looking at the machines and asking questions, Benjamina repaired Gracia's lips and removed her heavy earrings as well.

"I never knew these could be mended. This is so much better. We are all terrified of falling and landing on our faces. With those plates, we'd probably kill ourselves or smash our jaws in, which is just as bad. You are right. It's a little bit more freedom. Diego, look, she's fixed my lips up." Diego arrived, carrying their two year old Hermina.

Annie stepped in, "If you four will come with us, we'll take you to where you will be staying. Be prepared for quite a surprise. I am afraid it is a mile walk though, but a totally smooth one." Little Teresa hopped right after her. "She's a natural at it."

"Yes, she certainly is. We are seeing that with all the older children. Never having two legs and arms, they are not as terrified as we adults are. Honestly, she's fearless," Gracia replied, obviously proud of her daughter.

Benjamina added, "Once we get everyone here safely, I'll come by and we can all have a long talk. There is hope, Gracia. We just need some days to get all five hundred of you here."

Several hours later, Adalina Valen Donat appeared on the pad. Tim recognized her immediately. "Well this is a surprise. Adalina, the Sector ID Minister's wife, right."

"Yes, please just kill me now. I can't live like this."

"Please follow me, Adalina," Annie requested. Tim hastily alerted Benjamina.

A short hop later, Benjamina said, "Welcome Adalina Valen. I've some bad news for you. Your husband, Emeryk, is certain you are dead. Apparently, they teleported the remains of your arm back to the space port. Still we are offering you sanctuary here. I'll be removing your lip plates and healing up your lips now. That way you can use your mouth. After that, we've got a place for you, where you stand a good chance of being able to live well on your own."

"How can I ever live on my own? I was kidnaped and turned into this half-woman freak. I can't go back to Emeryk, not like this. Please, just kill me, because I can't even do that myself anymore."

"Let's get you fixed up and into a safe home. In a few days, I'll come by and we can talk more."

They all worked fifteen-hour days, handling ninety people per day. On the second day, they were all surprised to see Nita Valen appearing on their teleport pad. Like many of the women, she was in deep grief. She wailed an explanation, "I was helpless before and I saw this as a way to gain a better life. It was. I was actually helping so many people, making up for all the evil I have caused. Now I am worse off than before. Please, take care of my son here and put me out of my misery. I deserve it."

They heard hundreds of stories about the kidnappings and soon realized Antonio had gotten so many of his "volunteers" by outright abductions. Benjamina knew she would need to do an enormous amount of therapy work on these five hundred. Six days later, they finally finished the massive teleport project, though Tim stayed in touch with Inez for several more days, in case more women showed up later on. None did, however.

Leaving Tim to watch the monitors and Petrona to watch the children, the others then headed over to Madiera.

Elana pointed out the electric lights along the tunnel. “Looks like Alpha and Beta have extended their electrical system to this new tunnel. Cool. We don’t have to mess with keeping a lot of lanterns going.”

They found Gracia now inhabiting one of the quadraplex units. Originally designed in the shape of a cross, it provided separate living quarters for four families and gave them a common room at the center of the cross. This way the four families could help each other with their living needs. Considering the dependent nature of these women and the relatively few who had husbands, Gracia had moved more than four families into single quadraplex units. With the exception of her unit, she had at least one or two men in each quadraplex, along with their wives and children, and put four women into each of the four wings. That way each unit had at least one man there to help the sixteen women.

In her unit, she had with her the families of Alicia, Juana, and Renata. Plus, Natalia and Marcela were with her as well as Nita, Felipe, and Adalina. The latter two women she wanted to keep close to her so she could keep an eye on them. Nita, the woman who had handed out all the debilitating body modifications, did seemed reformed, but she took no chances yet. Adalina was the wife of the alien leader, even though he believed she was dead.

Benjamina knew she was taking a big risk by bringing all these women here to the secret spaceship. Gracia, Andres, Nita, and Adalina were all Valens and could well be considered by many as their enemies, though Gracia and Andres were never directly involved in any treasonous actions against the Midlands. She had explained this to her group earlier, “I have to believe people can change, that people can become better people. If we say once bad, always bad, then why are we working on a science of the mind and spirit? We have to believe people can change for the better.” However, for security reasons, they decided they would not tell them precisely where their spaceship was located. Besides, once inside Madiera, it looked like an actual world, only a small one.

They found the large group sitting in the large central

living room. Felipe and the three four year olds were running and hopping about playing games, truly happy. Upon seeing them enter, Gracia exclaimed, “This place is wonderful. We don’t know how to thank you. All these strange machines and bots – they are helping us immensely. Doors open if we just say ‘open.’ These other arm machines, we can sort of work them. I actually was able to eat my own breakfast, awfully slow and cumbersome, but I did it. What we women really love are the hair bots. A minute in one of them and our long hair is fully brushed, all the tangles gone! Simply amazing.”

“We are so glad things are improving for you,” Benjamina replied. “I had hoped it would.” Everyone had many questions, and they spent some time trying to answer them. Then Benjamina got down to business. “What we are going to do now is to use our new therapy methods on all of you. When we finish, you and we can evaluate the results.” She realized this meant nothing to these people as yet.

The ten divided up and began to give the seven mermaids, along with Marcela, Andres, and Diego their needed therapy sessions. While they all had already used their own katalyein skills to erase the lip surgeries they’d endured, the emotional trauma they’d experience when they lost their Calder-given powers was severe and rested upon the similar terror incidents when their bodies had been transformed by Calder and the diablo rojo fish. More often than not, these lay upon events that had occurred during their births.

It turned out to be a long day of therapy sessions. However, the men progressed rapidly, as well as Emilio and Carlos. When they finished up, Diego and Andres had fixed supper for everyone. Over dinner, Nita asked, “I feel so alive now, so happy, in spite of my physical limitations. Can I learn to give these sessions to others? If so, I can continue to really help others.” The other women agreed with her, begging to be taught how to do it. “If you do, then we eight can help with more of our women,” she added, begging to be allowed to help.

“Of course, you can learn how to do it. It is very simple really. Tomorrow morning, we’ll return and get you eight all hatted up on how to do it. Then we’ll tackle eighteen more of you,” Benjamina promised. “I was so hoping you would all want to learn how to do this."

Nita spoke up, "I feel so good now. I wish everyone could have these kinds of benefits, but will I ever really and truly be able to make amends for all the evil that I have done? Is there really any hope for me, honestly?"

Everyone looked at Benjamina, who considered her answer carefully. "Nita, we have to believe people can change for the better. If not, we are all doomed eventually. We've all done some things we are not proud of, things we should not have done, even things we failed to do when we should have done something. We have regrets. Yet if we recognize them, that is the first step towards recovery. Taking responsibility for what we have done, and, as you put it, making amends, must then be done. As far as I am concerned, I believe you are well on your way towards doing just that."

Gracia added, "Me too, Nita, I am very proud of what you have been doing. Benjamina, we owe you and your friends here more than we can ever repay. Do you realize we would all have likely died if you had not come to our rescue? It is still beyond us all here, how you few got to us so fast and got five hundred of us to safety."

"It is what we do, Gracia, helping people, but I admit, we had a little help from Lysandra," Benjamina answered her.

"But until now, we've never heard of you and your people here," Adalina broke in slightly confused. "It's like you were all sort of under ground somehow. Did any of you know of her and these people before?" she asked.

"Diego and I met Benjamina once a few years back, that's all," Gracia admitted.

Adalina's eyes flashed, "You are not the supposed Underground that Emeryk has been searching for the past five years are you? My god, you must be!"

Benjamina merely smiled.

"But you killed Valen's army, if what Emeryk supposes is so," she added.

"What would have happened if that army of three thousand were allowed to proceed with their objectives?" Benjamina asked. "All of the Midlands would be under siege now, war and horrors over all the land. Thousands of people killed, untold suffering. And for what? Just so Lord Valen could rule the world?"

Gracia spoke up, "Hey, he was trying to kill off us priestesses in Villa del Rey. Look, we priestesses all know Valen Tower has not been providing any of the Blackwater Ultimatum services they are supposed to be providing. Not one of the coastal cities has ever had any help from them. No healing, no *mentales* aid, nothing. We were providing it. If Valen can't even take care of its own towns and cities, what the hell are they doing by trying to take over the whole world?"

Adalina admitted, "Oh, I think his plan was to then to get the aliens to open up our world to the galaxy. We'd receive all their advanced technology and machines. Medical machines could be very valuable. Electricity-operated things would be very nice to have, like in their buildings at the space port. Even space travel would be ours for the asking. I think that's what he had in mind."

"She's right, I think," Nita added. "Open up Tierra to the galaxy. Now I am not so sure it's the right thing to do. All men would soon have blasters and nowhere would be safe anymore."

These revelations of the motives of Lord Valen came as a surprise to Benjamina and her group. At long last, they knew why Lord Valen had done what he'd done. She replied, "I think the question is simply, are we ready for such technology and what goes along with it?"

Gracia answered that one, "Not if the only way we have to settle disputes is by fighting. Pedro Valen's army left me no choice but to fight. Calder's modifications to my body left me no other choice than to do what I did to keep us all alive. I can see now Empress Amy Blackwater's order to settle disputes with a sword was the right one. I killed a thousand young men by using my godlike powers over water. I never saw any of their faces, yet surely they were not evil men. Tierra is not ready for the technology of the aliens; we're not ready to have blasters."

By the end of January, they finished up with the women's first round of therapy sessions. Benjamina now had four hundred of the mermaids trained in her therapy methods. Their emotional traumas associated with their kidnaping and horrific body modifications were gone, leaving the women at least mentally at peace. On the physical side, Alpha and Beta had not been idle. At this point, they invented and installed robotic kitchens. All a woman had to do was to vocally order up a meal and the many bots took care of preparing it. Only now did Gracia finally relax a little. Her women could at least survive in this strange world of Madiera.

Other changes occurred as well. Hernandez married both Gabriela and Francesca, providing support for the both of them as well as the other fourteen other women in their quadraplex. Three more daughters were born and were also mermaids like their mothers. This caused Alpha and Beta to begin a detailed chromosome analysis of the women and men now living here. Perhaps in time they could work out some kind of genetic modifications so that future children would be born with normal bodies.

Natalia and Marcela, discovering the special methods developed by Alpha for the women of Madiera to breed with each other, begged for the robot's aid. At the end of January, both were happily pregnant with each other's child. They didn't have to shag some guy, as Marcela had suggested earlier.

Gracia took care of the older children of the Underground during the daytime hours. The five year olds, Ken and Luisa, became constant playmates with Felipe and the mermaids Teresa, Inez, Isabelle, and Elmira. As Gracia put it, the physical body differences between the four and the three five year olds did not seem to matter much at all. True, the mermaids had almost no lateral movement in their leg, but to the children, this didn't matter at all. She knew Diego loved her and that her body's strange form didn't matter to him either. Summed up, she began to have some hope for the future.

As February came, Benjamina and the Underground shifted their attention to any possible ways they could undo more of Calder's impact on the mermaids. The medical machines examined several of the women for hours, but offered up no additional remedies. "Well, if we can't do anything about their physical bodies, what about their minds? Can we possibly turn them into *mentales* gifted?" asked Rafaela.

"There is always the possibility ingesting enough psi-dust over time that they might develop it," Tim suggested. "After all, that was what started all of us in the first place centuries ago."

"Hey, what about doing what our mothers did?" Benjamina asked. "They worked on their *mentales* gifts and trained themselves to do many, many things that they did not originally possess. I know there are only a few of the mermaids who have the gift now, but we could work with them and see if they could develop telekinetic skills. I think we should also try Tim's idea too, but we ought to get each woman's permission to try that on them."

Venerada Marisol agreed to supply them with ordinary psi-crystals. Dawn, Darcy, Eric, and Sally ground the crystals into fine powders. Andres and Rafaela then mixed measured doses into their test batch of two dozen mermaids, keeping careful records of the dosages given, from a small amount to a rather large one. Theirs was a carefully controlled experiment, which greatly interested Venerada Marisol. Why? If this proved successful, then she had another way to increase the dwindling number of *mentales* gifted individuals.

By spring, Rafaela and Andres finished plotting their results on a graph. They were successful in creating *mentales* gifted from the head blind! Their curve was exponential. Beyond a certain amount, the extra amount given made no difference either in getting the desired result or the speed of getting it. Below a certain weak dosage, nothing happened, though perhaps if they continued those low dosages over a long enough time period, something might happen. Now given the proper dosage from their three-month experiment, they began in earnest on all the others.

During this same time period, Benjamina worked with the few who already had the gift to see if they could be coached into developing more "gifts," namely telekinesis. She began with Gracia. In time, they discovered what Amy and Jan had:

new skills can be developed with a whole lot of practice and patience. While Gracia's newfound telekinetic skills were barely half of what Calder had given her, she was ecstatic over them. Now she could do far more things for herself. One by one the other gifted had this skill developed in themselves.

What they all found most interesting, but not unexpected in hindsight, was all the newly made *mentales* gifted had telekinesis as their primary gift. Benjamina began to believe the nature of one's gift depended largely on the environment of the person. Darcy, Dawn, and Eric were raised around the training of hawks and eagles, so that was the direction their gifts had taken. Sally, on the other hand, had been around the raising and training of horses and her gift lay in that area. Curiously enough, none of the new *mentales* gifted had any real healing skills, much to their disappointment.

Gracia and her group took the responsibility of training the new *mentales* gifted. That much, they could do easily. While it took the rest of 1251 to get everyone handled, for the mermaids, their lives were salvaged, and now they began to want to help others in some way.

Late December, Nita, Gracia, Rafaela, and Benjamina sat around the commons of the quadraplex discussing their work. Nita said, "You know, I am now convinced we humans of Tierra are simply not ready to expand to the wide galaxy out there. We need your science of the mind and spirit broadly known, Benjamina. In groups, we play follow the leader all the time, even if that leader is leading us into destruction."

"What do you mean?" Gracia asked.

"Look, in every group, every town, every village, there are key men and women who, for whatever reason, are looked up to by the rest of the people. Call them the opinion leaders, for want of a better word. I was once an opinion leader. Whatever I wore, from dresses to heels to jewelry, in time, all the other noblewomen and ladies of the courts simply had to have and wear that too. I learned to do this from my mother Carmen Valen, who had this down to a fine art. I began to wear the pipe corsets. Soon, women had to have them too, then later, even men. I got toe shoes and women soon had to have them as well. I got my lip plates and earrings and soon others had to have them as well."

"Follow the leader, peer pressure, call it what you will, but we humans are at this time more like a herd of animals, doing what their opinion leaders say, dressing like their peers. Look, I will be the first to admit those pipe corsets, toe shoes, lip plates, and fetter gowns were absolutely horrible, designed to cut one's mobility down to nearly nothing, making life extremely miserable. Yet hundreds of the nobles, lords, and ladies just had to have them too. It didn't matter to them I was leading them down a terribly wrong path."

Gracia nodded and expanded, "I saw this with my priestesses. Originally, none of us had those awful lip plates and huge earrings. Then Natalia joined us and she had them because she was 'nobility.' Within a short time, I had other priestesses begging me to let them have them too. We met as a group and the group decided we all should have them. I am now convinced if you allow a whole group to make key decisions, those decisions will not necessarily be good ones. I knew better, but I was too weak to stand alone against them. I could see that if I let the eight or so who wanted to get them and look like Natalia, then soon the others would feel pressured into having them too. We are just a bunch of herd animals, when it comes down to it."

She went on, "Another thing. You've told us what was happening at the Council of the Lords this year. My family, who have written me off as good as dead now, were all body modified years ago. They and the lords of Villa del Rey showed up at the council with their many modifications, in stark contrast to the current styles of the Midlands which is basically a reversion back to the gowns and heels that Nita wore before the body modification phase began. I predict there will soon be a resurgence in women wanting to get body modifications once more. I don't know if it will be among the Coastal City-State women and men or if some of the Midlands and Easterlings will do it. Mark my words, my father and mother and the other lords will be setting new trends. Donkey see, donkey do."

Rafaela chuckled and added, "True. Plus, they will find reasons for doing it, justifications like the ones we were fed.

Great power must be physically tempered to avoid the abuse of that power."

Benjamina cringed. "Yes, I know, mom started that one. I can see her point. She saw one weird planetary system, the Wasp Worshipers. That was their philosophy, physically temper their leaders so they had no way to abuse the immense powers placed upon them. She and Jan went there and got modified, seeing that as the only way they could return here to their home world. Yet in doing so, to be frank, they got aberrated by that society. Even though they apparently felt no pain from the many surgeries they endured to get their bodies modified to the wasp culture, we now know they had severe physical pain trauma that was wholly buried from their conscious minds. We know those traumas most definitely affect one's conduct in the present. Words spoken during the trauma are particularly nasty. 'I can't ever do anything right.' Given those words said to a person while they are unconscious and in pain, later on in their lives, they will always be seen to be doing the wrong things."

"Hey, it gets worse," Rafaela pointed out. "They are then likely to say those same words later on around one of their children, who gets hurt and is recording a trauma incident while they are unconscious. Now their children will thereafter tend to display the same aberration. I've seen that happen several times now in some of the people with whom I was giving therapy sessions. Aberration is contagious. I think it may well be vastly worse between mother and her children because they both share a common traumatic incident, the birth of the child."

"Golly, I never thought of that," Gracia exclaimed. "What about accidental traumas while we are pregnant? If a mother got hurt, got a blow to her womb, while she receives a trauma, won't the unborn child also receive a similar one? I would think the words spoken around the mother would be particularly important since both the mother and the child would have them in common from there on out. At least with we mermaids, I insisted we do very little physical hopping during our last two months before we gave birth. I figured all that jumping would be too hard on us, but now I can see it would also harm the unborn child, if they are actually recording these things, pre-birth that is. Do we know if they do that? Experience these traumas before they are actually born?"

"More research," Benjamina declared. "Before this crisis of yours, we were doing extensive research on this, particularly Rafaela and Andres. She had begun to discover indeed several subjects did seem to have pre-birth traumas."

"Well, we were both suited to doing this work," Rafaela explained, "because we both had lost our arms, when the Valen group captured us and tied us up and our arms froze. We nearly died, but Ben and Tim saved us. What with the body modifications we'd had, we couldn't do much useful work, but giving therapy sessions and doing the research for Benjamina – that we could do. We can't wait to get back to it."

"Say, what about us?" Gracia asked.

Nita caught on to what Gracia was thinking too. "Yes, what about us? We now know how to do the therapy sessions. Can we start delivering them to others around here, wherever we are at?" She laughed. "You know we haven't the foggiest notion where on Tierra that we are? Where is this Madiera world we're in right now? Anyway, couldn't we help you with the research? We can't do much else to help, but we can do that."

"Maybe we look too strange for normal people to accept us," Gracia countered. "We're not priestesses anymore. Plus, each of us doesn't have our own guardian any longer. We are incredibly vulnerable."

"Your help is welcome. Elegant Fashions Inc has given us some rooms in their facilities around Tierra to conduct our therapy sessions. Originally, she gave them to us so we could erase the many traumas of those who were body modified in their towns. I'm sure she will allow us to continue to use those rooms," Benjamina replied, thinking fast. She had here a trained group of therapy givers, ideal for a large research project. Logistics would be the problem with these mermaids.

No one in Brom had ever seen them before, though a few who had been on long trips down to a coastal town had brought back strange tales of these mermaid-looking priestesses. The biggest problem she saw was the fact they couldn't write or take notes on what they did with a subject or the results found. Well, neither could Andres and Rafaela, for that matter. In their case, when the two finished a session, they then told her about it, and she had written up the notes of the session for them. With something like four hundred of these women giving therapy sessions, she couldn't possibly keep up with the necessary record keeping, so vital in any research project.

"Okay, your help is accepted. Give me some time to work out how we can best do this, especially the needed record keeping," Benjamina replied.

"Thank you, you are giving us a way to continue to help other people, besides our own selves. Thank you," Gracia gushed, extremely grateful to have a way to do something useful with her life and those of her fellow mermaids.

Venerada Marisol looked over Rafaela's charts of the optimum dose of psi-dust that turned on the *mentales* gifts in the many mermaid women. "In a way, this could be the answer to the dwindling number of *mentales* gifted. I suspect your results have been substantially influenced by the fact these women had already been given the *mentales* gifts by Calder and then taken away. I suspect they were thus more susceptible to the dust than a person who never had the gifts in the first place."

"You are probably right, venerada," Rafaela agreed with her.

"Still, Rafaela, I am not going to make use of these findings just yet. You see, how am I or anyone else able to determine who out there in Brom should suddenly get this *mentales* gift? With the mermaids, it was desperately needed for their very survival. In our case here in Brom, would not I be playing the role of a goddess, if I determine that man or that woman should get the gifts? What if I should make a misjudgment and turn out another Paco Valen here in Brom? I don't think I have the right to pick and choose who should get the priceless gifts and who should not. So I will keep these findings to myself. Perhaps one day when we are all wiser, then we can play god."

"I think that is a wise decision, venerada," Rafaela again agreed with her. "The misuse of the gifts cost Andres and me our arms and very nearly our lives. Perhaps if Benjamina gets us a workable science of the mind and spirit, we will be able to make such judgments." Thus, the knowledge of the single largest man-created batch of *mentales* gifted was known only to a few, mostly the Underground members.

Chapter 11 Moves and Countermoves

"Well, this is a fine mess," Venerado Fons declared. "All of the priestesses have lost their powers. Incredible. Still, they have given us what we needed. They might as well die at this point; they haven't any real life without their powers. Let's forget about them. We simply cannot take care of them. Gracia is lost to us. Hopefully, Andres will return to us soon."

Capo Roberto replied, "True. Without their powers, they can't even live without someone constantly with them, and we can't spare anyone to waste all their time wiping their butts. Still there is no doubt they fulfilled the vacuum in all those coastal cities with their healing and curing skills. We now have the full support of all these coastal towns."

"But we need to keep that support, Roberto. I think we need to talk with Antonio about this. I'm sending for him," Fons declared and did so.

An hour later, the slow moving Antonio and Julio finally entered the Renegade Hacienda. "Have you heard? all the priestesses have lost every bit of their powers! Natalia is totally helpless," Antonio began after taking a seat in the gardens close to Fons. "I thought this priestesses thing was too good to be true. Still, it has accomplished its objective. I have the cities and towns along the coast of Tierra in my pocket. Are we going to do anything about those priestesses now?"

"I don't see there is anything we can do for them, except let nature run her course. Do you want to pay five hundred to provide them 24-7 care? I certainly can't afford that nor do I want to. They will never be able to do anything productive ever again, except leech off someone else for everything," Fons replied.

"My thoughts exactly. Nature run her course. I like that. Of course, I hate to lose Natalia, but she's wholly useless now. She's better off dead than the way she is," Antonio stated without any regrets over abandoning her to her obvious fate. "So why have you summoned us here?"

"The loss of all the priestesses must be handled. As you

well know, a major factor in our success in all these towns has been providing healing and curing for the locals, something long denied them by the supposedly ruling tower at Valen. With the priestesses gone, what is to keep them continuing to back you and us?"

"I see your point. For once, you are ahead of me. I was rather shaken by the sudden news of the priestesses," Antonio admitted.

"Quite right. Understandable. We need somehow to fill the vacuum they've left behind. We need *mentales* healers in these towns. Simple enough," Fons said dryly.

"But how? I can see we need to act fast before the locals start getting other ideas," Antonio pointed out.

"We've gone over all our records. There are six who have some healing skills including our own Anita."

"Six? Pathetic. I've got twenty towns and cities where the priestesses worked."

"We know. I've a plan. What we need to do is place a *mentales* gifted in each of the towns. When someone comes to the former priestess hacienda for curing, he or she will contact us telepathically. We will then summon one of the few who can heal and Roberto's circle can teleport them there and back later."

"Brilliant. I like that. I see where you are heading with this. You want me to provide the twenty *mentales* gifted and pay them to sit around the old priestess haciendas."

"Exactly. You provide the watchdogs and we'll supply the healers. We need to act fast. Word of the demise of the priestesses will travel fast. We dare not risk losing the ground we've gained," Fons stated passionately. "Our survival depends on their continued support."

"And our money," Julio added.

"Precisely," Roberto joined in.

"Accepted. We have a deal. I find it's incredible what just providing the minimalist support that Valen Tower should have been providing all these years has done for us. Incredible, just incredible."

"Yes, Antonio, a little healing goes a long way. Besides, we've added some fifty *mentales* gifted to those who are tower trained. That's even better. I just wish more had healing gifts," Fons replied with a sigh. "No controlling what gifts a person will get."

"Say, doesn't breeding with the right people help?" Julio asked.

"Some, yes some. Even that seems to be dying out considerably," Roberto sadly pointed out.

"Next, we should be attending the Council of the Lords come spring," Fons put forth.

"Which one?" Julio asked. He was referring to the one held at Castle Valen for the Westerlings and the one held in Exchange City at which Lord Valen wasn't permitted to attend. Both meetings would begin on the same day, the first of May this year.

"Both," Fons said with a wry smile. "Look, Antonio, Julio, you now control a large number of the cities and towns in the Midlands and Easterlings. That alone entitles you and the lords from those cities to attend the one in Exchange City. By the same argument, you and the other city lords here in the Westerlings are entitled to go to Lord Valen's council."

Antonio laughed. "You are the devious one. Yet, how can we be in both places at the same time?"

"Simple, you go to the more important one in Exchange City. Julio can attend the one in Valen. Perhaps I should accompany you, Antonio. Roberto can accompany Julio, if you think that wise."

"Devious, devious. I like how you think, my good man. Yes, I have been contemplating attending the council in Exchange City for the last two years. Now that we've expanded as much as we have with the priestesses, it's time I put in an appearance. Shake things up a bit. Julio. You go to Valen. Just watch your back! I don't trust them in the slightest," Fons explained.

Spring of 1251 had come. Exchange City was a hive of activity. Hundreds of visitors had arrived, booking all available rooms at the inns. Now that the emperor and empress had been effectively abandoned, the Council of the Lords met in the old throne room. Amid a trumpet fanfare, Lord and Lady

Rusden took their seats on the throne. Each meeting, a different major lord, that is, one who had one of the seven towers in his city, took the throne and ran the meeting. While Lord Rusden wore a fine suit from Elegant Fashions Inc, Lady Rusden wore the women's old style six-inch stilettos, a pipe corset, and a light brown satin gown. Like many women, she greatly desired to wear the most fashionable apparel, as fitting her high position. The former Lord Henry Rusden, who had given up the throne because of all his massive body modifications, slowly moved into his assigned position behind him, while his wife got behind Lady Rusden.

As with all the former *mentales* gifted rulers who had been so heavily body modified, when they resigned their positions to a head blind relative, they became head of the newly formed Elite Protection Squad, to which all the former modified *mentales* gifted staff were members. Thus, they both used their psi gifts to help defend the new rulers and also to act as truth sayers. all these men and women had been healed by the Underground, though they did not know whom it was that had done this priceless thing for them. Both the men and women wore the old style six-inch women's stilettos, the lowest they could wear with their partially repaired feet. The women often chose to keep their tiny waists, but wore gowns similar to the reigning ladies. Most all of them wore the new, top of the line alien prosthetic hands, which worked drastically better than the cheap ones they were originally given.

Just when the many lords thought all the entrance fanfares were finished, the trumpets sounded again. The deep bass voice bellowed, "Lord and Lady Gabino Rosa, Villa del Rey, Lord and Lady Antonio del Rey representing the Coastal City-States and Venerado Fons Valen of their Renegade Tower." Besides Gabino and Margaretta and Antonio and Marcelina, the lord's advisor Alvaro Rossi and his wife Ria and Venerado Fons followed them along with Delfina, Fons' wife. Behind them, a dozen other city lords and their wives walked into the huge throne room.

A study in apparel contrasts was quite apparent. Gabino's group was fully body modified, with lip plates and toe shoes. The other city lords were dressed in nice suits, while their wives also wore the old style stilettos and gowns similar to all the other women.

Someone called out, “Lord Rusden! Do something about them!”

He rose, “Here, here. You are not part of this council.” His tone suggested long withheld anger. These were Valens and cohorts!

Lord Gabino yelled, “Oh, but we most certainly *are* part of this council. With me are a dozen city lords, who make up our new territory. Whether you like it or not, we control all your shipping. Regrettably, the other Westerlings cities are not with us, since you’ve outlawed all Westerlings attendance at this council. However, if you care to check, all these with me belong to the Midlands or Easterlings. That gives us the right to attend this Council of the Lords.”

His face flush with anger, Lord Rusden glanced over the minor lords moving into the room behind the impossibly slow moving Gabino. He spotted Lord Nasik. “Lord Nasik. Have you turned traitor to me?”

“Nay, Lord Rusden, it is you who have betrayed us for over a century now. Not once have you sent your *mentales* healers to us, despite my repeated requests. Not once did you send anyone help to our people who came down with the Verge Sickness, many of whom died of it. Nay, you have never lived up to your Blackwater Ultimatum rules. Yet, year after year, you send your tax men to collect from us. Now we send our taxes to Lord Antonio and Lord Gabino, who are doing for us what you and your tower have never done. We owe you no further allegiance. I speak for my colleagues here, we have formed a new territory, the Coastal City-States. Our Renegade Tower *does* provide for us what Rusden Tower never has and many times over.”

“I’ll send my army down to Nasik and teach you to spout treason,” Lord Rusden spat.

“If you do that, I guarantee you not a single ship on Tierra will ever carry your cargo again. Our harbor will stand idle and you can carry all your precious grain overland in wagons thousands of miles to the Easterlings. Oh, I would send very strongly armed forces with those shipments to protect them from bandits. Just try it, Lord Rusden. That goes for the rest of you lords. If you attack our cities and towns, we lords guarantee you all sea trading will cease forever," Lord Nasik spat back quite sharply.

"You, you, you can't do that," Lord Rusden yelled.

"Oh yes we very well can do it and you all know it. Ask your advisors how valuable your sea trading has been the last few years. I guarantee you the loss of that large an amount will cost you incredibly dearly!" Lord Nasik shouted back.

Acting as a friendly, kindly mediator, Lord Antonio interrupted the angry outbursts. "Gentlemen, gentlemen. If I may have a word. All of you major lords are just as guilty of failing to provide the basic services to your coastal towns as Lord Rusden and you well know it. Further, as you likely know, the Coastal City-States does not now nor likely ever will field an army, unlike yourselves. While it is your decision to attack our member cities and towns with your army, our defense is an economic one, total loss of all sea trading. In the end, while you may control a coastal city by force of arms, the economic losses you will suffer from there on out will be staggering. Check with your own financial advisors if you doubt me."

He then added, "Let me also point out that since we do not field an army, we will not be 'attacking' you. We have no intentions of marching a conquering, plundering army over the Midlands or the Easterlings. We are shipping lords, merchant lords, if you please."

Standing behind Lord Rusden, his *mentales* gifted uncle sent, *He has a valid point. Fully one quarter of your yearly income comes from the extensive trading done through your southern ports. If you lose that, you will be financially crippled!*

Lord Rusden calmed down. "The meeting will take a brief recess while the ruling lords meet to discuss this. Lord Bolivar, with me." He motioned to the other lords who had a tower in their city. The men made a hasty exit to a side room. The other lords and ladies began chatting. While some were most unfriendly, all were not.

Lord Hayden of Hayden's Crossing came up to Lord

Nasik. "Welcome again. I do hope this does not come to blows. Honestly, over a third of my income comes from hauling grain down to your docks. I think that it is high time that some of us stick up for what was supposed to be our rights according to that Blackwater Ultimatum. We've never seen any healers either. We've heard that you have some very strange priestesses who do the healing?"

"Welcome to you, my friend. Yes, we had those priestesses from Renegade Tower. They did their job and have now moved on. We don't know where they went. These days, the Renegade Tower responds directly and immediately. All we have to do is what we used to do with the priestesses: bring the sick or injured to their building. A *mentales* gifted is always on duty there. He magically contacts the tower and they send a healer at once. We have found it is simpler to group the sick and injured into one batch and send for the healer only once. Still, my people are singing the praises of these priestesses and their Renegade Tower."

For a half hour, the group had similar conversations, while others were condemnatory. Meantime, the ladies had their own chats on entirely different matters. "Oh Lady Rosa, I am surprised you are still wearing those awful lip plates and toe boots," Lady Hayden commented with a teasing smile. "We all got rid of those years ago. So awful to wear, I'm told."

The *mentales* gifted wife of the ex-lord Rusden pointed to Lady Delfina's grey alien hands. "I see you are still wearing those really horrid original alien hands. We've all got these new models. See. They more closely match our skin color and they work so much better. Life got so much better too, once we had our feet partly healed. As I understand it, once your feet get reformed for toe shoes, mind you they are most elegant, just impossible to walk in, the healing only goes a little ways. We can't wear anything lower than these six inch ones. But honestly, dear, walking is so much easier in them."

"But we like our lip plates immensely, though I have always thought these toe shoes are going way too far. Do those new hands of yours fall off as easily as these do?" Delfina asked, curious about them.

"Oh no, not at all! We're told that they can lift up to five pounds before coming off. We can't lift heavy pots, mind you, but they stay on so much better. It's a shame that you didn't get yours," she replied.

"I suppose so. Say, you speak as if you somehow got healed. Is there a special *mentales* healer that you went to?" Delfina asked, growing more curious.

"Well, as a matter of fact yes. They live up in Brom somewhere. We all were invited to Brom Castle, where a man and a woman used some kind of strange machine to heal our lips and feet. They also provided these new hands for us all," she replied. She couldn't help adding, "But then there is so much hatred against this treachery of Valen and the Westerlings, I can't imagine those healers would have helped you. Really, convincing us all to get our hands cut off, why, that is not likely to ever be forgiven."

Delfina could have reacted angrily, but chose a different path. "We were victims of that treacherous man too. Thank god, he's dead. Yet, we live on, relics of the untold suffering he caused all of you and us as well. I am so glad you were able to get some healing, my lady. Say, were those new hands terribly expensive? How much did the healers charge you?" She hoped it was a steep price.

"Well, thank you. Yes, it has made such a difference in our lives. Honestly so many of us were ready just to give up, you know. Yet with all this healing and new hands, life is so much more bearable now. Not perfect, mind you, just much better. Oh, they gave us the hands for free and also the healing. Such generosity. We are so grateful to Lord Brom."

Delfina decided she had to run into Lady Bolivar of Brom before the council ended. Could she possibly get some of those new hands for her group? She doubted they could get the healing, but maybe the hands. She found it ironic that Lord Paco had fully hobbled all the ruling *mentales* of the Midlands, even removing their hands, and now they were back to battery, more or less, and she and her group, who had only done these things to help Lord Paco "convince" the other *mentales* to have these things done to their bodies, were stuck with them, living miserable lives. If nothing else, she wanted the new hands for her people.

Just then, the major lords returned. As a hush fell, Lord Rusden spoke, “We have agreed to accept the representatives of the Coastal City-States at the Council of the Lords and this Renegade Tower. They will not have a major vote, however.”

“Ah, so Wye does not have a major vote either?” Lord Gabino replied. “Come, come, we are a major player. Full voting powers or we slow down your shipments and let your produce rot before it arrives.”

“This is blackmail!” Lord Rusden fumed.

“So is denying a territory with its own tower full voting power, as all the other major towers,” Lord Gabino replied, refusing to back down.

“All right, then, full voting power. Now then can we get on to the business that we all came to discuss?” Lord Rusden gave in.

While the lords discussed relatively minor issues between them, Delfina moved as quickly as she could in her toe shoes towards Lady Bolivar. Unfortunately, her two-inch steps could not keep pace with the much larger ones of Lady Bolivar, who moved around the room, chatting with other ladies. It was nearly time for supper before she finally got herself close enough to talk with Lady Bolivar.

“Excuse me, Lady Bolivar. Might I have a word with you?” Delfina asked. She began to inquire about the new alien hands that were given out nearly five years ago.

“Oh dear, that was so long ago. I don’t know if there are any more of them still around. I will ask when I get back and let you know,” she replied.

The second day of the council, several of the minor lords began asking if the towers would soon be sending help their way. The major lords at least left them with the suggestion that they would talk to their towers about it.

A week later, word finally reached Benjamina and Tim about Delfina Valen’s request for twenty-one pairs of the new alien prosthetic hands. “Those people were Lord Valen’s helpers. They were backing his plan to mutilate us all. I say no way do we give them the good hands,” Tim argued. “And I sure as hell am not going to heal them. They are the enemy of the Midlands; look what they help do to us all.”

"Quite true. Still at this time they appear to be changing their ways, helping to heal others," Benjamina countered. "I think for goodwill and good faith, we should send them the hands, but no more. Leave them hobbled with the toe shoes."

"Good faith? What good faith did they show any of us?" Tim grumbled, remembering how awful life had been for him and the rest of his group when they lost their hands to Valen's nasty hoax. "Well, I see your point. Perhaps a little good faith may be in order. They've at least gotten the attention of the towers."

The next day twenty-one pairs of the hands appeared on the Renegade Tower's garden floor. Their protection network prevented Tim from landing them any closer.

When Lord Bolivar returned to Brom Castle, he summoned Venerada Marisol to him. "We've got a major problem coming." He outlined what had happened at the meeting. "Look, already all the coastal cities and larger towns have basically seceded from their governing territories, citing the tower's failure to provide services for them under the Ultimatum. I don't pretend to know what magic things you all do up there in your tower, but what exactly are the towers supposed to be doing? I gather healing the sick. I got blind-sided on this one, so did the other major lords. We've decided from now on, we are to bring our veneradas with us to the council meetings."

"Well, it said that, 'As the circles of all towers have been routinely ignoring the needs of the people within their lands, every other week, all circle members will spend an entire week out among the various towns and villages of their territory tending to the needs of the common man, whatever that need may be, from healing to constructions.' I admit that we have been lax in fulfilling these, but as you know travel in the winter is extremely dangerous up here. We routinely visit Hilliard Heights and occasionally Chester. We should do more. I will see to it, my lord."

"Good. I don't want any rebellions going on in my lands, not like that fool Rusden has down south. My god, he's lost control of his major coastal cities and towns. The idiot! At least their economic war threat won't bother us much up here," Lord Bolivar justified.

"I would not be so sure of that, but I suspect it won't come to that. There is too much at stake on both sides. I will be hard on me to attend the council, but I will do as you ask. Will that be all?" she asked. He nodded and she turned and left, but had to wait until the guard realized he needed to open the door for her.

A half hour later, her three capas met with her, and Marisol outlined the situation. "There is no escaping it; we are going to have to somehow get tower assistance to all the smaller towns and villages on some kind of a regular basis. Apparently, in the coastal towns, the Renegade Tower has one of their people stationed there at all times and that person lets the tower know when they need to send a healer. They must have an awful lot of the gifted to spare down there. I'm open to ideas? Do we bust up circles?"

One replied, "Well, Hilliard Heights is pretty well covered, since Anita spends half of each year there with her husband and his horse breeding and training. I can't see one of our tower technicians sitting around some office day and night twiddling their thumbs waiting for someone to break an arm and come to see him."

"I agree, our tower personnel are way too valuable to waste them like that, even if we just replace them every month," another agreed with the first. "How about hiring some emissaries — like head blind even. Pay them to sit and watch the office and have our Comm Network routinely check in with them. When something comes up, we can then use a circle to teleport a couple of healers or whoever is needed."

"Good idea," Marisol answered. "I like it. The emissaries can watch and observe and make suggestions for other things we can perhaps do for the town or village. I wonder how many we're going to need? Okay, that's my problem. I'll get us a workable solution. Thanks."

During June of 1251, she assigned one circle to visit the key towns and villages in their territory. In each, they purchased a small building, usually a home, and then hired a local person to be Brom Tower's official emissary. Once hired, the circle then made sure all those operating the Comm

Network became familiar with the emissary. The agreement was the emissaries would be contacted by telepathy every three hours during the day. If someone came by for assistance, the delay would be just a few hours. Further, the emissaries were also to see what else the tower might be able to do for their town, make suggestions at least.

By the end of July, all twenty towns and villages were quite pleased with their new connection to their mighty tower at Brom. Hardly any had actually been to Brom, but a few had at least seen Brom Tower and Castle at one time or another. When Marisol reported their initial success at the end of July, Lord Bolivar was pleased. *At least I won't be having mutiny problems in my lands.*

Part III Westerlings and Easterlings Mutinies

Chapter 12 Malaca Mutiny

Malaca was the largest city in the ancient kingdom of Abvera. Located nearly eight hundred miles from the coast up the Salamanca River, Malaca was nearly three thousand miles northwest of Valen and approximately eight hundred miles from the frozen northern coast of the Westerlings. With the sudden climate shift centuries ago, Abvera suffered massive changes, but not as severe as had the extreme northern kingdom of Zamora, which was now almost inhabitable, frozen solid all year round. Its once thriving city of Zona was a ghost of its former self, where a few hardy souls scratched out a living raising and training reindeer. Many had fled Zamora south into Abvera, swelling Malaca's population as well as other smaller towns.

Boasting some twenty-five thousand inhabitants, Malaca was the largest city in old Abvera. Still, its climate was a harsh one. Winters were long. Located on the southern bank of the Salamanca River, the lands around it were rolling low hills covered with fields of waist-high grasses, interspersed with groves of dense pines. Across the river from Malaca lay the Bosque Verde, a dense resinous pine forest roughly oval shape and some two hundred miles northwest to southeast, but one hundred on the other axis. The town of Manca lay within the forest at near its northwestern edge. Both south and east of Malaca is the Castilla Hills, a rough, rounded hilly land with mines and some patches of the resinous pines. Toledo lay some two hundred miles southeast of Malaca smack in the middle of this mining country. Iron, silver, copper, and some gems were mined here, one of the largest mining centers in the Westerlings. Toledo also produced swords.

Located far from the coast and ever farther from all other major cities that lay a thousand miles or more to the south, the culture and customs of Malaca were substantially different from that of Valen. Women wore their long black hair up in buns and wore wool caps with earflaps over their heads to keep warm. Men wore similar caps, often heavily embroidered with gay red and yellow angular designs. The women's heavy woolen dresses often had several petticoats beneath them and thick, tall socks. Men wore soft fleece-lined leather pants that ended at their knees, tucked into their tall boots. Women wore similar boots. The depth of winter snows dictated these styles. These were a hardy people, superstitious and fiercely independent.

Valen's annual taxation and soldier recruitment came in July and was always met with arguments and grumbling. "Robbing us of our young men, that's not fair." "What do we get for all these taxes we are paying?" Such were the blandest of the side comments those from Valen met when they came to collect and conscript men. Always, though, the Valen collectors came with a hundred soldiers to back them up and to protect them from perceived threats.

As a result of being located so distant from Plateau Grado, the center of the psi-dust from the massive explosion centuries ago, there were very few *mentales* gifted in Abvera and thus Malaca. Centuries ago, the witches were thriving here, curing the sick and healing the injured, but the Church of God had wiped them out. When the towers were first built, their tower was at Portillo, about fifteen hundred miles to the southeast of Malaca, but long ago Lord Valen had destroyed the tower, his first victory over the towers. The *mentales* gifted families, which were in that area, fled northwest and some settled in Malaca.

That didn't work out well. Soon Valen Tower came around and conscripted all young *mentales* gifted, forcing them to become tower circle members. Again these families fled and settled in the rugged Castilla Hills and in the dense forests of Bosque Verde. Only a few still remained in Malaca proper, many serving as advisors to Lord Ferdinan Malaca and Lady Luisa, who were now in their early forties and did not possess the "gift."

Yet there were a few other *mentales* gifted in Malaca around 1250 with entirely different stories. One of these was young Gervasi Quito, twenty-one. He was tall, well over six feet, a robust figure, and fighter trained. With thick eyebrows and a jet-black moustache, he cut a striking figure. His yellow eyes seemed to pierce others, giving him a very dominating look. Gervasi didn't know who his real father was, only that he was most likely a fosterling. He did have his mother's cheek bones and chin; everyone said so. Imelda Quito was forty. Though age lines had formed already, one could tell that in her youth she must have been quite a beauty. Gervasi didn't look at all like his supposed father, Fernando, a forty-five year old, heavyset blacksmith and weapons maker for Lord Malaca. That much he was certain of. As much as Fernando treated him like a son, he knew the man wasn't his real father.

Until now, he'd just accepted Fernando as his father. At least Vasco Lorancio, the *mentales* gifted advisor to Lord Ferdinan, had been kind and compassionate enough to take him under his wing six years ago, teaching him how to control his telepathy, that is, blocking out the thoughts of others around him and to keep from broadcasting his thoughts to everyone else. Vasco, along with another nobleman, had also helped him with his gifts, which primarily dealt with fighting and combat with a small amount of healing thrown into the mix. Gervasi's two prized possessions were the germanium crystal that he always wore around his neck, a gift from Vasco, and his high quality short sword made by his father, Fernando. Quito blades were the best in Malaca, unless one could get a Valen-made blade forged from the alien iron.

Gervasi had a younger sister, Ramira, eighteen. She also was a skilled fighter, wielding a short sword made especially for her by their father. Five inches shorter than Gervasi, she was just as well-toned as he; their practice fights often ended in a tie. She looked quite a lot like her father and had his friendly, extroverted disposition, unlike Gervasi who kept more to himself. They also had a younger brother, Tomaso, who was sixteen. Unlike his two older siblings, he wanted to become a blacksmith like Fernando and was now his apprentice. He wanted nothing to do with fighting.

Both Gervasi and Ramira worked as fighters for hire. Often they would provide security on ore runs for their father and gem and silver runs for some of the Malaca dealers, as they made the long trip to and from Toledo in the Castilla Hills. A few times, they helped provide security for Lord

Ferdinan or his associates on "city business." Those times, they did not ask questions, naturally. The brother-sister combination unit was well known around Malaca.

Late one night in July 1250, the two were at their usual watering hole, the Cabeza del Verraco, sharing pitchers of their famous dark ale. A friend of theirs had just returned from a job down by the coast. Just before that, he'd been at the Valen Council of the Lords with Lord Ferdinan and his party. Now that Vito was back in town, for the price of the pitchers of ale, he was telling all the latest news to anyone who would listen.

"I tell ya, this meet'en was somethin' else! The coastal towns have rebelled. They are now their own country, call'en themselves the Coastal City-States, whatever that means. Oh, you should of seen the fire in old Pedro Valen's face when he found out about it. They claim they have their own tower too, callin' it the Renegade Tower. Sounds fitten' to me. I says more power to 'em."

"Why did they rebel?" Ramira asked, refilling Vito's mug.

"Claims Valen Tower taxes them every year and never does what they are supposed to be doing. Something about visiting them and healing or curing, stuff like that, stuff he knows," Vito nodded towards Gervasi, who sat across the table from him. His sister was sitting on his right.

"Hell, don't look at me. Damned if I know anything about those towers. Never seen one, that's a fact," Gervasi countered and then shut up. That bothered him and Ramira knew it. He had the yellow eyes and the mind gifts. It was common knowledge they were supposed to somehow been taken under the care of the tower, though for what, none really knew for sure. Those who did, like Vasco Lorancio, never spoke openly about that topic. All this was a sore point with Gervasi.

Vito rambled on, ignoring Gervasi's obvious discomfort. "That tower and the lords somehow made a lot of priestesses, same as you with the yellow eyes, Gervasi, and they've been a healing and a curing for nigh onto five years some say. Old Lord Julio del Rey, he up and says to Lord Pedro Valen, he says, 'We're our own kingdom now, we secede from Valen

Tower, got our own tower now. No more taxes, no more conscripting our young men. You've taken from us for years and given nothing back. It ends now. You've seen what happens when you send armies to attack us. Send more and they will meet the same fate. This is the only warning you'll get from us. If you attack us again, we will shut down all shipping along the entire Westerlings coastline. Last year, that amounted to a quarter of your inland income. See, it's a new kind of warfare, called economic wars.' Did that ever shut the old pig up!"

"Now me, I keeps my ears open. Hear a lot of interesting things that way. Lots of local lords are making similar talk. I heard Lord Malaca saying that he's thinking along the same lines. Why keep paying Valen Tower our hard-earned money and letting them conscript our lads and get nothing back? Lots of the local *Jefe* are thinking the same thing. Going to be big troubles soon, I'll wager!" He hastily dipped his finger in his ale and made a hasty "+" sign on his forehead, the symbol that brought good luck to someone by warding off the bad luck that might soon be coming their way.

This interested Ramira, "So you think that we'll soon be fighting Valen's forces? Will they even bother with Malaca? We are so far from them."

"From what I've seen of Lord Pedro, he's an angry bastard with a nasty temper. We don't got none o' them priestesses here to do in his army like they did down in Ville del Rey. So I's be 'pecting 'em to try somethin' here. Best get yer sword sharpened señorita and yer hole filled, if'n yea wants."

Ramira smirked, replying coyly, "And I suppose that you'd volunteer to bed me and fill it, eh?"

Vito smiled, revealing two missing teeth, "Well, don't mind if I do. You asken'?"

"Oh sure, Vito, but afterwards, I'd have to cut it off so I can hang it on my trophy wall."

Vito roared, sending a splatter of ale from his mouth over the table. "Oh, I'll pass on that, señorita." She laughed too. Gervasi didn't, he had gotten moody again.

He was still moody when the two finally entered their

family home. Fernando and Tomaso had already turned in and Imelda was finishing up putting some beans on to soak overnight. "You two been to the pub? What news?" she asked as the two took off their cloaks and hung them on the pegs just inside the door.

"Lord Malaca is likely going to secede from the grip of Valen Castle and Tower, mom," Ramira announced. "Probably going to be a big fight over it, I'll wager. Not much else news. Going to bed, bit too much ale." She left the two alone.

"Wars, wars, always fighting. I suppose you two will be in the thick of it," Imelda said sadly, sitting down. Already Gervasi had plopped down on one of the kitchen chairs. "Ramira seems happy about it, but what's the matter with you? Don't tell me that you've had a sudden change of heart about all this fighting," she asked sitting down opposite her eldest son.

"No mom, that's not it. You know I'll always look out for Ramira and all of you. That's not it and you know it," he said at last looking at her directly in her eyes.

Imelda didn't need telepathy to know that look. She'd seen it many times before. She sighed, "You know if I tell you what you want to know, your life will be in danger. Lord help us all." She tried to deflect what was eating at her son, but this time, he wasn't rebuffed.

"Hell, mom, I'm likely to be killed in the coming battles, and I'll die without ever knowing who my father is," Gervasi spat out.

"Fernando is your father, well the only one that counts. You know that very well. He's treated you like his own son. Some things are best left unknown, for the good of everyone."

"For the good of you, mom. Why don't you just say what you mean?" he slammed her antagonistically.

"You know that's not true, not entirely. I know I made a mistake, but I was only eighteen then," she tried to counter and justified.

"Oh, so I am just your mistake," he continued to hammer her.

Tears formed. "No, Gervasi, you know that isn't true. I was waiting for the right time to tell you, when it would be safer for you. I don't want anything bad to happen to you because of my foolish mistake twenty-two years ago. Hell, we both were foolish, he and I."

"So what happened, mom?" Gervasi softened, hating to see her crying.

Her eyes clouded, as distant memories returned. "We were so young and he, so handsome and gallant in his fine suit. I was just a barmaid back then. I never had a noble paying any attention to me. I was excited and thrilled and believed what he was saying to me. Well, I was rather attractive back then, I suppose, still it all sort of went to my head. We only did it the one time, but then you know it only takes one time. He never came back, and I fled that part of the city and met your father, who is one hell of a better man than your paternal father ever was. Still, if I tell you, your life could well be in the greatest danger, especially if he finds out about you."

"Mom, why don't you let me be the judge of that? I am not going to do anything about it. Hell, I've never seen him and he obviously doesn't know about me. So what's the harm?"

"You must promise me never to tell anyone about it."

Sensing after all these years, she was close to revealing it, he agreed. "Promise, mom. I only wanted to know. How can I blame you?"

"No one knows, not even Fernando." She paused and finally made up her mind. "Lord Ferdinan Malaca. He was only eighteen then and probably hasn't a clue about you. Just be careful when you are around him. He's got two sons, who are fighting it out to see who is going to be his heir. If they find out about you, both are likely to come after you."

"Lord Malaca? Donkey's ass!"

"You see why it is best no one knows?" she asked, looking at him with a pitiful expression.

"Yes, I see why, mom. I sure as hell am not telling anyone. You're right, that could well get us killed. I don't hold it against you, mom. He took advantage of you, the pig." He came around the table and put his arms around her; she buried her head in his shoulders for a time.

A day later, a messenger came to see the two fighters.

When Gervasi and Ramira came to the door, he said briskly, "Lord Malaca wants to see you two immediately. He's got a paying assignment for you two. Come with me now."

"Okay, we need the money," Ramira said. "Give us a minute." She fastened her short sword around her waist and donned her cloak. Gervasi did likewise, but began to see their several year relationship with Lord Malaca in a different light. For three years now, he had been giving them some special assignments, guarding shipments from the hills to Malaca. Perhaps, this was just another one of those, he mused.

A half hour later, the messenger led the two into Malaca Castle's Great Hall, where Ferdinan sat on his throne. Standing beside him was his elder son, Pino, who like his father did not have the gift. Pino, a year younger than Gervasi, was Lord Malaca's designated heir to the throne, had been for many years. His younger son, Poncio, was eighteen and did have the *mentales* gifts. As adamant as Lord Ferdinan was about not having *mentales* gifted running the city and surrounding lands, that alone would have kept Poncio from inheriting the throne, perhaps. Poncio was not present and neither were any of his advisors. As soon as the messenger led the two into the room, he too left, leaving only the four of them present. *How strange,* Gervasi thought. *Here is my father; he doesn't even know I am his first born, his fosterling son. Donkey's ass!*

"Okay, Gervasi, Ramira, I have a special assignment for you both. Pay is a thousand silver," Lord Ferdinan spoke barely above a whisper.

Both sibling's eyes opened wide. This was ten times their usual rates. What was going on here? "My lord, that is a huge sum. What is the mission?" Gervasi finally found his voice.

"Guarding Pino here. He's on a secret mission for me. You are to go with him to Toledo in the Castilla Hills. There, he will be meeting someone and bringing back a certain package. You are to guard him with your lives. That is all that you need to know. I don't trust my usual Elite Guards. Too many wagging mouths. It will just be you three. He will go disguised as just another fighter. You need to leave tomorrow morning.

Ten days there, ten back. Pino will have all the packhorses ready. Be here at dawn." He tossed them a heavy bag containing the thousand silvers.

"We accept. See you in the morning, Pino," Gervasi said, now noticing the similarities between himself and Pino.

On their way home, Ramira was extremely pleased. "Now this is far more like it! Five hundred each – that's more than we made all last year. Sounds like a simple mission, though. Why so much money? Why not send his guards along? I know I would do just that, if I were him."

"Don't know, sis. Secret mission, Pino disguised? Something is going on here we don't know about. But for five hundred, I don't need to know. Pick up a package? How hard can this be anyway? Still, he's the lord's heir, and we damn well better not screw this one up, sis," he added emphatically.

Saddlebags loaded with spare clothes, dressed in their oil skin cloaks against the early morning dew, the two rode up to the castle gates. Pino was already there. Instead of wearing his usual suit, he looked little different from the two. He had two pack horses loaded with supplies, one tied to the other so that only one of them had to lead the horses. From the amount of supplies, both guessed they would not be staying at too many village inns along the way. Well, that suited the two just fine.

"Morning. Ready? Call me Pedro on this trip, okay? We'll camp out mostly especially closer to Malaca. Once we get into the hills, I'm not well known there so it'll be safe to spend a few nights in inns, if that doesn't slow us down. Need to be in Toledo by the 20th. Meeting is at nine the next morning. We'll head back right after I pick up that package. Gervasi, you lead; take back roads out of town for at least fifteen miles before hitting the main track to the hills. Ramira, you fall back and make *damn* sure that no one is following us. I'll bring the pack horses."

"Yes, my – er Pedro. This way," Gervasi said, barely stifling his accustomed "my lord."

Late that afternoon, they were back on the main path to Toledo. Ramira saw no signs they were being followed, but "Pedro" continued to insist she hang back and keep looking.

"Dangerous mission?" she asked Pedro, now that they were on the main path.

"Very. I fear someone is following us. I've just got that feeling. Keep alert back there," Pino replied nervously.

Shortly before dark, they made camp in a thicket of resinous pines. Ramira took care of the cooking. Gervasi could blacken a pot making tea and his cooking wasn't any better. After eating, the trio sat around the dying campfire before turning in. "So do you know who you are to meet in Toledo?" she probed a little.

"No, we're to exchange a secret code word only dad and I know. Let's just leave it at that. There are those who want this mission to fail. I aim to see it through for Malaca's sake. You know that dad is planning to secede don't you?"

"Yes, we heard rumors of that. So it's true then, he's going to drop out of Lord Pedro Valen's realm?" she asked.

"Sure hope so. You know Valen Tower has not lived up to even a single one of their obligations to Malaca or most other cities. For years now we paid our taxes and saw our young men being conscripted into Valen's army, most never to return. What have we gotten in return? Not a damned thing. It has to stop, but I best not say anything more on that. Dad trusts you two more than he does any of those in his Elite Guards. Just get me there and that package back to dad, okay?"

"Sure. You can count on us," she replied with a smile. He grinned back.

The last two nights before reaching Toledo, they stayed at village inns, where they could take a hot bath and wash their clothes before reaching the largest town in the mining hills. Toledo lay in the center of the rugged hills. The boulder-strewn valleys did have some tall prairie grasses fighting with resinous pines for the thin layer of soil. The hills themselves were jagged and rough. Dark openings and talus slopes dotted the hills around Toledo, but what ore was being mined in them was not obvious from a distance. Toledo was in the center of the squarish portion of the hills, some three hundred miles across. However, a narrow tip of the hills extended nearly five hundred more miles to the west, but was only eighty miles wide. This was a natural barrier. South of the hills, open rolling range land stretched all the way down to the Brozas River, the second largest river in the Westerlings, second only to the Alcantara River. Their own Salamanca River was third.

Home to close to twenty thousand, Toledo was definitely a mining town. Smelters, blacksmiths, and even gem smith shops seemed to be in every block. Wagons hauling ore filled the streets, though some were empty or carrying supplies back to the many mines. "Pedro" led them to the Silver Boar Inn where they took lodging for one night. While Gervasi took care of their horses, Ramira and Pedro got them their rooms. "Okay, you two will be in the next room to me," Pino insisted on still having his own room.

That night as they dined, Pino said, "Okay at nine tomorrow, I will meet my contact here in the dining room. That should take maybe two minutes. Then, we will leave immediately, so have the horses ready."

"If it is this dangerous, don't you think that one of us should stay in your room to stand guard over you?" Gervasi asked.

"No, the door has a lock. I'll be safe enough. Just wake me a half hour before, if I should oversleep. I want you both rested and ready to head back. I'm sure we were followed here. Maybe they will be attacking us on the way back."

"But I saw no signs at all of anyone trailing us," Ramira protested.

"Me either, but then that's not my specialty. I just have this bad feeling, that's all. This is a super important package dad must have. It comes from Valen Castle, but I probably should not say any more, not just now."

"And you don't know who you are to meet?" Gervasi asked.

"Nope, just the code words. That should be enough. Best get some sleep; we'll be riding fast tomorrow," Pino replied.

"We'll be up in a few minutes," Gervasi replied. He and Ramira sipped on a pair of ales, but really, they were casing the pub. "Look, if he is so sure we're being tailed, they might already be here in the pub. See anyone who looks suspicious?"

"Only that man in the shadows by himself. Can't get a good look at him, but he's definitely been watching our table here. Now he's not paying us any attention," Ramira replied.

"Well, we can't go challenging anyone we see just because he's been looking our way. Come on; let's see if we can get a look at him as we head up to our room," he suggested. They rose, finished their mugs in one gulp, dropped a few coins on the table, and headed to the stairs, passing as close as they could to the man in the shadows.

When they were in their room, she whispered, "He looked like an Easterlings man. Must be like you, yellow eyes. They were cold though, unfriendly. Best warn Pino," she suggested.

After joining Pino in his room, he replied, "No, my contact isn't from the Easterlings, I know that much anyway. Keep an eye on him in the morning. I'll lock my door after you leave." Though Pino looked even more worried, he still refused Gervasi's request to bunk with him for the night. Gervasi heard him lock his door before he joined his sister in their room.

Dawn came and the two got dressed and ready to leave. "Shouldn't Pino be up and about by now? Maybe you should check on him?" Ramira suggested. "All packed here." The two stepped out into the hallway. Just in front of Pino's door, Gervasi raised his hand. "Look there on the floor." Both bent down for a closer look. "Dried blood?" He knocked on Pino's door. No answer. Now both became worried. They knocked and called to him. Nothing. Gervasi put his shoulder to the door and forced it open, splintering the door jam. Both rushed into the room.

"Shit!" exclaimed Ramira. Pino's body lay on the bed, blood soaked the sheets and pooled on the floor. Much of it was already dried. Gervasi moved over to make sure and then the two fighters studied the scene.

"Looks like two cuts, one on his neck and shoulder causing the massive bleeding, the other here in his chest. Two different blades," Gervasi pointed out.

"Right, one about short sword size, the other, perhaps a dagger. Easterlings style. Pino was assassinated, but how the devil did someone get in here?" Ramira asked, moving over to examine the only other entrance, the window that was some fifteen feet above the ground. "Window is secure, hasn't been open for ages. I doubt it could even be opened without falling apart. The door was locked from the inside."

"Only way possible is the assassin must have teleported inside and then back out again. Look, here's a blood trail but it stops five feet from the doors. See, same dual patterns as we saw just outside, as if he were holding a blade in each hand. Typical Easterlings style. What the devil is going on here? Who would want to assassinate Pino?" Gervasi asked, his anger slowly mounting.

"Must have something to do with his secret mission. I wish we had been let in on what this is all about. Lord Malaca is going to be furious with us. Still, what's going to happen when the stranger comes at nine to hand Pico the package and Pico's dead? Should we try to intervene and return the package to Lord Malaca?" Ramira asked, growing even more worried. Their mission was now a total failure.

"Say, you're right. We ought to see first if we can get that package somehow. Come on. It's nine now. Let's go see if we can see any stranger down in the pub. We can at least bring him up here and show him that Pico is dead. Come on," Gervasi headed on down the hall.

As the two started down the stairs, they could see most of the pub tables. Hardly anyone was in here at this late morning hour. Gervasi stopped and hand signaled her to silence. Both stared in disbelief. Below them, Pino's younger brother, Poncio, was sitting at a table with a stranger. "Yes, I am Pino. You have that package for me?" Poncio said.

"Aye. Here you go Pino. Guard it well." The stranger rose and left at once. He was a Westerlings man, probably from Valen from his clothing, which looked a bit too rich for these parts. He carried a short sword, but no dagger. Both ruled him out as the assassin. Further, he obviously didn't know Pino personally and had given him the package, which was rectangular about a foot by a half-foot and several inches deep. Why was Poncio pretending to be his older brother? Lord Malaca had made no mention of Poncio being involved in this.

Just as the two were about to call out to Poncio, that strange Easterlings man moved from the shadows over to the table. Poncio slid a heavy money pouch across the table. The stranger picked it up, turned, and vanished from sight. He'd obviously teleported out of the inn. Poncio then rose, package in hand, and headed out of the inn.

"Follow him, but don't let him see you. I'll take care of Pino," Gervasi whispered. She nodded and slipped quietly down the stairs, while he headed back to the bedroom. He wrapped Pino's body in the blood soaked sheets and then a blanket, tying both ends. Then, he summoned the innkeeper, who was quite shocked that someone had been assassinated in his inn. He vocalized all manner of apologies and helped Gervasi carry the body down to the front door. By the time they got there, Ramira stepped back inside.

"He mounted up and rode out of town, heading for Malaca. I brought our horses around," she reported somberly. "Now what? Go after him?"

"Yes, we've seen enough to at least damn him to Lord Malaca. Come on. Let's get Pino tied to his horse," Gervasi ordered. Between the three of them, they got the body secured and left the still shocked innkeeper to deal with the bloody mess they left behind.

Once out of the town, they picked up Poncio's trail. "Two others have joined him," Ramira pointed out. She took point, leaving her brother to lead the packhorses and Pino's mare. "Shall we try to take them? I sure as hell want a word with Poncio!"

"We best try to get to the bottom of this before he gets away with whatever that package is," Gervasi replied. "They are now riding hard. I'm going to leave these other horses here, we can come back for them." A couple of minutes later, the two were galloping full speed after the fleeing trio.

A half hour later, they overtook the three. However, the moment that Poncio saw the two coming after them, he yelled, "You two, kill them. Kill them!" He kicked his horse into an all-out gallop, while his two henchmen wheeled around to face the charging siblings. All four drew their swords.

As the two neared the henchmen, who were wildly kicking their horses in an attempt to get some momentum from them, Gervasi called out, “Lean, let the sword do the work. Don’t stop.” From the corner of his eyes, he saw her obeying. As they galloped full speed into the pair, as expected the two fighters tried to swing their swords at them, but both siblings leaned over in their saddles, the henchmen’s blades missed entirely. However instead of swinging, the two allowed theirs to just touch the men’s necks. Their horses were flying and thus so were their blades, which cut deeply into both their necks, ending their vain attempt to obey Poncio. The two flew on past them without even glancing back.

Poncio turned to look back over his shoulders and saw the two charging after him. Wildly, he kicked and slapped his horse, urging more speed, but slowly his horse lost ground to the two behind him. He’d ridden his horse all night to get here in time and the horse was worn out. As the two closed the gap, Poncio resorted to using his *mentales* gifts. He conjured a wall of fire, placing it before the two charging riders. Gervasi focused and countered that one just in the nick of time. Both riders flew past where the wall of flames had been just an instant before. Again, Poncio tried to blast them with conjured flames. Riding so wildly, his aim was totally off and he missed entirely. Then his horse dodged a tree, but with his attention on the two behind him, Poncio didn’t see the resinous pine. He hit it, snapping his neck and knocking him off his horse. The mare continued racing down the track.

“I’ll get the mare,” Ramira called out. Gervasi reined in, turned around, and walked his lathered mare back to the fallen man. He dismounted and checked for signs of life. None. He searched him, but found no package. All he could do now was wait for his sister to return.

A half hour later, she came back, leading the mare. “Got her. Is he dead?” she called out.

“Yes, broke his neck. Let’s see if this damnable package is in his saddle bags.”

“Already did. It’s there. I didn’t open it, though. This package must be damnably important. Lord Malaca has lost both his sons and heirs over this mysterious package. I hope he thinks the cost is worth it!"

"Thanks, sis. Now the real question is how do we let Lord Malaca know that both his sons are dead. I know he despises telepathy. Yet the shock when we get back is going to be pretty heavy on him," Gervasi replied, as the two began tying Poncio's body over his mare's saddle.

"Better ask how are we going to get these two bodies back before they decompose badly. It's summer you know," she replied. "We could ride double time, dump most of the supplies and swap horses periodically or even get fresh mounts as we go along."

"Probably it would be best to get them both back to Malaca, sis. If they weren't the lord's sons, I'd just bury them here. Okay, we best ride double time," he agreed with her.

Six days later, they rode hard into Malaca and went straight to the castle. Gervasi did at least telepathically let the gatekeeper know they were coming, that Lord Ferdinan's two sons were dead, and that they were bringing them back with them. He let the man know as they entered the city, giving the lord time to get down to the gates, as they came cantering inside leading the two mares.

Lord Ferdinan's face was white, staring in disbelief at the two riders, whose horses were lathered. Both siblings had had little sleep, riding all day and far into the night to cut the journey as short as possible. "What the hell happened? Both?" he bellowed angrily. "I paid you to protect Pino. What was Poncio doing there? He knew nothing about this mission."

"We beg to differ, my lord. Poncio knew all about it, and I believe it was he who hired an Easterlings assassin to kill Pino," Gervasi began. "Let's get the bodies unwrapped and we'll show you what happened." He and Ramira explained everything they had seen and overheard. She then handed him the still unopened package. He added, "We don't know what all this was about, but that sure is one extremely costly package, my lord."

Lord Ferdinan and his Elite Guards' captain examined the body of Pino carefully. Both agreed with Gervasi and Ramira's findings that two blades were used, one likely a dagger, typical of the Easterlings fighting style of using a wicked, curved scimitar in one hand, dagger in the other. Lady Luisa and her ladies in waiting arrived and as expected began crying. The loss of both her sons was almost too much for her to bear.

After ordering the captain to see to the bodies, he motioned for the siblings to follow him inside to his study. Fighting back tears, he said, “At this point, you ought to know what this was all about. I am seceding from Valen’s territory, but I managed to have someone in Valen Castle smuggle one of those alien blasters out of the castle. He was to bring it to Toledo where he would hand it over to Pino. I didn’t trust Poncio at all. He was totally against my decision to secede, he was constantly arguing with me against it. Pino and I told no one about this deal to get the blaster. Somehow Poncio must have found out – that damned gift of his! The only thing I can figure is he had someone in Valen Castle get him that assassin fellow.”

“Here it is, the alien blaster. With this, we stand a chance, if Lord Valen sends his army up here to force us back into his fold. Without this blaster, we don’t stand a chance. He’s got lots of these wicked weapons. I was going to let Pino wield it when the time came. Now I’ve no sons, no heirs, and a lot of *mentales* gifted relatives, who will be demanding I pick one of them as my heir. Donkey’s ass!”

“What about your daughter?” Ramira asked.

“She’s a worthless *mentales* gifted too. I married her off to her kind in the Bosque Verde. No, I am just plain screwed now,” he replied, fighting back his grief for a while longer.

Do I or don’t I? Is now the time or ought I wait? Oh hell. “You’ve still got one more son,” Gervasi said softly.

“Huh? No I don’t.”

“Yes, you do. Me.”

“What?”

“Remember that barmaid some twenty-one years ago, Imelda? Your one night stand?” Gervasi said with a hint of antagonism and disrespect in his voice. Ramira gasped.

“What? Imelda, the barmaid? But it was just one night, I was drunk. She, she never said anything and she moved away somewhere,” he said, shocked. “If I had known. . .” His voice trailed off.

"Yes, well, she was ashamed and fled. I only found out myself just before we left with Pino. So you see, I've lost two brothers I barely knew," Gervasi added sadly.

"I can't believe it, but that explains why I have always been drawn to you, Gervasi. I never could put my finger on anything tangible. You look so much like your two brothers." He finally lost control of his emotions. Wet, salty tears trickled down his face, though he wiped them away several times. Wisely, neither Gervasi nor a very surprised Ramira said anything.

"Is she, is Imelda still living? Is she all right? Is she the wife of the blacksmith and weapons maker, Fernando Quito?" he finally asked, sniffing and clearing his nose.

"Mom's fine. Yes to all of them."

"Forgive me. I never knew. If she would have said something to me. . ."

"What would you have done?" Gervasi asked, a little hostility in his voice. He'd abandoned them when she needed him the most, as far as he was concerned.

"Point taken, my son. But now that I know, I will see Imelda gets the long overdue public acknowledgment she deserves for raising my son. Fernando too, he raised you well. Does he know?"

"No. Only mom and now us. I can see why mom wanted it kept a secret. Otherwise, I could well have been assassinated too, my lord."

"Damn, so many things are going wrong. Still I aim to get Malaca out of the hands of Valen Castle and Tower. The cost has been great, but that is the price leaders must pay. Will you come and stay here in my castle and manor house? You've much to learn as my heir to the throne of Malaca."

"Where I go, so goes Ramira. I trust no one but her at your castle. Obviously, Poncio learned all about this secret mission of yours. Who knows who else was in on it. No, we'll come by to learn but we'll stay put outside of the castle where we know we can be safe, my lord." Ramira grinned; her brother was not going to abandon her, which was what she was fearing most.

"I accept that. After we bury my sons, I will make the announcement you are my son and now my heir. After that, lord knows what plots will arise. It will sure shake things up a great deal."

"Okay. I just wish all this had come out before we left on this mission. Pino might have trusted me more and allowed us to share his room. Then, we might have stopped that assassin," Gervasi said with a sigh, recalling Pino's continued refusal to allow him to sleep in his room that fateful night.

"And then perhaps you would both be dead and I would have no heirs at all. No, I think this has all happened the way fate has chosen for us, my son. Go now. Tell your mother and father. I will see they want for nothing from now on."

As they rode through the streets, Ramira teased him. "Well, mister lord, now you have no excuse to not marry Rosita." His cheeks colored a little. She was the eighteen year old daughter of Amando Medio, a nobleman of Malaca. His family all had the *mentales* gifts and thus was not welcome at the castle. Yet the two were friends of the family. There were few who had the gifts actually living in Malaca; most had chosen to flee to the safety of the dense forest, Bosque Verde to the north. Because of his gifts, Gervasi had been taken under old Amando's wing. He'd seen to Gervasi's basic training. Over the years, he and Ramira had also performed a number of missions for the nobleman. He and Rosita were quite infatuated with each other, and Ramira was likewise quite taken with her brother, Antonio, who was nineteen. Until this moment, neither sibling really considered they would have a chance with these two young nobles, figuring Amando wanted to marry them off to other nobles. That Gervasi was now heir to the throne suddenly changed everything, at least for him, she assumed.

Gervasi quietly reminded her, "She's down at Govia visiting her cousins." Govia was their closest port at the mouth of the Salamanca River, home to perhaps ten thousand.

The next afternoon, the funeral for Pino was held, though Poncio was buried in total disgrace, labeled a traitor and murderer. Gervasi and Ramira were present, along with hundreds of other key men, women, and a few children. Later, when Lord Ferdinan announced Gervasi was his son and now his heir, more than a few heads were shocked and surprised. Indeed, the whole fabric of his court was visibly shaken. For two hours afterwards, Gervasi was pummeled with questions, comments, advice, and offered hands in marriage of young women, some of whom he'd never met. Ramira merely smirked, thinking, "Hypocrites!"

The Fall Council of Valen was to be held on the 21st of September. Normally, Lord Malaca would have left on the long overland journey to Valen some six weeks beforehand. This year, he merely sent a dispatch rider carrying his seceding document to be given to Lord Pedro Valen at the meeting. Winters came early this far north, and he wanted to take no chances with ambushes along the way back, once Lord Valen knew he'd withdrawn all of what had once been the Kingdom of Abvera from the territories under Valen's control.

Daily, the two siblings came to the castle to be "educated" in the castle's affairs, and in what Gervasi would have to know, if he were to one day become its ruler. The two took this in stride, but were continually vigilant. After all, there were others in this court that had backed the traitorous son, Poncio. "Keep on watching my back, sis," he whispered to Ramira more than once.

Lord Ferdinan anticipated some reaction to his dispatch of secession from Lord Pedro Valen. He kept the entire castle on alert as October came, bringing with it the first light snows. Winters came early this far north, though accumulations would not really begin until November. His fears were justified.

Just after lunch on the 20th of October, guards on the southern walls of the castle sounded the alarm. Great gongs echoed through the complex. "What's that?" asked Gervasi. He and Ramira had never heard these before.

"Attack. Malaca Castle is under attack! I knew Valen would strike!" Lord Ferdinan yelled. "Get to the south walls; that's where the alarm indicated they are at. Follow me. To arms!" he yelled to the captain of his Elite Guards, who'd just rushed into the throne room, still wiping the grease of his lunch off his face. He dashed off, while Ramira and Gervasi followed after Lord Ferdinan.

They raced across the cobblestones of the huge courtyard and took the steps to the walls two at a time. As they got to the top of the twenty-foot tall wall, men were pointing to the sky to the south. Two gleaming, copper colored air cars were heading their way, some five hundred feet above the ground and city. "What the hell are those?" yelled Gervasi. Neither he nor his sister had ever seen such strange flying machines.

"Air cars of Valen. They have three of them, left over from the Age of Chaos and powered by alien engines," Lord Ferdinan yelled back. "Where's their damned army? Anyone see their soldiers?" His concern was not for the flying machines, but for the massive ground forces that would be assaulting the castle. "Why haven't we had any word of their army before now?"

"My Lord, we've had no advance word of any army marching here. It's almost winter; surely they would not march an army here now," his captain suggested. Indeed, even if there was an army outside of Malaca at this moment, they would either have to winter over here in Malaca until April or march back to Valen through the deep snows and blizzards of winter. Neither were reasonable solutions.

They watched the shiny flying air cars as they approached the castle. There was little anyone could do against them, Gervasi noted. If they had bows and arrows, perhaps they could lob arrows up and into the cars somehow. He felt extremely vulnerable for the first time in his life, and he didn't like that feeling at all. Then, they saw an arm drop something over the side of the air car. It made a whistling noise as it fell. It landed on the roof of the manor house. Boom! A deafening explosion followed, when it struck the typical red tiled roof, sending shattered tiles flying in all directions, along with bits of the heavy timbers and stone walls. Boom! Boom! Two more bombs fell, destroying more of the roof and structure. Gervais quickly estimated that they were aiming for the private rooms of Lord Ferdinan!

"You cowards!" Lord Ferdinan screamed and pulled out

his blaster. He aimed at the rear air car and fired. Gervasi and Ramira saw a beam of blue energy flying from the alien weapon upwards. It struck the air car, a circular hole a foot across appeared in its bottom. Part of a man's leg fell slowly down out of the hole. The air car rapidly fell from the sky. A loud crash reverberated around the castle, but Gervasi estimated it had fallen beyond the walls close to the river. He hoped no one on the ground was injured where it struck. The other air car suddenly gained altitude and rapidly accelerated to its top speed, heading back the way it had come, heading due southeast.

"I got one! I got one!" yelled Lord Ferdinan. All around them, soldiers cheered their lord, who just waved the alien blaster around in the air. To Gervasi, he said, "It was worth it. Without this weapon, those two air cars would have destroyed us, and there would not have been a damned thing we could do about it. Now he's only got two of those flying machines left. I doubt Lord Pedro will try that wicked scheme on us ever again! Now he knows we have the blaster, so he'll think twice about attacking us. I was right; he did try to kill us all. Captain, go find that air car and kill anyone who is still alive in it! Come on, son. Let's go to the north walls and see if we can see it."

Later they saw several homes had been partially destroyed when the air car crashed into them as it fell from the sky. Two women were killed and several more injured. One man onboard the flying ship was dead, two more were wounded and quickly slain by the Elite Guards, who rushed to the scene. A day later, the men had hauled the remains of the machine into the courtyard and began studying it. A dozen more unexploded bombs were in it. The thin copper skin had been ripped and some of its supporting framework bent, but Lord Ferdinan was hopeful it could be rebuilt, giving them an air car for future attacks.

"Son, now we can relax until spring. As mad as Lord Pedro must be now, he can't do anything more to us until the snows have melted and he can march an army up here from Valen. We should be safe for many months," Lord Ferdinan declared, now greatly relieved. To others, he pronounced, "See, my son did not die in vain after all! This alien weapon has proved it worth!"

Ramira whispered to her brother, "I don't think any weapon is worth a human life."

"Neither do I. If we had archers, we might have found a way to stop those flying machines. Pino didn't have to die for a stupid weapon." He felt a little hostility towards his father's declarations to the contrary. However, things did settle down after that as winter came.

Then, in mid-December, the nobleman and *mentales* gifted Amando Medio came to the castle to meet with Lord Gervasi, as he was now being called, much to his distaste. "A private matter, Lord Ferdinan. If you will permit me to speak to Lord Gervasi and Ramira, please?" he glared at the ruler, but Gervasi knew if Lord Ferdinan didn't comply, Amando would use his gifts on the ruler, forcing him to allow the private meeting. Evidently, Lord Ferdinan also knew this and left, glaring hatred towards the nobleman.

"Good. We are alone. Gervasi, Ramira, I desperately need your help. Rosita has been abducted, kidnaped down in Govia!"

"What? Kidnaped? Is she hurt?" Gervasi reacted with surprise and anger. "When? Who? Ransom?"

"Let me Mind Link to you both and show you what she sent me," he said, visibly upset. It took him a minute to gain control of his emotions to be able to focus. His crystal energized and the two felt his mind join theirs. Four men were grabbing her, forcing a smelly cloth over her face. They were also kidnaping her cousin, who was with her, right on the main street of Govia in broad daylight! The two saw the four men's faces clearly, as well as their saddles and uniforms. Gervasi burned those images into his mind. He would kill them, showing no mercy; his anger swelled in his breast.

The contact broken, Amando continued, "That's all I got. She went unconscious. I've tried for two days to make contact with her, but nothing. She is either still unconscious or she has been put on that nasty *bacal* tea. Please, I need your help in finding her before it's too late."

"You can count on us, my lord! When can we leave?" Gervasi exclaimed, heedless of his new position as heir.

"Will Lord Ferdinan even let you go?"

"Leave him to me. When?"

"Antonio has gone to Basque Verde to see about getting us there more quickly. I'll be heading down the Salamanca River on a barge today with my wife. We should be there in a couple of weeks. I am hoping Antonio can get you two and himself there in a couple of days. If so, you three must find her somehow, before we get there. We will bring you all back via the barge once you've rescued her from her kidnapers. I only trust you two. Please find her. I know you care for her and she, you."

"You can count on us, my lord! We will get her back, and I will kill those who took her, I so swear!" Gervasi declared vehemently.

"Likewise, my lord. We'll get her back!" Ramira swore. "But how are we going to get there so soon?"

Amando looked around the room. Satisfied no one was listening in, he whispered, "If Antonio is successful, there are enough of the *mentales* gifted, who can join together, to teleport you three to Govia. Antonio will bring along enough funds for your needs once there. Travel light, just what you are wearing. Just don't let Lord Ferdinan know about this. He hates anything having to do with the gifts and those of us who have it."

"Will it hurt? I don't know how to do this," Ramira asked worriedly.

He laughed. "You won't feel anything and you just have to stand there. Don't worry, Antonio will take good care of you. I don't know how I can ever thank you both for this."

"You already have, my lord. You've watched over us both for many years," Gervasi replied. "No thanks is needed. We'll get her back. Will Antonio be contacting us?"

"Thank you both anyway. Yes, he will make mental contact if and when he can arrange it. I best get going. I'll let you handle Lord Ferdinan," he grinned. Amando turned and left, Lord Ferdinan entered, staring after the departing lord, disgust upon his face.

"Well, what did he want?"

"His daughter has been kidnaped along with her cousin

down in Govia. We're pledged to help them rescue them," Gervasi explained.

"What? You can't go there. It's far too dangerous," Lord Ferdinan countered and protested.

"If I am to be a good leader of Malaca, I must be seen as responding to the urgent, critical needs of our people, my lord. You would not have me be seen as a coward hiding within the castle walls, would you?" he tossed out the hint he knew would strike a chord in his father.

"Well, no, but son, you are my only heir. What if this is another of Lord Pedro's dire plots against us?"

"If it is, I will handle it totally, sending him a similar message to the one you sent him. However, if I have been following all your advisors right, Govia is part of the Coastal City-States lands now, not Valen's. They have seceded too, so I think Lord Valen is not involved. It is probably just a kidnap for ransom situation," Gervasi defused the situation.

Begrudgingly, Lord Ferdinan agreed, but urged him to return as soon as possible. The two headed to Gervasi's new suite in the manor house. They checked their weapons. "Guess we will have Antonio get us a change of clothes when we get there, horses too," he said to Ramira, but noticed she was a little nervous. "What?" he asked.

"Oh, this teleport thing. I don't know what it is all about. Is it dangerous?" she asked. Ramira was used to being wholly up front with her older brother. This was no exception.

"I don't know anything about it either, sis. We'll have to ask Antonio when he contacts us. It must be safe. Relax, we need to figure out how we can locate those four men when we get there. Distinctive uniforms. Maybe someone will recognize them," he suggested hopefully.

Chapter 13 Malaca Mutiny Expands

“I hope that Rosita is okay. Are you really worried about her?” she asked, knowing the two were close. For that matter, she had a crush on Antonio, but knew he would likely never be allowed to reciprocate. She was neither of noble birth nor gifted as he was.

“Worried, you bet. She’s not got any fighting skills, but her gifts ought to have allowed her to make contact before now, unless. . .” his voice trailed away, and she thought better of saying anymore. Instead, she tied up her long black hair into a tight bun, as she always did when going into the field. Unlike many other women, she preferred bangs that fell to just above her thick eyebrows. While Gervasi’s face was squarish, hers was more rounded with high cheeks and well-formed lips. That she was cute was not her concern, except when she was around Antonio. At those times, she felt like some childish girl, infatuated with some boy. Well, she was, she admitted, tightening her sword belt.

Near suppertime, Antonio made contact with Gervasi. *Hi, Antonio here. I’ve been successful in arranging for us to be teleported to Govia. Are you two ready? Okay then, first, they will bring me to you.* A moment later, Antonio appeared before them, stumbling slightly as he got his footing. He was an inch taller than Ramira, with piercing yellow eyes and a black beard outlining his cheeks. He was a handsome lad of twenty. Ramira’s heart fluttered slightly, but she was thankful she didn’t have to say more than hi to him just now.

“Okay, take hold of my hands. I am sure glad dad was able to convince you to help us find my sister,” his deep bass voice reflected both his excitement and worry at the same time.

“He didn’t have to convince us, Antonio. We volunteered the moment we learned she’d been kidnaped, Antonio,” Gervasi replied. “What do we do? We’ve never done this sort of thing before.” He glanced at his sister, saw her confused expression, and smiled, knowing she was grateful that he'd spoken this time. Normally, she was the conversation-maker, but not around Antonio.

"This is the only time I've ever done it — coming here. Just hold my hands. That's all there is to it, I hope. They didn't tell me anymore," he replied, grabbing hold of Ramira's hand. She wondered if he could tell how she felt, electrified by his touch. If he did, he didn't let on. Then, she sensed someone lightly touching her mind. The next instant, she found herself standing outside on a snow-covered street. The odor of the sea was heavy in the air, along with smoke from many resinous pine hearths. She stumbled but got her balance, keeping Antonio from taking a spill this time. "Thanks. Guess we are here. Let's find us an inn for tonight."

Several days passed. They rented horses and paid for a week's lodging. By day, they roamed the streets looking for sight of the four men and those unusual looking uniforms. They ruled out the city guards and the lord's Elite Guards. As the days passed by, they became more and more familiar with the port city. Finally, Ramira exclaimed in exasperation, "Men! Don't you ever stoop to just asking around? Come on! Now you two follow me!" She rode up to a city guard and began asking him if he knew of the strange uniforms.

"Sure, I've seen them around town. Usually, they are up in the east area, close to the edge of the city. Don't know any more," he replied. After thanking them, she led them into the eastern area where again, she continued to stop and ask men, who just might know of them or had seen them. Finally, she got the answer that she wanted.

"Yes, those are Lord del Rey's Special Forces. They've been here a couple of years. They barracks at a small hacienda at the very edge of the town." He gave her specific directions and finally they arrived at the designated location.

"See, men, ask and yea shall be rewarded!" she teased them both. Antonio flushed, but Gervasi merely grinned, nodding appreciatively to her. They tied up their horses a block away and walked past the hacienda, casing the place. A large gate blocked access from the inner courtyard and gardens, though only the dead plants and evergreen shrubs could be seen inside. Three back sides contained a number of individual suites. Around back, they found a small stable with six horses inside. "This far from the heart of the city, there are only likely to be six men inside."

"Why?" asked Antonio, trusting her wisdom entirely. Still, he wanted her reasoning.

"Too far to walk in this weather. It's cold outside and the streets are starting to get slick from the snow. While back home, it's already accumulating day by day. This close to the sea, it's warmer and only now is it starting to stick. I'd hate to have to walk into town in this stuff. No, I reckon there are six men inside, one for each horse. Whether more are out on the streets and will be returning, I can't speculate. Well, yes, I can. Look, the other stalls are empty and show no signs of recent usage. Six. We can take them!"

"Brilliant. Can we take all six at once though?" Antonio asked. "What if my sister is inside there somewhere? They might harm her."

"Right, we need a plan," Gervasi agreed. "We need to find the four who kidnaped her. Keep them alive until they tell us where they've got her and why. Any others, just kill."

"Or we could keep watch from an alleyway and take one or more of them when they come out. Kidnap them and force them to tell us," Ramira suggested.

"Hell, she could be in dire trouble right now. We can't wait. We go in now," Antonio insisted. She wanted to say haste made waste, but thought better of it, especially since Gervasi liked this idea as well. Men, she thought once again. They headed to the main gates. To their surprise, they were not locked. As they stepped inside, a couple of doors opened and voices hollered at them. "This is a private hacienda. What do you want?"

The three recognized the speaker as one of the four men who'd kidnaped the two women. "We want you," Gervasi called out angrily, drawing his sword. More doors opened and the six men rushed out, drawing their swords, forming a battle line. Gervasi noted their movements carefully. They were trained soldiers and likely knew how to fight well. *Antonio, you get between us,* he sent, knowing his fighting skills were not equal to these men.

"What do you want here?" the man asked again.

"We've come for you. You kidnaped my sister. We want her back," Antonio blurted out in anger. The six men reacted visibly. Gervasi suspected that they more or less anticipated one day someone would come looking for them, and he also guessed the two women were not the only ones these men had kidnaped. The three moved cautiously towards the line of soldiers.

With a lunge, the six joined swords. Two took on Gervasi and two went after Ramira, but only one could get at Antonio, thanks to Gervasi's positioning of him. Almost at once, Antonio saw he was out matched, but did his best to hold his ground. Steel upon steel echoed in the courtyard. The well-trained soldiers were no match for the fighting duo, who refused to fight by all the standard means. Ramira took advantage of a missed parry of one of her opponents, delivering a solid kick to his privates, sending him doubling over in pain. Enraged, her other opponent tried to overpower her, but she dodged and thrust her sword into the opening he gave her, driving hers deep into his chest. Using her foot, she shoved the man off her blade, while ducking another who tried to take his place.

At the same time as she ducked, she got her sword to slice a deep gash in the leg of the soldier, who was giving Antonio the fight of his life. He seized the initiative and managed to finish that one off. Gervasi was doing equally well on Antonio's left. One went down, then the other. At last, the remaining soldier yielded, backing up, while the one on the ground struggled to his feet, still in pain from Ramira's kick. Quickly, Gervasi and Ramira kicked the swords out of reach of the soldiers.

"Now then, you kidnaped two women; we want to know where they are now and why you did so?" Antonio said gasping for breath. This had been more strenuous exercise than he'd had in a long time. To his dismay, the men said nothing. He repeated his request several more times, but the soldiers just glared at him.

"We'll do it the hard way then," Antonio finally said, calming down. He focused and Ramira watched, as the crystal resting on his neck began to emit a pale blue glow. As always, she wondered what was happening. She again felt left out of something her brother and Antonio shared. Just then, she felt Gervasi touching her mind, and she began seeing and hearing what Antonio was seeing and hearing from the minds of the men, one by one. Images of them snatching up a dozen young women appeared, until they saw Rosita and her cousin being snatched. Now, Antonio forced their minds to reveal where they were taken. They saw another hacienda similar to this one, but closer to the docks. He picked up the words "mermaids," "priestesses," and "Daughters of the Seas." Antonio was not through with them. He forced himself deeper into their minds and saw they were receiving their orders from Lord Antonio del Rey of Villa del Rey, a city thousands of miles south and east of here.

When Antonio finished, his crystal dimmed and he spoke, "For crimes against the young, innocent women of Govia, you are hereby sentenced to death." A few swift blows and the six kidnapers lay dead at their feet. "We should search this place though," Antonio ordered.

They split up to search all the rooms. Gervasi whispered to Ramira, "That was a mental rape. He tore all those images and ideas out of their minds. Mental rape. Nasty business, sis." She nodded, now she had a name for what she'd seen via her brother, and she didn't like it.

An hour later, Antonio found the clothes his sister had been wearing when she was abducted. However, there were a dozen more women's outfits in that same room, very disheartening to the trio. Carrying her things, the trio walked back to their horses and headed back to their inn. Once safely in their rooms, Antonio contacted his father, while the siblings waited patiently, though already planning their next move: locate this new hacienda with the twin fishes on its gates.

Antonio looked incredibly pale when he finally broke contact with his father. For a moment, he didn't say a word. Finally, with the two staring at him, he sighed. "We're far too late for Rosita. Dad is asking us to find this new hacienda and wait for his arrival in a couple of days. Rosita's alive, if you can call it that. She finally was able to contact him. These beasts have mutilated her body something horrible, claiming she's now a priestess of Calder, a Daughter of the Seas, whatever the hell that is. She. . . she begged dad to come and kill her. She only wants to die now! My god, when I get my hands on whoever did this to her, I swear I'll torture them horribly!"

Gervasi slumped onto Antonio's bed, crushed. Ramira fumed, "You'll have to be faster than me! I'll kill them myself! The bastards!"

The next day, the trio set out to find this second hacienda and to find out more about these priestesses. With Ramira taking the lead, they quickly found out more than they wanted to know! The ancient god Calder, God of the Seas, had awakened or so everyone said. His priestesses were in all the major towns along the entire coastline of Tierra. They blessed ships and sailors and many now swore by them. Some fishermen claimed they got record catches once the priestesses had blessed them and their ship. Further, these priestesses were great healers. The claims some of the locals expressed, the trio found hard to believe. "It's like there's a tower operating here," Antonio exclaimed. "Only a tower can heal to this degree. What the devil's going on here? Gods come alive? Why?"

Of course, when they got a physical description of these priestesses, all three were utterly shocked and if what they heard was true, the three could understand Rosita's begging to be killed. However, Gervasi couldn't see himself killing Rosita, no matter how terribly disfigured and mutilated her body was. However, they did wait for Amando's arrival.

Three days later, the trio met the barge when it docked near the mouth of the river, just as the muddy waters met the ocean. Amando looked tired and worn out. He hadn't shaved for days and his clothes needed a good cleaning. "Dad, we've got the place cased. We can go in anytime and get her," Antonio spat out the moment his dad set foot on the docks.

The older man pulled his heavy cloak around himself and stood there for a moment not answering his son. "I'm afraid if it's as bad as she claims, I may have to put down my own daughter," he finally said softly. He wreaked of grief. Ramira didn't need to have the gift to know he'd been crying a lot. His eyes told her. "We'd best rent a carriage, son." He turned to the barge captain. "Get it ready for the return trip. We may be back very soon." Gervasi sensed what Amando hadn't added, "with what remains of her," and he cringed.

While Antonio rushed off to rent a carriage for the day, Gervasi filled the older man in on what they had learned of these priestesses. "Apparently, they possess some godlike powers. They claim some god called Calder gave it to these priestesses. We've heard of over a dozen miracles they've performed. As near as I can tell, one of these priestesses is doing the work an entire *Círculo de mentes* does, though I really don't know that for sure, never having seen a *Círculo de mentes*."

"Tell me more specifics, please," he asked quietly. Ramira and Gervasi took turns relaying the different stories they'd been told had happened. Eventually, he finally smiled, "Yes, it would appear your conclusion is correct. One priestess is doing the work of an entire *Círculo de mentes*. I don't know how that can possibly be, but maybe Rosita can be talked into living because she's now able to perform such miracles, though from her explanation of her mutilations I seriously doubt it. Here comes Antonio. I just don't know what to think anymore. How could this have happened?"

Ten minutes later the four arrived outside the gates. A sign read Daughters of the Sea. As the four walked up to the gates, nothing could have prepared them for the grizzly sight just inside the gates. A dozen women were screaming, wildly terrified. All were hopping on one leg with no arms to help them balance. Each had extremely long earrings and five-inch lip plates protruding from their upper and lower split lips. Wailing and sobbing blended with terror. A dozen men with swords and wearing light blue uniforms were just inside some of the many suites. Through the open doors, they could be seen hastily packing.

Gervasi spotted what was left of Rosita and ignored the others, who stood rooted to the spot, unable to grasp what they were seeing. Seeing him move, Ramira snapped out of her shock and followed after her brother as he dashed through the gates and into the gardens. He headed straight for Rosita; she was right behind him.

"Rosita! Rosita! I'm here! We're all here! We've got you now!" Gervasi called out to her. She hopped a little to turn to him. She was shaking from terror and sobbing wildly, a terrible combination, but she recognized him.

"Kill me, please, Gervasi, kill me! We've lost all our powers! I can only barely hop without falling. Kill me, please!" she begged while sobbing. Just as her leg began to give out, he reached her side and held on to her, steadying her.

"It'll be all right, Rosita. I'm here, your dad's here, Ramira is here, Antonio is here. We have you now," he said softly, unable to think of anything reasonable to say to her.

Just then, another priestess came hopping over to him, sobbing as well. "It's gone! Our powers are gone. We are supposed to go to the Elegant Fashions Inc and wait for help."

One of the men came out carrying a bag. "We're out of here, priestess. You are on your own now. God help you!" He dashed off, leaving her crying all the more.

"Who are these men?" Ramira asked, drawing her sword.

"Our guardians who are supposed to help us, but now they are abandoning us too," the priestess replied. Bravely, she added, "Come on, priestesses. We have to hop to Elegant Fashions Inc soon. We can do it somehow." She began to take small hopping steps towards the gate.

"We're taking my Rosita," Gervasi told her.

"Whatever. We're all as good as dead. We're more helpless than helpless," the priestess continued to sob, while moving slowly away from the two.

Gervasi felt Rosita shivering. She was freezing, wearing nothing but the thin, light blue dress. "Ramira, go see if you can find something warm to put over her. Antonio, you get the carriage ready to go. Amando, come and help hold her. We can't let her fall onto the cold cobblestones," he barked orders, finally collecting his wits. Ramira ducked into a suite, Antonio knocked a guardian away from his feeble attempt to steal their coach and got to the driver's seat, waving his sword at the other guardians as they too fled the hacienda.

He watched in utter dismay as eleven shivering

priestesses came hopping out after the men. None even noticed him and the carriage. At last he yelled, “Priestesses, the store is only two blocks away!” He recalled having seen it as they cased this area beforehand.

Ramira soon came out with a blanket and the two wrapped it around Rosita. She ducked back inside, while Gervasi picked up what was left of his love and carried her out to the carriage. Still in shock, Amando followed slowly after him. Ramira came out carrying an armful of men’s clothing, heavy winter gear. She threw them into the carriage and climbed in beside Amando. On the other bench, Gervasi continued to hold onto Rosita, who was sobbing underneath the blanket. The carriage began to roll.

Gervasi, Vasco Lorancio here. Bad news, Lord Ferdinan has just been assassinated. We believe it was that same Easterlings man who killed Pino. You must get back here at once! You are now our Lord Malaca. Where are you?

Gervasi’s stomach lurched, and then tightened until he felt like he was being cut in half. *Govia. Don’t touch anything until I get there. I want to see the scene.* Ramira sensed something was horribly wrong with Gervasi. She’d never seen him go so pale and tense so quickly. She put her hand on him. The warm touch of her hand brought him to the present.

“It was Vasco. Lord Ferdinan, my dad, he’s just been assassinated. Likely that same Easterlings assassin that got to Pino. Antonio. Can you get your friends to teleport us back to the manor house as soon as possible, before I throw up?” He felt the shaking terror of Rosita in his arms. Too much was happening too quickly.

“Oh dear god, Gervasi! I’m so sorry for you,” Ramira whispered, keeping her hand on his shoulders.

Antonio halted the carriage and had his father repeat what Gervasi had just said. “Damn those Valen folks! Okay, on it.”

“I’m sorry Gervasi. I should never have asked you to help us rescue Rosita. I’m afraid all we can do now is to put her down humanely. I’ll take her from you, if you like,” Amando said, his voice choked with grief.

“No, she and I wanted to marry. I will take care of her.

She is still Rosita, no matter what they've done to her. Now I am the Lord, I will still take Rosita. Dear, hang in there a little while longer until I can get you home to the manor house. We'll figure something out. Hush, hush, don't cry. You've been through more than anyone ought to ever experience," he spoke softly to the sobbing form in his hands. "No one is going to harm you ever again. I give you my sworn word on that, dear."

"Okay, five minutes and they'll be ready. They'll have to make two teleports out of this because we're too many. Ramira, hold onto your brother. They'll take you three first. Dad, hold onto me, we're going second," Antonio replied, squeezing into the carriage. "Where in the manor house should they bring us, Gervasi?"

"The Great Hall," he whispered. "Just a little longer, my love," he whispered to the blanketed Rosita, who was still shivering from the cold and sobbing uncontrollably.

Five minutes later as the sun began sinking and darkness fell on the port of Govia, the rented carriage stood empty at the side of the street. The five arrived in the Great Hall, stumbling to get their footing. "I'll take her to my suite. Antonio, you and Amando come with me. I want you two to look after her, while Ramira and I go check out the assassination scene," Gervasi ordered.

Rapidly, he carried Rosita down the halls and up the stairs. Vasco came running after them, but politely didn't say anything yet. "You are now very light, my love," he whispered to her, still entirely covered by the blanket. After setting her down on his bed, he kissed her forehead. "I'll be back soon, my Rosita. Watch her, please," he ordered Antonio, who nodded grimly. Ramira and Gervasi dashed out of the room, joining Vasco, who began telling them in detail what had happened as he led them to the Master Bedroom.

"It must have happened during the night. We discovered their bodies late this morning," he said grimly, his teeth rather clenched.

"Hold here. Let me see that floor here." They were just outside the bedroom doors. Ramira was just ahead of him and they knew what to look for this time. She silently pointed to the two distinct sets of blood drops, one on either side of a man who had been holding the blades when he teleported out of the locked bedroom. Inside, the bed was a bloody mess, but nothing had been disturbed. The windows were locked from the inside. The ground below was some twenty feet down, a sheer stone wall, unclimbable.

From the wounds on his father and his wife, the assassin had used two blades, a dagger and perhaps a scimitar, just as had been used on Pino. "Yes, the wounds are identical to Pino's. Come on. Bring lanterns. I want to look on the grounds just below dad's windows," Gervasi ordered. Several of the Elite Guards responded quickly. A few minutes later, the siblings examined the grounds below the Lord's bedroom window and found nothing at all. "Footprints would easily be seen in all this snow. Our assassin was not out here before teleporting into his room," Gervasi concluded.

"I agree," Ramira added. "That can only mean the assassin somehow slipped through the main gates, walked into the manor house and through the halls, up the stairs to just outside the room. How can it be that no one saw him or stopped him?"

"We must have other traitors in this castle," Gervasi concluded.

"Damn!" Vasco swore. "I was hoping we didn't. Now what?"

"Go ahead and prepare them for burial. I've got to go to Rosita. She's alive and needs our help now. Come on Ramira," he said. Turning on his heels, he and his sister raced back to his suite.

Amando and Antonio had Rosita sitting close to the fireplace warming up. They'd removed the lip plates as well as the heavy earrings. When the two joined them, Antonio was feeding her some warmed up stew from supper. "Ah, you're back; we've got my sister warming up. Any news? Sorry about your dad; he was a good leader," Antonio said sympathetically.

"Thanks. Yes, we're quite certain it was the same Easterlings assassin who killed Pino, same method of operation. I'm positive there are traitors within the castle! The assassin just walked into the castle and up to dad's room. No one stopped him or saw him. That's hard to believe, but I'll worry about that tomorrow. Right now, we have to take care of my fiancé here."

"But My Lord," Amando spoke up, "she's no longer worthy of being your wife. As the Lord of all Malaca, sire, you should pick a more worthy woman." While her crying had ended, Rosita again broke down and began sobbing; his words hurt her.

Gervasi sized up the situation rapidly, his fighter training again proved valuable. "Look, Amando, we both know you're giving me an honorable way to end my long standing wish to marry your daughter. Until I found out who my father was, Rosita and I didn't make any long range plans about our future. We both knew you would want her to marry upwards or at least sideways in the nobility hierarchy around Malaca. So we didn't press the issue, what with me only being the son of a blacksmith. Now that I am Lord Gervasi Quito Malaca, that's all changed. I still want to marry Rosita, if she will have me. Look, she is alive and healthy. She still has her *mentales* gifts; she is still my Rosita. What kind of man deserts his love when she's in desperate need of his help and love? I will not abandon her like those pathetic blue uniformed guardian men back in Govia."

"That's most honorable of you, My Lord," Amando replied, choosing his words carefully. "But sire, she has been mutilated something horribly. It's my responsibility to urge you to use caution in this matter. When a mare breaks her leg, we do the humane thing and put her down. Surely you can see this, My Lord." Rosita sobbed more, but nodded her head, agreeing with him.

"My Lord Amando, I beg to differ. Your daughter's a woman, a human being. We put down animals who can't survive their injuries, but we are not animals. I'll have no more of this morbid talk. If you insist, then I order you to allow me to marry Rosita at once. Tomorrow morning, sir, it'll be done. That's my final word. I have three enemies to focus on now: the Easterlings assassin, Lord Pedro Valen, and now this Lord Antonio del Rey, who was behind this awful mutilation of my Rosita and the other young women. Focus your attention and efforts on finding those guilty men and obtaining the justice that honest men demand, My Lord. Now please, you both should return to your home. Return at nine tomorrow for the wedding, if you desire. I have spoken," Gervasi declared forcefully. Both men nodded, rose, kissed Rosita on her forehead, and left.

"I'll head home and tell mom and dad and Tomaso what's happened, Gervasi. Let me know if you want me back here later tonight," Ramira said softly. Then she added, "Congratulations, Rosita. I'll be back by eight to help you get ready for your wedding day. It should be your special day." She smiled at Rosita, who'd stopped crying, but lowered her head.

Finally alone, Gervasi put his arms around Rosita. "Rosita, I still love you. I'll never abandon you. I'm here for you, my love."

"But Gervasi, I'm so helpless like this. I'm barely half a woman. I do love you. I always have, but I'm just a hideous burden and freak."

"You still have your mind and spirit intact, wounded perhaps, but you're still you, the woman I love. You love me, so finally, Rosita we can be together. Not quite the way we'd imagined, but we're together at long last. I dreamed of this day, when I can hold you in my arms."

"But I can't hold you," she whimpered.

"Sure you can, use your gift like you used to do when we slipped into rapport with each other," he suggested. She did so, using her telekinetic powers to press into his body a little. "See, that's my woman. Look my love, soldiers often get wounded on the battlefield. Some lose limbs as well. We just don't give up and die. A fighter regains his strength and health and fights on. You are a fighter too, dearest. Don't give up, fight back. You're alive; you can do it."

"Do you really think so?" she asked timidly.

"Of course, my love. Otherwise, I wouldn't be marrying you in the morning. Come on. Let's get you into bed. I'm exhausted and I bet you are too. It's been one awful day for us all."

"My body is now so weird," she whispered.

"Who cares? It's you I want to marry, not your body," he said lovingly and softly. He rose and headed to his bed, preparing it for them. Rosita swallowed hard. She leaned forward and gave a little lunge with her torso, getting up onto her foot. Sighing, she bravely began hopping over to the bed. "See, you can hop just fine, but I bet it's damned scary."

"No kidding, terrifying really. Before when I had all those powers, I could use them to easily keep my balance and even teleport, only they called it jumping," she explained.

"You have to tell me all about it, love. Here, sit on the edge and I'll brush out your hair for you." She did so and began to tell him everything that had happened to her, beginning with the four men who'd stopped them in the street weeks ago. As she continued, he took her light dress off her and both got a good look at her modified body's actual form. Realizing the depths of her helplessness, he continued to have her tell him all about what had happened. Later beneath the warm covers, she rested her head on his shoulders and he draped them in her long hair.

On a hunch, he said, "Rosita, tell me all about it once more, leave nothing out." She did so, yawning several times. When she finished, she felt greatly relieved. He knew everything she knew and felt, and more importantly, he still loved her and wanted her as his bride. He had indirectly begun to erase the huge traumas she'd endured.

In the morning, he dressed her, brushed her hair, and had their breakfast brought to their room. Ramira arrived as they were eating. "Okay, I brought a white wedding dress for my new sister-in-law. You can't get married without a white dress, Rosita. I know it isn't going to be much of a good fit, but it's the spirit that counts. Big brother, if you will go change into your suit, we women have to get your bride-to-be all ready for her big day."

"Thank you, sis! I owe you a big one," Gervasi exclaimed and did as she asked.

As nine o'clock approached, Ramira finished her magic on Rosita, who beamed. Her white gown had extremely short sleeves that wouldn't get in her way. Her long, black hair was parted down the middle of her head, her thick hair falling over her shoulders down to her knee. A garland of greens rested on top of her head, a circle of color pinned to her hair. This last day of December, there were no flowers to be had, unfortunately.

"You look ravishing!" Gervasi exclaimed, getting his first look at Ramira's handiwork. "Thank you, sis." Ramira grinned broadly. "Shall I carry you to the Great Hall?" he asked.

"I should hop as much as possible. I can't do the stairs, so you'll have to get me down them. Before I lost my powers, I could have jumped or teleported down them. It's just I'm going to have to do what little I can do and hopping's about it, I'm afraid."

"Hopping it is then, my love. Shall we?" She took small hops at his side, occasionally glancing at his face. Seeing him smiling so much, she too began to relax and smile as well, though her lip loops bobbing up and down across her mouth and chin didn't show it. He gently carried her down the stairs but sat her back on her foot at the base of the stairs. Proudly, she hopped beside him into the Great Hall, ready to face the hundreds of people gathered there to witness their new lord's wedding and of course to stare at her. Word had spread overnight.

If Gervasi had any concerns about how Rosita would be able to handle the wedding, they evaporated at once. She held her head high and hopped proudly to the front alongside of him. Ramira was at her other side, acting as her bridesmaid. He spotted his father, mother, and younger brother in the throng. They were smiling too, and he relaxed, but sensed the overwhelming emotion was one of great sympathy for Rosita and her terrible physical shape. That she bore it with determination and self-pride made him feel more like bursting out, shouting his love and admiration for Rosita.

The wedding was short and simple. He kept the reception fairly short, citing the need to beef up security and to make the arrangements for his father and his wife's funeral the next day. He also sent to Antonio and Amando, *I need to see you both right after the reception. It's critical.*

An hour later, the two men joined him in his suite, while Rosita, Ramira, and some other women met in an adjacent room of the suite. "Look, we have traitors among us here. Can you get word to the *mentales* gifted in the Bosque Verde that I need several of them who are truth sayers to come to the castle and help me check on everyone here? Further, let them know from now on, anyone with the gifts is welcome here in my castle. No longer will they be seen as outcasts. We need their help in keeping Malaca and the surrounding lands free from the claws of Valen. Also, is it possible to have them send a message from me to Lord Pedro Valen via the Comm Networks?" They agreed and left to handle it for him.

Next, he returned to his wife and sister. Ramira said, "We've got two dressmakers coming shortly. We are going to get special outfits made for Rosita, ones that will keep her warm and fit her body's shape."

"Terrific, sis. Rosita, I need to talk to you about teleporting. I've only been teleported twice and know absolutely nothing about it. I need to know because we have this Easterlings assassin who's using his teleport gift to assassinate people, and I have to find a way to stop him."

"Sure, I did quite a bit of it; we called it jumping to differentiate it from our hopping," Rosita replied, eager to be of some slight use to her husband. A half hour later, Gervasi thanked her and left the arriving seamstresses to do their handiwork. He had plans to make.

He rounded up Vasco, his father's advisor. "Look, I need you to gather up all the bits of wire you can find around the castle. Do it on the quiet and bring them to dad's bedroom. Don't let anyone see you doing this."

"Wire? What on Tierra for, son?" Vasco asked.

"I can't tell you now, but if I'm right, the assassin will be returning here." Vasco nodded solemnly and left to carry out his new lord's strange request.

That afternoon Amando returned. "They can send the message verbatim. When do you want to do it?"

"Now. The sooner, the better," Gervasi replied. He sat down and wrote out what he wanted to say, changing his mind several times before he bounced it off Amando.

The older man grinned. "My god, son. That will certainly get his attention! Won't you risk bringing that assassin back after you this time?"

"That's the idea. I have three men to bring to justice. We'll start with the easiest."

An hour later, his message was sent to Lord Pedro Valen, via the telepaths of Bosque Verde. He'd sent: Lord Pedro Valen. You have assassinated my father and brother. In no way does that change anything here in Malaca. I am now Lord Gervasi Quito Malaca. I guarantee you Malaca and all of old Abvera has seceded from your territories. We will remain an independent kingdom. We owe you no allegiance and will never give you any support whatsoever for any reason. In fact come spring, I will be seeking your death, as payment for your assassinations of Lord Ferdinan Malaca and Pino Malaca. Watch your own back from now on! I have spoken and my word is law.

"Well that'll certainly shake him up some," Vasco teased Gervasi once the message had been sent. "Now what?"

"Come, you can help me lay a trap for the assassin," he replied. Vasco and Amando followed Gervasi to the master bedroom. Here, they began laying out a grid of metal wire throughout the room. When they finished, the whole room was filled with inner connecting strands of wire, both iron and copper. All were between a foot and three feet above the floor. No one could walk more than a foot without running into the taught wires. Both men looked at Gervasi as if he'd lost his mind, but he was extremely pleased with the room when they finished.

"Gentlemen, now let everyone in the castle know Rosita and I will be sleeping in the master bedroom from now on," Gervasi ordered.

"When do you want to scour out the traitorous rats around here?" Vasco asked.

"Later after we catch the assassin, Vasco." Both men shook their heads and left to carry out his request, while he headed back to his own suite to talk to Ramira.

She followed him back to the master bedroom. After he explained his plan to her, she suggested placing a number of boards with protruding nails on the floor as well. He grinned, liking her devious idea and headed off to see to them.

That evening, the two began to play their game. After

announcing to everyone they would be sleeping in the lord's master bedroom from now on, they gave the appearance of doing so, but snuck over into his old suite just down the hallway. Ramira then joined them, along with Antonio. The three of them shared guard duties, each taking a three-hour shift.

Three nights later, Antonio woke Ramira and Gervasi. "I heard something, sounded like a cry of pain!" The three dashed out of the suite and down to the locked door of the master bedroom. Hastily, Gervasi opened it, while Antonio held a lantern high. There in the middle of the room was the Easterlings assassin, writhing in pain. Several of the wires protruded from his abdomen, blood dripping down his cloak. One wire went through his lower left leg. Nails protruded from his feet, and he was chopping wildly at the wires, trying to cut them. His pain was so great he could not focus to teleport out of the room and trap in which he was enmeshed. He tried to turn to see his opponents, but the wires mercilessly tore into his abdomen. He couldn't move his feet and he swore vehemently.

"Well, well, well, the rat is finally caught in his own game," Ramira called out.

Gervasi quickly ended the game, unwilling to allow the assassin any chance to escape. "Now that was clever!" Antonio exclaimed, once the man was slain. "Who would've ever thought of that?"

"Rosita gave me the idea. Your sister is a well of knowledge, Antonio. Like she said, he teleported into the room, but materialized with the wires inside of his body and with the nails through his feet. Those immobilized him. The pain kept him from being able to teleport himself back out of there. If he had, he would still be hobbled up. Either way, we got him. One down, two to go. Let your dad know we can use the truth sayers anytime now. We can begin to root out the other rats in this castle."

The next morning, Antonio left to fetch the City Guards. Following Gervasi's orders, these men took up positions just outside the castle gates and periodically along its walls. Their orders were simple. No one was to be allowed to leave the castle. At breakfast Gervasi made his announcement that there were traitors among them and that truth sayers were on their way here. Everyone in the castle would be tested. As he expected, a number of men and women attempted to flee and were taken into custody by the City Guards. Even two members of his Elite Guards tried to flee as well.

When the purge was over, Ramira and Antonio came up to Gervasi and Rosita, who were eating their supper. "We have an announcement to make," Antonio said with a wry smile. The two looked up. Gervasi noticed his sister was grinning from ear to ear. "Ramira has just agreed to marry me!"

"Wow! Terrific, sis, Antonio!" he replied.

"Wonderful, congratulations," Rosita added her enthusiasm to her husband's.

"I know, we're defying dad's wishes, but the hell with them. We love each other and that's that!" Antonio added.

"Rosita, I want you to be my bridesmaid," Ramira interrupted him. "Please, say you will."

"Me, well, if you want me I will. You were mine. I'm so happy for you both," she replied.

Antonio added, "Now you have two to constantly watch your backs." During the past few weeks and for the first time in his life, Antonio finally felt like he mattered, that he wasn't always standing in his father's shadow doing only Amando's wishes.

After the wedding a week later, Gervasi and Rosita moved into the master bedroom suite allowing Antonio and Ramira to move into the old suite next door. Now they began the real work, taking stock of their resources and planning for the future.

Gervasi expected come spring Lord Valen would send a small army to Malaca in an attempt to squash the rebelling territory and city. He had no army to counter them — that was the biggest problem Gervasi faced. It was the dead of winter, entirely the wrong time to try to raise an army from the vast lands of old Abvera, let alone from Malaca.

He and Antonio sat around a table with a large map of the old kingdom. "We are ill equipped to fight off an army. A siege of Malaca castle will do more damage than good; we can't hold out indefinitely," Gervasi explained. "What we need are some miracles here."

"There are quite a lot of *mentales* gifted living in Bosque Verde," Antonio suggested.

"Hey, that's an idea. Why not let them come to Malaca and form up our very own *Círculo de la Torres*? Just like they did down in Villa del Rey. I hereby appoint you to be their Venerado, Antonio. Rosita can be your healer or maybe your Regulator, if I understand these tower things properly. What say you?"

He grinned, "Okay, I'll see what can be done. You know there are a lot of archers living in the forest. They hunt deer and game. Maybe those would be useful too, somehow," Antonio suggested.

"Hey, they just might be. We are not following any rules here because Lord Valen sure isn't. Why not use arrows as a weapon? Look, the most likely route their army will take is a straight line from Valen to Malaca, passing squarely through Castilla Hills — perfect ambush country. We could pick them off one by one."

By May of 1251, Antonio Medio was officially Venerado Antonio, the leader of the first *Círculo de la Torres* of Malaca, temporarily housed within the castle's manor house. Their own tower was being designed with construction slated to commence in the summer. Rosita became one of their adjunct healers. Gervasi had about one hundred in his Elite Guards, plus the Volunteer Archers of Bosque Verde, who numbered some two hundred men and women. Additionally, twenty other *mentales* gifted from Bosque Verde volunteered to act as advanced scouts. They fanned out across old Abvera and began watching for the approaching Valen army.

Around the first of June, word finally came to Gervasi via the scouts. Valen was sending a small army of around a thousand men to squash the Malaca rebellion. After a week of plotting their course, they were heading in a straight line for Malaca, just as Gervasi had anticipated. Now, he acted.

"A lord must lead his troops into battle," Gervasi explained to his advisors and others. "While I am gone,

Antonio is in charge of the castle." He and Ramira led their meager forces out from Malaca. As they rode out, the streets were packed with those who came to see them off. It was unheard of that their own lord would be leading the attacks! This, they had to see for themselves. Gervasi was playing a dangerous game, but, if somehow he could win against this army, preventing them from reaching Malaca, he knew he would thereafter command the respect of everyone in Malaca and the surrounding lands. He had to take this gamble. He was a fighter and this was a fighter's duty. He had to lead his forces.

At the first ambush sight, he ordered the archers to aim first for those on horseback, some fifty of them, if the scouting reports were accurate. They were to fire off two volleys of arrows, then retreat to their horses and head for the next ambush location. His Elite Guards were broken into smaller squads and sent out to eliminate any of the Valen army's advance scouts and to look for additional good locations for the subsequent ambushes.

His tactics worked to perfection. With each attack, between fifty and seventy of the Valen soldiers were either killed or wounded by the archers. As their losses mounted, Gervasi took another approach. When the few remaining riders came galloping after the fleeing archers, he led several squads of his Elite Guards down on their supply wagons, trailing along behind the men, a mile or two back of them. Now they were denied both food and tent shelters. After the tenth ambush, the remaining soldiers routed and retraced their path, heading back towards Valen. Again, Gervasi instructed his scouts to make sure they did cross the Brozas River, the old boundary of Abvera and Trujillo.

In early August, Lord Gervasi and his troops returned victorious to Malaca. Wild cheering and celebrations broke out spontaneously throughout the city, and he encouraged them. They were free at long last from the many, many years of Valen dominance.

However, Antonio and Rosita also began routine healing operations for anyone who could get to their "tower." As expected by Rosita, this quickly had a very positive effect on the entire city. Now the *mentales* gifted were truly using their gifts to help their fellow man.

In September, Rosita's former Daughters of the Seas priestess leader, Ria, thought of her and how, in their terror-filled escape to Elegant Fashions Inc, she had been left behind. Ria had been healed, received her therapy sessions, and was also giving them. Her life was somewhat better, what with all the bots in Madiera. At this point in time, she felt responsible for having left Rosita behind and thus deprived of all these miracles that had given her a whole new life. Hence, she reached out to see if Rosita was still alive, using her newfound gift of telepathy.

Ria? Is this really you? Are you all right? Yes, I am fine and married to my boyfriend – the one who came to rescue me that terrible day.

After a lengthy chat, Ria sent for Benjamina. When Benjamina arrived to chat, she explained, "She was left behind when we evacuated Govia. Her family and boyfriend came to rescue her and took her back to Malaca. He married her, and she is now Lady Rosita, the wife of the new Lord Gervasi Quito Malaca. He's taken all the old kingdom of Abvera out of Lord Valen's grasp. Seceded. She's been using her native *mentales* healing skills on those who need it in Malaca. Isn't there some way we can get her lips healed and all that awful trauma she endured erased like we have? I would be more than willing to run her therapy sessions, if only she were somehow here. I can't go to Malaca. Too far to hop," she jested.

Benjamina chuckled. "Let me see what we can work out. To heal her, we'd have to bring her here to our Underground. We still need to keep that a secret."

"I know. I've not told her anything about Madiera. Please, I feel responsible for her, since I was her leader back then," Ria pleaded.

Two days later, Tim ran the teleport machine. Both Rosita and Lord Gervasi appeared on the low pad. He had his sword at the ready, while holding securely onto Rosita. "Welcome, I am Benjamina and this is Ria, of course. If you will follow me, we'll get your lips healed first thing. It is painless and takes only twenty minutes or so."

"Where are we?" Gervasi asked, sheathing his sword and making sure Rosita was able to hop down off the pad without falling. They followed Benjamina and the hopping Ria.

"We need to maintain secrecy because we're helping all those in need on Tierra. I can say this much, Lord Gervasi, you are somewhere in Brom," Benjamina replied as best she could.

In the next room, the two saw all manner of alien medical machines. "All these are alien?" he asked rubbing his eyes, not trusting what he was seeing.

"Yes, while I work on Rosita, why don't you take a close look at Ria's lips. See if you can tell where they were sliced," Benjamina deflected his attention somewhat.

"I can see a very faint line, that must be it," Gervasi replied. "Will my wife's lips look the same?"

"We'll know shortly," Benjamina replied. Twenty minutes later, she held up a mirror for Rosita to see her face, while Gervasi looked her over closely himself.

"Incredible, I can only see the faintest scar line, just barely visible. Thank you very much," Gervasi said, his voice carried just how grateful he felt to the two women.

Next, they walked and hopped into the next room where chairs were setup. Here Ria ran her therapy sessions on Rosita. Benjamina and Gervasi watched from some distance. "You know, this is so similar to what I did with her that first night we were together," he pointed out.

At noon, Rafaela brought in lunch trays and then later on, supper trays. That evening, they were led to a guest bedroom, but both wanted to talk about the therapy. Already Rosita was greatly impressed with it; she was feeling more and more alive and less and less like some freak. When Ria finally finished her up, Rosita felt better than she ever had in her entire life. Her eyes were alight with the brilliant flame of life. "I have to learn how to do this!" she insisted.

The next day, Benjamina hatted her up on the basics and turned her loose on Gervasi, while she sat back and oversaw Rosita's first session. Ria stuck around as well. First she had him return to the moment when he learned of the death of his paternal father, who he'd only known for a brief while. Of course soon they were into the earlier loss of Pino, his half-brother. "I always have to look out for myself. No one else will," he continued to say during the several runs through of those two emotional loss traumas.

Following the principles of the therapy, Rosita then asked him, "Is there an earlier moment similar to this one?" She had to ask him several times before he realized there was something there, but it was all black.

Two hours later, he'd run through his birth. His mother had kept saying those very words, while she was giving birth and then just afterwards. Suddenly, Gervasi began laughing wildly. "So that's why I always felt that I had to look out for myself! That's silly. I feel great now. This stuff really does work, Rosita! Thank you, love, thank you."

"Benjamina, we desperately need this therapy of yours in Malaca and all of old Abvera! Please, is there any way we can get it in use there?" Gervasi pleaded.

Benjamina saw this as a huge breakthrough. Now she had at least one tiny foothold in the otherwise empty Westerlings. She agreed to come and help Rosita work on others at Castle Malaca until Rosita had it down well. She also agreed to help anyone else there who wanted to learn how to do it. "Afterwards, you can always consult with me via telepathy. I will relay any new techniques and tips I develop. We are inventing the science of the human mind and spirit here."

On the lighter side, at the Fall Harvest Ball that Gervasi held in the Great Hall, hundreds gathered, dressed in their finest for the celebration dance. While Rosita wore a newly made blue pod-silk dress that was designed especially for her, she felt wholly out of place at Gervasi's side. "I feel terrible. I can't dance with you."

Gervasi sensed how much this was hurting her and, during the break between tunes, he called out to the musicians, "Play a fandango now." They complied. This was a hopping dance, in which all the rapid movements were done by making little hops, unlike the other slower dances. "Now you can dance with me," he said with a grin. She wasn't so sure about it, but with his steadying arm around her waist, she tried. Soon, both discovered she could still dance their traditional fandango dances. After that, Gervasi made sure nearly every other tune was a fandango.

Word soon spread among the musicians of Abvera. By the spring dance, many more new fandangos had been written in their Lady's honor. That began the explosion of new music being written and composed in the Westerlings. Thus, the renaissance of music in the Westerlings began up north in the old Kingdom of Abvera. Soon it began spreading southward to the other larger cities.

Of note, no one attended the Fall Council of the Lords of the Westerlings held in Valen Castle, much to the anger of Lord Pedro. Worse, Benito, Arabella, and Villa del Rey, embolden by Lord Gervasi's secession in the far north, expanded their territorial claims further inland some thousand miles. This left Valen controlling only the lands immediately around it, out to about a thousand miles. Lord Pedro had now lost control of three-quarters of the Westerlings! Worse, he no longer had large numbers of young men to conscript into his army to retake them. He sat that winter fuming and brooding in his castle, utterly unable to counter the massive uprisings. In short, Valen's total control over the Westerlings was destroyed. The real power now lay in the hands of the lords of four key cities: Malaca, Benito, Villa del Rey, and Arabella.

Chapter 14 Tragedy in the Easterlings

The situation in the Easterlings took a different turn. After the massive climate change, the old Kingdom of Matruk became the breadbasket land of the entire Easterlings. Southbend, its traditional capital saw explosive growth and in 1250 boasted a population approaching fifty thousand. The city continued to expand physically and now was divided into the Old Town, which lay at the center of the city, and New Town, which entirely surrounded it, nearly four times its physical size. Old Town was full of crumbling adobe buildings and became a den of thieves and assassins.

The single *Círculo de la Torres* of the Easterlings was at Adelmira at the southern edge of the Buku Hills, the start of the massive desert regions of the Easterlings. It was only natural the tower there had a very close relationship with Matruk, to the near exclusion of all the rest of the vast Easterlings territory. While there were good crop lands just south and west of the tower, just a few hundred miles further south, the land became arid. This was the old Kingdom of Alba, with the huge coastal city of Turda its capital city of some thirty thousand. Just north of Alba lay the old Kingdom of Arad with its large capital city of Tecuci. The northernmost old Kingdom of Domei, now a harsh winter desert zone, had one major coastal city, Teraspoli, which lost population and was down to some twenty thousand hardy souls. These three huge old kingdoms had been mostly ignored by their supposed rulers at Adelmira Tower.

Then in 1249 and 1250, the Daughters of the Seas arrived at the major and minor coastal towns and cities. They brought with them a huge resurgence in trading and fishing. Additionally their vast healing powers soon brought them to the complete attention of all those who lived along the coast of the Easterlings. By late 1250, word of these miracle healers reached far inland into the vast deserts of the Easterlings.

In the larger cities, other changes had occurred in their culture, which had a long history of physical binding of their women. Primary among these were concessions won by the Empress nearly a half century ago. Among the wealthier classes, women now no longer braided their hair, but kept it brushed out and tied in the back with the Midlands bluebird clasps. They also adopted the arm-fetter-gowns and six-inch heels as well, whose sales were pitched heavily to them by the Elegant Fashions Inc stores in the largest cities. In addition, the five-inch lip plates and long dangling earrings were also worn by the wealthy.

However, most all other women wore their hair in twin braids, wore their traditional fetter skirts, and had their arms bound to their waists at their elbows as they had for centuries. Made of heavy silk, these gaily-colored skirts fit extremely tightly all down their legs to their ankles with no walking slit. This forced the women to take a shuffling-like two-inch step at most. Women's movement was thus extremely slow and shuffling. None could climb stairs, but that was not a problem since all buildings had only one floor.

Important at this time was the simple fact there were only a handful of the Elegant Fashions Inc storefronts in the Easterlings, primarily in the four major cities. Thus, when disaster struck the Daughters of the Seas in December, 1250, over a hundred plus of these mermaids had no store to which to flee to be rescued. Some would have to somehow travel a couple thousand miles to the nearest store, wholly impossible for them. All this led to an unexpected outcome that impacted the stability of the entire Easterlings. Some might say the slow breakdown of the centuries-old Castas system was behind it.

What remained of the three old kingdoms (Domei, Arad, and Alba) abided by a strict three caste system called the Castas. The Lords Castas consisted of the rulers and those who controlled the power-base. The Craftsman Castas consisted of those who did the fine work, the coppersmiths, the millers, the rug makers, the cloth makers, the smelters, the blacksmiths, the soldiers, the guards, and the weapons makers. These were the gentry. The Labor Casta consisted of the lowest servants, the menial laborer, the wholly unskilled workers.

To help denote one's Castas, fingernail length was used. The Lords Castas kept their nails at least four inches long, though none was allowed to exceed the length of their actual Lord, whose nails were often six inches long. The Lords Castas seldom fought; their weapons were primarily ceremonial. Rather their fighting was done by proxy, utilizing their soldiers or personal guards instead.

The Craftsman Castas men were allowed to have their nails as long as two inches, but often their occupation prohibited such and that was acceptable. The Labor Castas could grow theirs to a half inch beyond their fingertips, but no more. Few could afford such luxury however.

Their women were also bound by the same Castas, and their nails uniformly spoke of the Castas to which they belonged. With both sexes, it was possible to marry into a higher Castas. That is, a Lords Castas could marry a Labor Castas, which would then elevate the Labor Castas man or woman into the Lords Castas. One never moved into a lower Castas, for that was not allowed. Ordinarily one was fixed permanently within the Castas in which he was born, excepting by marriage elevation.

Near the end of December 1250, the three large coastal cities each had a dozen Daughters of the Seas operating out of a large adobe compound. Eleven other smaller coastal towns each had six of the mermaids actively healing the sick and injured and blessing the sea going ships. While a few managed to get to their Elegant Fashions Inc outlet in time to be rescued, most did not. In many ways, what happened with three sets of these mermaids is indicative to what occurred with all fourteen such groups.

In Turda, Alba, forty year old Enzio Franco considered himself the ultimate businessman. It had started with the appearance of their Elegant Fashions Inc outlet in the heart of this huge coastal city. Those in the Lords Castas were plainly visible on the streets. Men wore thin, white suits made of silk. Black belts and shoes contrasted sharply, adding to the impressive appearance, along with their gem encrusted scimitars and daggers.

Their women wore the elegant new arm-fetter-gowns, discarding the long-standing waist chains. Again, these were primarily white silk and light, excepting re-enforcing bands at their ankles and along the sides of the gowns to prevent accidental ripping either by their arms or feet. Garter belts held up their black stockings, which contrasted sharply with their white gowns and white, six-inch heels. The pipe corsets had not been accepted here, but the lip plates and huge dangling earrings had. With their brown hair always now un-braided and falling down their backs and with their often six inch long nails, these women cut striking figures, especially when shuffling along the city streets.

Indeed styles and fashions were changing, and Enzio saw his opportunity to take advantage of these new erotic styles. Like many traditional men, Enzio believed that these styles were indeed erotic. So why not make money off this new trend? He opened up Enzio's Escort Service to provide some of these erotic women to accompany men for a night's entertainment. He chose his original beauties carefully, picking young teens from the lowest Castas and altering them into new style, elegant women. To the teens, they believed they were being elevated to the Lords Casta, and they jumped at this golden opportunity that came miraculously their way. One trip to Elegant Fashions Inc and they left as elegant women, wearing the new jeweled lip plates, incredibly long earrings, black silk hose, and white silk arm-fetter-gowns with matching white six inch heels. Leaving their hair un-braided and draped across their backs flowing down to just below their knees was the hardest change for these women to accept.

Only men who came to Enzio's Escort Service wearing one of the new white silk suits were allowed to choose one of his beauties to be their companion for the evening. His reasoning was simple, if they could afford the suits, they could afford his escort women. He had no fear the women would be mistreated. Unwritten law throughout the Easterlings condemned to death any man who physically harmed a bound woman or even failed to assist them when they needed some help with something.

In early December, Enzio's Escort Service had four beauties from which to choose. Lia was twenty and had worked for Enzio for nearly four years. Jemma and Mona were nineteen, and Gabriella was the youngest at eighteen. While at first they enjoyed being dressed in such finery and treated as if they were Lords Casta, they soon discovered they were being used as men's sex toys. To keep them from causing trouble, Enzio had two holes drilled in each of their lip plates. He inserted pad locks through them. Now they were unable to open their mouths to speak. "All women talk too much," he explained to them when he first locked their plates shut. Only at mealtimes did he unlock them. This solution had been working perfectly for the last three years now.

During the daytime when the women sat around their bedrooms in the back of his store, they could not chat or complain to each other. Further, when they were on the job in the evenings, again, they could not speak and thus could not cause "difficulties" with their clients. All in all, Enzio believed this was a perfect solution to his kept women. Then, in 1249, the Daughters of the Seas arrived in Turda. Of course, their strange body forms caused quite a stir among everyone from all Castas. Everyone assumed that these young women were of the Lords Casta, since they wore the lip plates and earrings.

Enzio saw a drop-off of his usual business clientele. Even he found himself staring at these most unusual women. More than one of his customers teased him, "Enzio, you should get some of those mermaids for your service. I bet you could make a fortune hiring them out for an evening's entertainment." He'd always followed the principle of what the customer wants, I should provide. His principle had so far made him a small fortune. If money alone allowed one into the Lords Casta, he was there and then some. As early as late 1249, Enzio began scheming to acquire one or more of these priestesses.

Of course, there were two key barriers to this. One, they were priestesses with enormous *mentales* gifts. Telepathy alone would pose enormous problems, to say nothing of their inherent teleportation gifts. If he somehow got a hold of one, she would leave his bedroom at will. Two, they were always accompanied by their own personal guardian fighter. Enzio was not a fighter; his own six-inch nails prevented even holding a scimitar properly. Still, fighters could be hired to take out the guardians, but then what? The mermaids would simple teleport back to their place.

No, these exotic women were simply out of his reach for now, he decided. "One day, one day," he kept telling himself. His dreams of possessing some of these women kept him from "acquiring" additional younger women to expand his escort service. He waited patiently for the right time to act.

Then came that fateful day one warm December day in 1250. Word spread rapidly. The Daughters of the Seas had lost all their powers! He acted instantly! Enzio rounded up six fighters-for-hire and one carriage. Within minutes of learning of the disaster that had befallen the mermaids, he and his men arrived at their adobe complex, close to the sprawling docks.

Chaos was all around him. Guardians were packing their things and fleeing. The dozen Daughters of the Seas were sobbing hysterically, but some were also begging their guardians, "Please, we must be taken to Elegant Fashions Inc. Please, you must help us. We are now completely helpless, please." Their pleadings fell on many deaf ears. Enzio saw the guardians recognized these priestesses without their powers would be useless. Further, they would be out of their well-paying job and hence they were clearing out, for the most part, though one or two seemed to be trying to get the women together.

Into the hysterical madness and grief, Enzio stepped calmly and surely. "You, you, you, and you, come with me, I will take you there. I have a carriage waiting for you. Men, grab them so they don't fall," he ordered his guards. They did as ordered, picking up the four prettiest of the twelve, but not their leader priestess, who was still trying to get the guardians to fulfill their obligations to the Daughters of the Seas. Before anyone realized what was happening, Enzio climbed into his carriage and watched as his men lifted the four young women into his carriage, depositing them on the benches. All four were crying hysterically. Wisely, Enzio didn't say anything.

Once at his business, he had his men carry the mermaids into his large adobe home, depositing them on the edge of a bed, side by side. After paying the men, he returned to look at his prize catch, eyeing them greedily. At long last, he could satisfy his clientele's erotic desires in a big way. While he knew he could have easily taken all dozen, he had not. Enzio knew these mermaids, stripped of their magical powers, would be entirely dependent upon someone for their every need. He had four other women here, and they would now provide all the help his new acquisitions would need.

“There, there, my beauties, it will be all right. You now work for me. I am Enzio Franco and you are now part of Enzio’s Escort Service. In the morning, I will get you all elegantly dressed for your new roles as my top escort models. Now what are your names, please?” he explained.

“But we are supposed to go to Elegant Fashions Inc and be rescued,” the older teen pleaded.

“There, there, there will be none of that silliness. You are all beautiful young women. I will see that you are of the Lords Casta in the morning. You are already rescued. Now, what are your names?”

Between sobs, they replied. Daniela was the eldest at sixteen. Then came Alessa, a year younger. Arianna and Floriana were both just fourteen. Leaving them continue to sob out their hearts, one by one he removed their lip plates and made his alterations to them. Once reinserted, he then locked their plates shut, effectively ending their futile attempts to speak. That accomplished, he brought his other four women into the room.

“Now then, here are your helpers. This is Lia, this is Jemma, this is Mona, and this is Gabriella. Ladies, I want you to pick one of these new mermaids to be your charge. You will help them with whatever they may need. First thing, lead them to their new bedrooms and get their hair brushed out. I must see to getting them proper gowns and heels.”

The older women in their heels shuffled very carefully over to one of the young teens and helped her get up onto her foot. The mermaids tried to talk, but with their plates locked tight, they were unable to be understood. They wanted their helpers to put an arm around them to keep them from falling. Enzio watched as his new exotic beauties hopped slowly and carefully out of the room, down the hall, entering other unused bedrooms. He began dreaming of the vast profits that he would soon be making.

Realizing he best not use Elegant Fashions Inc because the mermaids had wanted to go there to be somehow rescued, Enzio instead hired a couple of local dressmakers to make his four new additions some proper white silk gowns. Later he traced each one's foot and purchased white heels to match the ones worn by his four normal women. Of course, he tossed the extra shoe from each pair.

Three days later, he had Daniela finally dressed properly for work. She wore a sleek, light, white silk fetter-gown. Of course, the fetter portion had no effect on her; she had only the one foot, nicely covered in the fine, black silk hose. Daniela shook her head from side to side trying to tell him that she couldn't wear the six-inch stiletto he was fastening to her foot. Unable to speak, she tried saying, "No, I can't keep my balance or hop like this." Her words were unintelligible.

"Sorry, but all elegant women are wearing them. I am sure with a little practice, you can manage to hop in them." She continued to protest. Then he forced her up on her heel. She wobbled wildly, frantically trying to stand on it and not fall. He gave her a push forcing her to hop or fall down. Soon Enzio saw just how unstable his elegant mermaids were in these heels. It didn't matter to him though. He just adopted another rule. Those who hired them would have to promise always to keep an arm around their waists or they would take a nasty tumble. Further, this also meant that they could not "escape" on their own, should they get such a wild notion.

That very evening his clientele immediately hired all four of his new mermaids. All four cried and complained by talking through their teeth that they couldn't do this. It fell on deaf ears. One by one, the lecherous men put an arm around his woman's waist and pulled her forward. Daniela went first. She had no choice but to try to hop beside this strange man, who was leering at her. If he hadn't been holding her, she'd have fallen. Thus began her nightmare evenings. That she was raped each night was the least of her terrors. Her greatest fear was being left alone. She was now deprived of the only thing left to her, her ability to at least move by hopping.

Enzio's profits began to soar to new heights. Some of

the funds he spent on his eight women, purchasing them more fine dresses and heels. This only depressed the four even more. Quickly however, the hearts of the other four women, who were tending the daily needs of the four mermaids, went out to them, as they saw how much they were suffering. The only times that their lip plates were unlocked were meal times. Enzio enforced a strict policy of no talking while eating. The women ignored that as much as they dared.

"Don't worry, Daniela, I will always be here to help you, always," Lia whispered between bites. Likewise, the other three promised their mermaids the same thing. The growing bonds between these eight women was all that kept them alive. Their lives had turned into a living nightmare with no end in sight.

Around this same time up in Tecuci, Arad, the second largest city along the coastline of the Easterlings, Sultan Fausto Ferro had gained total control over the entire city. Old traditions were breaking down and he led the way. He kept his fingernails short, for he was a superb fighter and a master of strategy. At thirty-eight, he and his ever-growing force of fighters had finally gained total control over the port city.

He had a small harem of wives. Sonia was the eldest at twenty. Already, she had born him a son. Then came Susana, nineteen, and Rosetta, eighteen, his latest wife. Each now wore the latest fashions, emulating their far distant empress from many years past. That is, they wore the new arm-fetter-gowns, lip plates, long earrings, pipe corsets, and toe shoes. He was immensely proud of their magnificent appearance, though they didn't hold the same opinions entirely. That breathing was terribly difficult was not a problem. They mostly sat around their gardens during the daytime. This also meant they did very little walking, which in the toe shoes was quite challenging. That their palace complex had solid surfaces of cobblestones make walking in them possible. Beyond the palace, walking on the soft sandy streets was exceedingly difficult for them, if not impossible. Still that too was not a problem; they were carried when needed by the Sultan's men.

In November 1250, Sultan Fausto explained to his wives

over dinner, "You know, these new Daughters of the Seas priestesses are doing an admirable job. For once, we have true healers in Tecuci. Not once has any healer come here from Adelmira Tower."

"Aren't they supposed to come here and help?" asked Sonia.

"Yes, that was the deal. Not once have they come. Yet out of nowhere, these priestesses have come. Impressive."

"Dear, haven't they been a boon to the fishermen? I heard stories from some of the women in town that is so," Susana asked, politely.

"Indeed, my pretty Susana. That they have. Record catches. Besides that, we are now eating bread made from Midlands' wheat, the real thing. The merchants of my city are making profits like never before. I've received a request to join the lords from Villa del Rey, making Tecuci a part of their new Coastal City-States, independent of Adelmira Tower," he pointed out what the latest dispatch had said.

"But dear, their tower is even further away than Adelmira," Sonia pointed out.

"My thinking exactly. If Adelmira never comes here, why should their gifted come here? They are three times farther away," he countered.

"So what are you going to do?" Sonia probed.

"I say let's make Tecuci and all the Arad independent once more. We used to be our own masters, the mighty Kingdom of Arad, before those damnable *mentales* gifted destroyed our old kingdom, forcing us under the thumb of Adelmira Tower. With these priestesses healing us, it is time I take back what is rightfully ours, the entire Arad! No more taxes to Adelmira. No more letting them steal away the very few *mentales* gifted from us. Besides, this is a good thing, now that our merchants are making a small fortune. Those funds should support us and the Arad," he declared.

He continued, "Starting tomorrow, I am going to send out my forces to all the oasis clans and bring them under my control, releasing them from Adelmira Tower's grip. Let's see how many *mentales* gifted we can find. Perhaps we can have our own tower here in Tecuci." None of them had the slightest idea what a tower actually did, but the idea was appealing.

Later that night, the three women helped each other undress down to their pipe corsets. After brushing out their long brown hair, Fausto joined them, undressing himself. "Ah, my pretties, it is time for bed once again." One by one, they lined up, oldest to youngest, the order of their marriages. Each one put their upper arms at their sides and put their lower arms behind their backs one on top of the other so that he could slip the leather tubes over their arms, binding them for the night. One by one, in the proper order, the women tossed their hair back and climbed into bed. Fausto doused all the lanterns save their small night light and gently slipped in among his harem. "Whose turn is first tonight?" he whispered.

Late December brought the disaster to the Daughters of the Seas. Sultan Fausto was one of the first to hear about their total loss of their powers. Like many other men, he was captivated by their erotic body shapes, but he was also shrewd. The men of Villa del Ray, Westerlings, had brought them here. Yet now their powers were gone. Could this be some diabolical means to enforce their will on him? He'd not joined their political alliance, instead declaring his independence of Adelmira Tower, reclaiming Arad as his kingdom. Could this be retaliation? Or was it something else entirely? One thing he did know. Without their powers of telekinesis and teleportation, they would be almost entirely helpless, but would they one day regain their powers?

Sultan Fausto acted swiftly, accompanying some of his men to the adobe complex of the priestesses near the docks. As he suspected, he found a dozen terrified, sobbing women and chaos among their guardians. Some spoke of getting to the Elegant Fashions Inc, but he ignored them, his keen eyes sizing up each of the dozen mermaids. He picked out the three prettiest and had his men snatch them up and bring them out to his carriage. Then he climbed in and finally spoke to the sobbing young women.

"My ladies, this is a catastrophe for you. I am saving you three. Soon I will marry you and you may take your places in my harem. Then you will not want for a single thing," he said softly and as lovingly as he could, though he felt no love for them, just an erotic arousal. Still if in time they regained their powers, he would have three of them as his own wives. For such incredible powers, he was willing to treat them as his wives. Then again, he really didn't love any of his wives, for that matter. They served him as he served them.

That at least caused them to cease their hysterical sobbing. Arriving at his well-guarded complex, he lifted each one down from his carriage. "Okay, follow me, my dears," he commanded. Terrified out of their minds, the three did their best to hop after him, wiggling and wobbling to keep their balance. Their whole world had just been turned upside down; they felt completely helpless just like they had before they received their enormous psi powers.

Inside, Fausto explained to his three wives what his plan was. He ended with, "You three will look after their needs. Perhaps one day soon, they will regain their enormous powers and that will benefit all of us." He then summoned the local priest and within an hour had married them. Sonia was careful to note the precise order of the marriages, however. Custom dictated that the first wife always was handled and satisfied first, then the second and so on. Renata, sixteen, became his fourth wife. Natale, fifteen, became number five, while Sandra, fourteen, became number six.

Quickly, the three original wives took charge of the new wives. By suppertime, they realized just how much work this was going to involve. These mermaids were practically helpless in all ways. Still, it was not their place to complain. Later when the six removed their clothing for bed, they finally saw how altered the three mermaid's bodies were. Pity and sympathy replaced their annoyance and they began to develop a close relationship with them. More importantly, they discovered that all three were virgins still. This they pointed out to Fausto.

"Hum, virgins. My mermaids, unless you have any objections, I will keep your virginity intact a while. Perhaps that may play a role in the regaining of your lost powers," he decided. The still frightened women readily agreed, believing they had somehow put off the marriage consummation. Still, he did pleasure the women, which they did enjoy. Although they were well treated, Natale, Renata, and Sandra felt they were kept prisoners. They'd lost their lives and were now merely being the sultan's play toys. They were emotionally miserable as well.

Over a thousand miles farther on up the coast of the Arad, Warlord Luca Marco had similar notions. He ruled over Tetrano Oasis, located twenty-five miles inland from the coast, at the edge of the semi-arable strip of land along the coast, where some crops could be grown. He was a ruthless warlord of forty-five. His longtime wife, Romana, was two years younger, and had born him two sons and a daughter, Valeria, who was now eighteen. During the past two years, he'd seen a sudden, huge demand for the crops grown in and around his controlled lands. Wisely, he traced this sudden growth to the nearby port town of Po.

Accompanied by ten of his trusted men, he visited Po to discover what was causing this sudden demand for their crops. Mind you, he greatly appreciated the sudden increase in wealth this brought him. Rather, he wanted to know why it had come about. Luca soon discovered the source was these new strange priestesses and the great ocean going caravels from the Westerlings. He learned of the great powers these most unusual women had and was deeply intrigued by them. Great healers were perhaps the most important people to have in one's employ, especially if you anticipated fighting battles, which Warlord Luca certainly did.

He began hatching a plot to kidnap some and bring them to Tetrano Oasis. However, since they had teleport skills, he knew that this would be futile. They'd just teleport back home to Po. He left six of his men in Po and returned to his oasis with the rest. They would keep an eye on things for him, while he attempted to work out a way to keep the mermaids from teleporting back to Po, once he'd kidnaped them and brought them to Tetrano.

Late December, one of his men came galloping into Tetrano with startling news. The Daughters of the Seas had lost all their powers. Luca acted immediately. With another ten of his men, he rode hard back to Po. He had one man steal a wagon, while he and the others stormed the priestess' compound. Other lords had similar ideas and Luca found himself in a battle over the spoils. Although he lost two men, he was able to snatch two of the women and hastily evacuated Po. The women, Tina and Zita, were both fifteen and were placed in the wagon and then covered up, out of the way of prying eyes. Later after dark, they finally arrived at Tetrano Oasis.

"Here we are, your new home. Out of the wagon, please," he ordered.

"But we can't," Zita sobbed. Both women had been sobbing and crying, sometimes hysterically, most of the long ride home. He had to lift them both down, much as he often did for his wife. Hopping in the soft sand was almost impossible for the two, who wiggled and wobbled, as their foot shifted positions in the soft sands of the approaching desert. At last, both fell, but managed somehow not to smash their lip plates into the ground.

Luca now saw their plight and realized they would not be able to go far at all in the sands without help. He kindly lifted each to her foot. With an arm around each of them, he nudged them forward again, supporting them, as they valiantly tried to hop in the warm sands. Once inside, he led them to the large bedroom of his daughter. "Valeria, your job now is to attend to Zita and Tina's needs. They will be many. They can't hop in the sand without help. Take care of them. One day they will regain their powers, and we will have two great healers for our oasis!"

Valeria protested, but knew it was in vain. However, soon she began to feel a deep sympathy for Tina and Zita. That they had been kidnaped, turned into these freaks, and were now almost completely helpless tore at her heart. Before long, she devoted herself to caring for their needs. The three quickly became good friends, sharing their deep-seated fears with her. Valeria was a good listener, but had no idea of how she could really help them out of this mess with her father. All feared if they did not regain their powers, then Luca would simply rape them, adding them to his new harem.

Similar events happened at the other towns and cities.

Only a handful of the Daughters of the Seas in the Easterlings actually made it to the safety of the Elegant Fashions Inc and were subsequently rescued. Yet, there are two other events of significance that also occurred.

Far up in space, Calder and Wystan trailed after the fleeing spaceships. Both were fully intent upon finding where these ships came from and then settling down there. The incredible technologies that these possessed, especially the powerful energy beams, had impressed both gods, that is, free beings who did not need a physical body to operate. Wystan was imagining the mighty battles that could be fought using them. Unfortunately for both spiritual beings, the raiders had other ideas. Discovering the two were following their retreating ships and with the assumption they had come from Tierra, they therefore must be Imperium spies of some new and unknown kind.

The fleeing frigates suddenly opened fire with all their energy weapons trained on the energy fields around Calder and Wystan. The two unsuspecting gods took the full force of the blasts. Surprised and knocked wholly unconscious, both gods, both spiritual beings, began drifting in space. Gravity slowly made its presence felt, dragging the electronically zapped and unconscious beings back down towards Tierra. What happened next, some might say was poetic justice. Lysandra merely thought, “How marvelous!”

Wystan landed out upon the vast arid, frozen steppes of Domei at a small town called Viterbo. He sailed into the adobe home of Carlo and Abelie Donatello, where Abelie was just giving birth to their first son. Totally confused, Wystan saw the tiny baby body and put a communication line onto it, hoping to get himself re-oriented. Instead, the pain of its birth sucked him squarely into the baby body’s head. As zonked as he was, he tried to energize a beam to push himself back out, but that only pulled him in more tightly. Then the overwhelming unconsciousness hit him and he slept. When he awoke, it was morning and he felt starving. He eagerly began suckling on his mother’s huge breast. Thus, Wystan found himself not only stuck in a human body, but he somehow felt he *was* this body. His confusion only added to these convictions. After all these centuries, Wystan had finally himself become trapped within the human bodies with which he had been playing around with for his own amusement for centuries.

One of the guardians of the priestesses at the town of Po had married his charge. Beppe Venuto married priestess Elda, who was pregnant with their first child, when the awful disaster stuck the priestesses. Before long, armed men began raiding their compound, and fighting broke out among the various raiders. Most of the guardians chose this opportunity to flee for their lives. Beppe and Elda were at the back of their complex when the large-scale fighting broke out. "Quickly, Elda, hop to the rear door. I will protect us. We have to get out of here!" he ordered. She did her best, hopping as quickly as she could. Before she could reach the doors, two of the fighters rushed them, engaging Beppe. He fought bravely, refusing to give ground, fighting to protect the priestess and his wife, as he had been paid to do. Outnumbered, the odds were against him. He was not a great fighter. Four blades to his two were most daunting.

His scimitar finally found its mark, cutting deeply into one of his attacker's arm. Unfortunately for him, the other took this opening to nearly sever his left arm at the elbow. Howling in pain, he made a thrust towards his attacker, and his scimitar again cut into the man's abdomen. Both attackers fell back and Beppe, gushing blood, did the same. He dropped his scimitar and ran to the door, opening it for Elda. After she hopped out, crying hysterically for his wounds and her own helplessness, he followed after her.

"You are bleeding badly. I can't even do anything to help you, Beppe!" she sobbed.

"That's okay. Come on. I know someplace we can go before I pass out." He led her through the streets to a small adobe home, some four blocks away. He pounded on the door and then slumped to the ground, passed out.

When he came to, he was lying in a makeshift bed. Elda was sitting on the floor close to him. "What happened?" he whispered.

"They had to take off your arm where it was just

hanging on a little. They say you will survive. Oh Beppe, whatever will we do now?" she again started sobbing. Both of their lives were now ruined. His right hand found her head, and he rested it on her, then fell asleep.

Several weeks later, Beppe was healed enough to travel. He gave his friend the last of their coins and in return received a small wagon, horse, and supplies. Elda had been asking for days what they were going to do now. At last, he came up with the only answer he could think of: to return to his home oasis and live there in safety. After thanking his friend profusely, he helped her into the wagon and climbed aboard himself. Taking the reins in his hand, he began the long trip through the desert of Arad to his home oasis, Campo, some three hundred miles as the crow flies due west of Po.

Campo was a poor oasis, perhaps a thousand eking out a meager living. Once there, his parents helped him to quickly build a small adobe home for himself and Elda, a one-room affair. His task now was to find some way to support himself and Elda and their child soon to come into the world. He finally found with only one arm, his choices were severely limited. Finally, he discovered he could make adobe bricks, something which most here hated to do. Beppe then began his business, providing adobe bricks for the constructions around the oasis. While it offered only the barest survival potential, they did manage. Once their child was born, Elda discovered she could jump in the mud pile, helping to mix the straw, dung, and clay into the proper consistency for the bricks, thereby helping Beppe earn a meager living.

In March 1251, Elena was born. "She looks just like her pretty mom," the proud Beppe announced as he struggled to get the newborn cleaned up and over to her side for her first nursing.

The god Calder, also wholly unconscious, was pulled by Tierra's gravity and finally landed solidly on the ground with a heavy thump. The collision roused him slightly and his first sight was the tiny infant, Elena, who was semi-unconscious from her birth as well. Vaguely, he recognized the strange body form, one of his mermaids, and put a communication line out to her. As dopey and confused as he was, Calder was instantly sucked into the body's head, where he experienced the pain and trauma the small body had just experienced during its birth. He fell asleep again, awakening a bit later, frantically sucking for life-giving milk. He forgot everything else and focused on getting more and more milk.

After that, he had vague notions he had been something other than this tiny baby, but no more. He was now tiny Elena and was loved by Elda and Beppe. He was warm and secure, which was all that mattered now. He had no idea he was now playing the game of being human beings, the creatures which had amused him for so many centuries. As Elena grew up, she continued to have the thought she was supposed to have some incredible powers. They never materialized, however.

Thus, by early 1251, the old Kingdom of Domei and the old Kingdom of Arad had declared their total independence from Adelmira Tower. Turda, Alba chose to join the Coastal City-States alliance, since Adelmira Tower lay at the very northern edge of old Alba. They didn't want to risk trying to retake all Alba from the tower. Adelmira Tower now controlled the breadbasket Matruk with its large city of Southbend and the northern half of Alba, which was also part of the new breadbasket lands.

Chapter 15 Lysandra's Move

When Calder abandoned Tierra and his Daughters of the Seas, the Goddess Lysandra anticipated she'd be heavily called upon. By early January 1251, she had been. She'd heard at least a dozen prayers from these women, most all in the Easterlings. Further, she knew the vast majority of Calder's women didn't even know about her, much less that they could pray to her for help. Already she had gotten an enormous boost from Ben Blackwater, now Benjamina, but he or she was in Brom, Midlands, far, far from these Easterlings women, scattered all up and down the long coastline.

At first she toyed with the idea she could just teleport these abandoned women to Benjamina's location. However, doing that without demanding a sacrifice on the part of the woman being teleported would violate her basic working principles. A gift from the goddess must be accompanied with an appropriate sacrifice from the recipient. These mermaids had nothing left physically to sacrifice, except their sight and a single leg. Further, she could not undo Calder's massive body morphing because she had no idea of what he'd done or how he'd done it, and she simply couldn't ask for more from these women. Yet they were women and were praying for her help. Lysandra had to do something, but what and how? By March, she had little choice but to do something. At long last an idea formed.

Some twenty women lived at Turda's Sisterhood Guild House. Fifty year old Guild Mother Luciana Vitalia addressed her assembled twenty sisters. "Yes, it is official. I've received the document from Lord Turda today. Officially Turda is now part of the Coastal City-States, governed by the lords and tower in Villa del Rey, Westerlings."

"But what does this actually mean Guild Mother?" thirty year old Felisa Sandro pointedly asked. She had a reputation for being rather antagonistic towards those in power. She was also the best scout in the Turda Sisterhood.

The portly Luciana replied, "Heavens knows, Felisa!

One thing we do know is Adelmira Tower has not ever given anyone in Turda any real aid like they were supposed to be doing per that Blackwater Ultimatum."

Felisa replied, "Darn right they haven't! No, we have to take our wounded almost a thousand miles overland up to their tower to get any healing." She was tall and thin, with thin eyebrows and thin lips. Felisa bore her mistreatment at the hands of men plainly visible as the ugly scar on her right cheek.

"Yes, Felisa, but what about all the priestesses they sent here," Bianca Alessandra e Freda countered. She was thirty-nine and one of their best fighters, along with her free mate Angelica Freda e Alessandra, a year older. "They've lost their healing powers and have literally vanished. Are we to expect this so called Renegade Tower is now going to come here to Turda? Thousands of miles away? To take their place? I think not!" she retorted.

"She's right. Don't look for healing from them," her free mate Angelica added, backing her longtime lover. "So what's to be gained? We send our taxes to the Westerlings instead of to Adelmira? Makes no sense to me."

"Are you forgetting the fresh apples you so love, Angelica? Or the many other new things that we can now buy in the markets?" Donatella Alba e Falda countered. She was twenty-eight and the only *mentales* gifted in the house. Her free mate was the fighter Marcella Falda e Alba, two years older. Donatella had a noble birth but had relinquished her birthrights for her own personal freedom. She too was quite thin and tall. She continued, "This Coastal City-State alliance has opened up all Tierra to vast commercial trading, the likes of which we've never seen before. That alone is vitally important to everyone's future, but I agree, the loss of the priestesses and their healing is a sore point."

"Hey, I like all these new spices and delicacies we're able to get in the markets these last few years. You all like the variety," their cook, Savina spoke up. She was somewhat overweight and had a jovial personality. "Trading has been good for us. Think about your bellies for once." She chuckled and several others cracked a smiled; she had a point.

"Hey, speaking of those priestesses who aren't priestesses," Gina Vanetta broke in, "I saw one of them all dressed up in the company of one of the city noblemen the other night. He's married. She looked miserable though." Gina was short, thin, and incredibly agile. Something of a contortionist, she was their resident thief, though she preferred to be known as their "Returner of Rightful Property."

"You mean she's become a whore?" asked Felisa, her voice full of disgust.

"Can't say about that, Felisa. But what's she doing with that nobleman?" Gina answered coyly.

Just then, the dimly lighted room with its crude wooden tables and chairs that had seen better days became illuminated in a warm yellowish glow, startling all twenty women. Then a form materialized within the glow. Lysandra appeared before the assembled house of the Sisterhood.

"Lysandra?" asked Luciana, her eyes wide with wonder and awe. It was her place to address anyone new to the Guild House.

"Yes, Sisters. I have come to ask for your aid in helping the very women you were just talking about — the priestesses of Calder, the Daughters of the Seas. These women have been horribly, terribly misused by men and by Calder, who has abandoned them. Yes, they have lost all their powers and are now almost completely helpless women. There are about five hundred of them. A courageous woman and her associates in Brom, Midlands, have rescued nearly four hundred of them and are in the process of salvaging their lives for them."

"As you have heard, here in the Easterlings, over a hundred of these priestesses were not able to be rescued. They have been kidnaped by ruthless men and are now being forced to serve their wicked needs. Many have prayed to me for help and for a quick death. As you know, for my help, I demand a sacrifice of the woman. In this case, the poor women have nothing left to sacrifice thanks to Calder! By the way, Calder is now suffering as one of them."

"So I have come to you to ask a great deal of you. I want you to travel the coast of the Easterlings and find these mutilated women and rescue them. In time, they will be taken to Brom, where they will be able to be salvaged and live fruitful lives. This will be an exceedingly dangerous mission to ask of you, but I have no other choice, if these victimized women are to be helped. The only other alternative open to me is to give them a merciful death, which I am loathed to do, since they are victims of men and Calder."

"Hey, you came to the right place!" Felisa broke in. "We here have all been victimized by men, one way or another. We'll do it. Tell us what we need to do. Are the rest of you with me?" she asked, waving her hand at the other nineteen women around the tables. A chorus of "yes" echoed in the small room.

Lysandra appeared to smile. She said, "I had so hoped you would volunteer to help rescue these women, though at great peril to yourselves."

"Yes, that is all well and good, but what's in it for us?" asked their resident thief, Gina. "I don't mind danger, but there has to be a profit in it."

"Is not helping these otherwise helpless women not enough profit for you, Gina?" Lysandra asked pointedly.

Gina flushed, "Well, certainly, I supposed so." She regretted her outburst. "I mean it will cost us quite some funds to travel this extensively. Food, horses, oasis fees. We here aren't exactly rich."

"Glad you see it that way. I will give you a money pouch from which you may withdraw unlimited silver coins, Gina. Expenses will be covered. When you have rescued all that can be salvaged, I will see that each of you receives a most priceless gift from those at Brom." That brightened Gina up completely, who wondered what this priceless gift could possibly be. Gold? Gems?

"Your contact in Brom is Benjamina Blackwater. Begin here in Turda. There are ten women being held captive here. Rescue them and bring them in total secrecy to your Guild House. Take care of them until there are twenty here. Daily Benjamina will contact Luciana to see if she has twenty women ready to be taken to Brom and safety. When there are, she will coordinate the teleport operation. I would suggest you make up a strike force of some eight of you to travel forth and do the actual rescuing. The others here will soon have their hands full caring for the many needs of these poor women."

Felisa spoke up, "I should go. I'm the best scout here."

"Me too, I've got the *mentales* gifts and can keep us in contact with the Guild House as we go along," Donatella quickly volunteered.

"Hey, where my free mate goes, so goes I," Marcella added with a broad grin towards her lover.

Angelica looked at Bianca, who nodded barely perceptibly. "We'll go. We're the best fighters here."

"I'll go," Milana Mirella added her alto voice to the mix. "You need someone who is good with horses and that's me." She was thirty-five.

"Hey, you can't keep me from coming," Gina insisted. This sounded like a real adventure to her.

"I'll come; you are going to need a cook," Savina volunteered. "Besides, I can also drive a wagon."

"Thank you all," Lysandra again spoke. "Angelica will have the money pouch. I will guide you to each location where a woman is being held. We begin here in Turda with Enzio's Escort Service."

"I knew it!" Gina interrupted the goddess. "I just knew there was monkey business going on there! Poor women." She shut up, realizing in her enthusiasm, she'd just interrupted a real goddess.

"Make your preparations and begin as soon as you can. Again, I thank you, as will the many women you will be rescuing." Lysandra's form dissolved, leaving behind the soft yellow glow. Then that too vanished. Silence reined for a minute before they all began talking at once.

Gina headed off to case their first target: Enzio's Escort Service. Meanwhile, the others acquired three wagons, horses, and supplies. Next, they prepared two of the wagons for desert traveling. That is, they put a tall wooden frame over the wagon's beds and hung thin sheets over the framework. This way, the occupants of the wagons would be shielded from the harsh desert sunlight. Since they would be traveling along the coastline, this wasn't necessary, except the sheets would hide their passengers from view, which is precisely what Angelica desired. No prying eyes.

Gina walked down the densely packed streets, mentally checking her armaments. Her two daggers were strapped to her waist belt, one on either side. She wore a light blouse and pants with tall soft-soled boots, men's ware as most saw it. She had long ago abandoned the nonsense tradition of the Easterlings physical binding of women. She wanted the freedom of action all men had. Each boot contained a hidden knife, while a pair of throwing daggers was strapped to the outside of each pant leg. Her lock picks were concealed in her hair. Her double braids were tied up in a bun on the top of her head, out of the way in case of trouble. The double horse head earrings clearly identified her as a member of the Sisterhood, though these days, anyone could tell that much from her dress, totally non-conformist.

She also had her own special weapon tied to the backside of her belt. Three one-pound stones were each tied to a two foot long leather thong, and the thongs were tied together. She was short and not a fast runner. If she needed to stop someone running away from her, she'd whirl the stones around her head and throw them. Their spinning action would encircle her opponent's legs, tripping him. Of course, if she aimed for his neck, the stones would probably kill him, if not choking him first. Picking up her pace, Gina felt secure and confident, though she kept her eyes open. Pickpockets were also walking the streets.

The Escort Service occupied a large adobe building which was a hundred feet long and forty wide, taking up a good quarter of the entire block. A food market and candle maker were just across the street. Gina stopped at the mart, picked up some dates and sat down in front of the mart, leaning her back against its adobe wall. From here she had a clear view of the long front of the building across the street. A large sign advertised the service. The wide double door entrance was watched by one guard, who paced up and down past the door. The windows were frequent, but too small to allow a human to enter them. Her eyes roamed to its roof, its weak point. Like many of the cheaper constructions here in Turda, the roof consisted of several heavy timbers with thin crossbeams, covered in an oily paste mixed with palm leaves. Inexpensive and cool, it sufficed to keep the infrequent drizzles out. It never rained significantly here in Turda, but nightly the sea breeze brought heavy dew and sometimes a light drizzle.

After a time, Gina noticed a young man had walked past her spot some ten times now. Curious. On his next pass, he quietly stopped and sat down beside her, pretending to chew on a piece of straw. “Back door, but it has iron bars. Don’t think it’s ever used. Four guards inside, one outside, if you’re curious.”

Startled, Gina asked, “Who the hell are you? What’s your interest in yonder establishment?” She noticed he didn’t have a lot of money. Either that or good quality clothing was not what he spent his money on. He carried only a small dagger, no scimitar. Hence, she immediately ruled out a fighter. He must be a tradesman from the callouses on his hands, as opposed to a thief.

“Gianni Mazo, ma’am. They are holding one of those Daughters of the Seas in there, forcing her to escort men at night. Four of them actually. What is your interest in them? I couldn’t help noticing you staring at the place where they are being held.”

“So they are being held against their will?” Gina replied in a non-committal manner. *Just who is he and what’s his interest in them?*

“Yes, that much I’ve determined. I’ve been watching them for several days now. They only get taken out by lecherous men at night, along with some other women, who also look like they are being kept. They all have those strange lip plate things, but the owner has got the two plates locked together so that the women can’t open their mouths to talk. What’s the Sisterhood doing here? Are you going to try to help them too?” he replied.

He seems sincere, but what’s his real interest in them? “Damn, that’s downright wicked of him. So why are you so interested in them?” Gina again framed her key question.

“It’s Arianna. There’s a life between us now. How do I say this properly? Months ago, I had cut my hand and it got infected. I very nearly died, before someone told me to visit the priestesses. Well somehow, I got myself to them. I was at death's door, fever and all. Bad infection, Arianna later told me. She healed me, saved my life with her incredible healing powers. A few weeks ago, I heard all the priestesses had completely lost all their powers. The more I thought about Arianna, the more I worried about her. Without her powers, how can she even live? There is a life between us. I am sworn to somehow rescue her from this wicked den of iniquity and take care of her."

He went on, "I checked and he wants fifty silvers just to take her out for an evening's entertainment, plus a coach, of course. I don't have much money; otherwise, I'd have paid it and taken her away to someplace safe. So I am trying to find another way to rescue her and the other women too, if I can, though I don't know if I can care for that many's needs. Still, I am honor bound to die trying. I had been thinking I could stop the carriage of whoever had rented her for the evening and steal her from him, but I am not a fighter. So far, those rich men always come with several strong fighters. I've tossed that idea away. Still, I owe her my life and I must repay Arianna somehow. Say, would it be possible for me to hire your Sisterhood women to help me break them out of that awful place? I can pay maybe twenty-five silvers, and I promise to work hard to make up any more your people would ask of me for your help, ma'am."

Gina was impressed with Gianni's story, if it were true. "Well, I will take your case to the Guild Mother and see what she has to say."

"Thank you, thank you! I can't ask for more than that. I will be here watching as I have been for several days now. The women are never allowed out during the daytime. A cook always comes early in the morning and leaves at suppertime. He has six guards around during the prime evening hours, but they leave, once the women are returned. Another two guards then come and watch the place during the night. The only way inside is through those double doors, which he locks after the night guard change," he added helpfully.

Gina smiled, "Thanks for the info. I'll go check with our

Guild Mother." She rose and quickly merged into the crowded street, walking briskly. *Damn meddling man anyway! Well, he has a point, honor — a life between them. Still I wish he'd just go home. Gina, don't even think that! He's acknowledging his obligation to her and that's a rare quality among men.*

"Do you think this Gianni can be trusted?" Angelica asked. Gina had just finished explaining what she'd discovered at their first target and the man who was asking for Sisterhood aid.

"He's honor-bound to repay his debt to this young teen, Arianna. He seems most sincere, and, if we don't include him, I think he'll be there helping her anyway. Can we ethically deny him this opportunity to repay his debt to her?" Gina answered. "Still, we should keep a close eye on him. You never can trust men, you know."

Several smiled in agreement with her last point. "All right then, we move tonight, but we need a plan."

Gina interrupted her leader. "Okay, I can get the front doors unlocked. They won't be expecting that. Maybe the guards will be drowsing and you can take them by surprise. Do we kill them?"

"Gina, you have a point as always. I agree. We'll let Gina try to pick the lock, but do it quietly please. We must take them by total surprise or else we'll have a battle on our hands. I don't want any of us to get wounded on our first rescue. We've got many more to go. No, we don't kill the guards, not unless they attack us first. We'll try to overpower them and knock them out. Now this Enzio fellow — he's signed his death warrant by his wicked actions against women."

"But Angelica," Gina again interrupted her boss, "if the guards see we are women, then by tomorrow everyone will know the Sisterhood raided this Escort Service and that could bring big troubles for our guild."

"Point taken. I've got a set of black blouses and pants for each of us. We'll wear black masks as well. Just make sure we take the guards by surprise and they don't see who we are," Angelica replied sternly. "We'll make our move at three in the morning. Gina, you best go let this Gianni fellow know, but tell him to stay the hell out of our way!"

Near three in the morning, the two wagons rolled quietly up to Enzio's Escort Service, parking a block from the building. As the women climbed quietly out, Gianni came walking up to them, leading his horse. Gina noticed he had two large bags tied to the saddle. Naturally, she wondered what was in them. "How much do I owe you for your help in rescuing my Arianna and the others? I am Gianni Mazo, instrument maker," he whispered, looking from one black clad woman to another.

"You owe us nothing. Stay out of our way, but you can help with Arianna when we get to the captives," Angelica replied tersely. "Quiet everyone. Gina, you are up. Remember, we have to take them by total surprise." The band of six, less two women who waited with the wagons, walked quietly to the adobe building. Gianni tied his horse to one of the wagons and hastily joined them at their rear.

Gina first observed the dim lights coming from the small, open windows. One was near the double doors, but the other came from the back right side. Her guess was Enzio kept a night light going in the women's room. At the door, she bent down and looked into the key hole. No light. That meant the key was still in the lock. Carefully she slipped a small leather roll off her belt, opened it up, and slid it beneath the door, aligning it with the keyhole. Using her lock picks, she pushed on the key and heard a faint thump as it fell out and onto the leather. Gently she pulled the leather strip back out and triumphantly picked up the key. A moment later, she had the doors unlocked and stepped back, leaving the battle to the fighters.

Damn, Gina! That was incredibly fast, Donatella sent her. *You're good at this.* The small thief smiled.

Angelica and Bianca moved to the doors with Marcella and Donatella right behind them. Felisa and Gina stayed back along with Gianni. As quietly as she could, Angelica opened the door a crack and looked inside. She saw a dim light coming from her right and signaled Bianca. Ever so slowly, she opened the door enough to slip inside. Bianca was right behind her. Both quietly drew their weapons, moving very cautiously through the hallway to the room where the two guards were sitting around a table playing cards. Donatella focused and directed a blast of psi-energy at the two men's minds. Their hands went up immediately to their heads, reacting to their sudden splitting headaches.

Angelica and Bianca acted. Both rushed the two men and cracked them over their heads with the hilts of their scimitars, knocking them out. Hastily, the two tied the men up and blindfolded them. Now came the hard part. They were not familiar with the layout of the large complex and thus didn't know where Enzio was sleeping. The four fanned out and began searching the rooms. Minutes later, Angelica found Enzio's bedroom. He was sleeping soundly. Without any hesitation, she moved silently to his bedside and brought her sword down on his exposed neck. He bled out swiftly. As he did so, she then placed a small paper on his forehead. It read: Guilty of gross mistreatment of bound women.

"All clear. Enzio's dead," Angelica called out. "Find the women and let's get them into the wagons." Felisa slipped back out and signaled to Savina and Milana, who responded at once. Soon, the two wagons were waiting at the front doors.

"In here," Felisa called out. One very large bedroom held the eight small beds and two commodes. A line hanging from the roof beams held a rope on which numerous women's dresses were hung. A soot covered lantern provided dim nightlight. "Ladies, wake up. We are here to rescue all of you and get you to a place of safety!" As her companions filed into the room, she began relighting several other lanterns.

"Dear god! He's really locked their mouths shut," exclaimed Angelica. She watched as the four older women struggled to get themselves into a sitting position in their beds. All were wearing their pipe corsets, severely limiting their motions. The mermaids didn't even try to get up yet. Each woman had a pair of locks holding their ornamental lip plates together. Still they tried to speak, but the rescuers couldn't make out what they were saying.

"Leave them to me," Gina ordered. Lock picks in hand, she moved over to Lia and began to undo her lip plate locks.

Meanwhile, Gianni found Arianna and rushed to her bedside. "Arianna! At last, I've found you. I'm Gianni Mazo.

You healed me from a bad infection in my hand last fall. You've saved my life. Now I am here to save yours, Arianna. I will stay with you always and help you with everything. There's a life between us and I have to repay you. Let me help you up and get you dressed." He proceeded to help her sit up in her bed, and she mechanically swung her leg over the edge of the bed. Her eyes met his, recognizing the young man, but tears swelled in her eyes. She tried to say something and then stopped. With her plates locked together, such was useless; she could only mumble.

For the next few minutes, chaos reigned as the many women set about getting the eight women dressed and ready to be evacuated to the wagons, while Gina went from woman to woman unlocking their lip plate locks. Of course, as soon as that was done, the freed women began talking rapidly. Angelica quickly interrupted them. "Look, we are taking the Daughters of the Seas to the place where they were supposed to be taken to be rescued in the first place, Elegant Fashions Inc. From there, they will be taken elsewhere." Benjamina had already contacted them and suggested this would be safer than taking them to the Guild House.

Lia interrupted her, "Please, you must take us too. We've been helping the mermaids and we want out of here too. Enzio, he's done terrible things to us all. . ." Her voice trailed off, embarrassed to be more descriptive or precise about what he'd forced them all to do.

"Of course you are all welcome to go with them, but we must hurry," Angelica added hastily.

"We can't hurry, not in our toe shoes," Lia sobbed. "Please don't leave us behind because we are so slow."

"No one will be left behind," Angelica answered. "Just get everyone dressed and ready to go. Don't worry about Enzio; he's dead. He's paid for his many crimes against you women." Several cheered.

After Gianni got Arianna dressed and Gina freed her lips, Arianna begged him, "Please, Gianni, use your dagger and kill me, please. I can't live like this, I beg you, please."

"Oh Miss Arianna, no, I can't do that. Not ever. You saved my life, now I must repay you. It's horrible what's happened to you — deserted by your god. Still you are alive and healthy. I will take care of you always; you can depend upon me, Arianna. You are so young and have so much life ahead of you. Let's not talk of such depressing things. We shall just have to make the best of it. You'll see. It's not the end of the world. You and your fellow priestesses have helped so many of us, and now it is your turn to be helped by us. It is the very least I can do for the life you've given back to me."

Lia, who had been watching over Arianna these past weeks, interceded. "While that's very noble of you, young man, you don't realized just how bad off these women actually are. We do. They are almost totally helpless and need assistance with everything. You best leave her care to me."

"Miss Lia is it? I do sincerely thank you for all you've done for Miss Arianna here and the others, but it is my responsibility now to help care for her. She saved my life and there's a life between us. If it's the last thing I do, I will repay my debt to her, but I am not a fool, I would appreciate all the guidance you can give me on her care, Miss Lia. Arianna is so young, she could almost be my sister. She must be protected and helped and I aim to do just that. Not all we men are lecherous perverts like Enzio was. Oh, they want us to go now. Please, let me help you too," he replied. He put a steadying arm round Lia and his other around Arianna's waist. "Okay, follow the leader out to the wagons, please."

Lia nodded, grateful for his steadying arm. Walking in her toe shoes was extremely challenging, especially once they left the house and reached the uneven street. Arianna merely focused on trying to hop and not fall down. Lia whispered, "At least Arianna still has her virginity intact. The rest of us have not been so fortunate."

"I understand, Lia. Mum's the word on that. You've been courageous and brave," he replied. "If you will permit me, I will help you as well." She gave him a curious look.

Walking behind them, Gina just shook her head in disbelief. *Gianni must be incredibly naive,* she thought. *He has no idea what he's getting himself into with Arianna, poor thing. She's probably right; we should just put her down. What kind of a life is she facing now? God, if that ever happened to me, I'd want to be put down for sure!*

The women were grateful for Gianni's strong arms. One by one, he lifted each of the eight women into the wagons. A half hour later, he lifted each one down carefully, noting how much care Lia also required. Again, his arms provided support for both women, as they made their slow way into the fancy establishment. Ahead of them, other Sisterhood women were doing the same thing as he did with the other six women.

Once inside, the eight thanked them profusely for their rescue, and Angelica bid them all the best of luck. She and her women quickly left, they had nearly ninety more women to rescue.

During the next few days, while the Sisterhood continued to bring in more of the mermaids from around the city and outskirts, Gianni proved he was sincere in helping both Arianna and Lia. If fact, he became invaluable in helping all the many women, much to Lia's amazement. For the first time in Lia's life, she began to see that here was a real man of worth.

Once all the women around Turda had been rescued, they were all teleported to Brom. There, Benjamina oriented them, healed their lips, and got them into Madiera homes. Immediately, others began therapy sessions on them, while Gianni continued to provide all the assistance anyone needed. When their therapy was finished, Benjamina got them onto the proper dose of psi-dust. In time, they would regain some of their lost *mentales* gifts. However, Lia, Mona, Jemma, and Gabriella — the four who had looked after the mermaids — also got the gifts, along with Gianni, who continued to live up to his word with Lia and Arianna.

Months later, the Sisterhood rescue squad rolled into Tecuci, the capital of old Arad. After dropping off the mermaids they'd rescued along the coast south of Tecuci, depositing them at the local Elegant Fashions Inc, they focused on how to retrieve the three mermaid wives of Sultan Fausto Ferro, the ruler of Tecuci. His royal palace was impenetrable to their small number. Well-guarded, they were forced to take a new approach for these three, Natale, Renata, and Sandra, who were officially his wives.

Donatella took charge this time, arranging a meeting with the sultan. While they chatted over formalities, she probed his mind to ascertain what his intentions towards the three mermaids actually were. Then she acted. "The reason for our visit, Sultan Fausto, is a simple one. The Goddess Lysandra has asked us to find all the young mermaids who have been so horribly mistreated by the long gone God Calder and to get them to a safe place. Once there, the mermaids will be greatly helped and will receive some of their old powers back, though that process will take many months to complete. The mermaids were supposed to have been taken there shortly after they lost their powers, but, as you know, quite a few were unable to get to the safe house of Elegant Fashions Inc and from there to Lysandra's place of safety. Hopefully in a year or so, the mermaids will be back in operation."

"Ah, so it is like I originally thought, in time, they will regain their lost powers and be most powerful once more," he exclaimed, adding, "I have kept their virginity intact just in case this might occur. Yet, they are my wives now."

"Yes, of course they are. Still, if you truly want them to regain some of their lost powers, they will need to come with us to the safe place Lysandra has prepared for them," Donatella replied. "It might take a year for them to regain what they can. Surely you want them to regain some of their powers, sultan."

"Yes, of course. Then, I will have three most powerful wives!" he replied greedily.

"Excellent, Sultan Fausto. The sooner we can get them to Goddess Lysandra's safe house, the sooner they can be helped to regain some of their powers," she replied, carefully avoiding mentioning they would be returned to him. "I am sure the Goddess Lysandra appreciates just how well you have cared for them until now."

"Yes, I certainly hope so. I've treated them as my honored wives, most well indeed," he answered rather boisterously. "Come here, my lovely brides," he gestured to the three. All three were sitting on pillows with their foot extended out before them. From this sitting position and lacking their telekinesis powers, they could not easily get up onto their foot. At once, his other three older wives rose and helped them to stand up. Donatella picked up their surface thoughts. All three of his older wives were *very* glad to be rid of the three mermaids. Their entire care had fallen onto them, and they really wanted out of this untenable situation.

Once safely in the wagons, Renata asked, "Do we really have to come back here? Are we really going to get our powers back?"

"No, you don't have to come back to that oversized pig," Gina replied before Angelica or Donatella could. "As far as your powers go, we don't know about that. I think you might get some, but certainly we've not heard of any of you, who are now as powerful as you once were. Sorry, we just had to get you out of the sultan's clutches."

Late November, the rescue squad pulled into Tetrano Oasis, where Warlord Luca Marco ruled. Some two thousand lived here in adobe buildings that surrounded the oval water pool. The Sisterhood women paid their two silvers to be allowed to park their wagons beside the waters for the night. Naturally, nearly everyone in the oasis stuck their heads out to stare at these amazon women. Some women envied their apparent freedom, while others detested them as did all the men. The eight women mostly ignored the villagers and went about setting up their camp for the night. Still, they did not have any real plan on how to extricate the two mermaids, Tina and Zita, from the clutches of Luca. Angelica hoped an idea would come to her as they sat around their wagons eating the warm supper Savina hastily whipped up for them.

By now, Valeria, Tina, and Zita were best friends. The two mermaids were wholly dependent upon Valeria, however. "Is it true? A Sisterhood caravan is at the oasis?" asked Zita. Valeria had just returned to their adobe dwelling.

"Yes! There are eight of them, all well-armed! Tina, Zita, this might be our only chance to escape. I have to try to get away. Dad's going to force me to marry next month. Once that happens, there'll be no one to help you both. We simply have to try to escape now! I need you both to be very brave. It will be hard for you, I know, but we have this one chance," Valeria explained.

"Okay, we will do whatever you ask," Zita replied. "We know he'll rape us once you are married and gone. Your mother hasn't ever helped us; we can't do anything ourselves, so we have to try."

At midnight, Valeria rose and stepped quietly out of their bedroom. She paused by her parent's room and listened carefully. Both were sleeping soundly. She slipped back into her room where Zita and Tina were sitting on the edge of their beds, their hearts pounding, scarcely daring to breathe. "Okay, they are asleep. Come on, up you go. Be as quiet as you can," Valeria whispered. She put an arm around each. Taking small, barefooted hops, the two began moving towards their bedroom door. At the door, they paused. Valeria headed back and worked her magic on their beds. Stuffing her extra clothes and some pillows, she made each of the three beds appear as if they were still sleeping there beneath the sheets. Her idea was to buy them a little more time in the morning before they would be missed. She then rejoined her two dear friends.

As quietly as they could, Tina and Zita hopped through the home, again scarcely daring to breathe, their hearts racing. If they were discovered, they'd never get another chance to flee the warlord's harem. At the main door, Valeria held the rug flap open, while one by one, the two hopped outside, wobbling as they reached the soft sands on which they could just barely keep their balance. Both mermaids relaxed a little, once they again felt Valeria's arm slip around their waists. "That way," Valeria whispered.

Slowly and carefully, the trio made their way the quarter mile down to the water's edge where the three wagons were located. "Who goes there?" Felisa called out softly, nudging Marcella awake. She was on guard duty, for none of the eight trusted these villagers.

"It's Valeria, Tina, and Zita. We beg you to let us join you. We have to escape from here, please! It's our only chance to get away," Valeria whispered.

"Oh! Tina, Zita, you are the ones we've come to rescue! Come on in. I'll wake the others!" Felisa whispered excitedly.

A minute later, a sleepy eyed Angelica introduced herself and the others. "We've come to take Tina and Zita to a safe house. I guess you can come too, Valeria."

"Thanks, these are my best friends and they need my help," Valeria whispered back. "Thank you, thank you."

"Come on. Let's get you into the wagon now. Break camp quietly. We'll leave immediately and before morning, try to put some miles between us," Angelica whispered. The eight women hastily went about their duties, hitching up the horses and breaking camp, both efficiently and quietly. Meanwhile, Savina made a place for the three in one of the wagons and helped them into it.

Fifteen minutes later, the wagons began rolling out of Tetrano Oasis, back on the east track towards the small coastal town of Po, some twenty-five miles away. Once clear of the oasis proper, Angelica set a swift pace. She rightly assumed come morning, the three would be missed. With the Sisterhood wagons gone, the warlord would very likely send a party out to intercept them and search their wagons, looking for the three teens. Hence, she wanted to get as far away as possible.

At seven in the morning, they rolled into Po, and Angelica steered them immediately onto the south coastal road towards Tecuci, some twelve hundred miles to the south. As the sun rose and anticipating the worst, Angelica had Savina hide the three women beneath their many supplies.

Around noon, Donatella, who was riding as rear guard, sent, *Angelica, Riders coming up fast from Po. Probably after the three teens.*

"Okay everyone, here comes trouble. Act bored and pretend we've never seen their women, but be prepared for a fight if they find them," Angelica ordered. Before long, twenty men came galloping up to the three wagons, rapidly encircling them. Angelica signaled for them to halt. "What's the meaning of this? You are stopping a Sisterhood caravan."

"Three of Warlord Luca Marco's teens have mysteriously disappeared. We believe that you have taken them. Prepare to be searched!" one grubby man ordered.

"Sorry, I don't know what you are talking about, but if

all you want to do is have a look in our wagons, that alone is not worth spilling blood over. Go ahead, just don't damage our goods, because that *would* be worth fighting over," Angelica retorted in a hostile tone.

His men dismounted and began rummaging through the wagons. "Nothing here, boss," one said. Shortly, two others commented similarly.

"Damn! Where the devil have those three gone? Okay, sorry Sisterhood women. We had our orders. Be on your way. No offense taken," the grubby man ordered.

"None taken. Move out," Angelica ordered, breathing a sigh of relief. Savina had done her job well. Once the men had disappeared, she called out, "Well done, Savina!" Several others added their praise to hers.

"I buried them good," she called out from her perch on the driver's seat. "Let me know when it's safe for them to get unburied." Angelica thought it best for the three to stay hidden until they camped for the night.

As the women made camp, Valeria helped Zita and Tina out of the wagon. Together, they relieved themselves, and then she helped the two sit beside the campfire. Angelica came over to them. Zita said, "Thank you for helping us. Where are we going? Valeria must come with us; we can't live without her. We've lost all our powers and can't do much of anything for ourselves. Are we going to be Sisterhood members now?"

Angelica laughed, "No you're not. We are taking you to the safe place where you were supposed to be taken when you lost your powers. As close as you three are, I wouldn't dream of separating you from Valeria. You are safe now. I don't think they will be back. In two days, we'll have you at an Elegant Fashions Inc store. From there, you'll be taken to a safe house. You'll have a chance to regain some of your lost powers, at least enough to be able to survive better."

"Valeria too?" asked Zita.

"Valeria too," Angelica smiled.

"Did Lysandra really appear to you?" asked Tina, curiously. While Savina began cooking, Angelica launched into her tale once more. The three listened fascinated. The goddess must be real, they thought.

As Savina began dishing out the supper stew, Valeria said hastily, "Please, just one large bowl for us. I always feed them. We eat together." Before the two days had passed, Angelica saw just how much these three worked together and how invaluable Valeria actually was for Zita and Tina. She relaxed, no longer worrying about how they would have to care for the two rescued women. So many of the others had required enormous care from the eight women.

The last night before they reached the port town, which had a small branch office of Elegant Fashions Inc, to everyone's total surprise, Lysandra appeared before them. Zita, Tina, and Valeria were very shocked and surprised to see the golden form of the goddess appearing.

"Well done, Sisterhood. These two here are the last of the many mermaids who can be rescued. Several others are happily married and are doing well enough. As I promised when you accepted this assignment, you will be given priceless gifts. Hence, when you get to the store tomorrow, you will be teleported to Brom along with these three. There, you will receive the gifts, and in time they will teleport you back to Turda. I cannot begin to thank you enough for what you've done for these many women. I can say this, the future repercussions of your efforts will be monumental in proportion. It is time the Easterlings women throw off their heavy bondage and live like women were meant to live. In your own way, you are helping to bring this about. Again I thank you all." Her image flickered and vanished, followed shortly afterwards by the soft, yellow glow that had first announced her arrival.

Of course, Gina began speculating on just what this gift would be. Later, she and the others received their basic therapy from eight of the mermaids. As expected, they erased very significant traumas they'd suffered at the hands of men in their lives. All eight felt a strong resurgence of life force within themselves. Further, Benjamina also allowed them to gain the *mentales* gifts, via feeding them controlled amounts of psi-dust — all except Donatella who already possessed the gifts. June the following year, the eight finally returned home, vastly more able and powerful. Gina was more than pleased. She could now teleport!

They all had seen this mysterious Madiera town and its incredible machines or bots. That the mermaids were now able to do some things for themselves brought tears to the eight Sisterhood women's eyes. Gina checked on Gianni, Lia, and Arianna. To her amazement, she found he and Lia were engaged and both were caring for Arianna as though she was their daughter. The eight knew firsthand the world would slowly become enlightened and a better place for everyone to live, to flourish and to prosper.

However, the world had not yet seen the last of Wystan or rather Damiano Donatello as he was now called.
The End.

Other Books by Vic Broquard

Without Warning (fantasy)

The Trident Series: (fantasy)
Volume 1 The Trident and the Book
Volume 3 The Trident and the Scepter
Volume3 The Trident and the Resurrection

The Adventures of Elizabeth Stanton Series: (science fiction)
Volume 1 The Evolution of the Path
Volume 2 The Great Messiah
Volume 3 Of Kings and Queens and Troubadours
Volume 4 Chaos in the Aftermath
Volume 5 Power Plays
Volume 6 Age of Exploration
Volume 7 Abducted
Volume 8 The Emperor and Empress
Volume 9 A Job Worth Doing
Volume 10 Degradation
Volume 11 The Second Crusade
Volume 12 When Worlds Collide
Volume 13 Dark Ages

The Lindsey Barron Series: (fantasy)
Volume 1 The Rod of the Apocalypse
Volume 2 The Board of Governors
Volume 3 The Crown of Moses
Volume 4 Dominus for President
Volume 5 The National Health Care Program
Volume 6 States Justice
Volume 7 Cross and Double-cross

Zoran Chronicles Series: (fantasy)
Volume 1 A Dragon in Our Town
Volume 2 Dragons, Power, Courts, and War

Planet of the Orange-red Sun Series: (science fiction)

Volume 1 When Kingdoms Fall
Volume 2 Dark Ages
Volume 3 Age of the Towers
Volume 4 Difficillis Exitus
Volume 5 Age of the Lords
Volume 6 The Renegade Tower
Volume 7 Rebellions
Volume 8 The Aliens Return
Volume 9 Power Struggles
Volume 10 Guilds, Genetics, and Gods
Volume 11 Magi, Witches, Swords, and Superstitions
Volume 12 The Voyage of the Eagle's Seed
Volume 13 Justifications
Volume 14 Responsibilities

The Return of the Wizards: Twelve Companions – The Making of Wizards (fantasy)

www.ingramcontent.com/pod-product-compliance
Lightning Source LLC
Chambersburg PA
CBHW060852250626
47159CB00008B/2706

* 9 7 8 1 9 4 1 4 1 5 2 3 8 *